THE ZOOKEEPER'S WAR

Steven Conte was born in 1966 and raised in Guyra in rural New South Wales. He has travelled widely in Europe and Australia, lived in Sydney and Canberra, and is now living in Melbourne.

THE
ZOOKEEPER'S
WAR

STEVEN CONTE

Quercus

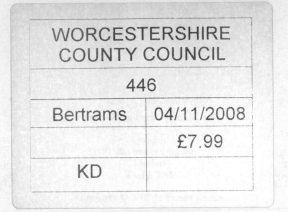
Originally published in Australia by
HarperCollins Publishers

The moral right of Steven Conte to be
identified as the author of this work has been
asserted in accordance with the Copyright,
Design and Patents Act, 1988.

A CIP catalogue reference for this book is available
from the British Library

ISBN 978 1 84724 727 8

This book is a work of fiction. Names, characters,
businesses, organizations, places and events are
either the product of the author's imagination
or are used fictitiously. Any resemblance to
actual persons, living or dead, events or
locales is entirely coincidental.

10 9 8 7 6 5 4 3 2 1

Printed and bound in Great Britain by Clays Ltd, St Ives Plc.

For my grandmother, Marion Marcus, 1901–2003.
With love and thanks for other stories.

ONE

The air-raid sirens bayed. Searchlights probed the dark and Berlin's outer flak ring opened fire, setting the birds in the aviary screeching and flapping. The zoo's blackout was total. Weeks had passed since the last air raid, and Vera was shocked by her body's quick recall, the lurching of her stomach and the trembling. As usual she felt the vulnerability of the animals. Always there were casualties.

Alongside her strode Axel, snow flicking off the boot of his good right leg. His limp was bad tonight. From the corner of one eye Vera sensed the swaying of his shoulders, then she turned and saw his barrel chest and felt oddly reassured, as if Axel were built of tougher matter than muscle and bone.

They passed the waterfowl lake, the kitchens and the administration, Vera longing to be back at the villa asleep. A flare lit the minarets of the primate house, and on the snowy hub of the roundabout she glimpsed Artur Winzens,

1

the Head Keeper, a small straight-backed man. He was too elderly for the army, though Vera feared that soon even Herr Winzens would have to go — since Stalingrad the regime had called up youths and older men. The keeper's breath was wreathed.

In the west the drone of bombers joined the rumbling of flak, and the searchbeams flailed like the legs of an upturned beetle. Axel greeted Herr Winzens in a jovial tone then paused to watch a flare tinge the aquarium green, and silently Vera gave thanks for her husband's aplomb — a legacy, she supposed, of his service in the trenches half a lifetime ago, a gift to weigh against the shrapnel in his hip.

Cut into the soil at the centre of the roundabout was a staircase that led down to a steel-plated door. Herr Winzens drew the bolt and Vera followed him into the air-raid shelter, which stretched beneath the garden bed as far as the sculpted elephant gates at the front of the zoo. Cantilevered planks along each wall could seat two hundred people, but apart from nuisance attacks there had been few raids in daylight when visitors were about, and at night only she and Axel and Herr Winzens sheltered here. Locals used the two tower-bunkers in the Tiergarten, which together held thirty thousand people.

Herr Winzens lit a kerosene lamp and hung it from the ceiling, bolted the door and handed out blankets and electric torches. From a thermos Vera poured hot chicory into mugs, warming her gloves on the enamel. The droning of the bombers was louder than usual and she glanced at the concrete ceiling.

Axel tore newsprint into narrow strips, which they each dipped in a bucket and crammed into their ears just as the flak on the tower-bunkers opened up, shaking the earth. Vera straightened on the bench, her spine a spear, then leaned into Axel's loose embrace.

Flak shrapnel clattered on the promenade, and overhead the bombers roared. The first explosions raised a wall of noise, beyond anything Vera had heard before. She seized the plank beneath her thighs and the explosions rolled nearer, a *Bombenteppich* — the carpet she had thought was a metaphor. It was vast this time. Axel let go of her and jabbed a finger at his throat, shocking her until she realised he was pointing at the cork tied around his neck. She tugged her own from inside her collar and bit down as a thousand-pounder hit, jolting her seat and punching the air, then a brace of bombs detonated in sequence, juddering the walls. Vera drove both hands to her ears but the din increased as explosions and the engines of the bombers merged, whole squadrons indistinguishable from one another. The flak towers barked. Vera pressed on her ears and felt her blood hammer.

Overhead she heard whistling that started high and sharp and deepened exponentially, making her think of mathematics, the brutality of numbers. As she lunged, the

3

force of the blast snatched her up, drove her spine against concrete and emptied her in space. Idly she wondered if she was about to die, then a blow stunned her chest and she skidded and stopped. There was an oddly domestic tinkling of glass. She was lying face down in darkness, breathing dust. One of the men was writing on her legs. She called Axel's name but couldn't hear her own voice, then a torch, Herr Winzens', lit swirling dust and she turned and saw Axel's face, a powdered mask, his mouth shaping her name. She tried to answer but coughed. The air stank of cordite, smoke and kerosene. Herr Winzens flashed the torch across her eyes, and she got to her knees. Axel was yelling, demanding to know if she was wounded. Just battered, she said. He raised a thumb. Herr Winzens was bleeding from a cut on the chin but claimed to be unhurt.

The blast-door was dangling and edged with glare, and through the gap came the crash of more bombs and flak. Axel got up and shouldered the door into its frame, leaving Vera to imagine what was happening on the surface.

Axel lay beside her and put an arm about her shoulders. Air raids had lasted two hours before, but never at this ferocity, and if another bomb didn't kill them, there was a chance they would suffocate.

For several minutes more the bombs kept falling, then abruptly the explosions stopped, leaving flak and the machine guns of *Luftwaffe* night-fighters, until these too fell away. Vera gagged on smoke, and sweat drenched her back.

She scrambled to the blast-door, gripped the latch and felt its heat on her gloves. Herr Winzens looked aghast — there was no all-clear — but Axel helped heave the door off its hinges, letting in heat and a blood-red light. Most of the steps were missing. Flames billowed in the sky.

Vera followed her husband to the lip of a crater that flickered with pale-blue phosphorus. Splashes of the incendiary had pockmarked the snow. The bird house was a pyre and the music rotunda a tree of flame; the conservatory on the top floor of the administration was burning. Only the aquarium was not on fire, though a red glow silhouetted a bite in the roof. The air was dense, a hot sirocco. No creature of any size could have survived above ground.

In the tenements to the south a time-bomb exploded, sending a pulse through the earth under Vera's shoes. Axel asked Herr Winzens if he'd go to the Civil Defence for help, and looking relieved to have orders the old man set off for the entrance gate, which Vera could see had been hit. Beyond it, Kurfürstenstrasse was a gully of flame, sharp gusts tearing slate off the rooftops. Embers jerked upwards on spirals of heat. Vera felt the earth begin to shake, looked down, and saw that her knees were trembling.

Axel pointed to the fire in the conservatory and said there was still time to get the studbooks from his office. This made sense, though meanwhile more animals would die, and she would have gone alone to fight the fires if one person

5

could have handled the water tanker. Instead she took Axel by the arm and together they entered the building.

The lobby was dark, the air full of ash, the stairs funnelling wind to the conservatory. Vera followed Axel into the office, leaning into a gale that howled through smashed windows. On the walls, framed photographs chattered in the wind, most of them of Axel's father: Herr Frey beside a newborn giraffe; shaking hands with the Kaiser; watching black men loading wildebeest onto the deck of a freighter.

Axel opened his desk and started yanking out the studbooks, and Vera began pulling the pictures off the wall and jamming them into the crook of her arm, leaving only an obligatory portrait of the dictator. Axel opened the gun cabinet and retrieved the Mauser.

She was anxious now to get away and hurried Axel through the foyer. Outside, the wind was scorching and gaining force, turning the snow on the promenade to slush. She shivered — last summer in the Hamburg firestorm many had died from burnt lining of the lungs. The horizon glowed as if circled by sunsets. She had no idea how to begin to save the animals.

In a blizzard of sparks from the burning rotunda she saw a dense, moving light — a fire that drew nearer, leapt and veered, until she recognised a zebra mare in flames. The animal's eyes were big with fright and, what seemed worse, a kind of injured amazement. Axel tried to block the mare's path but she swerved with ease, her back a cape of flame. She galloped through the wreckage of the entrance gate, struck a lamppost, lurched sideways but somehow kept upright and, before Axel could reach her, clattered off into the darkness.

'The zoo is finished,' said Vera.

The thought had stalked her all day and now she had voiced it. Axel didn't respond. In the lamplight of Flavia's tiny flat, his face was weary.

'It might not be so bad,' said Flavia. 'Tomorrow you might see things differently.' Her optimism sounded genuine and Vera was touched — usually it was Flavia who needed consoling. Incongruously, she was decked out as a 1920s flapper, still in costume from a party the night before, despite a day spent striding through the smoke and rubble.

Vera shook her head and listed the losses: the elephant pagoda, the camel and antelope houses, the aviary and aquarium. The primate house half destroyed, the woodland enclosures burnt. Thousands dead across the zoo. Axel said nothing, and his silence confirmed all her fears.

She couldn't yet bring herself to speak of the villa. Four years earlier she had told herself that she could endure the war if her home was spared, but staring that morning at the ruins of the villa the absurdity of this bargain had struck her in full. A contract had to be enforceable. She would have fewer possessions now than when she'd left Australia a decade ago.

'Well, you're alive and that's the main thing,' said Flavia, injecting the platitude with fierce conviction. She got up, apologised for the lack of proper food, and offered them a plate of canapés from the Hotel Bristol. The canapés, she claimed, were a gift from the Rumanian ambassador, though she was just as likely to have tipped them into her handbag by stealth. With the Soviets advancing on Bucharest, the Rumanian legation knew their days were numbered, and according to Flavia they planned to enjoy whatever time was left to them. The party had moved underground at the start of the raid and gone on until morning.

Flavia brought water from a pail she'd filled on the street. Her narrow dress made her look half starved, though in reality she scrounged more in a week than a heavy-worker ate in two. The electricity was down and the canapés unheated, but Vera devoured them anyway. Axel ate in silence, hunched under a blanket.

When the food was finished, Vera offered to tidy up, the habit of courtesy stronger than exhaustion, but Flavia gently pushed her back into the chair.

It was good to be cared for. After a day fighting fires and tending animals with burns, most of which had died regardless, Flavia's sympathy left her teary with gratitude. It was Flavia who had found her in a trance of fatigue at the zoo, and Flavia who had persuaded Axel to come away at last.

She had led them through a city that Vera had barely recognised, no longer a place of concrete and stone but of smoke and shifting light. The air was scarcely breathable. For all Vera could tell, they might have been on Mars, so it was a surprise to reach Meinekestrasse, behind the old synagogue, and see that number sixteen was virtually untouched.

Flavia washed their plates in a pail then poured each of them a glass of schnapps. The forecast was for cloud, she said. 'With luck the British won't come tonight.'

From Flavia, this was tactful. Usually she welcomed air raids and would try to provoke Axel by saying so, arguing that the raids would shorten the war, since people repeatedly forced underground would behave like worms when it came to a fight. Axel would only laugh and accuse her of masochism. The raids stiffened public resolve, he said, and Vera suspected he was right.

Flavia finished her schnapps and began to make a bed on the sofa. 'For me,' she explained. 'You two take my room.' Vera tried to argue, but Flavia had more energy. 'Anyway,' she said, 'I owe you.'

Twice before, she'd been bombed out herself — in 1941, when it was a novelty that drew sympathy from strangers, and in the big raid of the previous August, when only her friends had cared — taking refuge at the villa on both occasions until the Air-raid Damage Office had found her a flat, each smaller than the one before. Vera had hoped never to call in the favour.

Flavia hustled them into the bedroom and found two sets of men's pyjamas. Vera felt filthy and her skin reeked of smoke, yet she clambered gratefully under Flavia's eiderdown, sensed Axel's weight beside her and slept.

Hours later she woke, not knowing where she was, then smelt smoke and remembered the animals. Even now, she couldn't grasp that so many had died. Would not. Not yet.

Flavia's room was windowless, the only light coming from under the door. On the ceiling Vera could make out two fissures that collided and forked apart. Beside her, Axel was snoring softly, while in the other room Flavia was already up, a sign that morning was well underway. Vera lay still, reluctant to trigger another day's events — there would be bureaucracies to deal with, necessities to find. In the past she had always dismissed platitudes about the futility of plotting a course in life, since in her case she had chosen more often than drifted, but the war had narrowed choice and lately she had felt like a passenger on the train that according to rumour had torn through the *U-Bahn* in a previous raid when shrapnel killed the driver.

Axel shifted and stopped snoring. He would want her to wake him. She could smell his odour, a blend of smoke and stale sweat. His hair was thick and — unjustly, given his added years — had no more silver in it than hers. His expression was tranquil. While the war had ground her down, making her vulnerable to coughs and colds, Axel had stayed robust. For all the worry of the zoo, he'd remained optimistic. He was the constant in her life. However forbidding the future might be, the man who lay at her side would make it endurable.

That afternoon she entered a school gymnasium commandeered by the Air-raid Damage Office. Queues ran the length of the hall to where officials sat at school desks interviewing each person in turn. Cursing herself for arriving so late, she joined the queue that seemed shortest.

The hall was unheated and Vera tugged her coat tighter. Ropes and gymnastic rings dangled from the ceiling, reminding her of the gibbon enclosure, one part of the primate house that had survived the raid. By the gymnasium doors stood a bored-looking policeman — there on the off chance, she supposed, that this crowd of old men and housewives might riot. But the mood, though sullen, was subdued. Every class seemed represented here — as Flavia liked to say, bombs were a great leveller, especially as no insurer covered loss from acts of war. Vera remembered how in her childhood the neighbouring house of a lawyer had burned to the ground. The worst thing, claimed the lawyer's wife the next day as she sobbed in Vera's mother's arms, was not the burning of the house but the loss of precious photographs and keepsakes. To Vera this had sounded noble, yet now she would give up all the photographs she had saved if such a sacrifice could in some way resurrect the villa.

For several minutes the queue hardly moved, then the doors swung open and a brawny old man in a tailored suit paced into the hall. He was bald and sported a white walrus moustache stained yellow at the tips. The effect was half gangster, half circus-strongman.

The man surveyed the room and groaned, strode past the queues and planted himself before a desk, arms crossed, feet apart. The queue shivered with annoyance, and to Vera's relief an official ordered the intruder back. The man blustered and waved his identity papers, then he turned away, grumbling, as if to leave, only to change direction and stand behind Vera.

'Don't they know there's a war on?'

Vera half turned in acknowledgement. Today she wanted quiet.

'Some of us have better things to do,' said the man. 'They should give priority.'

She surrendered a brief, chill smile. Lately she'd encountered more than her share of the eccentric, the bombastic or the downright crazy — people attracted, she supposed, by the friendly expression that she wore to offset suspicion about her accent.

The man in the suit spoke in barking Prussian. 'It's not enough that you've lost your house — they have to sabotage the war effort.'

She murmured vaguely but he continued. Some were fighting the war, he said, and others hindering it. If people only stuck together, the nation would reach the final victory. He looked at her expectantly and Vera sensed that she would have to respond or appear defeatist. She said *ja*, facing sideways, fending off conversation. Mercifully the queue began to move.

'The enemy will pay, *gnädige Frau*, you've no need to worry. He won't know what's hit him when the *Führer* unleashes the wonder weapons.'

The *Wunderwaffen* — Vera doubted they existed, but she wasn't about to say so; the old fool was a Nazi through and through. Though no taller than Axel, he was bigger, better fed. Perhaps twenty years older. His hands were large as dinner plates. The suspicion came to her that he might be trawling for subversion, but even if not a paid informer he was the type who'd denounce you if given half a chance. She let him rant. Until now she'd managed to craft a life in which she rarely had to mix with Nazis, confining herself either to Axel's friends — scientists who, like him, had no interest in politics — or else to Flavia's tight-knit theatre crowd, who in private heaped contempt on the regime. Sequestered at the zoo, she'd avoided the fanatics, and for that matter the patriotic majority.

The suited strongman paused, perhaps sensing her dislike, and Vera leaned towards the woman in front and commented on the slowness of the queues, speaking quietly to stop the strongman overhearing. The woman was middle-aged, brown-haired, sinewy, with anxious eyes crouched deep in their sockets. Forgetting why they were here, Vera asked her where she lived, bringing a look of anguish to the woman's face. Her flat in Neukölln had been destroyed, she said. She worked as a seamstress in a nearby factory and had an elderly mother to care for. Her sentences were hesitant and brief, as if the full stops were burrows she had to scamper between. Vera explained that until two days ago she had lived at the zoo, and the seamstress looked intrigued. She'd been to the zoo as a girl, she said, and had never forgotten the giraffes. Vera spared her the news that the giraffes had all been killed.

The conversation lapsed, and the seamstress began to look awkward, then a minute later she blushed and in a halting voice asked Vera if she would mind holding her place in the queue. They were nearer the front now, and the lines had lengthened. Vera nodded and the seamstress scurried away.

The man in the suit grunted. 'More fool her.'

Promotion in the queue seemed to improve his mood. With both hands he twirled the ends of his moustache. 'Got a husband?'

She almost laughed — this was no informer. He was at least twice her age. She admitted to a husband.

'Fighting, is he?'

'Working.'

'Z-card?'

She nodded.

'I'm exempt too, though I'd fight if they'd let me.' His chest inflated — the strongman likeness was surely deliberate. 'As it is, I do my bit. Manufacturing. On contract to the *Wehrmacht*.'

She was saved from replying by the return of the seamstress, who crept back to her place, strewing apologies. The strongman demanded to know what she was doing, and the seamstress tensed in fright. She murmured about her place.

'Too bad,' said the strongman. 'You leave, you start again.'

The seamstress looked stricken.

Vera sighed, turned to the strongman, and for the first time spoke a whole sentence to him. 'The lady was here first and I'm letting her in.' She watched as her accented German struck home and then turned and crossed her arms, feeling her scalp contract in the silence at her back.

Thank God they were nearing the front; the seamstress was next in line. Abruptly the strongman left his place, marched over to the policeman and started speaking in a hushed but animated way. He pointed at Vera. The policeman gazed at her and ambled forward. The whole room was watching as the policeman stopped and asked her name and nationality.

She gave her name and announced *Deutsche*, holding the strongman's gaze. The policeman asked for her papers and she reached into her handbag and took out two envelopes: the first for documents she resented or tolerated — ration card, residency permit and certificate of naturalisation; and the second for those she genuinely valued — her marriage certificate and an employment card that listed her profession as zookeeper. The policeman checked each one in turn, handed them back and told the strongman that everything was in order. The strongman mumbled about duty; the policeman shrugged and returned to his post.

Vera seethed. She was used to extra attention from officials, but never at the prompting of another civilian. From time to time it was all she could do to remember the kindness of individuals and not curse the entire German people, their language and their works, and above all the strange *mittel*-European passions that had led them to disaster. She looked at the rows of grey-clad people — to suffer alongside them seemed grossly unjust.

The seamstress took her turn at a desk and began telling her story.

At times Vera longed for the lazy ways of her own countrymen, who fought wars readily enough at Britain's behest but were otherwise happier at the racetrack or the beach. Space and warmth nurtured apathy. She imagined the heat of January and gave in to the mawkish homesickness that often afflicted her these days. Her yearning for Australia seemed physical, and who could say that her flesh didn't hold a molecular memory of eucalyptus? There was little else to remember it by. The only object she still had from home was a 1938 penny that showed the king on one side and a kangaroo on the other, a gift from her brother who'd had it turned into a necklace.

The seamstress finished at the desk, turned around and risked a smile. Vera waved her goodbye then stepped forward and answered the official's questions: address, occupation, number of dependants. She couldn't have said how many animals were left.

The official was kindly enough but made no promises about housing, and instead handed over coupons for clothing and food. Vera thanked him and turned to leave, staring in contempt at the strongman before striding out the door.

On the street she wrapped a scarf around her head and put on sunglasses against flying cinders. Coal and lignite stored for the winter burned steadily in cellars, clogging the air. Although daylight was fading, the temperature was warm, a sinister Indian summer.

In the Mitte, the old city, bombs had caved in the skyline, dropping telegraph poles, power lines and tram cables onto burnt-out lorries and trams. Shops were destroyed or boarded up, and glass, chunks of plaster and shrapnel paved the streets. Field kitchens had sprouted at the major intersections, and in alleys off Alexanderplatz girls were already soliciting. Outside one bombed-out tenement Vera read the chalked inscription, *Everyone in this shelter has been saved.* Around the corner: *My angel where are you? Leave a message for your Sigi.* In a house without walls on Unter den Linden, a man played Bach on a grand piano, and below him, in a lake fed by a burst water main, a fur stole clung to a hatstand. Half the people on the streets wore a uniform: police, air-raid wardens, women postal workers. Soldiers moved in squads and the only vehicles were staff cars and *Wehrmacht* lorries, as if the army had conquered Berlin and deployed clerks and shop assistants to the front in a fleet of private cars.

For all the pre-war pomposity of Berlin, the Reich capital, Vera couldn't help grieving for that other Berlin, an unruly city whose emblem was a crudely depicted black bear. It was the city she had entered in 1934 after arriving by train at Bahnhof Zoo. Berlin had been unimaginably hectic, a maelstrom of human and mechanical traffic. Axel had sent their luggage ahead then insisted on showing her the city on foot, and though tired from the journey she had happily agreed. Her first impressions were disjointed and had little in common with the city she later came to know. Axel was exhilarated, stabbing the air with his hands like the fishermen they'd seen in Naples. A city of four million people, he enthused, ringed by parks and forests, lakes and rivers. Canals and Europe's biggest inland harbour. More bridges than Venice. She laughed and smiled, sensing for herself the immensity of Berlin in the churning crowds, the cars and lorries and double-decker buses, trams squealing and spitting sparks overhead, trains thundering along the elevated *S-Bahn*, and a zeppelin in the sky; and later, when she understood the layout of the metropolis, it would seem to her like a wheel on the hub of her home — the green thirty hectares of the zoological gardens.

Outside a bombed apartment on the Linden, some prisoners of war, Badoglio Italians, pumped air into the ruins through a large canvas pipe, while Hitler Youth and girls of the *Bund deutscher Mädel* laboured in the wreckage. A row of bodies lay on the pavement, a scene she had witnessed after previous air raids, though not so often that she could look away. The nearest victim was an elderly woman, her skirts obscenely rucked to the waist.

The Tiergarten was ploughed up like a Flanders battlefield, with many of its oaks and beeches shattered. Camouflage netting above Charlottenburger Chausee had fallen on the road or vaporised.

Vera turned into the park towards the zoo, and the noise of lorries fell away. At the goldfish pond she passed a marble statue of a bow-wielding Amazon on horseback, the arrow poised to fly eastwards — towards Moscow.

The trees thinned and through a gap in the branches she glimpsed the tower-bunker next to the walls of the zoo. Flak cannons gleamed on the roof. Rows of shuttered slit-windows made the tower resemble a castle keep. Beside it was a smaller but still imposing structure — the headquarters of Berlin's anti-aircraft defences. Along with its own battery of cannon, two dish-like aircraft detectors rotated on the battlements.

At the Landwehr Canal she crossed a footbridge that led to the zoo's northern gate. Behind her the revolving dishes scooped the last of the sun.

Axel watched as a fire crew doused the zoo's restaurant and concert hall. Only the walls remained. Smoke cast mustard-coloured shadows at his feet, and his gaze swirled about with the eddies. He and Vera had feared a truly massive raid, and now the worst had happened. As best as he could estimate, two-thirds of the remaining fifteen thousand animals had been killed. A single attack had demolished a century of building.

He turned away from the hall and began a final leg of inspection. At the woodland enclosures, trunks and branches were smashed. All the deer houses were destroyed, including the reindeer chalet, though some of the reindeer had escaped and were pressing against an outer fence. Further north, the sea-lion pool was miraculously unharmed, but beside it a bomb had destroyed the zoo's hospital and breached the northern wall, revealing the Landwehr Canal and beyond it the Tiergarten. To the right of the hospital the Head Keeper's cottage was gutted, adding Herr Winzens to Berlin's homeless. As Axel gazed at the ruins of the cottage, an African hunting dog loped by with an ibis in its jaws.

The zoo had closed only once before, in the wake of the last war, but there had been no structural damage and the visitors had returned. As an assistant to his father in the 1920s he had gathered animals from every continent, including Antarctica, and when the Board had appointed him Director he had inherited an institution that had not only overcome the Great War and the Depression but surpassed the *belle époque* in the breadth of the collection and numbers of visitors. The main difficulty, in fact, had been a lack of space for displaying animals in open-plan enclosures, and though he and Vera had added monkey rocks and the alpine peak, past success had limited expansion. The zoo had remained his father's realm. Vera had wanted to knock down some of the animal houses, which Flavia liked to denounce as hideous follies, remnants of an imperial grandeur that had always been half imaginary, but visitors adored the animal houses, and members of the zoo's Governing Board were traditionalists. Secretly, Axel had been relieved. He'd grown up among the palaces, temples and lodges, loving them with a child's uncritical eye.

He made his way to the carnivore house, which was still standing but badly burned. Oskar and Zoe, Sheba and her cubs — not a single lion had survived. Bombs had crushed but not burned the northern wing — the nearest cages held the bodies of a puma and two jaguars. The next cage was Gogol's, a Siberian tiger they had raised from a cub. His body lay beneath fallen masonry.

The trouble with being born into a golden age was having to live through its decline. War had started the slide, though at first the only signs were mild rationing and the loss of younger keepers to the *Wehrmacht*, and if anything there were even more visitors than usual. When the bombing had started, however, Berlin's children had been evacuated, forcing the zoo to depend on soldiers visiting with their girlfriends, or on workers from the armaments factories that ringed the city. Later, when rationing grew stricter, the health of the animals began to suffer. With good food even African animals could flourish in Europe, but without it the cold had taken its toll.

And now bombs had finished the job. With nothing left for visitors to see, there would be no income, only costs. The Board had long ago written off its losses, and the only hope now was government charity.

Axel trudged along the cratered banks of Neptune's Pool. In the middle the bronze god was still straddling his dolphins. The wind was warm and smoke slid in layers, merging with a ceiling of cloud.

He mounted the front steps of the aquarium, saw that the front doors had blown outwards, and in the vestibule found a freshwater crocodile bleeding from its ears and nostrils. A hind leg lost and a lacerated flank. Dorsal scoots missing, leaving narrow wounds. Axel knew he should act but couldn't stomach another killing. He would have to send a keeper. He stepped over the crocodile and limped into the tank room.

Inside, the devastation was total. Something big — an aerial mine perhaps — had crashed through the glass roof and detonated in the central atrium, smashing the crocodile stream upstairs and bringing soil, rocks and palm trees down onto the tanks. Thousands of fish lay dead on the floor, among them stingrays and sharks, as well as crocodiles. Axel waded into the wreckage. The smell was bad and would only get worse. He stooped to right an upturned turtle, but its shell was cracked and the turtle dead.

The aquarium had been his favourite part of the zoo, a haven where he had liked to watch the fish: curtains of herring, grave-eyed perch, porcupine fish like thorny barrage balloons. Where the tropical tank had been, dead fish carpeted the floor: mottled blenny, banded perch, damsel-fish and painted moki; then in a pool edged by jagged glass an octopus stirred. Valvular gills pulsated in her jowls. Her eyes, which were banded and shrewd like a goat's, pierced his own as he loomed above her. He made a mental note to arrange a rescue.

In the freshwater tank a giant catfish lay thrashing in knee-deep water. Axel hooked his arms beneath the fish, hoisted it up, and staggered to the door, feeling the stab of its whiskers through his coat. Outside, the smoke stung the lining of his nostrils. Feeling foolish, he struggled through the slush to Neptune's Pool. The catfish was probably riddled with glass; this was a sentimental act. He stopped and lowered it into the water where it lay sideways as if already dead, then quivered and sank into the murk.

His overcoat stank, and on one sleeve a fish scale gleamed. He heard Herr Winzens call his name and turned around and saw the Head Keeper on the bank with a man at his side dressed in a black suit and butterfly collar. Men in overalls, some with notebooks, were gathered on the promenade.

Axel climbed the bank and shook hands with the visitor, a tall thin man, who grimaced and wiped his palm on his trousers then introduced himself as an *Oberinspektor* from the Reich Ministry of Agriculture. Hair receded from each temple above a narrow face. Mid-thirties, Axel judged, certainly younger than himself — always odd to meet younger men in positions of authority. Axel had lost count of the number of times he had lobbied the Ministry to have some of the animals evacuated to regional zoos, but all the hours in anterooms had come to nothing. Evacuation smacked of defeatism, they'd said, and would send the wrong message to the populace.

The *Oberinspektor* cleared his throat and announced that the zoo would be audited.

'What sort of audit?' asked Axel.

'Of surplus food.'

'We've no extra food. As it happens, our kitchens were spared, but there's only a week's extra food in storage.'

The *Oberinspektor* gazed about him. 'You've taken a battering here.' His tone was concerned.

'That's right.'

'And lost quite a few of your stock.'

Axel caught the man's drift. 'You're here to count corpses.'

'Herr Director, I wouldn't put it like that. We're avoiding waste. As for counting, it's living stock we're interested in. Once the numbers are established, we'll adjust your rations.'

'Reduce, you mean.'

'In all likelihood, yes.'

The *Oberinspektor*'s tone was reasonable, and despite Axel's annoyance he could see the man's logic. His own reaction was more of disappointment than disgust, as already he'd mentally assigned the dead animals to feed the surviving carnivores. If the *Oberinspektor* was a scavenger then so too was he, and like any vulture he'd have to wait his turn.

'I've also noticed that your walls have been breached,' said the *Oberinspektor*. 'I'll arrange fencing to keep out intruders.'

'Other than yourselves, you mean?'

This was a childish protest, he realised, perhaps even dangerous. The *Oberinspektor* scrutinised his face and then explained in the same unruffled tone that his men would need some of the keepers as guides. This would slow the rescue and recovery work, but Axel was keen to get the audit over with and asked Herr Winzens to make arrangements. The aquarium would have to wait.

'And I'll need a map,' added the *Oberinspektor*.

'Our maps were destroyed.'

'Could you draw one?'

Axel considered this and nodded. There was nowhere else that he knew so well.

He led the *Oberinspektor* across the promenade and toward the kitchens, a long low building left oddly naked by the destruction of the administration block. Inside, the kitchens were cold and gloomy — echoes, tiles and stainless steel. He lit a candle, poured tea from a thermos and drew up two stools at a bench. The tea was lukewarm and tasted of grass, and the *Oberinspektor* set his cup aside. Axel tore a page from an exercise book.

The map was more awkward to draw than he had imagined. Scale was the problem, and his first attempt went into a bin. He rushed his second effort, feeling uncomfortably like a schoolboy under the gaze of a teacher. The finished map looked askew, as different from the surveyor's version as an early map of exploration would be from a modern naval chart, but all the enclosures were there and he was anxious now to be alone.

The *Oberinspektor* thanked him and made his own way out. Axel ripped another page from the exercise book and again drew the lemon-shaped outline of the zoo, but rather than add the enclosures as he had done before, he sketched in the streets to the south and west, the Canal and the Tiergarten to the north. He paused. At the centre of this new map lay empty space. He put down the pencil and gazed at the blankness.

Twilight had come on by the time Vera arrived. She looked surprised to see him there and frowned. Her hair was dishevelled, which in candlelight made her look unexpectedly like a gypsy. Soot marked creases he'd never noticed at the edges of her eyes.

'I've just seen men pushing dead deer in wheelbarrows,' she said. 'What's going on outside?'

The *outside* held a hint of reproach. He told her about the *Oberinspektor*.

Vera looked annoyed. 'We don't have the time.'

'I know, but this way we get rid of them sooner.'

He asked how she'd gone at the Air-raid Damage Office and was relieved when she launched into a story about queues. He was thinking about that empty map, and all the ways he might fill it. Vera described her trek from the Mitte to the zoo. 'On the Linden, a surrealist could have painted straight from life.'

He would explain his thoughts another time — Vera had enough to manage. Marriage had long ago taught him the importance of knowing when to speak and when to stay silent.

TWO

Cutting up an elephant was like demolishing a shed, Axel decided: the same search for weak points to bring down the structure and, if you could overlook the gore and the sadness, the same satisfaction in a job well done. By rights this should have been Herr Winzens' job, but for years the old man had worked as the elephants' mahout, taking children for sedan rides on top of old Siam, the bull of the herd, and it would have been heartless to make him pack Siam off for soap.

Beyond the western gate, trains were lumbering in and out of Bahnhof Zoo — whatever might be said against the authorities, they could work miracles with transport and public utilities.

Through trial and error the men from the Ministry had streamlined the job, first hacking off the legs and head and loading them onto a lorry with a block and tackle. The next part was awkward and had caused the most grief:

slicing the hide but not the membrane of the belly, which had to be opened by someone fast on his feet.

With the muck of the belly cleared away, the hide became a tent you could crouch in. They'd left Siam to last, and half from curiosity and half to ward off the cold Axel took up a cleaver, cutting the meat and the hide away in sections. The task was absorbing, and when he stopped and saw Vera he had no idea how long she'd been watching. Axel gave the cleaver to the next man, took off his gloves and went to her side. '*Liebling*, you don't need to put yourself through this.'

She was staring at the carcass. 'No, but I ought to.'

Axel couldn't see why.

'To remember,' she explained.

And then to brood, he suspected, though from experience he knew that trying to persuade her to leave would be pointless. The men began sawing the weakest joints and knocking down bones still shaggy with meat. He would have liked to do his part but hesitated, sensing that Vera wanted him at her side while she paid her respects.

'Isn't it time to go back to the Ministry?' she asked.

The Ministry again. He wasn't sure he could face another futile visit.

'They'll have other priorities.'

'What about your *Oberinspektor*? You've co-operated. Surely he owes you.'

'I doubt he'd see it that way.'

'Axel, I'm asking for the animals.'

It was arguable whether an evacuation would help any more, given the risks of transportation, and with rationing in force throughout Germany. A lingering death in some provincial pen would be little better than what the animals faced here. The truth was the rest of the stock was probably doomed, though he couldn't say this to Vera. To salvage something from the wreck, he had placed the studbooks and his father's photographs in the shelter.

The men from the Ministry swung Siam's carcass onto the back of the lorry. Axel looked sideways and promised to go to the Ministry if that was what she wanted. Vera smiled a little — in satisfaction, he thought, and perhaps also to apologise for stubborness. She kissed him, and they arranged to meet at nightfall.

The workmen collected their cleavers and saws and climbed aboard the lorry, and though Axel knew they'd come for their own purposes, he felt strangely abandoned. He stared into the ruins. The elephant pagoda had been hit dead centre, scattering granite and coloured roofing tiles. Two of the herd were still under the rubble and would have to stay and rot. The lorry started up, pulled away between the craters and disappeared through the western gate.

The *Oberinspektor* rose from his chair, shook Axel's hand and smiled, something his colleagues had never done. Times had changed. The Reich's defeats had triggered one of two reactions from public officials: redoubled callousness or growing circumspection. The *Oberinspektor* seemed like one of the latter breed. On his leather-topped desk were two trays marked IN and OUT, both filled with documents. A file lay open on his blotting pad, showing Axel's most recent letter. Behind him hung the *Führer's* portrait.

The *Oberinspektor* motioned Axel into a seat and drew up his own chair nearby, more like a friend in a café than a public official. 'Herr Director,' he said, 'please forgive me, but I must say straight away that your request has been denied.'

This was no surprise. Axel would have liked to leave immediately but wanted to tell Vera he'd tried his best. In a polite tone he reminded the *Oberinspektor* that the Ministry had already agreed in principle to evacuate the big cats if the bombing worsened. 'The big cats are now dead. I'm asking you to evacuate our other stock.'

The *Oberinspektor* leafed through the file, scanned a page then raised his head.

'The concern was for public safety. It was thought the bombing might release dangerous animals.' His long face was composed.

'My point is that having agreed to an earlier evacuation there's no reason to oppose one now. The zoo is closed. Defeatism is no longer an issue.'

'That may be, Herr Director, but to be frank there are other obstacles — the shortage of cattle cars, for one.' The

Oberinspektor fingered both ends of a pen and then suddenly set it down. 'Furthermore, I regret to inform you that the zoo must lose more staff. Remaining men between the ages of sixteen and fifty are to be called up for service.'

This was a shock — he'd expected disappointment, not punishment. Already he'd attended too many funerals of former zookeepers killed at the front. 'Without those staff the stock will die,' he said. 'If that's your aim, just say so, and we'll pack off the animals to an abattoir. They'd suffer less, and the Ministry would save on fodder.' Stripped of sarcasm, he realised, the idea was unpleasantly plausible.

The *Oberinspektor* replied with exaggerated patience. 'Herr Director, you're upset. That's natural. The zoo's plight is regrettable, but you must understand that the war effort comes first.'

Axel stood up. 'Then thank you for your time.'

The *Oberinspektor* waved him down. 'There *is* something we can do for you. After reading your letter I approached the Reich Labour Front, and I am happy to say that they have agreed to give you twelve *Ostarbeiter*, all males, mostly from Poland and the Protectorate of Bohemia.'

Axel's shoulders stiffened. 'I'm sorry, I can't accept.'

'Oh? Why is that?'

'We want our existing staff, not foreign workers.'

'The *Wehrmacht*'s needs are paramount, Herr Director.' In a perfunctory tone he added, 'Your staff will be returned at the end of the war. Until then you can use the *Ostarbeiter*. You will find that they cost far less to employ.'

'Cost is not the issue.'

The *Oberinspektor* examined him closely. 'I see. And do you wish to explain the issue?' From the wall the *Führer* stared into the room with unfocused discontent.

Axel could barely explain it to himself. Vera wouldn't like it, he was sure of that, but he could hardly say that he'd be in trouble with his wife.

'It's a question of training. And there's the language barrier. Inexperienced staff would be a burden.'

The *Oberinspektor* raised his palm. 'Forgive me, Herr Director. You don't understand. This is not an offer but accomplished fact. Cynics maintain that a letter posted to a government ministry is destined for oblivion, *Vergessenheit*, that it vanishes like vapour.' His hands mimed a puff of air then settled together on the blotting pad. 'Nothing could be further from the truth. A letter reaches in-trays. It clogs pneumatic tubes. Eventually it necessitates a response.' The *Oberinspektor* waggled a forefinger. 'Now you, Herr Director, have sent not one but many letters.'

'Simple. I withdraw them.'

The *Oberinspektor* shook his head. 'Even now, the Reich Labour Front is diverting the *Ostarbeiter* from other projects.' He closed the file. 'Go back to the zoo and await your new workers. Try to be more grateful. Foreign labour is better than no labour at all.' He rose to his feet, performed the salute, picked up the file and transferred it to the out-tray.

Axel stood up and inclined his head, determined not to utter another word. He crossed the room and grasped the doorknob.

'Herr Director.'

Axel stopped, half turning around. The *Oberinspektor* was standing with studied casualness, busying his hands with a fresh pile of papers.

'There's no need to blame yourself, you know. You needn't be concerned. No one, *niemand*, who survives this war will escape with honour wholly intact.'

'It's wrong,' said Vera, 'that's all there is to say.'

Axel doubted it was this simple, but as usual when Vera took to arguing he was stumped for a reply. What came to mind first was one of his mother's maxims, though she had been dead for more than twenty years. 'Vera, what can't be changed must be endured.'

She set her iron back down on the stove. 'We're not discussing the weather. This is slavery.'

'They *are* paid.' This was quibbling, but accuracy mattered.

'Nonsense,' she said. 'It's a pittance, a fig leaf. They're forced to hand the money back to pay for their own *konzentrationslager*.'

'Barracks. They're kept in barracks.'

Vera scoffed. 'This will count against us when the war is over — whoever's in charge.'

Flavia was due home soon, and Axel hoped she'd be on time. 'The *Ostarbeiter* will be better off at the zoo than a factory. Whoever's in charge when the war is over will see that we've tried to look after these men.'

'But how? With what food? Whose money?' A worrying quaver of emotion filled her voice. 'Anyway, this goes beyond all that. What you're proposing will diminish our souls.'

Metaphysics now — she was impossible in this mood. Oddly, she resumed ironing.

'You're better than this,' she said, 'that's the frustrating thing. Good heart, thick head. A Marxist would rank you with the unschooled peasants.'

So her sense of humour hadn't disappeared. Axel spoke in a gentle voice. 'Now that the other keepers are going, we really have no choice.'

'Even the zoo isn't worth this.'

'Maybe so. But someone has to look after the animals.'

'I know, I know.'

Suddenly she seemed beside herself with despair. He changed the subject.

'I've been thinking about where the zoo goes from here. After the war,' he explained.

'After?'

'We need a plan. Fortunately, I've had some ideas.' Vera seemed troubled, but he persevered. 'For years you've wanted to build more *Freigehege*, and what's stopped us is lack of space. Remember what you once called the animal houses? Mausoleums. "What idiot thought of houses for animals?" you said. A lot of those houses are gone now, and in a way the British have done us a favour because when the war is over we can start again, without walls, without cages.' Vera frowned and drove the iron over one of his shirts. Even to his own ears the speech sounded gushing. 'Fewer displays, but larger. Proper breeding, not the half-hearted kind we've done before ...'

'And the animals we have now?'

'There's a limit to what we can do for them. There's not enough food. We can't stop the bombing. Some species could have priority: the hamadryas baboons, or any others that might be bred later — but for individuals there may be little we can do.'

She worked in silence until Axel couldn't wait any longer. 'Well?'

She set down the iron. 'It's all so calculated — "These ones are done for, so let's plan for the next lot."'

'Vera, you know that's not it.'

'It sounds like that.'

'I'm saying we may have to sacrifice some to save others.'

'By *sacrifice* you mean starve?'

'If needs be, yes.'

'I don't want that on my conscience,' she said, 'any more than I want to exploit slave labour.'

He took a deep breath. It wasn't as if they had choices. He had meant to inspire, but instead they were back on the *Ostarbeiter*. He tried one last time. 'Vera, for years you've argued for redesign. The bombing, the *Ostarbeiter* — I wouldn't have chosen any of it, but can't you see it's an opportunity?'

Through the door came the sound of Flavia pounding up the stairs, and Vera answered him quickly. 'We didn't build *Freigehege* for beautification. It was all for the animals. The zoo's for them, not us, or we're no better than gaolers.'

The door flew open and Flavia swept in, and without hesitation Vera asked about her day, ironing as she spoke. Flavia launched into an obscene anecdote about an actor at the Theatre Rose, but though Axel chuckled at all the right moments he was also still puzzling over Vera's reaction to his plans. How could she champion the animals and yet reject the *Ostarbeiter*, the only way of keeping them fed? And what did the issue have to do with his plans to rebuild, something she'd wanted for years? The more he recalled what they'd said to each other, the more it seemed like a pantomime for the venting of emotions.

They ate some dinner, then he settled down and tried to read the newspaper, but the paw prints of the Propaganda Minister were on every page, and the words stopped making sense. Flavia was cursing at a needle and thread, while Vera laboured over a government form.

How he hated arguing — Vera could be reckless when angry. Their one-sided rows reminded him of one of his worst mistakes in zookeeping, when he had herded chamois and ibex together, only to learn that the chamois' rearing challenge laid it fatally open to the horns of the ibex, whose fighting instinct was to charge.

At least arguments with Vera were rare, and really he couldn't complain about her forthright nature, since he'd known about it from the start.

They had met in Sydney, April 1934, in a Salvation Army Hall in Woolloomooloo. He was on a collecting trip, and in return for help from the German Consul he had agreed to make a speech to the Australian–German Friendship Society, which had been established to mend relations after the war. His speech was remedial Darwinism — meant to correct the impression formed by a film like *Tarzan* that species such as lions and pythons commonly fought to the death. In the wild, he'd argued, aggression was never pointless: lions and pythons were no threat to one another's vital interests and therefore had no need to fight. Aside from hunting, most aggression occurred within species, usually in competition for territory or mates.

After the speech, all the questions concerned man-eaters, terrestrial or aquatic, and venomous snakes or spiders, and he'd all but given up on a sensible question when a woman at the back of the hall raised her hand. Her German was halting but accurate. He had mentioned that aggression within species was caused by struggles for territory or mates, said the woman, instincts that presumably benefited the species in some way. Axel nodded. In the case of humans, continued the woman, what possible benefit could have accrued from the slaughter on the western front?

The audience shifted uneasily, and the Consul, Axel noticed, was visibly irked — no doubt it was awkward representing Germany in the country of a former foe.

Axel met the young woman's eye — for a short time in Belgium he'd faced Australians in battle. The last war, he said, could indeed be interpreted as a contest for territory, however she was right to imply that the loss of life seemed disproportionate to the amount of land that ultimately changed hands.

'And competition for mates?' asked the woman. 'Surely the men who chose *not* to fight — those who were free to choose — survived in greater numbers to procreate. Hasn't the machine gun made Darwinism obsolete?'

The Consul rose but Axel waved him down. He looked at the young woman. 'I'm not sure we can say that. For all the randomness of death in the trenches, natural selection may have done its brutal work. It's arguable that returning soldiers enjoy a higher social standing, and as a result secure more desirable wives.' Some of the audience tittered. 'But I see that I'm straying into sociology — a vice of many of us who make a study of animals. To speak in strictly Darwinian terms — and with apologies to those here who may have lost relatives — the men who died in the Great War were expendable. Among mammals, it's the survival of females that's paramount.'

As he was speaking, Axel watched the young woman's face — nods of comprehension, a wrinkled brow. It seemed natural when she challenged him again.

'And female aggression? What accounts for that?'

In the front rows people turned around, craning to see the questioner's face.

'The same, I'd say — territory and mates. And hunting, of course, among carnivores. As a rule, though, aggression is less marked in the female. All too often, in the animal kingdom, it's the fate of the female to be a prize for the aggression of males.'

He fell silent, aware that some in the audience looked uncomfortable, perhaps even hostile — not about his views on aggression, he suspected, so much as his suggestion that the glorious dead were dispensable. The Consul stood up and moved a vote of thanks, and Axel glanced again at the young woman. She had straight black hair, a well-formed face, dark eyes and probing questions.

When the applause subsided and the audience began to leave, the Consul approached the lectern and shook Axel's hand. Vera was lingering at the rear of the hall, rearranging books in a bag. Axel could see that she was beautiful, though perhaps too young. Cutting short the Consul's thanks, he strode up the aisle. Propositioning strangers wasn't really his thing, but one of the advantages of visiting a foreign country was not having to face the consequences of mistakes. He invited her to tea, and she smiled and said yes.

★　　★　　★

Vera stopped at the enclosure to let the Czech *Ostarbeiter* rest. He had struggled to carry only half the feed. His face was emaciated, his cheekbones ridged. A blade of a nose and narrow nostrils, which he'd wiped several times with a rag. Sores in the stubble of his shaven scalp. His head looked unsteady on the stem of his neck, while his shirt might have been draped on the back of a chair. The points of his ankles stuck out from the gap between his clogs and the cuffs of his threadbare trousers. Once or twice he had tottered and skidded on the snow.

She leaned against the parapet, disguising her concern at the state he was in by gazing over the moat, where hamadryas baboons were scouring the rocks for scatter-feed: chestnuts and acorns gathered by children evacuated to the Prussian countryside. The animals scampered from ledge to ledge and raked up nuts until their cheeks were bulging — when the rocks were bare, there would be time enough to eat.

Vera glanced sideways at the Czech. He was labouring to breathe. On the walk from the kitchens she'd thought to offer him some feed, then seen the baboons and decided not to risk offending him. He could help himself to food when no one was looking, though there was little enough to spare.

On the rocks the tribe began to eat. Otto, the top male, lolled at the summit, submitting to the grooming of a pair of females, one of whom probed his grey fur flanks, the other his mane. He reached backwards and scratched his rump, wrinkling the scarlet skin. His tail twitched. He stretched and yawned, showing arcs of fangs. He was as big as a Doberman and twice the size of the females, who were mostly grooming each other or fending off juveniles: dark-furred homunculi with agile eyes. On the lower ledges sat several scowling young males with swept-back manes, separate not only from the group but each other, as well as elderly males with baffled, rheumy eyes.

She scanned the Czech's face for signs of interest in the exhibit, but he looked weary and indifferent. His clothes were urban and might once have been smart, as if he'd been plucked from a café in Prague. His hands were delicate, notched and scabby. She knew from Axel that he understood German, though so far he'd said nothing, as the law commanded. Around other people in the kitchens, Vera hadn't dared to ask his name. Now that the *Ostarbeiter* were here she could see that accepting them was the latest in a series of compromises — from tolerating propaganda to patronising shops that refused to serve Jews. Necessity eroded whatever morals you might have had, leaving only confusion. Even if Axel was right that the zoo was a sanctuary for the *Ostarbeiter*, some like the Czech were so malnourished they would be lucky to survive the winter, however kindly they were treated.

One of the females grooming Otto stood on all fours and sauntered away, revealing a swollen rump, and a ripple of disturbance spread through the tribe. On the ledge below Otto, the female stopped and settled down on the cushion of her rear.

The Czech's upper lip was flared in distaste. He noticed her watching him and made his face a blank.

'Our baboons repel you?'

The Czech hesitated. 'The baboons do not concern me.' His voice seemed too deep for the narrow chest. If he spoke with an accent, she couldn't detect it.

It was strange to see the zoo through the eyes of someone to whom it meant nothing. His indifference to a few baboons was not only understandable but also just, yet even so she felt slightly piqued. The exhibit combined so many of the features that she and Axel had laboured to perfect: tilted layers of naturalistic rockwork, climbing branches, overhangs and caves, and an elevation that made visitors look up to the animals. If she'd been superstitious, she might have felt vindicated by this enclosure's escape from the bombs.

There was a burst of shrieking as Otto sprang upright and loped towards a male sniffing at the female in oestrus.

The female bolted, spreading squawk and scramble, juveniles clinging to their mothers' bellies like upside-down jockeys. The younger male braced and held his ground, and from the corner of her eye Vera saw the Czech tense. Otto struck with his entire weight and the two animals rolled. The tribe whooped in panic. Like a boxer, Otto drew back and then reattacked, and seconds later he was in pursuit.

The chase was brief. On the far side of the enclosure the younger male braked and then lifted his buttocks in the air. Otto swaggered up and with a bored expression mimed thrusting in his rear.

Vera stepped back from the parapet, noticing with annoyance that the routine display had unsettled her. She asked the Czech his name.

'Krypic,' he said. His face was sullen. She worried that her question might have sounded peremptory, and sensed from his tone that if he'd been a soldier he might have added a rank and serial number. A friendly gesture might sting like a slap.

'Herr Krypic, I'm Vera Frey.' She picked up two of the empty pails. 'And I'm afraid it's time we returned to work.'

The Czech nodded, bent down and lifted his pails. He was short for a man, not much taller than she was. A similar age or older, at least that was her impression, until she noticed that the skin around his eyes was smooth and realised that privation had made him seem older than he really was. He walked with a shuffling gait. Above the breast-pocket of his shirt was an oblong patch, roughly embroidered with the single word *OST*: a point on the compass, a classification, the direction of a wind.

THREE

From the open bathroom came a clatter of cosmetics. 'Is it true there are crocodiles in the sewers?' called Flavia.

Vera said no, and Flavia mewed with disappointment. 'I also heard that a tiger broke into Café Josty and died after eating a pastry. That's untrue as well? What a pity. Though I don't suppose anyone could contradict me. Tonight it's important to create a sensation.' Her throaty voice bounced off the tiles.

'You cause a sensation every night.'

Flavia peered around the doorjamb. 'Darling, that very much depends on who I'm with.' She winked and ducked back out of sight. 'It just happens that tonight I want to cause a bigger sensation than usual.'

Vera waited for the explanation she knew would follow.

'There's a man.'

'You're joking,' said Vera.

'Go ahead and scoff. This time it's different. We met

underground on the night of the bombing. I was rocked to my foundations.'

Flavia told all she knew about Friedrich Motz-Wilden. A *Junker* family with an estate in East Prussia. Privileged schooling. At twenty-one a fighter pilot with numerous kills. Shot down over the North Sea and rescued, badly wounded. Partial rehabilitation. Transfer from active service to the Foreign Office as *Luftwaffe* liaison officer. Encounter with the marvellous Flavia Stahl in an air-raid shelter beneath the Hotel Bristol. Invitation issued to same for attendance at a Foreign Office cocktail party. 'I'm reliably informed there'll be food,' said Flavia.

Vera knew better than to take the attraction seriously. This flyer couldn't be more than twenty-three, and Flavia was a mercenary lover in any case, manoeuvring from one man to another according to the rewards on offer. If it hadn't been for her political convictions — she never slept with Nazis — she might have been an out-and-out courtesan, though it was hard to condemn her unscrupulous streak, as she could never have survived on a make-up artist's wages. Thanks to a lover in the Reich Labour Front, she'd avoided the production line.

She emerged from the bathroom in full get-up: silver earrings, elbow-length gloves, a black satin dress and her usual exquisite make-up, scavenged from the Rose. In nostalgia for the 1920s, a decade she'd been too young to enjoy, she bared the back of her neck with a layered bob.

'You look like an otter,' said Vera.

Flavia stopped and swivelled. 'That's an outrageous accusation.'

'Glossy and sleek. It's a compliment.'

Flavia gaped in mock revulsion.

'Howler monkey,' said Vera. 'The likeness is superb. Any chance they'll put on *Aesop's Fables* at the Rose?'

Flavia tossed her head, snatched a packet of cigarettes and crossed the room — Nordic furniture, Parisian prints, and a suitcase full of banned jazz records that Flavia claimed she sometimes shared with her *Blockleiter*, a former Social Democrat. She put on a coat and together they went out onto the fourth-floor balcony. Pale sunlight angled low over the opposite block as they sat down at a circular table. Most of the windows in the street were boarded up or sealed with blackout paper. To the north, at the intersection with the Kurfürstendamm, hoardings fenced off half of a block where a direct hit had brought down a tenement. Traffic on the Ku'damm shunted past in shadow, while above the double-decker buses the sun lit a pair of stone eagles on pillars.

Flavia lit a cigarette, her cupped hands echoing bracket lines on either side of a muscular mouth. Languidly she waved the match, failing to put it out, then calmly lowered it into an ashtray where it curled like a dead worm on concrete. She inhaled sharply and fell back in her chair. 'A smoke in sweet tranquillity! You know, yesterday on the

U-Bahn some sow tried to stop me — The German Woman Does Not Smoke. A *Hausfrau*, by the look of her. I could have slapped her jowls.'

Vera scanned the nearest balconies. All were empty. 'An informer, probably. Lucky you didn't.'

'Lucky for her.'

She blew a stream of smoke, as usual leaving Vera feeling tame for complying with state propaganda. At times she was tempted to take up smoking as a gesture of defiance against the regime, but her father — a free-thinker in other ways — had disapproved of cigarettes, and though she'd defied his memory, five years after his death, by smoking at university, she hadn't enjoyed it and had soon given up. A loved parent's beliefs were the hardest to reject.

Flavia lunged and tapped ash off her cigarette. 'Soon we'll get them,' she whispered. 'Just see if we don't.' She pointed at the eagles perched high above the Ku'damm. 'In no time at all they'll be swinging from the wing tips.'

Vera glanced backwards, a reflex action. 'The *Hausfrauen* too?'

'Them as well. We might need stronger gallows, but they won't miss out.' She beamed savagely and Vera returned a half-hearted smile. Though every inch the anti-Nazi, Flavia could sound as rabid as the authorities.

Thoughts of home overcame her, as they had done all week. Soon it would be summer in Australia, but beyond that she couldn't be sure of anything. For a few months of the previous year she had worried about the threat of the advancing Japanese but, from what she could gather from Radio London, they'd been stopped and, like the *Wehrmacht* in Russia, were now in retreat. There was no way of knowing how her family and old friends were getting on. Letters had once tethered her to home, but in the silence since 1939, Sydney had grown more distant.

Flavia stabbed the ashtray with her used cigarette. 'What's up, Vera Frey?'

'I want to go home,' she replied.

'You mean Home home?'

Vera nodded and Flavia took her by the hand.

'It's natural you're homesick after losing the villa.'

Vera tried to smile. If only it were just homesickness — there was so much on her mind. The animals had become a daily sorrow, and so far she hadn't even found the courage to tell Flavia about the *Ostarbeiter*.

'Trust me,' said Flavia, 'you're upset about the villa. But soon you'll get a flat, and after the war you'll rebuild. This is just a temporary inconvenience.'

'Be sure to warn me of a major disruption.'

Flavia grinned, checked her watch and announced that it was time to leave for the Foreign Office. Vera wished her luck, submitted to a kiss on each cheek, and Flavia left the balcony. A short time later she emerged on the street, waved and set off up Meinekestrasse, stepping swiftly in high-heeled shoes as if aiming at a series of targets at her toes.

Vera buttoned her coat, pensive again. She would be alone until Axel returned from the zoo. Twilight had come, yet no lights were visible, the city sinking into a darkness as complete as any that would have fallen when the land here was forest and marsh, and suddenly her presence in a darkening city on the northern plain of Europe seemed utterly strange. If this were a dream, she wondered, would waking come as a relief? Would she unwish Berlin, the zoo, or even Axel, for the chatter of rosellas on her mother's veranda?

She shivered. These were pointless thoughts, and there was nothing like cold to bring you back to your senses. She stood up and went inside to wait for Axel. A brass doorknob, blackout paper, a cold dark flat. The facts of her life were unalterable.

★   ★   ★

At twenty-eight she had been a teacher of German to daughters of the Sydney elite. Her mother fretted that she'd never marry, the Great War having culled potential husbands, but it wasn't marriage or even men that Vera was looking for — she'd had lovers and might have had husbands too, though her mother didn't know it. What Vera longed for was travel, if possible to Europe. Her brother had fought in France, and along with some oddly bloodless tales of the trenches he'd returned with more vivid stories of passing through Egypt, then of later taking leave in London and Scotland. Like her, Selby hadn't married, though for different reasons: he was prone to tearfulness, and sometimes to violence in public bars. He couldn't hold a job. Vera was fully grown before she realised that Selby had not escaped from the trenches unscathed, but his war retained an air of romance for her and she longed to make journeys of her own.

She had liked Axel Frey from the moment she had seen him standing behind a lectern, a solidly built man speaking with passion and intellect. She wasn't surprised when he introduced himself. He took her to tea, and they visited Taronga Zoo. He was twelve years her senior, witty and warm. He'd fought in the trenches, though for the other side, travelled widely and led the kind of expansive life that Vera wanted for herself. Quickly she saw him as a possible liberator. Three days later they were lovers.

Axel was wary when she asked to go with him to Europe, and made it clear that he couldn't be her keeper. She told him she was able to care for herself. She wanted the world, not new dependency — this would be a cheerful affair of convenience. Axel booked them two cabins on the *Einhorn*, a freighter bound for Hamburg.

To her mother, running off with a man meant disgrace, and running off to Europe meant never seeing her daughter again, whether Vera married or not. Selby's objections were political: the National Socialists had suspended elections in Germany. Hitler was talking about rebuilding the army, and if that happened Britain and France would invade. Vera told him that she wouldn't stay in Germany long.

Saying goodbye before sailing was difficult: though Selby behaved cheerfully, their mother was tearful. Vera kissed and half embraced her then broke away and marched up the gangplank. An uncomfortable hour followed, during which she stood at the rail while friends and family waited on the wharf. Axel had thought it best to take to his cabin. When the *Einhorn* pulled away, she waved wildly at the cluster of her loved ones, at least partly in relief. The ship passed Fort Denison and Axel came back on deck. The harbour was unnaturally still. When Sydney Heads clamped shut at the stern, she was startled by misgivings, then a breeze blew up and the moment passed. An escort of gulls saw the *Einhorn* out to sea.

The voyage was pure pleasure. Axel was a keen conversationalist, and within days her spoken German improved. They spent hours in Axel's cabin making love and then lying back and talking as daddy-longlegs slung gossamer cables overhead.

Several times a day Axel checked on the animals he'd collected: dingoes, wallabies, koalas and possums — eighteen creatures in all. The animals were in crates on the *Einhorn*'s rear deck, extremes of hot and cold being less harmful to wild animals, said Axel, than a lack of fresh air.

Tarpaulins protected them from sun and rain. Vera visited the animals from time to time and worried about their cramped conditions, though Axel promised they'd have more space in Berlin and live much longer than in the wild.

Most of her knowledge of animals came from well-loved family pets — a cocker spaniel, two cats, some ferrets that her brother had kept and a dynasty of budgerigars — and she felt a similar affection growing for the animals in the crates, and suggested naming them. Axel agreed and asked for Aboriginal names, forcing her to admit that place names were the only Aboriginal words she knew. Berliners wouldn't know the difference, he said, and so with the help of an atlas they named all eighteen.

When the ship reached the equator and all three koalas — Wollongong, Goodooga and Guyra — died in quick succession, she felt ashamed of the fun she'd had in naming them. Axel explained that koalas were notoriously hard to transport. The idiosyncrasies of some species were a mystery, he said, which was why they were needed for study in zoos.

The ship reached Aden, on the Arabian Peninsula, and Axel showed her the old fortress overlooking the port. They rode on donkeys from the edge of the city to the rim of a dead volcano. This was the life she'd dreamed about, and she had Axel to thank. His chatter and booming laugh were addictive.

Two days out of Aden the ship was overrun with fleas, and as a precaution against plague the captain ordered fumigation. Vera went to the cabin to fetch books and stationery for a long stay on deck, then Axel arrived with a half-full hessian sack. He was smiling and clearly plotting a surprise, and she obliged him by looking puzzled. With a magician's flourish he opened the sack and pulled out an empty jar. He unscrewed the lid, stepped onto a chair and, with the jar in one hand and its lid in the other, he trapped the nearest spider and grinned. He passed her the jar. 'Hand up another. We'll put in breathing holes later.'

At this instant, shortly after lunch, in the Red Sea at latitude twenty degrees north, she fell in love with Axel Frey.

★   ★   ★

With only herself, Axel and Herr Winzens left of the original staff, Vera took charge of one of three work teams and set about sandbagging buildings, sealing windows and stockpiling food for winter. Her work team was made up of three Poles and the Czech, Krypic, and for all her misgivings she was thankful for their labour. Most soon wore coats that must have come from the blackmarket, probably in exchange for stolen zoo feed. Vera worried about those without. The scarecrow Krypic was one who hadn't provided for himself — whether from bad luck or apathy, Vera couldn't tell — and to give him a chance to recuperate she had him moved to the kitchens.

The next day she brought ingredients from her own rations to feed a white-cheeked gibbon with influenza — precious protein: a little milk and a single egg. Like all the primates, the gibbons were dear to her.

Inside, the Czech was scrubbing trays, deep in clatter and splash. Twin cords of sinew ridged the back of his neck, and she saw that his fingers were clawed with cold — the kitchens were not quite the sanctuary she'd imagined. She said hello and he jolted. He glared when she apologised.

She found a whisk and a mixing bowl and returned to the bench-top. Water splashed in Krypic's tub. His neck looked thin, so vulnerable to injury. She let her hands taste the curves of the egg and then cracked the shell. Krypic fell silent. Vera paused, holding the shell together, then the awkwardness of waiting seemed worse than going on and she emptied its contents into the bowl. She added the milk and seized the whisk, and at last the Czech went back to his scrubbing.

She churned the mixture till it bubbled and then draped a cloth across the bowl. The Czech tapped water off the last of his trays, gripped the handles of the tub and hefted it off the bench, making the sinews splay at the base of his neck. He staggered towards the drain, starting a wave in the tub and splashing his shirt. Vera rushed to his side and seized one of the handles, freeing him to take the other with both hands, and together they tipped the tub over the drain. An arc of filthy water slithered into the floor.

'Thank you,' he said and straightened up. His wet shirt clung to his belly, and already he was shivering.

'We'll have to find you — all of you — some warm clothes,' she said. That evening he would march through the snow with the other *Ostarbeiter* to their barracks in Moabit.

His face tilted towards her. 'The accent — you're not German?'

He'd hardly finished speaking when he flinched, as if scared by his own temerity. Quickly she said, 'No, no. Australian.'

Krypic nodded. He frowned then suddenly looked resigned. In English he said, 'So your mother-tongue is English.'

She felt a flutter of surprise, though English speakers were hardly rare. In her own language she replied, 'Yes, English. You know it?'

'To read, perhaps.' He switched to German. 'My spoken English is not so good.'

He stopped, perhaps remembering the prohibitions. She would have liked to set him at ease but felt inhibited herself, not from fear but embarrassment. His face was angled and planed like some avant-garde sculpture.

'We can talk another time. By then I'll have seen about extra clothes.'

He looked sceptical. She hesitated, fetched her bowl and left the building.

Axel watched as Herr Winzens measured the boiler-room floor. The air was hot and close. A feeble light shone on the keeper's iron-grey hair. Finally he turned and shook his head. 'You'll never fit a generator in here. *Unmöglich, nein,* it can't be done.'

The old man crossed his arms, looking gloomily satisfied. He was right, that was obvious, but Axel knew not to give up.

'No space next door, either,' said Herr Winzens. As if to check this, he peered into the annexe.

Patience was the key. The keeper was an able foreman but pessimistic by nature. Years ago he'd resisted Vera's enclosure plans, making her mutter for weeks about dismissing him, but by then Herr Winzens had been an institution at the zoo. Axel could remember trailing behind him as a boy when they'd accompanied Axel's father on the morning inspection. He had loved watching the men working, yet he had also liked to steal away to favourite nooks in what he had liked to consider a private domain. Once, Herr Winzens had discovered him behind the pagoda moulding animal figures out of elephant dung — a game that Axel had suddenly realised was surely very bad. On the way back to his father, he'd pictured the keeper betraying him in the careless jokey way of men, yet Herr

Winzens had kept mum — out of forgetfulness or compassion, Axel never knew, but even now he felt an echo of gratitude.

The old man glanced from one side of the wall to the other. 'Not load-bearing by the look of it.' He tapped the brick. 'Knock a hole through, and there's space for your generator. Then, so you won't choke, run an exhaust pipe outside.'

You had to lure Herr Winzens with a problem. When he had grumbled about the construction of the monkey rocks, Axel had feigned incompetence and, when the crane arrived, the old man had clambered around the site all day, signalling and yelling orders at the operator.

'I'll sledge a hole through the wall then.'

He drew a pencil from behind his ear and made a series of marks on the wall, as if he'd known the solution all along. He began to talk about angles, tools and materials, and Axel joined in, discussion now being as vital as patience at the start.

The keeper was still talking when Vera entered the annexe. She strode over and stopped in the doorway.

'It's getting cold. Those *Ostarbeiter* need uniforms.'

Axel sighed inwardly. Vera could be tactless at times.

But she was right; he should have thought of it himself. Herr Winzens stowed the pencil behind his ear and straightened up.

'They're wasted in storage,' added Vera.

Axel tried to reply but Herr Winzens was faster. 'We'll need those uniforms for when the lads come home. After the war.'

Vera looked impatient. 'Are all our lives on hold until after the war?'

Axel made a move in the direction of the boiler-room door, but neither Herr Winzens nor Vera paid any attention. Most of the keepers would never return, though he wasn't about to say so.

Herr Winzens said, 'Give away those uniforms and how will we replace them?'

'We'll get them back,' said Vera.

'You'd be lucky, I reckon. And in what condition?'

'Those workers need warm clothing.'

Herr Winzens rolled his eyes at this, giving Axel a chance to speak. 'If the men get sick, they'll be useless, Artur. We can fit them out with jackets and keep the trousers in storage.'

The keeper looked gloomy but unsurprised. He shook his head. 'If they're getting part of them, they can wear the lot.'

He grunted in reply to Vera's thanks and returned to his measuring. Vera raised a furtive eyebrow then left the room, while Axel lingered, vaguely hoping to make amends. The last few years had been hard on Herr Winzens, and the loss of his cottage had been a heavy blow, forcing him to take refuge in Kreuzberg with a hated niece.

Axel asked about ventilation for the generator, but the question sounded forced and, rather than risking more embarrassment, he left the old man to his work.

Outside, the air was biting but fresh. He set out between the battered enclosures, glad to be in the open and free to wander for a while. Above the bare arms of the trees, a cloud swept low across the sky.

At the ostrich house he paused as a stranger might, seeing its oddness in the field of snow. Though scarred, the ostrich house wasn't structurally damaged. A mural on the hieroglyphed façade showed men with switches herding a queue of ostriches, flanked on either side by a row of rigid women with baskets of eggs as big as river stones. If the temple were destroyed, how might an enclosure for ostriches look?

Axel rounded the building and reached the outdoor pen, where the living ostriches paced and paused.

Irritating others, he reminded himself, was an inevitable result of wielding authority. He did his best to be fair, and at times even tried to fool himself that he could befriend the staff, but zookeeping was a practical affair, and when theory became action someone always seemed to suffer. Command had come more easily to his father, who'd ignored the opinions of others and never doubted his own, and even when the staff had grumbled they had seemed to respect him. His self-assurance had made them feel safe, like animals.

Overhead, a band of sunlight pierced the cloud and flashed white on the snow and the ostriches' plumes. Axel squinted and turned away. He had uniforms to organise. Burying his head was no option here — the ground was hard as iron.

That evening, Vera watched the *Ostarbeiter* march out of the zoo in the dark-green uniforms of keepers. She threw an arm around Axel's waist and drew him close. Three days until Christmas and goodwill to last a year.

They followed the workers onto the street and Axel locked the gate: a flimsy structure of planks held together with barbed wire. Vera linked her arm in his, and they set out for Meinekestrasse. In the absence of streetlights, the Milky Way was a radiant stream.

She had never doubted her husband's kindness; it was his lack of political wisdom that sometimes troubled her. On board the *Einhorn* she had challenged him about National Socialism, and he had dismissed it as a passing aberration. He'd lampooned the misfits in the Party hierarchy and ridiculed the Nazis' mania for uniforms, and mistaking his assurance for political insight she had set aside her questions.

Three months after her arrival in Berlin, Axel's father had been diagnosed with stomach cancer. Since the death of his wife in the '20s, the old man had lived alone at the villa, visited daily by a housekeeper-cook. At the dinner table he spoke of only two topics: his transformation of Berlin's Zoological Gardens into the greatest in the world, and the good work that Hitler was doing for the nation. National Socialism had brought the people to their senses — as if the Party were a national dose of smelling salts. Hitler knew how to dispose of troublemakers, and Germany needed someone strong. Early in the new year, Herr Frey had died and, for the first and only time, Vera had witnessed Axel weep.

At Meinekestrasse they found the flat empty, though Flavia was due back soon — plays and films were scheduled early to avoid interruptions from the British.

Vera led Axel into the bathroom and lit a candle. Now that water was reconnected, baths were permitted twice a week. She ran the hot water and the air filled with steam. She took off her clothes and loosened Axel's belt. He beamed. 'And to what do I owe this good fortune?'

'You need to ask?' She stabbed a toe into the tub.

He smiled and pointed at the taps. 'I'll take the gentleman's end.'

She shook her head — he'd been gentleman enough already. She turned off the taps and eased into the water, revelling in the heat. Axel undressed, stepped into the bath but immediately sprang out, hollering about the heat, then gingerly he tried again and settled down, raising the water to the brim. Vera tucked her feet against his ribs. She gazed through the steam. 'Thank you for today.'

'No, it was your doing. Let's just hope that Herr Winzens forgives us.'

She linked her legs with his and kneaded his calves. Axel touched the clefts of her knees, and she lazed backwards beside the taps and thought of nothing for a while. Axel was idly stroking her thighs, outwards then inwards and back again. The skin had memory. She could trust in this.

At last she sighed and clambered onto her knees, easing Axel backwards and splashing the floor. He giggled. She kissed him, stroked the snowy hair on his chest and wriggled higher.

She loved the merging, the letting go of who was who — male, female, either, both. From one of their chests came a humming sound. Her knees were rocking on the bath's enamel, but any pain had given way to pleasure, a torrent of stars. She closed her eyes and emptied her mind, but then Axel's body slackened. He said sorry and groaned. The heat, he said. He apologised again.

She felt breathless with need — a type of shock, she supposed, then almost giggled at the hyperbole of the comparison. She took a deep breath to steady her voice and told Axel she didn't mind. Men were fragile as flowers, and how she acted now could affect the whole evening. Carefully she slid backwards into the bath and gave Axel's calf a squeeze. She tried to nestle against the cast-iron tub, but she was restless, still stirred. She longed to reach down and touch herself, but what he might have welcomed another time was out of the question now.

For a minute they lay still, then Axel sat up, sending more water onto the floor. He clasped her wrists and raised her to her knees, and Vera felt his arms around her waist and the warmth of his mouth on her hip. She gripped both sides of the bath as he continued. The water lapped her thighs. She shivered, part immersed, part exposed to the air, and familiar noises invaded her throat. This was quick, quick. She strained and braced, seizing Axel by the arms, gasped and then slumped across his back.

Axel sank and resurfaced, pretending to splutter for air. She kissed him hard, invigorated by relief, and in mock helplessness he began to wave his arms about.

She was still laughing when Flavia's key rattled the front door and, though the bathroom door was shut, Vera shrank back in the tub. Flavia came into the living room.

'Vera, is that you in there?'

'It's both of us.'

'*Ooo la la*! I'm afraid you'll have to stop. I have news.'

'Can't it wait?'

'No it can't. Are you ready? I'm coming in.' She threw open the door and stepped inside, saw the floor and threw up her hands. 'My God, a gale!'

Vera crossed her arms. 'You could have told us through the door.' Axel looked relaxed.

'This is too important,' said Flavia. She paused for effect. 'I'm getting married!'

Vera hesitated. 'To your fighter-ace?'

'Don't be ridiculous. I like him too much. No, to a friend of his, another pilot.'

'His name?'

'Franz. Or Fritz. Something like that. Aren't either of you going to congratulate me?'

'Would it be out of place to ask why you're marrying a stranger?' asked Axel.

'Ration coupons. There's extra for weddings, and I need some for a New Year's party. You're both invited, by the way, though on one condition: I need witnesses for the wedding.'

On the last day of 1943, Vera arrived with Axel at a registry office in Charlottenburg. Flavia was pacing about the waiting room. The groom's friend, Friedrich Motz-Wilden, wouldn't be coming at all, she explained, as he was busy scrounging alcohol for the party. Would Axel mind very much standing in as best man?

The groom arrived late, infuriating the Registrar, a short, bald Bavarian in the grip of a cold. The groom was young, too young for marriage — Vera doubted that he'd reached his twenties. Blond hair cropped close at the sides, with a lengthy fringe brushed low across his forehead. Blue eyes in a squarish face that was almost handsome. A small, lithe build. When he made his vows he grinned as if drunk, but it was ten in the morning so this seemed unlikely. Pinned to the breast of his uniform was a knight's cross with oak-leaf clusters, awarded for extreme acts of valour in combat.

When the ceremony was over, Vera helped witness the certificates of marriage and racial purity. In defiance of custom, Flavia had elected to keep her surname. Though plainly bored during the vows, she now stared intently at the marriage certificate and motioned at the date stamp on the Registrar's desk. The Registrar sniffed, refusing to be rushed, and rummaged his pocket for a handkerchief. With his spare hand he stamped the documents and presented the originals to the groom.

Outside on the pavement the wedding party broke up then went separate ways: Flavia to claim ration cards, the groom to organise the party, Vera and Axel to the zoo.

At the kitchens, Herr Winzens greeted them with bad news: overnight the colony of two dozen fairy penguins had died for no detectable reason, though malnutrition had no doubt played a part. The penguins were the only birds that Vera had felt no qualms about keeping, and the death of her 'little men' was desolating.

By eight that evening she felt exhausted. At Flavia's flat she reluctantly dressed for the party, then caught the *U-Bahn* with Axel to the suburb of Dahlem, where the groom was staying with his parents. Flavia had gone ahead to prepare the rationed feast.

From the station, Dahlem looked almost normal, each house sheltering behind a garden fence, but a rising moon showed that bombs had fallen here too, destroying every fourth or fifth home. Broken tree trunks gored the pavements. An air raid was unlikely while the moon was full, as Flavia would have known when she planned the party — these days, everyone knew the lunar calendar as surely as any peasant.

The house was shielded by a high brick wall and a line of fir trees epauletted with snow. Vera followed Axel through the gate and onto a gravel path. Ahead, through more trees, a cigarette glowed, then the moonlight revealed a man dressed in a greatcoat and the cap of a military officer. From the shadows the stranger wished them good evening and asked to see their invitations, and Vera drew nearer and produced them. With the same hand in which he held the cigarette he took the invitations and raised them to the moonlight. His greatcoat was *Luftwaffe* issue.

'Follow me.'

He turned and led them along the path until the trees parted in front of a two-storey house, the home of well-to-do bourgeoisie. Its windows were dark, the blackout impenetrable. From inside came chamber music played on a gramophone, the chords made spectral through the walls. The *Luftwaffe* officer opened the front doors and motioned Vera and Axel into a foyer. He called the bridegroom, who appeared a few seconds later by a central stairway. In the lamplight he looked even more youthful than at the registry. He welcomed them and took their coats and hats, spilling Axel's hat onto the parquetry. The groom gestured at the officer. 'Not too startled by our ghost? We always have one at parties, in the buffer zone. The best thing about a garden, really.'

'Motz-Wilden,' said the officer. He stubbed his cigarette in an ashtray and extended his left hand to Axel. 'I've been careless enough to lose the other, you see.' His right sleeve was pinned to the elbow. A strong jaw line, full lips. He turned and Vera caught sight of seared flesh on the left side of his head and neck.

The groom promised to find Motz-Wilden a replacement for guard duty, then showed them into a drawing room heated by an open fire. Immediately he fetched two tumblers of aquavit from a sideboard, which also held the gramophone Vera had heard from the garden. Otherwise the room was empty of furniture. A Persian rug on the floor. Overhead a chandelier.

It was still early and only a few guests had arrived. Vera left Axel talking with the groom and went looking for Flavia, tracing a smell of burnt pastry down a corridor that led to a kitchen with a flagstone floor and a big wooden table. Copper pots lined the walls. Flavia was working with two other women, both in long, glittering dresses. Their polished fingernails looked purpose-grown for making hors d'oeuvres.

Flavia saw her and squealed with relief. The strudel was burnt, she said, the bratwurst in trouble. She introduced the two women as Trudie and Heike. 'Vera, darling, we need your help.'

By the time the snacks were ready, the party was well underway. Vera counted at least twenty guests, most younger than she was — a large gathering by recent standards, and disproportionately loud. Most of the men were uniformed, a number in the blue of the *Luftwaffe*. Some were wounded and on crutches. One had bandaged, foreshortened feet, the signature of frostbite. Another was blind. Flavia's theatre friends chatted to the wounded men as if nothing was amiss, and it was almost possible to look around the room and only see ordinary young people at play.

With a tray of hors d'oeuvres, Vera circled the floor then joined a group made up of Axel, the groom and Friedrich Motz-Wilden. Motz-Wilden had removed his cap, revealing a head of black hair above the lava of his burn. His left ear was livid but whole. Judging by the fold in his sleeve, he'd lost half his forearm as well as the hand.

The groom had seen her watching Motz-Wilden and winked. 'Friedrich is the luckiest man alive.'

'Oh?' she replied, aware of having hesitated.

'Shot down over water and lived to tell the tale. What's most remarkable, though, is that Freddie's happy. Nothing bothers him. Not the imminent loss of the family estate to the Russians. Not the lopped-off limb, or the state of his face.'

'I was never good-looking,' said Motz-Wilden.

This was clearly untrue. The scar had added flamboyant criminality to what must have been already striking looks. His eyes were deep blue. It was the face of a gunrunner or a mercenary, though he spoke with a cultivated *Junker* drawl.

'Freddie's a diplomat,' said the groom.

'I was just describing my trip to Stockholm,' explained Motz-Wilden. 'Undertaken at some risk to get the Swedish firewater that glimmers in our glasses.'

'So that's how the diplomatic corps keeps busy these days,' said Axel.

'Idle hands,' said Motz-Wilden.

'But you're too hard on yourself!' protested the groom. He raised his glass and in a martial voice said, "The Reich, I assure you, is grateful for your efforts!' It was a poor impersonation, but good enough to interest an informer, though no one seemed bothered, least of all Axel. The groom took another slug of aquavit.

Vera asked Motz-Wilden what his impressions were of Sweden.

'Hard to say,' he said. 'The term I favour is neutral. It's the winteriness partly, yet there's more colour in Stockholm than in Berlin — on awnings, in shop windows' — he gestured at his uniform — 'in the clothing. No, it's not the streets that are colourless but the tone of the place. Drugged, somehow slumbering. Neutral.'

'Whereas Germany?' prompted the groom. Vera tensed in alarm.

'Germany is red,' declared Motz-Wilden, then noting the groom's amusement he added, 'whatever the ideologues might say. We're alive, but deepest red.'

The group fell quiet, all but the groom, who was warming to the game. 'And what colour is Russia?'

'The Soviet Union is brown. Potato-sack brown. The colour of the future.'

Vera excused herself and left the room. In the kitchen she seized Flavia and dragged her into the corridor. 'You have to do something about your *Luftwaffe* friends.'

'Why? What's wrong with them?'

'They're talking treason.'

'They always talk treason. That's why I like them.'

'I mean serious sedition.'

'Vera, there are no informers here.'

Vera gave her a look of frank scepticism.

'All right,' said Flavia, 'if it makes you feel better, I'll quieten them down.'

She fetched Trudie and Heike and led them up the corridor, promising to introduce them to eligible men, beginning with her husband. In the drawing room she took the groom by the arm and pressed against his shoulder. On stilettos she towered above him. 'Don't we make the most adorable couple?'

'Irresistible,' agreed Trudie, '*unwiderstehlich*.'

'The blush on those cheeks!' cried Heike. 'It makes you want to tweak them.'

The groom beamed, looking indistinguishable from a man just wedded to the love of his life. Axel led a toast to the happy couple.

'Where will you go on your honeymoon?' asked Trudie.

'London,' said the groom, 'maybe Dover. By the docks there's a quaint little hotel I want to wreck.'

'Tonight's the honeymoon,' said Flavia. 'I'm back at work tomorrow. Schiller again. What I'd give to work on a contemporary play!'

This statement was as reckless as some of the groom's had been. Flavia regularly bemoaned the end of the avant-garde, having come of age in the dictatorship, missing the long golden night on the town that was Berlin in the '20s.

'Any chance you might get a role?' asked Axel.

'You're sweet to keep asking but you needn't anymore. Make-up is enough. Knowing your true calling — isn't that the key to happiness?'

'Not even spear-carrying?'

'You must be joking. If I can't be a star, I won't act at all.'

'Truth is,' slurred the groom, 'I'm honeymooning with Papa and Mutti. Here, at home. They can't deny me a thing. My revenge for childhood. Take tonight — "I'm having a party," I told them. Mutti angled for an invitation, but I put a stop to that. Packed them both off to my

73

uncle's, with them tumbling over themselves to agree. Didn't tell them I was getting married.'

'But that's cruel!' cried Heike.

'Not cruel. Kind. They need sacrifices to make on my behalf — the harder the better.'

'National Socialism's greatest crime,' said Motz-Wilden. 'Begetting a generation of monsters.'

The groom snickered. 'At least we know what monsters we've become. Aren't I right, Freddie?' He took a playful swing at Motz-Wilden's chest and missed. 'Totally heartless.'

Flavia wrapped her arms around him. 'No, *Liebling*, you're wonderful. Why else would I marry you?'

The groom shook his head. 'You're just pretending. I'm a beast. When I got home this time, Papa and Mutti had a gift. Party membership. A certificate. You know where I put it? On the toilet hook. Uproar. Ungrateful son.' He looked forlorn. 'But even that, they overlooked.'

'Let's dance,' said Flavia. 'I'll change the music.'

Vera edged Axel to one side. 'You realise we ought to leave.'

'Already? It's not midnight.'

'If someone calls the Gestapo, the party won't reach midnight.'

'Vera, our host is a highly decorated pilot. And Motz-Wilden's patriotism can hardly be questioned.'

'If you ask hard enough, there's nothing unquestionable.'

'So would you like another drink?'

She tried to look stern.

'If there is an informer,' said Axel, 'his notebook's full already. We might as well enjoy ourselves.'

He nudged her and made off to the sideboard, and ruefully she watched him refill their glasses. After dodging bullets and shells in Flanders, Axel couldn't calibrate risks that weren't made of metal. There was nothing for it but to take his advice and have a good time.

The gramophone crackled and then filled the room with the unmistakable strains of Billie Holliday, one of Flavia's banned records. Across the room, Flavia caught her eye and winked, and Vera couldn't help smiling. Axel returned and handed her another aquavit; they touched glasses and she took a heavy swig.

Two soldiers rolled up the carpet and Flavia led the groom onto the floor, quickly followed by more couples. Other guests were talking and joking, voices raised in competition with the gramophone. Even the men who were maimed seemed happy to be there, propped along the walls like boys at a country dance. Vera finished her drink and was about to take Axel's hand when Motz-Wilden appeared at her side and cupped her elbow. His heels clicked faintly together. 'May I?' The question was addressed half to her, half to Axel. Axel smiled and toasted them onto the dancefloor.

Motz-Wilden guided her between the other couples, the stump of his arm pressing against her back. 'No use nursing it,' he said when she glanced behind her. 'It never seems to grow.' He led with a two-step and they started to dance. Light from the chandelier polished his scar.

The record ended and Flavia put on Duke Ellington: saxophone, trumpet, cymbals and drums, with bass like an undertow in surf. Motz-Wilden began to spin her around in circles, blurring the view beyond his shoulder, and Vera felt the day's tiredness falling away. Beneath the worsted cloth of his uniform, Motz-Wilden's shoulders flexed. Self-assurance gave him the air of an older man.

The music slowed, a melancholy clarinet, and Motz-Wilden drew nearer, tingling her throat and scalp. Their cheeks were close but separate.

'It's a long time since I've danced with such a beautiful woman.'

She threw back her head in noiseless laughter.

'What's so funny?'

'You're a comedian.'

'I'm serious,' he said smilingly.

'Look around. There are younger women here.'

'Perhaps,' he replied, not looking away.

'All of them better-looking than me.'

'I don't have to look to know that's a lie.'

She felt herself blushing and silently cursed.

'Tell me,' said Motz-Wilden, lifting her left hand and tapping her wedding ring. 'Does this come off?'

'Goodness! Are you always so direct?'

'Are you always so evasive?'

'Am I being evasive?' she asked.

'An evasive question.'

'The answer is no, the ring doesn't come off.'

'Another night, perhaps?'

'Not on other nights, either.'

He gazed at her for a time and then shrugged. They kept dancing, a fraction less close than before.

Vera said, 'Tell me, does a request like that work? Do women say yes?'

'Sometimes. Mostly. You'd be surprised.'

She considered this. 'Not really. The war, that changes things. And you're good looking,' she added, leaving out the *still*.

It was his turn to scoff.

'The scar improves you,' she said, 'and even the rest — women don't seem to need a man in one piece.' She hesitated, anxious that she might have gone too far, but Motz-Wilden looked unfazed.

'So you'll take me after all.'

'That's not what I said.'

'Is there too much of me left, is that what you're saying?'

Clearly there was no risk of hurting this man — tonight he was at play.

'Nothing so perverse. Just that my marriage comes first.'

'That's too bad.'

Flavia put on another record, releasing a steeplechase of fiddles and castanets, accordions and zithers — wild, disorderly, eastern music, Romany or klezmer, that carried Vera back to her earliest years in Berlin, though she could not recall where she'd heard music like this, or remember the moment it had vanished.

Flavia strode back onto the floor, arms outspread, snapping her fingers. She drew up beside Motz-Wilden and, as if the move was rehearsed, Vera passed him into her arms, catching Motz-Wilden's eye for a final time as Flavia swept him away.

Axel was waiting by the gramophone. 'You'll have to watch yourself,' said Vera. 'I have an admirer.'

'Motz-Wilden?'

She nodded. 'He tried to seduce me.'

'The cheek. Has he succeeded?'

'Of course. It's all arranged.'

Axel feigned horror then tilted his glass in her direction. 'Can't fault the man's taste.'

'Impeccable,' agreed Vera. She looked at Motz-Wilden again and then spotted the groom. 'Do you think he'll get a chance to consummate the marriage?' This was prurient, but she blamed the alcohol. Axel looked amused.

'The question is, would he want to? In my opinion he only has eyes for Freddie.'

Vera looked more closely at the groom. 'Are you sure?'

'As I can be. He gazes at Freddie and speaks of no one

but Freddie — apart from Papa and Mutti, that is. Looks to me like a man in love.'

Vera looked from Axel to the groom and back again. Though her husband often seemed inattentive, he sometimes surprised her. She liked the idea of being married to a surprising man.

They danced for a while, then met more of the guests. A few had drunk too much on near-empty stomachs, though Flavia was in no hurry to return to the kitchen. 'I'm the bride!' she protested when Vera reminded her of the food. 'I can't be expected to do everything.'

'You're a fraud and I won't let you hide behind a veil. We'll do it together. Otherwise half your guests will pass out.'

In the kitchen they grilled the wedding-ration of sausage, then cut it into slivers, which they put onto rolls snaked with mustard. Flavia raced off to announce a smorgasbord. The crowd came in and swarmed the table then stood around eating and talking.

At five minutes to midnight, the groom climbed onto the table and spread his arms above a squall of talk and laughter.

'Friends! Honoured guests!' The noise abated. 'Unaccustomed as I am' — from the *Luftwaffe* came guffaws — 'unaccustomed as I am to speaking in public, I want to welcome you to my wedding, which by chance is taking place on the brink of the New Year.' The groom scanned the crowd. 'Some of you I know. Some I've forgotten. Some of you,' he said, staring at Motz-Wilden, 'I barely recognise anymore.' The laughter this time was tentative. Motz-Wilden smiled and shrugged.

'What's important, though,' continued the groom, 'is that you're here. If you *are* here. In body, that is — we're all here in spirit.' He was swaying slightly. His boyish face was flushed.

'Here at the dawn — and I'll hold you to that — at the dawn of 1944. Uncanny, that number, don't you think? Those fours like sawn-off swastikas.'

There were shouted reminders that midnight was near; the groom looked at his watch and spoke in a rush: 'I'll end by saying, have a happy New Year. Oh, and for a gorgeous dinner, thank delicious Flavia. She's my wife. A lovely girl and I know we'll be happy.'

He gazed at his watch and began conducting the passing seconds, reached ten and counted down aloud. The crowd joined the chant and at zero erupted, throwing streamers that wove into a net about their necks. Vera kissed Axel deeply and long, until the moment to kiss anyone else had passed.

Above the din a radio caterwauled, and a big-band number, sublimely American, boomed around the room — unmistakably from the BBC. Vera spun around to see who was risking execution, and by a radio in the corner she saw Friedrich Motz-Wilden. He adjusted the dials and, as the whole room watched, left the radio and vaulted onto the table beside the groom. The men swapped a signal, crossed their arms and dropped onto their haunches then started kicking double-time to the swing from London. Vera glanced at the other party-goers — the BBC was one thing, Cossack dancing another. In her experience, even anti-Nazis had qualms about the Soviets — these *Junkeren* no doubt more than most — but while a few looked troubled, they were soon clapping in time with the rest. With each kick, the two men edged clockwise, heels clipping wood, until Motz-Wilden barked an order and both men fell sideways, balancing on one arm and still kicking in time. Motz-Wilden was piston-booted. Still supporting himself on his one good arm, he began to clap with his forearms, palming the table on the downward stroke and launching himself back into the air. This was too much for the groom, who fell down flat and lay back laughing. Motz-Wilden pressed on, undulating in flight. He wore a fixed smile, though his nostrils pulsed, then he squatted again and lashed the timber with his boots, the crowd urging him on with whistles and cries. At last he was gasping and, as if on cue, he sprang to his feet and bowed. The audience thundered. He wiped his brow.

Flavia was clapping wildly, her thighs pressed against the edge of the table, while behind her Trudie and Heike were leaping like sequined trout on lines. Motz-Wilden leant forward, grasped one of Flavia's wrists and lifted her onto the table, where they launched into a dance that might have been swing. The groom reversed away then clambered off the table. Vera reached out and shook his hand.

'Bravo! I take it you've done that before.'

'A bit,' he admitted. 'In the mess, on a slow day.'

'That's not dangerous? Political?'

The young man laughed. 'What can they do? Kill us? Who'd fly the planes? And we're going to die in any case.' He was breathing flares of aquavit. Trudie and Heike climbed up beside the others, and the crowd stormed the table on every side. Trudie danced the charleston, Heike a shimmy. Motz-Wilden had Flavia bound up in a kiss, the aristocrat claiming seigneurial rights. The groom saw them too and his smile disappeared.

Axel was stomping across the flagstones like a Greek, but Vera longed to be up on the table. She pressed a knee to the timber and butted between calves, striving for a foothold, then the room fell away beneath her. She was up. She was dancing. Her sinews sang. The edge of the table was under her toes. Around her were swooping, frenzied bodies: young, middle-aged, truncated, whole. They were dancing like the possessed, on the rim of a crater, without heed or care or caution, and Vera knew with a fiery certainty that there was nowhere — not Sweden, not even Australia — that she would rather be at this moment than here.

FOUR

A week into January a letter came from the Reich Housing Authority announcing that a flat was available in Kreuzberg, south of the Mitte, and the next day Axel left to take a look while Vera packed what little they'd salvaged from the villa. Axel returned in the afternoon and would only say that the flat was small.

'Smaller than this?' she asked, sweeping an arm around Flavia's flat. He nodded and she didn't press for details.

On a freezing winter's morning they drove in the zoo's last lorry to 412 Reichenbergerstrasse, Kreuzberg, not far from where Herr Winzens had moved in with his niece. The street had been heavily damaged by the bombing, its buildings blackened and the rubble swept into heaps on the pavements.

'At least the streets are wide,' said Vera, the only consolation she could find in the scene beyond the windscreen.

'For a clear line of fire,' said Axel. Last century, he continued, peasants had flocked here from the country to work in the new textiles and heavy-engineering plants. 'The state was terrified of an uprising and planned for it.'

He turned off the street and eased the lorry through an archway that ran beneath a tenement. Beyond this was a courtyard, five-storeys high, sunk in twilight like a castle keep. Masonry choked the corners. Overhead there were timber baulks. Three of the walls were windowed, the fourth a blank of bricks. Snowflakes corkscrewed onto a cobbled pavement.

In the last courtyard they found Flavia arm in arm with Friedrich Motz-Wilden — since the night of the party, Flavia had rarely been home. Flavia's new husband stood off to one side, smoking a cigarette and looking sullen.

Axel pulled off the lorry's tarpaulin, exposing the last of their belongings: a suitcase holding clothes, an armchair, a cupboard and a drinks cabinet minus the glass panels in the doors. There were chairs and a table, courtesy of Motz-Wilden, and according to Axel the flat had a cast-off double bed.

Vera looked about and shivered. Number 412 resembled a prison. Incendiaries had added scald marks to layers of soot, and parts of the upper walls were missing.

On the threshold she stopped to get accustomed to the gloom. The vestibule smelt of fried fat and boiled cabbage. Flavia appeared at her side. 'Think of it as an adventure. A story to tell on the terrace of your chateau when you retire.'

The stairs were concrete, and in the elbow of the flights between the floors was a bathroom shared by four sets of tenants. Behind the doors to the other flats came voices and footfalls.

On the third floor, in near darkness, Axel stopped on the landing and stabbed with a key at the door of flat number six.

As he'd warned, the place was tiny: two rooms, one window and a coal-grimed stove. There was no running water or even a basin, and certainly no electricity. The glass of the window was broken. Fallen plaster revealed wooden ribs in the ceiling. The abandoned bed almost filled the bedroom. The sagging mattress was stained.

They returned to the courtyard and began unloading the lorry. Motz-Wilden couldn't help with the furniture, but Vera noticed that he ignored the smaller items too. On the landing he kept Flavia in a lengthy kiss.

The move was over in a depressingly short time. Flavia took Vera by the hand. 'It looks bad, I know, but you can make it better. And this won't last forever.' She crossed to Axel and poked the breast of his overcoat. 'Don't forget to look after her.'

'Vera looks after herself.'

'Well, I'm holding you responsible.'

'Flavia, please!' said Vera.

'All right, I'm going.' She ran her arm around Motz-Wilden's waist, pinched his buttocks and hustled him out of the flat. His pilot friend followed. He'd said very little and had smoked throughout. He was due back soon to his squadron in France.

Axel left after the others to return the lorry to the zoo, and Vera put away their belongings. The flat was freezing. Its skeleton creaked. The prospect of even a month here was awful.

When she had finished unpacking she swept the floor and then went downstairs to get coal for a fire. Where Axel had parked in the courtyard, another lorry had pulled up, also loaded with furniture, much of it upholstered with expensive-looking leather.

She found her way to the coal store, which lay opposite a converted air-raid shelter in the cellar. On the way back she passed two men hefting a wardrobe up the stairs, then on the second-floor landing she came face to face with a man she recognised, though it took a few moments to place the stocky build, the hairless head and walrus moustache.

'*Gnädige Frau*! I was wondering when we'd meet.' The strongman grinned. 'Seems those pen-pushers at the Air-raid Damage Office know how to keep a tidy record.'

Vera was startled but saw it made sense — this was how the authorities operated: methodically, by numbers, bringing specious order to catastrophe.

The strongman looked enormously pleased to see her

and introduced himself as Reinhardt Schiefer. 'Came by yesterday and bumped into your mousy friend, the one I let into the queue. She's moved in as well, along with her mother. Guessed it wouldn't be long till you showed up too.'

Schiefer explained that the Air-raid Damage Office had re-registered several flats it had earlier condemned. 'It's not the Adlon Hotel, but we're all in this together, eh?'

He seemed to be serious. Vera made noises of agreement, all her defiance at the Air-raid Damage Office lost. The strongman already looked at home. He said good day and continued down the stairs, leaving her standing with the coal and new misgivings.

When she told Axel that night, he didn't understand her concern.

'Isn't it a good thing to know the neighbours?'

'This man is abominable. A thorough Nazi.'

'I expect we'll have to put up with some of those.'

She recognised his soothing tone, and tonight it annoyed her. 'Schiefer said something strange: that our flats had been empty, declared uninhabitable.'

'So?'

'This place might be shabby but I wouldn't call it uninhabitable — the bomb damage is upstairs. Why would a flat like this have been empty?'

Axel grinned and wrapped his arms around her. 'Here for less than a day and already you want to know all there is to know.'

In bed that night she was kept awake by scratchings in the walls. Axel was restless and around midnight he began to snore. The sag in the mattress made her roll against him, and her last conscious sensation before falling asleep was the grumbling vibration of his breath.

The alarm clock rang early, and though Vera wasn't planning to go with Axel to the zoo she got up and brewed chicory. The stove billowed smoke. The living room was dark and bitterly cold. Axel drained his mug, said goodbye and then departed, and hoping for a few more moments of rest she climbed back beneath the bedclothes.

Four hours later she woke again, saw the clock and struggled out of bed. Outside, pale sunlight touched the roofs but not the courtyard, yet even this much light was cheering. She ate a breakfast of porridge then scrubbed the flat and stuck blackout paper on the empty window frame. In the courtyard she pulled three planks from the bomb debris, carried them upstairs and laid them under the mattress. She felt almost happy and guiltily realised she hadn't thought of the animals all morning.

There was the seamstress to locate, but the thought of facing strangers was too daunting for now. The idea made her think of sewing, however, and for the first time in months she picked up a needle and thread. There were socks to darn, a gift to Axel from Flavia, who had found them in her laundry. The sewing was strangely therapeutic, but she'd hardly started when she heard a knock and had to answer the door.

In front of her on the landing stood a man and a woman, both middle-aged. The man was plump, wore a brown Party uniform and sported the same postage-stamp moustache as the dictator. He was holding a flowerbox brimming with soil. The woman was very small and finely built, her head almost shrunken. A coin-slot mouth slashed with lipstick. Bleached curls in a hairnet. She was wearing a black sable coat. The pair were standing close together but not touching. Vera sensed that they were married.

'Heil Hitler,' smiled the woman and saluted. Vera pretended to smooth a snag in her stockings, then was saved from responding when the man handed her the flowerbox.

'Daffodils for spring,' he said. 'Grew the bulbs myself.'

The woman welcomed her to the building. 'I'm Klothilde Ritter. This is my husband, your *Blockleiter*. May we come in?'

Mentally Vera checked the flat then invited the couple inside. She set a pot of chicory on the stove.

Frau Ritter sat in the armchair, got up again and wandered about the room. She was very small and thin, with a face explicitly shaped by her skull. She peered into the drinks cabinet then picked up the telephone that Axel had recovered from the villa. 'You won't find a socket in here for this. You're not in the West End now, you know.'

Her laugh was grating. A *Berlinisch* accent, working class. The coat was oversized, as if stolen.

Vera served the chicory and the *Blockleiter* toasted her in thanks. He had heavy jowls, a snub nose and a scar that zigzagged from one eyebrow into thinning hair. The skin around the scar was ridged.

His wife looked about her with obvious satisfaction. 'Not what you're used to, I bet.' Her teeth were small and pointed.

'Not really,' said Vera. 'But it's a roof. We can't complain.'

'These are difficult times. Our own son Norbert went missing at Stalingrad, though God willing he'll be back home soon.'

This was pitiably optimistic, and Vera mumbled assent. She paused for what seemed like a decent time then asked who the previous tenants had been.

'They moved on,' said Frau Ritter. 'So many changes in wartime.'

The *Blockleiter* frowned.

'I see you don't have books,' said Frau Ritter. 'That's good. Books are dangerous.'

'Oh?' said Vera, as evenly as possible. 'I like books.'

'A friend of mine in Tempelhof had a neighbour's bookcase fall through the ceiling. This was before the war, mind. White ants. Someone might have been killed.'

'We lost our books in the raid.'

'You're better off without them.'

'Oh, I don't know,' said Vera, unwilling to concede.

Frau Ritter leaned forward. 'You're English, aren't you?'

'I'm a citizen of Germany.'

'But you're *from* England.'

She thought of claiming to be Irish, as she had in the past
— somewhere in her family there'd been an Orangeman —
but today her instincts warned her not to lie.

'I'm from Australia.'

'Isn't that a colony of England?'

She was well informed, if out of date. 'Not for forty
years.'

The *Blockleiter* nodded benignly. Perhaps he was simple.
His wife sat back and opened her arms. 'But you're German
now and that's what matters. If the Reich welcomes you,
you're welcome in this block. And that reminds me — in the
vestibule you'll see a list of donations to the Winter Relief.
We collect every Sunday.' She stood up and beckoned her
husband, who gulped his chicory and followed her to the
door. 'Give my regards to your good husband,' said Frau
Ritter. 'If there's anything you want, anything at all, just see
me — my son-in-law's a district Party official. Another
thing: don't forget to register at the *Rathaus*.'

Vera closed the door behind them and went to the
flowerbox, plunged her hands into the soil and sieved it
through her fingers. On her palms rested half-a-dozen
daffodil bulbs.

*

After registering with the local Party authorities, Vera started back at the zoo, squeezing on to the *U-Bahn* each morning with passengers who looked as exhausted as she felt. She was always sniffling and often cold. Her gums were sore and sometimes bled, making her fear for her teeth. She longed for the war to end.

In mid-January the Reich Ministry of Agriculture cut supplies of straw to the zoo, forcing Vera to spend days with her work team digging leaves out from snow to use as bedding for the animals. The Czech, Krypic, was well enough now to work outdoors, and Vera added him to her work team. From his papers she learned that his first name was Martin. The Poles, she noticed, didn't call him by it, mostly ignoring him and he them. She hoped there was someone at the barracks who called him by name.

The work was wet and cold. Vera's ears and fingers stung, and she knew it must be worse for the *Ostarbeiter*, none of whom had gloves, though some had made mittens from rags. Vera comforted herself that all of them now had woollen uniforms. One of the Poles had shamed her with thanks; to her relief, Martin Krypic had said nothing.

One arctic morning the Czech let her know that the rhinoceros seemed disturbed, but when she asked for details he would only say that she should look for herself. The pen was just two minutes' walk away, but she would have liked to know symptoms. Krypic's uniform was hanging off him, but Vera could see that he was walking more strongly. His hair was longer and chestnut coloured, and the terrible sores had left his skin. His angular cheeks were rosy from the cold.

Before the cage came into view she could hear that something was amiss, an irregular, discordant striking on iron. Shrapnel had killed the rhino's mate in November, though the enclosure was still intact. She hurried ahead and saw the rhino pacing her pen, knocking her horn on the bars as she passed. The cage was old-fashioned, far from ideal, the symptoms of boredom easy to recognise. Vera met the Czech's gaze then looked back at the rhino striking the harp of the bars. Her horn resembled the prow of a boat, with the eyes a surprise on the hull of her head. A grey, wrinkled hide, heavy shoulders, an emaciated belly and nuggety haunches. A fly-swat of a tail.

'A barrel,' said Vera. 'A barrel will keep her busy.'

'Empty or full?'

Even his jokes were expressionless. Vera smiled. 'Empty. She needs something to push about.'

Krypic raised a single eyebrow, and Vera suggested he try the stores. The truth was she had no idea if diversion would help. The rhino might be sick or simply hungry. In these conditions, so much was guesswork.

Krypic nodded and set off, his clogs crunching the gravel through its pelt of snow.

The British returned under a waning moon, sending the tenement dwellers to the cellar, some in nightwear and carrying eiderdowns. The cellar was a dozen paces square, bricked and cobbled. When all the residents were inside, the *Blockleiter* shut the blast-door and Vera found herself enclosed with more than twenty people: a mother and her children, a woman with a baby, some middle-aged and much older couples, as well as a group of young women. There were no younger men. An oil lamp over a central table cast spokes of shadow off four brick columns, and around them lay a series of stretcher beds fenced apart by suitcases. By one of the walls there was a cast-iron bathtub full of water, along with picks and shovels, stirrup pumps and a stack of folded blankets. A chimney-sized tunnel led to a neighbouring cellar. To slow the circulation of fire-feeding air, the tunnel was loosely blocked with bricks.

Frau Ritter welcomed the new arrivals to the block and said how much cosier the cellar now felt — there was solidarity in numbers and they could all depend on one another for support. Vera noticed the seamstress beside an old woman in a bathchair, presumably her mother, while the strongman, Reinhardt Schiefer, had taken a seat at the table and was shuffling a deck of cards. Some of the people were familiar to Vera from the stairwell, and they must have known each other, but so far there were none of the wisecracks she had heard in public air-raid shelters.

The *Blockleiter* crossed the cellar and introduced himself to Axel. His voice was soft, seemingly at odds with the moustache. In the way of veterans they soon established that in 1917 they'd both fought at Passchendaele, where the *Blockleiter* had been wounded. 'The doctors put this in,' he said, tapping the scar on his forehead. 'Metal it is. On cold days it tightens.' He mimed a squeezing motion and smiled. Either he was touched in the head or pretending to be.

Apart from the baby, the children seemed to belong to one family. They were groggy with sleep and their mother settled them onto stretcher beds, and several of the adults also lay down.

At the table, the strongman began a card game that included Frau Ritter. The *Blockleiter* tipped his cap to Axel then went and sat with his wife, peering about as if on guard.

When the bombs began falling, Axel went to sleep, while Vera lay awake on the next stretcher bed. The raid was intermittent but long, the lulls only putting her more on edge. The seamstress, Vera noticed, was also awake, and so giving up on sleep Vera got out of bed and went to say hello. The seamstress seemed pleased and introduced herself as Erna Eckhardt, then she tried to get the attention of her mother, who frowned and looked away. Her mother was no longer all there, said Erna, though to Vera she looked alert, if cantankerous. The wickerwork armrests of her bathchair bristled.

With a little prompting, Erna was willing to talk about her work at the factory, which she said made uniforms for the military, but when Vera asked about other family members she grew cautious, admitting to a son fighting in Russia.

'So you're not from Berlin?' Erna asked.

To a true Berliner, a foreigner was anyone born beyond the city limits, and when Vera explained where she was from, Erna looked baffled. 'What language did you speak?'

The reply fell into a gap between the blasts, and in unison the card players all turned and stared. Vera tried a smile, then more explosions saved her from speaking.

Erna looked alarmed and even glanced over her shoulder. 'Are you meant to be here?'

Vera explained that she was German, but Erna seemed wary. She was sleepy, she said. There was work the next day.

Vera returned to Axel's side, mulling over the seamstress's final question. She had no idea of the answer. She looked at the card players and was just in time to see Frau Ritter turning sharply away.

'They're slackers,' said Herr Winzens. 'And they steal the feed.'

Axel leaned against the railing of the hippo pool. Herr Winzens had been grumbling about the *Ostarbeiter* since the day of their arrival.

'They don't understand a word you're saying. Couldn't work to save themselves. A German worker's worth ten of 'em.'

The sun was down and the air was freezing but two of the hippos were still nosing about the pool. Beyond stood the hippo house, squat and square, and looming in the distance the flak towers.

'To be honest,' said Axel, 'I'm not surprised they ease up when they get the chance. Wouldn't you?' He steeled himself. 'If the poor devils need food so badly, I think we should overlook their thieving.'

Herr Winzens gripped the rail. Axel could read the old man's thoughts, or a version of them: moral disintegration, barbarians at the gates. And he was right: this was the end of civilisation as they'd known it.

Everything had changed. Once he would have said that a rare lemur was worth more than a person — there had seemed to be plenty of humans to spare — but this claim had been rhetorical, and now that people he knew were being killed it also seemed tasteless. Bombs would destroy many of the remaining animals anyway, and in the meantime the *Ostarbeiter* might as well take what benefits they could.

Axel pointed at the hippo house. 'Ugly, isn't it. Like an electricity substation. Why do you suppose it's survived?'

'That I couldn't say,' said Herr Winzens.

'Do you think the Board would notice if we knocked it over on the sly? We could blame the British.'

Herr Winzens looked scandalised — he rarely recognised a joke — though this time Axel shared some of his uncertainty.

'If you ask me,' said Herr Winzens, 'we've lost plenty already. No need to make it worse.'

One of the hippos yawned, showing chalk-stub teeth.

'Animals, yes. But is the same true of the houses?'

As systematically as possible, Axel began to describe his vision for the zoo: animals living in conditions similar to the wild, as breeding populations, with whole herds on farmland open to the public. Herr Winzens continued to stare at the pool.

'What do you think?' asked Axel when he'd reached the end.

Herr Winzens let go of the rail and crossed his arms. 'I'm against it.'

Of course he was against it. Axel almost laughed aloud. It was as if he'd not wanted approval at all, so much as proof that the world had not changed irrevocably after all.

'Tell me why, Artur.'

'I'm just against it.'

Immovable — as it turned out, much more so than the animal houses.

'You'll have to make a better case than that. Give me a reason.'

'All right then: your father. He wouldn't have liked it.'

Axel stared at him. 'What makes you say that?'

'Half those houses he inherited, the other half he built. He would have wanted the zoo left the way it was when he departed.'

He made the death sound grandiose, and Axel pictured his father farewelling life in splendour, perched like a maharajah on Siam, perhaps — not as he had died in reality, his body shrivelled and his certainties intact. It would have been unkind to point out to Herr Winzens that he had described a man who in his day had been an innovator, and that if his old boss had faced circumstances like those of the present, he almost certainly would have seized the chance to start anew. If there was one belief of his father's that Axel could share it was that opportunity springs from adversity. Being caught in the collapse of a civilisation was not only a curse but a privilege.

He thanked the keeper for hearing him out, and for his vigilance with the *Ostarbeiter*. Herr Winzens nodded gravely, took his leave and shuffled away. Confiding in him had been rash, but Axel wasn't sorry. What it really showed was how much he missed sharing his plans for the zoo with Vera, though if he tried again it would only upset her. It was hard for her to accept that so many animals couldn't be saved, and she would suffer alongside them till they suffered no more.

One by one the hippos lumbered from the water and moved indoors, and he set off for the zoo's main gate. If he could have saved Vera the trouble of a broken heart he would have done it — she was only in Berlin on his account. For the last three months he'd been more conscious than ever that she had chosen badly all those years ago when she'd swapped the lion and the unicorn on her Dominion passport for the eagle and swastika on a German one. What was less clear was how to make it up to her.

★ ★ ★

Sometimes he doubted he would ever have married if Vera had not been a foreigner. At forty he had struck a balance between solitude and the company of friends, and though he had lacked the ruthlessness of a lothario, from time to time there had been lovers.

A holiday romance had suited him, and he had only agreed to let Vera come with him to Europe on the condition that she accepted a return ticket as a gift. They'd got on well, she was intelligent, and the lovemaking was splendid. Germany was on her itinerary, and so after they arrived in Hamburg he had invited her to Berlin.

Sightseeing was difficult, as his father wanted him back at the zoo, but somehow they found time. He let Vera stay in his flat, breaking a previous rule, and found himself enjoying her presence there. At a dinner party, he introduced her as his prize Australian specimen, confident she would prove she was firmly her own woman. When a drunken medical friend invited them to a see a dissection, Vera accepted, and a few days later they went to the university to view cadavers in various stages of dismemberment. As a veteran of the trenches he was unperturbed, but he kept a careful eye on Vera, if only to catch her if she fell. Instead she asked a series of questions. Had the blood been drained? How were the corpses preserved between lessons? What was tendon and what was sinew? They passed vats with cross-sections of torsos in formalin, then his friend put on gloves and fished out a block of flesh that Axel recognised as half a female pelvis, the reproductive organs revealed as if in a diagram. Mortifyingly, he felt the first flush of fainting. The vulva was bristled. Vera asked if the vagina was normally so small, and his friend said yes, though it expanded during intercourse and childbirth. Axel gripped the bench till his body cooled. Of the hundreds of corpses he'd seen or touched on the battlefield, none, he realised, had belonged to a woman. He wasn't sure that he liked his friend's tone.

That week, Axel's *Blockleiter* had complained about Vera's presence in his flat and threatened to check her visa. Though the regime massed adolescents at gymkhanas and rallies and gave the wink to the pregnancies that followed, professional people were expected to marry. Axel promised that Vera would be leaving soon.

The next day he took her to the forest to fire a gun. Vera had raised the idea after seeing the Mauser in his father's office, and though at first Axel had been doubtful, he had recognised the holiday impulse to try everything.

He made an excuse to his father, borrowed a car from a friend, stowed the rifle in the boot and drove out to the Grunewald, stopping first at Wannsee. It was a beautiful weekday in September and the artificial beach was nearly empty. They swam in the lake and then ate lunch in a restaurant that overlooked the water.

When the meal was finished and coffee on the way, Vera leaned forward and said that maybe it was time to leave Berlin. He was busy, she added, and his *Blockleiter* couldn't be fobbed off forever.

Axel hadn't thought beyond the present, but as the waitress arrived and served their coffees he realised he didn't want Vera to leave. He liked having her close, not just because of the lovemaking but for her presence beside him in the night. He loved her touch and the signs of their common physicality: her bad breath in the morning, the monthly flow of blood.

She was watching him closely. He wanted to ask her to stay but hesitated. This was a place he'd been before, a crossroads where he'd always chosen solitude.

He told her that he didn't know what to say.

If she'd known him better, she might have recognised it as a compliment, a sign that he needed more time to think. Instead she looked out at the lake, shielding her face with her coffee cup. Axel thought fast. There was the visa problem, accommodation, the demands of his father. Vera was resolutely looking at the water.

Coffees finished, he paid the bill and they returned to the car. The cabin was hot and Vera was silent. He started the engine, steered the car away from the lake and took a side road into the Grunewald, which at this time of year was dense with foliage. Trees bowered the road, lashing the windshield with sunlight.

Marriage had never appealed to him; he'd never seen the point. The marriage he'd known best was his parents', in which his father had ruled and his mother obeyed, and it was as much from sympathy as selfishness that he'd declined to make any of his lovers his wife. Most had forgiven him, and he was rarely lonely. He liked his life.

He parked the car far away from picnic sites, got out and fetched the Mauser from the boot. Vera was chatting again, apparently determined to recapture the carefree mood of the morning. They set off between the trees and walked half a kilometre or so before reaching a clearing, where he loaded the rifle and explained to her the actions of the breach. She asked how the trigger set off the charge, her voice all concentration, then he showed her how to stand with her feet apart and the rifle butt nestled between breastbone and shoulder. He warned about the recoil then explained how to align the sight on the stock with the bead at the tip of the barrel. No need at this range to make allowances for distance. It was time to demonstrate. He took the rifle and pinned a sheet of paper to a tree, told Vera to block her ears and aimed. The Mauser was more elegant than his old army rifle, but still he must have trembled. The shot echoed around the clearing, then he lowered the gun and saw that he'd only just winged the page. This was how not to shoot, he joked, and handed the rifle to Vera. Again he took her through it, step by step, then stood off to one side. Vera weighed the rifle in her hands and raised the barrel to horizontal. The juxtaposition of jutting metal with the human form was ugly, he decided, and yet he was moved — she was so slight, so vulnerable. She held the rifle still for a moment and then fired, jolting with the discharge but keeping her feet. She turned to him laughing, as excited as a child, pointing to a hole in the paper's heart. He smiled and applauded. She wanted another go. With the same deep stillness, she steadied herself. A rock in a glade. A bullseye again.

Back at the car he asked her to stay in Berlin, and then he asked her to marry him. They kissed and she said yes, smiling and smiling. He grinned and didn't feel afraid. On the drive home they forested the future with plans, then on the outskirts of Berlin Vera burst out laughing. What would Doctor Freud have made of such a proposal, she wondered. Whatever he liked, Axel said. Sometimes a gun was just a gun.

★　★　★

'Surely feeding, sheltering and medically treating your animals shields them from the struggle to survive,' said

Schiefer. He sat back in his chair. To Vera he seemed insufferably smug. His contribution to the war effort had turned out to be as the owner of a factory that made saucepans for the military, and he liked to hold forth about production levels, military strategy, and most of all about the *Wunderwaffen*, which he was convinced would win the war.

Axel looked unruffled. 'That's exactly what we're doing.'

'Then your animals are degenerate.'

The air raid that had brought them here rumbled from afar, an almost soothing sound. The cellar dwellers who'd stayed up all looked at Axel.

'If you mean that physically they're inferior to their cousins in the wild, then no, I'd dispute that.'

'I mean that your animals don't have to struggle to survive.'

'Then you misunderstand the purpose of a zoo. We reproduce only some of the behaviours of the wild. Partly this is practical: we can't care for big cats, for example, without gaining their trust — to tame them as a circus trainer might. This is for their own good.'

Schiefer looked triumphant. 'So you admit your animals are feeble?'

Frau Ritter nodded firmly, her head like some specimen bobbing in a jar.

'On the contrary,' said Axel, 'they're much healthier than in the wild.'

'Both weak and strong surviving indiscriminately,' said Schiefer.

'A zoo is designed to entertain and instruct. It's a place to see a version of the real. For complete authenticity you must visit Africa.'

'Wouldn't it be more instructive, especially for youth, to display animals in a genuine fight for survival, demonstrating what the world is really like?'

Axel laughed. 'Maybe. If my pockets were deeper. Exotic animals are too valuable to waste on demonstrations of how the world may or may not be.'

His voice was light-hearted but, knowing it well, Vera could hear a stony undertone.

Schiefer began to make another point then seemed to change his mind. 'Can't stand animals myself. Except for dogs. But your dog is more human than animal, isn't it.'

The conversation turned to dogs, then the relative merit of cats. Vera noticed that Axel joined in keenly, his irritation with Schiefer apparently gone. In private he had taken to calling their fellow residents '*der Stamm*', the tribe — an affectionate reference to baboons — and allowing for their reserve, he got on well with all. Vera liked his amiability as a rule, but his cheerful dealings with Frau Ritter and Schiefer bothered her. Frau Ritter liked to boast of her daughter's marriage to a Party official, and freely admitted that her husband owed his position to his son-in-law. She spoke adoringly of the *Führer*. Seeing the best in people presumed that there was a best to be detected.

Vera guessed that the *Blockleiter* was what he seemed: a decent if dull-witted man, though it was hard to ignore the moustache. On Sundays he wore his Party uniform to collect donations for official charities, softening extortion by fumbling for change. In the '20s he had owned and skippered a barge on the canal between Berlin and Hamburg, and his wife would complain to anyone who'd listen of the conspiracy of big business and Jewish financiers that had driven him broke in the Great Depression. Largesse from his son-in-law probably explained how the *Blockleiter* had stayed plump throughout the war, though it was possible he was dim enough to credit the ration system or his wife's good management.

The *Stamm* included four young women who worked sixty-two hours a week at the Siemens tank factory in Spandau. In the shelter, they mostly slept. There was also a retired omnibus driver and his wife, their daughter and her baby boy. The daughter had a husband serving on a U-boat and lived in terror of a telegram delivery.

The other children were German refugees from the Ukraine, where their parents had taken a farm after the *Wehrmacht*'s advance into Russia, enjoying *Lebensraum* for barely two years before fleeing the resurgent Red Army. Recently the father had been conscripted into the *Wehrmacht*, and his wife was resisting the evacuation of her children, aged three to fourteen, while she applied to return to her native Swabia. She was a worn-down woman whose prize possession was a silver Mother's Cross, presented after the birth of her sixth child by Magda Goebbels, wife of the Propaganda Minister and herself a mother of six. Generally the children played or slept through the raids, as if they were cooped up with only bad weather outside. The three-year-old could have had little memory of an era before air raids — in twenty years' time the sound of aircraft or a backfiring car would either terrify her or inspire nostalgia.

Vera, on the lookout for kindred spirits, had noted as possibilities a couple her own age — an engineer and a stenographer. Neither had so far greeted her with the salute. They lived across the landing from flat number six, and had a boy of seven and a girl of nine who'd been evacuated to separate villages.

Lastly there was Erna and her mother. As if gaining the trust of a nervous animal, Vera had accustomed Erna to her presence and, though they had little in common, Vera had begun to feel fond of her. Erna's every move was timorous, as if she was afraid of breaking something, possibly herself. She shared her mother's surname, and Vera guessed that Erna's soldier son had been born out of wedlock.

On a mattress in the corner, two of the youngest children, the little girl of three and her five-year-old brother, were squabbling over a broom. Their mother groaned in her sleep. When disturbed in the past, she had woken in a rage.

Leaving the conversation, Axel rose from the table and went over to the children, whispered in their ears and gently disengaged the broom. Schiefer grunted approval.

Wielding the broom like a rod, Axel made a casting motion. He led the children to the opposite side of the cellar, gave back the broom and crawled away, goggle-eyed and gulping and swirling the air with what were meant to be ventral fins. Schiefer looked at him in astonishment, Frau Ritter with disgust. The children mimed casting, and Axel sniffed imaginary bait. His expression was haughty, inquisitive then voracious. He snapped his teeth, the children jerked the broom, and he flopped and thrashed. His palms churned the air. The children pretended to reel, he came closer then veered away, then in mock exhaustion he tacked back again and pitched himself onto the cobbles at their feet. The children's squeals were lost in the bombardment but their gestures were clear. They wanted to play the game again.

A month of bombing had done less harm than the big raid in November, but in late January a direct hit destroyed the air-raid shelter at the zoo. Vera felt unnerved — if not for the November raid they might have been killed, though Axel said it made no sense to speculate, and that next she'd be wearing a rabbit's foot. Involuntarily she touched her kangaroo penny.

What was undeniable was the loss of the studbooks, as well as Axel's father's photographs. The studbooks had become less like working documents than rolls of honour for the fallen, yet their destruction struck Vera as an evil omen.

Despite Axel's talk about saving at least some of the animals, she was troubled to see that he spent most of his time poring over maps or using his work team to clear rubble. The odd thing was that Axel seemed happier now than before the bombing, as if the end of the zoo as a going concern had freed him from care. For Vera it was nothing but loss. The animals were like pets to her; to Axel they were stock. He loved them as an artist might love paints, for their collective effect.

Returning from shopping one morning, she entered the front gate and found him demolishing the last of the administration block with two work teams, her own as well as his. She'd left Krypic and the Poles distributing feed. Resisting the urge to complain, she walked along the promenade, plotting a course between the craters. From the ruins Axel called hello, saw her loaded with string bags and asked Martin Krypic to assist.

Krypic lowered a sledgehammer. He was the nearest of the men.

'Thank you, but I can carry it myself,' she said. Krypic hesitated and looked at Axel.

'*Liebling*, you're tottering. Let the fellow help.'

Fuming, she handed one of the bags to Krypic and set off for the kitchens. She'd given her work team equally trivial tasks, and her own annoyance mystified her.

'Let me apologise for this. My husband worries too much.'

'It's good for me to rest.'

'He's been working you too hard?'

For the first time she heard him laugh. 'I've known rather worse.'

'Even so, the work here is unreasonable?'

'Not so bad, considering. You and your husband are not unreasonable.'

They walked several paces in silence, then Vera asked how he'd ended up in Berlin.

He made a rueful face. 'Because of Mickey Mouse.'

After the takeover of Czechoslovakia, he explained, he'd avoided being drafted for labour in Germany by slipping into the countryside and finding work on a farm. 'After two years I got bored and went back to Prague — the worst mistake of my life. America hadn't yet entered the war, and at a cinema on Kaprova Ulice *Fantasia* was showing. It's ridiculous, but as a boy I'd been fond of Mickey Mouse. I was starved of films so I bought a ticket. An elephant was flying across the screen when the police came searching for unregistered workers.'

At first they had sent him to Münster he said. 'We had to dig for unexploded bombs, then for ruptured sewerage pipes and bodies. They didn't feed us well. I got ill. They sent me here.'

They reached the kitchens, went inside and put down the bags. The Czech crossed his arms.

Vera hesitated. 'Herr Krypic, this might — must — sound feeble to you, but please understand that I am sorry.'

He gazed at her and nodded. 'Can I do anything else?'

She shook her head. 'No thank you. No, not for now.'

The morning rush was over and the store was empty of other customers. The grocer examined Vera's ration cards. 'New here, aren't you.'

'That's right.'

He eyed her closely. 'And you're not German, I can tell.'

Vera tensed. In the past month she'd had to explain herself more often than in the whole preceding year.

The grocer must have noticed her baulking. 'Don't mind me, I'm just curious.'

'I'm Irish.'

He looked tempted to ask another question but instead measured off a slab of butter, hesitated, then cut a larger slice. 'Closed lips get extra, understand?' She handed over the money, trying to hide her surprise. He'd charged for the difference, and it wasn't cheap, but bonus butter was invaluable. 'Welcome to Kreuzberg,' he said.

Pleasantly bewildered, she said goodbye and left the store. So far, this was the warmest welcome she'd had to the neighbourhood, making her ponder the sullenness of some of those in the cellar. The engineer and his wife kept strictly to themselves, she'd noticed, and the omnibus driver rarely said anything to the *Stamm*, though he and his wife often chatted to one another. The more she watched, the more she was convinced that the long-stayers were deliberately reticent, unwilling at times to meet her eye; and though Axel told her she was imagining things, she couldn't be sure without knowing any of the long-stayers personally. The cellar felt like a minefield to which she alone lacked a map.

That evening she heard someone arriving at flat number five, and on an impulse she opened her door. On the landing, the stenographer was grappling with her keys. She looked up and Vera said hello.

'I was wondering if you'd like to come to tea on Sunday,' said Vera. Seeing the woman blush, she added, 'If you're able to make it.'

'Thank you,' the stenographer said, 'thank you.' She was smiling but fingering her keys like worry beads.

'Three o'clock?' suggested Vera.

Again the woman thanked her — there was no doubting the sincerity. 'I'd love to,' she added in a voice of regret.

'All right then,' said Vera, unsure if they'd agreed to meet or not, and too embarrassed now to clarify.

Two nights later in the corridor on the way to the cellar, the stenographer stopped and took her by the arm.

'Frau Frey, I have to tell you I can't visit on Sunday. My husband and I have lived here a year,' she said, as if this explained her change of heart. 'We think it's better to keep to ourselves.'

'I understand,' said Vera, not understanding at all. The stenographer looked away, and instead of annoyance Vera felt a spasm of fear.

FIVE

Motz-Wilden and Flavia arrived for dinner and Axel took their coats. Motz-Wilden was in uniform, a *Luftwaffe* tie-pin securing his right sleeve to the elbow. The effect was preternaturally neat, squared away, and with the scarring made him look, to Axel, like a fastidious pirate. He bit the glove on his surviving hand and tugged it free.

Vera emerged from the pantry kitchen and Motz-Wilden handed her two parcels.

'Coffee,' he explained. 'Plus oysters fresh and unrationed from Lübeck. There's a lemon as well.'

Axel was impressed and asked him how he'd come by such luxuries.

'Knowing the right people,' said Motz-Wilden.

Flavia flung her handbag onto the armchair. 'Have you heard? The Soviets have crossed into Poland. That'll give the Carpet-eater something to chew on.'

Axel smiled — Flavia's invective against the dictator was inexhaustible.

'It's true,' insisted Flavia. 'Freddie saw him at it after Stalingrad, didn't you Freddie. Fell down in a panic on a Persian rug and chewed the edge till it was slobbery.'

'A friend of mine saw it.'

'There!' cried Flavia.

Axel handed out schnapps, and Flavia downed hers in one gulp. She raised the glass. '*Prost*.'

'Another?'

She nodded, then her face became serious again. '*Dunder-head*, neanderthaler, moron.'

Axel dipped his glass. 'Cheers to you, too.'

She flicked out her tongue like a monitor lizard. 'If I could get near that man, I'd gun him down myself. Someone has to do it.'

Vera served the oysters and everyone sat down. Flavia herded half-a-dozen shells onto her plate, squirted lemon and started scooping with the dexterity of a munitions worker. Axel had never cared for oysters, preferring sugar to salt, and regarded the loss of pastries and cakes from Berlin's cafés as the worst effect of rationing. He forked an oyster into his mouth and tasted sea.

Flavia had finished already, and he leaned towards her: 'You know, tiger's whiskers will kill a man, finely chopped and sprinkled on food. An old Indian trick. Shreds the stomach and leaves no one the wiser. I ought to have some at the zoo.'

Flavia was galvanised. 'Truly?' Axel chuckled and she hurled a serviette. The pincer points of her hair stabbed the hollows of her cheeks.

While Flavia abused the regime over dinner, Motz-Wilden ate in silence, smiling now and again. When the main course was finished, Axel cleared the plates and took Vera's pudding from the oven. At short notice she'd concocted a dessert of mashed turnips and banana essence. He brought out the bowls and found Flavia still at it, though her tone had turned pessimistic.

'When the war's over, the rest of Europe will tear Germany apart, and what's more we'll deserve it.'

'It didn't work last time,' said Axel. 'Why would they try it again?'

It was Vera who answered. 'In retribution for forced labour?'

She had said little all evening, and Axel hadn't realised she was feeling testy.

'Vera thinks we'll be strung up after the war for having *Ostarbeiter*. I think there'll be bigger fish to fry.'

'Forever the optimist,' she said.

'Axel's done the right thing,' declared Flavia. 'Didn't you say yourself that the Ministry had insisted?'

Flavia was the last person from whom he had expected support, and judging by the look on Vera's face she was equally surprised.

'We look after them the best we can,' he said, 'and that has to count. I get on with my work team, and Vera with hers. One of mine was a lawyer in Warsaw, a likeable fellow. Another's a school teacher.'

'What their jobs were shouldn't matter,' said Vera.

'I only mean they're not labourers, and they know that I know. We chat a little.'

'Is that wise?' asked Motz-Wilden.

'The zoo's quiet at the moment, and the workers aren't likely to denounce me. To be brutally honest, they have more to lose.'

Motz-Wilden asked Vera how she got on with her workers, and she answered with a shrug.

'*Liebling*, you're too modest,' said Axel. 'One's your right-hand man, isn't he? What was Herr Krypic in civilian life?'

'He's still a civilian.'

Something had annoyed her — he supposed that after dinner he'd find out what.

'I don't know his profession,' she admitted.

'I'll bet he's a violinist or some such. They're an accomplished lot. If we get them through safely, there'll be reunions in later years, just wait and see.'

'I doubt it,' said Vera.

He saw that she wouldn't be jollied.

'It can't be easy for them,' said Flavia, 'but they'd be worse off in a factory. And my God, it's nothing to what's happening to the Jews. They've been carted off to die.'

Axel seriously doubted it, and he knew that on this topic, at least, Vera agreed with him. In the last war the Allies had accused the German army of everything from bayoneting Belgian babies to boiling down corpses for soap, and he could recognise propaganda when he heard it. He didn't doubt there had been hardship and even killings in the east, but the Nazis weren't so stupid that they'd sacrifice labour, and in wartime it was important to treat rumour with suspicion. Such stories only diminished true suffering. The deportations to ghettos had been bad enough.

Flavia noticed his expression. 'You don't believe me? Freddie, tell him.'

'Me? What would I know? I'm a humble diplomat.'

It was time to change the subject. Axel stood up. 'Anyone for real coffee?'

After dinner, he guided Flavia and Motz-Wilden down the darkened staircase. It was late, so when they reached the vestibule he was surprised to see Frau Ritter in her doorway — the air raids had disturbed the sleeping patterns of everyone in the block. He led Flavia and Motz-Wilden through the courtyards to Reichenbergerstrasse, and on the return journey Frau Ritter's door was locked.

Back in the flat, Vera was washing plates in a basin. Axel took up a teatowel.

'Those two are getting on well.'

'I don't like him,' said Vera.

Axel was startled. 'Why not?'

'He's a bad influence. Flavia's all stirred up.'

'I don't recall Flavia ever needing help in that direction.'

'This is different. He might get her into trouble.'

'Pregnant, you mean?'

Vera snorted. 'That's one kind of trouble she knows how to avoid. I mean political trouble. He played the innocent, but where else would Flavia have picked up those rumours about the Jews?'

'You know what her imagination is like. She doesn't need anyone feeding her stories.'

'He's too young for her.'

Axel smiled. 'There's a bigger age difference between you and me.'

'It's not the same the other way round. Women are more mature. Or they should be. Flavia and Freddie are like a pair of children.'

To Axel, Motz-Wilden had seemed older than his years. 'You're not jealous?' he asked. Vera looked puzzled. Sometimes it was possible to tease her out of a bad mood, restoring her sense of the ridiculous. Gravely he added, 'I'm a man of the world — I know that in marriage attention can stray. Motz-Wilden is handsome, why deny it? And what kind of woman could resist a war hero?'

'That's the stupidest thing you've said all night.'

In bed she was restless, and when he asked what was wrong she complained of sleeplessness. He wrapped his arms around her. 'I expect it's the coffee.'

They lay quietly for a time, then Vera whispered, 'Do you think there's anything in it? Flavia's talk about the Jews?'

Axel pulled her closer. 'She's an actress, remember.'

'A failed actress.'

'But all the same, a dramatiser.' He leaned over and kissed both her eyelids in turn. 'Just forget it. Sleep.' He sank back on the pillow, the flutter of her eyelashes fading from his lips.

Frau Ritter was at her usual post in the vestibule when Vera came downstairs on her way to work. Axel had left at the normal time, showing no sign of tiredness from the night before.

'A successful dinner party?'

'Thank you, yes.'

'That was a fine-looking officer. *Luftwaffe*, is he?'

'That's right,' said Vera, making a move to leave.

'Pity about those injuries. He still flies?'

'No.'

Frau Ritter barred her way. 'A desk worker then?' She tilted her narrow head, as if embedding a screw with her eyes. There was no obligation to answer, but Frau Ritter was no doubt capable of making false denunciations.

'A liaison officer.'

'Oh? Who with?'

'The Foreign Office,' admitted Vera.

'And the young woman, who is she?'

This was taking the interrogation too far. 'A friend.'

'Another foreigner?'

'Another German, like me.'

'Forgive me, I forgot.'

Vera looked at her watch and Frau Ritter apologised for delaying her. 'I try to keep abreast of what's going on in the block. My son-in-law at District Party headquarters likes to know what we ordinary folk are up to, and when my Norbert comes back from Russia I want him to see that I've done my duty too.'

Fifteen minutes later on the train, Vera was still deciding if she'd been subjected to a threat or a confession. Either way, Frau Ritter's moral compass was haywire.

Over lunch she described the encounter to Axel. 'Frau Ritter is fishing. We'll have to go carefully there.'

'She's just a busybody. That's how it is in tenements — everyone rummaging in each other's pockets.'

'She's a snake. I don't trust her.'

'Now you're sounding like Flavia. Frau Ritter is the sort of person for whom we ought to have compassion. Considering what the last few decades have thrown at her, it's no wonder she follows the Party.'

'I don't care what her motives are,' said Vera. 'She

worries me. It's wartime and I'm an enemy alien, whatever my passport says.'

'Give her a chance. Most people are well meaning if you allow them to be.'

It was just like Axel to take the rosy view. 'If that's true, why do we have to huddle for our lives underground every night?'

'Every second night, and sometimes not for weeks at a time. I still maintain that most people respond to friendliness. If Frau Ritter doesn't, you can make an enemy of her later.'

'She's an enemy now; you just don't know it. Whenever she looks at me in the cellar, it's like she's baring her fangs, only no one else can see it.'

'Vampirism. You're hallucinating. Nothing that a proper sleep won't fix.'

Vera sighed. There seemed little chance of sleep.

Most of the primate house was destroyed, its palm trees long since dead. Vera led the work team through the atrium and entered the intact southern wing, where the group divided by language: the Poles to the gibbons, while she and Krypic fed the lemurs. From there they moved on to visit Traudel, the last chimpanzee of a family of nine.

Traudel looked pleased to have company. Vera picked her up, cooed and stroked, then offered the chimp to Krypic to hold. He baulked and she smiled. 'Still disturbed by apes?'

'I was never disturbed.'

'Yes, now I remember — our apes don't concern you.'

'They have nothing to do with us.'

He had spoken gravely. If this was a denial of Darwinism, she'd be disappointed, having picked him as a more sophisticated thinker. 'You don't see the family resemblance?'

Krypic looked impatient. 'I don't doubt we're related. But you're holding a wild creature and we shouldn't presume ...' To Vera's astonishment, his voice wavered. 'We shouldn't presume to know them.'

He was breathing deeply, staring at her. Normally this argument would have irritated her, but the passion of its delivery demanded attention. Defiance suited him.

'You're right,' she said. 'We shouldn't presume. But we can aspire to know animals, and by knowing them better we can also know ourselves.'

'You're still talking about us. What about them? Your chimp,' he said, motioning at Traudel. 'What good is our curiosity to her? She'd be much better off in a jungle.'

'At present, undoubtedly. She's hungry — like I am. But in the right conditions this kind of animal does well.' She explained how they hoped one day to display a range of active species such as chimpanzees, noting to herself how she was lauding plans that she'd criticised Axel for raising.

'But no matter how well designed, your enclosures are too small.' He was jabbing the air with the blade of one hand, as if hacking out a version of his own angular face.

'Looks can be deceiving,' she said. 'In the jungle a chimpanzee's range is small.'

'As small as this cage? Or even this building?'

'No,' she admitted. 'But food is what they're seeking when they go further afield, and in better times they'd have as much as they need here.'

'In better times.'

He was right to be dismissive, she thought. Fine intentions counted for little while bombs were falling and the animals went hungry. Consciously or otherwise, he was surely speaking of himself, and he was entitled to his anger. She was glad he had the nerve to express it.

'It's bad here — I don't pretend it's not — but in principle, a zoo animal needn't feel its confinement, since even nature imposes territories or patterns of movement. We say "free as a bird", yet a linnet never ventures more than a stone's throw from its nest, while a swallow is compelled to migrate.'

'The tyranny of nature?'

'You could call it that.'

'Then what about the freedom to comply?'

Vera suppressed a smile. 'That's wordplay. Wild creatures are also free to be tormented by parasites, to starve or be torn apart by predators.'

He gave her a dubious look.

'What did you do before the war?' she asked, enjoying catching him off guard.

125

For a moment he hesitated. 'I conserved works of art.'

Dexterity — she might have guessed from those slender hands.

'Well?' she demanded. 'Will you tell me more about it?'

He shrugged, nodded. In Prague he had worked at the National Gallery, he said, though in a junior position. 'An apprentice, really — they hadn't let me work on anything important.'

'No Michelangelos?'

'No, but one or two imitators.'

'How do you work — with a paint brush or a scrubbing brush?'

'That's not so far from the truth. The tools are still primitive. By conviction, I'm a scrubber. The chiaroscuro of most Renaissance paintings was never intended by the artists — it's from centuries of candle grease and soot. Also flakes of human skin. I remove a layer of real skin to bring out the flesh in paint.'

'Using a scrubbing brush?'

'More like a tiny toothbrush. Some conservators can't contain themselves and scrape at the canvas, bringing off paint as well as grime. That's just vandalism.'

'Perhaps they're the older ones who can't wait for better tools. You have youth on your side.'

'If I get through the war, yes.' He sounded matter-of-fact.

Traudel's weight was becoming too much, and

126

reluctantly Vera returned the chimp to her cage. The Poles had gone ahead to the terrarium.

Krypic said, 'One day I want to restore a well-known portrait — one that people think they know, that is — and reveal its true tones: the lustre of hair, the moisture in an eye. To bring it truly to light.'

His face shone for a moment, then he collected himself. 'And now you, Frau Frey. What did you do before the war?'

'I was a zookeeper.'

'Yes, but how did you become one?'

Answering a question was more daunting than asking one, and Vera sensed how her curiosity might have unnerved him, yet this was a familiar question and she gave her stock reply, describing her meeting with Axel and their journey to Europe, the arrival in Berlin and Axel's proposal. The story was honed and polished with use, and telling it was a pleasure, so that at the end she was startled by the Czech's forensic gaze, and unprepared for his second question.

'Why did you stay in Germany?'

Vera hesitated. 'No one's ever asked me that.'

This was a delaying tactic, and only partly true — like Erna, he was asking whether or not she belonged, though she guessed he was hoping for a different response. Answering was no easier the second time around — too much history, public and private, packed into too small a space.

He was waiting for a reply.

'I was married,' said Vera.

This would have to do. She picked up the feeding pails and handed one to Krypic. Lurking somewhere in his question was politics, yet a personal answer came closest to the truth. More than any other choice in her life, staying in Germany had been a case of putting heart before head.

★　　★　　★

In the excitement before the wedding, she'd thought little about politics. After the ceremony and a reception at the zoo, she and Axel had left for a honeymoon in the Schwarzwald, where she had seen snow for the first time, skied cross-country and visited Freiburg, where Axel's sister had moved after marrying a doctor. There was the spoken language to adjust to, then Berlin itself, a metropolis that made Sydney look provincial, and above all there was the levitation of love, making every action effortless. Axel was generous and capable. By crossing the frontier of another's soul, she felt her own expand.

In the same month that Axel's father had died, the zoo's Board had appointed his son as Director, which for Axel meant returning to live at the villa, his childhood home. At first Vera was wary of making changes to the décor, but Axel welcomed her tentative suggestions, and so she replaced the dark carpets, swapped the drapes for blinds and had the wallpapered rooms painted white.

It was exhilarating to wake in the morning to the cries of toucans and macaws. A lion's roar was like the revving of an aeroplane, but even so the time before opening felt peaceful, the hum of traffic beyond the walls only emphasising the calm. When visitors arrived and thronged the paths, she would enjoy the thought that by evening the zoo would be hers and Axel's again.

At night she helped with emergencies — a sick giraffe, the first time, then an elk giving birth — and standing bleary-eyed in a stall, holding a blanket or a bottle, she felt more purposefully employed than she ever had while teaching German to schoolgirls. She joined Axel on his rounds and learned the idiosyncrasies of species that until recently she hadn't known existed, and though the smallness of some of the enclosures was unsettling, she chose to wait until she was better informed before querying their size.

It was the particularity of the animals that delighted her: the understruts of an ostrich's wing, the transparent shutters on the eyes of a sea lion. She became a connoisseur of smells, savouring the musk of each enclosure. In conversation with friends, she caught herself saying 'our animals'.

Axel took her to Stellingen Zoo in Hamburg where the Hagenbecks had pioneered *Freigehege*, separating species where necessary with hidden moats or trenches. Vera knew straight away that this was how she'd like their own animals to live. Two years later they were able to boast one completed enclosure — the alpine peak for mountain goats and other European ungulates — as well as plans for bear and monkey enclosures. As a teacher her achievements had been intangible, but in a letter home she boasted that here was concrete progress. Her mother asked whether she meant to have children of her own — raising a child would be a joy, she claimed. Vera suspected that a life devoted to children would be a life postponed, and she sent a prevaricating reply.

Her mother and Selby were the family that at times she longed for. Early in 1937 she invited them to Berlin, offering to pay their way, but her mother wrote back citing distance and the international situation as reasons not to come. Could Vera, she countered, come home for a holiday?

Vera replied that the threat to peace was exaggerated. True, there had been talk of war when Hitler had reoccupied the Rhineland, but the Allies had backed down and tensions had since eased. Her mother sent a noncommittal reply, and the idea faded. By comparison, claimed Axel, the Rhineland negotiations had been straightforward.

After the *Anschluss* with Austria, the regime turned on Czechoslovakia. Axel argued that the crisis would pass like all the rest — memories of the last war were still too fresh, or foul, for Europe to slide into another bloodbath — but the tone of her mother's letters grew worried. Wouldn't it be safer, she asked in one, for Vera to come home, at least until the tensions eased? Axel would be welcome too. Vera considered the letter carefully. Her mother was far away and knew little about international affairs, but her arguments were no longer so easy to dismiss. Axel had talked about one day revisiting Australia, but this was out of the question in summertime when the zoo was busiest.

A trip to England would make better sense. At the embassy she learned that Germans with money were still welcome to holiday in Britain, yet she hesitated raising the idea with Axel.

In September some of the keepers got their call-up papers, and with sudden clarity Vera saw how short a distance remained between the idea of a war and its execution. That evening she argued the case to Axel for taking a holiday in England, stressing how easy it would be now that the summer peak was over, and how short a time they'd need to spend away.

Axel listened from an armchair. It wouldn't come to war, he said, when at last she'd finished speaking, but what made her believe they'd be safer in England if it did? Had she considered that he, and maybe she, could be interned there? She admitted that she hadn't, and for the first time asked herself where Axel's loyalties might lie if a war broke out. Twenty years ago he'd fought for Germany. She gazed at the floor, considering the logic of his arguments, only to realise that her mind was already made up: she distrusted the German authorities, and if a war did start she wanted to be with her own kind. The trouble was how to admit this to Axel. At that moment he stood up and came to her side and wrapped his arms around her. It wouldn't come to a war, he repeated, but weren't they due for a holiday? For some time he'd been wanting to visit England again.

They travelled by train from Berlin to Ostende, then by ferry to Dover, crossing borders with ease. In the late-summer heat, Europe hardly felt like a continent on the brink of war, but when they arrived in London and caught a taxi to their hotel the driver could talk of nothing else. Chamberlain was in Germany to discuss the Sudentenland, and in the driver's opinion Hitler was welcome to it. 'I've seen war,' said the driver, 'and there's no dirt anywhere that's worth as much as blood.'

'Even English dirt?' asked Vera.

'That's different,' he conceded. Axel's face was impassive.

Despite having never visited London before, she had anticipated her arrival as a kind of homecoming, so she was surprised by how alien the city felt, the density of buildings, crowds and traffic more like Berlin than Sydney, the unfamiliar accents of her mother-tongue only adding to the strangeness. For the next week they took in the sights, but apart from two visits to London Zoo she took little pleasure in it. The leaders' negotiations had shifted to Munich, and the news was all bad. Londoners, like Berliners, opposed a war.

Axel claimed to be enjoying himself but no amount of sightseeing could disguise the fact that they were in limbo, not tourists so much as refugees-in-waiting, and suddenly it seemed foolish to have taken sanctuary in a country where both of them were foreigners.

It was in a telephone box at St Pancras Station that she learned that Europe would not go to war. She was about to book a restaurant table, juggling pennies in one hand and the telephone in the other. Axel had gone to buy a newspaper. Rain was falling outside and the booth was misted. She dialled and the telephone had begun to ring when the door behind her opened, toppling her umbrella against her stockings, and she spun round and saw that the intruder was Axel. He was smiling hugely — amused, she thought, at the joke of squeezing in to join her — but his shirt was wet and pressing on her blouse, and she frowned and made a shooing gesture. Instead of retreating, he held up a newspaper that bore the headline 'PEACE!'. She hung up the telephone as someone was answering. Axel embraced her and whispered in her ear, 'Didn't I tell you?' She squealed with delight. He picked her up and swung her from side to side, battering her shoes against the glass. 'Didn't I tell you?' he repeated. 'Didn't I tell you?'

★   ★   ★

Late in March, Krypic arrived at work in hobnail boots that could only have come from the blackmarket, probably in exchange for stolen animal rations. She made a fuss of admiring the boots, asked him the source of his newfound wealth and was amused to see him blush.

That afternoon, in front of the work team, she slipped on ice and fell, cutting her knee and spilling a pail of offal. Quickly she sprang upright, brushing dirt and slush off her stockings. The knee was bleeding, but she was more concerned by a rip in her woollen stockings, her only pair. Krypic put down his pails and squatted in front of her, and she told him not to worry. Taking no notice, he clasped her leg and peered at the wound, turning her calf from side to side. The Poles looked amazed, and to cover her own confusion she stared them down.

'It needs cleaning,' said Krypic. 'You should go to the kitchens.'

'The lake is closer.' She walked a few paces and winced.

Krypic offered to help, and leaning on his arm she hobbled to the bank of the Four Forests Lake, the zoo's largest open space. Ice had retreated from the centre but still ringed the edge.

Where the shoreline was flattest, Krypic prised off the ice. Vera crouched then jerked straight up again, startled by the stinging of her knee. She felt foolish and would have preferred to be dealing alone with the wound.

'The hem,' he suggested and pointed at her skirt. She

lifted the heavy fabric and Krypic splashed her knee, making her squeal, not from pain but the shock of the water. He asked if she had anything to wipe it with and she gave him an embroidered handkerchief. He looked at it doubtfully.

'Go on,' she said, 'there's nothing else.' He dabbed the wound, all concentration. She said, 'How does it feel to get restoration work again?'

Krypic smiled but did not look up. To fill in the silence, she added, 'This would never have happened if I'd had boots as fine as yours.'

But he would not be distracted and said nothing more till he was done. 'I doubt you'll need stitches. Maybe iodine if you've got it.'

She thanked him and Krypic let go of her leg. The ghost of his fingers held the crook of her knee.

Flavia's flat had once looked shabby but now seemed luxurious. Vera envied the bathroom, especially the bath, though for Flavia the key fixture was the mirror. For the last half-hour she'd been putting on make-up, and while Vera waited in the living room Flavia prattled about Friedrich Motz-Wilden: his *Junker* relatives, a recent mission to Paris, chances of promotion and post-war political hopes — even his plans for a prosthetic hook. 'I told him he should get a parrot and a cutlass to go with it.'

Vera had never seen her so obsessed by a man. 'What's so special about him, this Freddie of yours? Granted, he's handsome, but you've been with better-looking men. Less damaged ones, certainly.'

She had spoken with a deliberate edge in her voice, but if Flavia had heard it she didn't react. 'Yes, but isn't his damage seductive.'

'It's that simple then?'

'Well, no. Not quite.' Hearing a novel tone of seriousness, Vera stood up and went to the bathroom doorway. Flavia spotted the movement in the mirror and spoke to her reflection. 'He's very intelligent.'

'But also a bit cagey?' — in retrospect, no more so than on the night they'd first met when he'd charged her with evasiveness, though it would be unfair to bring up that episode now.

Flavia raised her eyebrows, suddenly arch again. 'Maybe he has perfectly good reasons to be cagey.'

'Such as?'

She laughed. 'Vera, darling, you know me — as close as the grave. I couldn't possibly say a thing.'

Normally this was the first move in a game that ended with Flavia telling all, but Vera was reluctant to play. For weeks Flavia had either been busy at the Rose or off somewhere with Freddie, and even now that Vera had her alone, Flavia could speak of nothing but Motz-Wilden. She planned to meet him in half an hour. Clearly she was bursting to reveal some secret or other, and Vera noted with satisfaction the effort it was costing her not to speak.

In Flavia's current state of mind there was little chance of her asking any questions in return.

Vera abandoned her place at the door and, perhaps taking the hint, Flavia left the bathroom and seized her coat.

'I'll come with you,' said Vera. 'We can walk.'

'But I'm wearing high heels.'

'Do they stop you dancing?'

'Vera, you're a savage, and if there were any taxis to be had in this town you could go to hell.'

On the street, she exulted in the surrounding bomb wrack. 'This will teach the bourgeoisie! For years they looked the other way and now they're reaping their reward.'

Vera tried to gather her thoughts but hardly knew what she wanted to say. That she was attracted to another man? Even thinking it was ridiculous. The first thing Flavia would ask was who.

And she was unsure what she hoped for in return. Advice? Absolution? Before speaking, she would have to decide.

What frustrated her was Axel's goodness. He wasn't a drunk or otherwise unreliable; to her knowledge he'd never had an affair. He'd done nothing wrong — in fact the reverse: since November he'd been remarkable, brushing off the destruction of his life's work. Resilience was one of his greatest qualities, yet it was precisely this that had begun to annoy her. Strength could resemble complacency. Seen in a certain light, Axel was just the sort of petty bourgeoisie that Flavia was railing against.

Vera groaned under her breath. Nothing made sense, and if she couldn't explain it to herself there was no point raising it with somebody else.

She breathed deeply and asked Flavia if she would ever marry. 'Marry seriously, I mean.'

Flavia turned and gave her a penetrating stare. 'Why do you ask?'

'No reason. Just curious.'

Flavia went back to admiring the wreckage. 'Nothing personal, but I've never wanted to. Why confine yourself to one man when there are so many to be had?' She gave a raffish grin. 'But lately, I must say, I've had sentimental thoughts. Maybe reaching thirty has turned me soft.'

'If you married, wouldn't it be a struggle? To stay with one man, I mean.'

Flavia feigned outrage. 'Goodness, what do you take me for?' Vera eyed her steadily. 'Oh, all right,' Flavia conceded. 'But if someone like me were to marry, fidelity would have to be the point. I wouldn't start if I knew I couldn't carry it off.' She looked almost prim. 'Why do you ask? Are you thinking of taking a lover?'

Even after knowing Flavia so long, her directness could surprise. Vera looked sideways to see how serious she was, but already Flavia was gazing back over the rubble.

'Hardly,' said Vera. 'Where would I find a lover? A good one's so hard to come by these days.'

'You're fussy, that's all. I've brought you lots of lovely men and you've turned up your nose at all of them.'

They were nearing Wilhelmstrasse and Vera knew that if she was to say anything more it would have to be now. In the most casual tone she could muster she said, 'Sometimes I wonder. The way Axel is.'

Flavia looked startled. 'Are you two having problems?'

'Not exactly. No. It's just that sometimes his practicality annoys me. His literalness. If a problem's concrete — say, a destroyed enclosure, a person in trouble — he takes action, and that's wonderful, but he's oblivious to abstractions. You know his politics. He's an innocent. He can't recognise malice. After you and Freddie had dinner with us the other night, the *Blockleiter*'s wife tried to interrogate me. She admits she's an informer, yet Axel thinks she's harmless.'

Flavia stopped. 'Did she ask about Freddie?'

Vera tried to explain it had come to nothing but Flavia cut her short. 'What did you tell her?'

'Nothing. The point is —'

'Because it could be very important.' She demanded to know everything about the exchange with Frau Ritter and wouldn't move until Vera repeated it word for word. At last she seemed satisfied. 'If anyone asks again, I want you to tell me.'

She started walking again and they entered Wilhelmstrasse, Vera simmering. Flavia had wrecked her line of thought and they were out of time. The Foreign Office stood alongside the Reich Chancellery, headquarters of the dictator. High explosives had knocked out chunks of ashlar, and incendiaries had blackened the walls of both buildings. Smoke stains swept like eyebrows from the upper windows.

They reached the front steps of the Foreign Office and stopped. Before the war it would have been impossible for Flavia to openly visit a lover in a government building, but as political paranoia had increased, moral vigilance had lessened.

Flavia leaned forward and kissed Vera on the forehead. 'Goodbye, and remember what I told you.' She sprinted up the steps.

Vera waved belatedly and continued along Wilhelmstrasse, heading for the station, then at the intersection with Leipzigerstrasse she caught sight of the post office, and as always at this spot remembered the outbreak of the war.

Berlin had been hot that day, the sky cloudless and still. At midday, news had come of the French and British declarations, and by one o'clock the loudspeakers on Budapesterstrasse had been blaring marching music across the zoo. After the reprieve of the previous year, Vera couldn't understand how it had come to this. Axel seemed stunned and repeated over and over that in 1914 there were cheering crowds. Vera couldn't trust herself to speak. Her emotions felt unwieldy — grief for humanity, fury at world leaders — but beneath these abstractions lay an unmistakable sense that she could never quite rely on Axel again. On the streets that afternoon, the few people about looked openly worried — at least Axel had been right about his countrymen's lack of stomach for a war. For a few minutes she consoled herself with this thought, but at the post office a clerk refused to accept a letter that she had hoped to send to her mother. Mail to a hostile nation was forbidden. She was trapped for the duration and there would be no more news from home.

★ ★ ★

On the sixth of April the sirens blew at midday and Vera joined Axel, Herr Winzens and the *Ostarbeiter* in heading for the tower-bunkers. Day raids were generally made by Mosquito bombers and did little more than fray the nerves, but with the zoo's shelter gone it was best to be cautious.

From Moabit, Wilmersdorf and Charlottenburg, people streamed towards the towers, which rose over a haze of budding trees. Queues had formed at the entrances, and parked by the walls were ranks of prams. At the door of the larger tower a bottleneck had formed. The sirens moaned.

After several minutes of waiting, Vera found herself in a crowded vestibule with vast walls like the set of a Wagner opera, then the roof guns opened up and the whole crowd flinched as if ducking a scythe. Air-raid wardens drove the crowd up broad stairs, the concrete shaking with each report of the flak. The steel shutters were drawn. On the ceiling, bundles of electric cables snaked between bulbs. Sirens had conditioned Vera to go downwards, so that even with the knowledge that the tower was impregnable it took a conscious effort of will to ascend. Young children cried and wardens barked orders, then a woman began shrieking and a warden hauled her aside.

On the fifth floor they filed into a cavernous room bordered by benches for the weak or the elderly. The rest of the crowd stayed standing, foreigners mixing with Germans, the poor with the wealthy. Awkward-looking youths in uniform were crammed against civilians. The building swayed from the recoil of the guns.

The zoo contingent stood at the centre of the crowd and Vera found herself between Martin Krypic and Herr Winzens, then above the flak came the noise of massed bombers, causing a hubbub of unease. A panic here would be disastrous. Axel nodded reassuringly over Herr Winzens' head, though he must have known they were helpless.

Outside the bombs began to fall — a serious attack, not the fly-stings of earlier daylight raids. Accidentally she brushed against Krypic and was appalled to feel her face and neck flush. Axel was hardly an arm's-length away.

The bombs kept falling and a few people squatted on the floor, forcing those left standing even closer together, then the lights blinked off and the room went dark. The crowd groaned. A man started sobbing and Vera sensed a pulse of panic cross the room. She stumbled and felt Krypic's arms around her, then she recoiled and their thighs interlocked. Behind her, Axel asked if she was all right, and with a calm that amazed her she answered yes. The crowd swayed as if in sympathy with the tower, and voices pleaded for calm. Krypic pulled her against him and she gave up all responsibility for balance, leaning into a thin but unwavering body. He kissed her neck and she clung to him, terrified that the lights would go on and primed to spring away. This was insane, crazy, but his scent was good and she gave herself to it. His hands were on her back and he pressed his mouth on hers, then their teeth clashed and she widened her mouth. His tongue was shocking in its slippery intimacy, the pleasure so intense that she forgot to be afraid, until somewhere a torch flashed and she drew away, glad that he couldn't see her face. Now that they were separate she wanted the lighting back on, but only the drunken beams of torches swerved above the crowd. Axel was talking with exaggerated calm.

Twenty minutes later the raid came to an end, but the lights stayed off. While the lower floors were cleared the wardens barred the door, then the crowd shunted and Vera joined the descent to the vestibule, nervous that the crashing of her heart might show on her face. The outside air smelt of smoke and she saw that the Tiergarten was on fire, an uncanny sight in daylight. People emerged behind her and peered about, blinking. Axel looked grave. She hardly dared to look at Krypic, and when she did was relieved to see a neutral expression. In daylight he seemed almost weakly again.

What had happened inside seemed unreal and this calmed her. It might be possible not to mention it at all. Unacknowledged, a kiss might starve.

She climbed through a hatch into the corn-snake display: rocks and sand and tufts of grass, three walls, a ceiling and a viewing window. The air was warm.

Of the two snakes, only the female was alive, her neck swollen by a rat and half of her own mate, the male having seized the opposite end of their prey then inched with it into the female's mouth. Now the female was exhausted, at risk of dying. Her agate eyes were pressed backwards by the body of the male, which trailed from her unhinged jaws. Her neck convulsed and her tail swept the sand.

Vera clambered into the service corridor and returned to the gallery where she sent one of the Poles in search of Axel. The remaining Poles lit up cigarettes while Krypic leaned against a wall, his eyes meeting hers then shying away. They had lost the gift of small talk. Of any talk.

To cover her embarrassment, she withdrew to gaze like a visitor at the iguanas and monitors. The terrarium had so far escaped real damage, but even so the viewing windows would have long since shattered if Axel's father hadn't used reinforced glass. Cracks flowered at random through the wire mesh.

Axel arrived and entered the enclosure, and shortly afterwards he came out looking grim. He ran his eyes over the work team and asked Krypic to fetch a saw, and Vera tensed despite herself, knowing that Axel's choice meant nothing but worrying that it might. Krypic caught her eye for what seemed an instant too long and then left by the stairs.

Ten minutes later he returned and handed over the saw, and Vera went back into the enclosure with Axel. He crouched beside the snakes and asked her to hold the female's neck. She had handled snakes before but again registered the strangeness: the scales were dry, like overlapping fingernails — a shared inheritance of keratin. Axel positioned the hacksaw and cut into the victim's back, a centimetre away from the female's mouth. She tried to struggle. Her gums were pink and her fangs massaged the other's spine.

Axel was through in seconds and set aside the dead snake's tail. What blood there was oozed, the victim having suffocated hours before. The flesh was ridged like a salmon's. Vera let go and backed away; the surviving snake thrashed, then slid into the torpor of digestion. Blood reddened the teeth of the saw.

She left with Axel by the hatch and returned to the gallery where they parted, he to his rounds and she to her work team.

Portents could mean anything, that was the trouble. Or nothing at all. She tried pushing aside the images but couldn't. The picture that came to her, that wouldn't go away, was of what the dead snake might have seen at the end: the other's jaws on his snout in a firm caress, the rising rim of the mouth and then darkness.

Vera pressed her nose against the mirror, which was barely big enough to hold her reflection. A corner was chipped and the backing had flaked. She didn't recognise the woman she saw, dark-haired, in her thirties. Around the eyes were wrinkles that she liked. Brown irises and tiny burst capillaries in the whites. She noted that the skin was less supple than a younger woman's, and threads of silver glinted in her hair.

She kept staring at herself, not from vanity — or not only that — but to absorb the strangeness of the image. This had happened before, on and off since childhood — the brain taking stock of change, perhaps. If she survived to old age, she hoped to avoid the sensation of not belonging in her body.

But the uncanniness was stubborn this time, or rather the oddness was not in her face but her person. She pronounced her name and watched the lips move, added her surname then her maiden name and listened to their vibration in her head. The sense of unfamiliarity was like numbness, and in its own way pleasurable, so that for a time she consciously tried to prolong it.

Then self returned, and she itemised her being: memories, convictions, a slew of instincts and emotions: mostly fear and despair, but love as well — a stubborn love of objects and places, animals and people, for her friends and her family and for Axel.

Yet it was Martin Krypic she longed to speak with now, Martin to whom she wished to describe the sensation of not knowing herself in the mirror.

SIX

Vera and the work team had gone ahead, and on an impulse Krypic set down the shovel and let the chimpanzee clamber into his arms. She smelt musky and weighed more than he'd expected. Feeling foolish, he cooed to her as he'd seen Vera do, and stroked against the lie of the fur on her back.

He heard a noise behind him and turned to see Vera stopped between the cages. She was looking strangely at him, as if angry or pained. Krypic lowered the chimp to the floor, took the shovel and left the cage, locking the door behind him. He thought of trying to explain but hardly dared to speak. Since his recklessness in the tower-bunker, Vera had been distant.

Like a statue brought to life, she walked towards him, her face so intense he expected a slap. Instead she set the shovel down and took his hands in hers, shooting a tremor through his arms and chest.

Now he was the one standing motionless, heart pounding, while Vera raised his hands to her face and turned them back and forth as if spellbound. He could barely breathe. She was kneading his hands, moulding them, bringing them alive, and then she kissed each palm in turn.

Keeping his hands gripped in hers, she reversed through the atrium and led him into the wrecked eastern wing: high walls, fallen concrete, an open sky. Spring had lured weeds out of gaps in the debris, and sunlight angled over the walls. She kissed him and this time he wasn't afraid. They kissed again and she loosened his belt and lay down on a tilted slab of concrete. She tugged away her underthings and drew him down on top of her. He felt the brush of her pubic hair, then without hesitation she drew him into herself and they began to make love, fully dressed, just her face bared and the silken exchange between their clothes, concentrated by the bordering fabric and surprise. They were silent and Vera's eyes were closed, and in wonder Krypic watched her fluttering lashes, until he groaned and couldn't keep control.

Vera opened her eyes and Krypic was startled to see uncertainty. He kissed her forehead and the lids of each eye, and it was only when a tear splashed onto her cheek that he realised he was weeping. He kissed the tear away and Vera brushed his eyes. He tried to speak but she hushed him.

They lay quietly, long enough for him to consider the risk — in a whisper he asked about the Poles, and Vera said she'd sent them on ahead. He didn't ask about her husband, but as if reading his thoughts she added that no one would think of looking for her here.

He untensed. What was there to lose after all? Six months ago he'd expected death — had never dreamed of this joy. He felt like a gambler with winnings to spare, and leaning forward he asked if he could see her naked.

Vera looked amused then shook her head. 'Not here.'

'You said we're safe.'

'It's cold.'

'The sun is warm.' He kissed her left ear.

Clearly she was tempted. She looked from side to side then took off her cardigan, then he stilled her hands and took over, removing each garment in turn and spreading them on the slab, until Vera was naked apart from her wedding ring and the small bronze coin she always wore around her neck. She looked away and tried to cover herself, and gently he pulled her arms aside and lowered her backwards. Her hair fanned the concrete.

'Let me look at you,' he said, calling her *du* for the first time, a liberty that made her smile. She closed her eyes and accepted his gaze.

She was lovely, like an angel, a dark-haired angel. The air stirred and goosebumps roughened her skin. He asked if she was cold and she opened her eyes.

'Not really. But this feels like a medical inspection.'

'No, no,' he said, shocked, and clasped her hands. 'You're beautiful.'

She made a sceptical face but closed her eyes. The sunlight smoothed her skin. On her forearms the down cast a thatch of shadows, and her face softened and she sank back further on the concrete. She looked utterly dignified. Consciously he branded the image on his memory, onto his very soul.

There was a scab on her knee where she'd fallen on the ice. He traced a finger around it and, before he could stop or even think, he'd leaned forward and kissed it. He drew back, expecting her to be repelled, but instead she kept her eyes shut and smiled.

'My Freudian slip.'

Warm, foolish words: he'd missed them more than food, more than touch. He kissed her mouth, her breasts and the ridge of each thigh, felt her hands on his temples and let her be his guide.

As usual of late, Flavia was hard to pin down, but Vera telephoned from the zoo and persuaded her to rendezvous in the Tiergarten on her way to the Rose. She put down the phone and felt a rush of exhilaration and nerves.

The days were getting longer and the air was warm, but weather was the only similarity with springtime in the Tiergarten of old — trees were shattered and the goldfish pond, she discovered, was a cratered morass. Sandbags buried the equestrian Amazon.

Flavia was late, and while having to wait was no surprise it stirred the brew in Vera's belly. However brazen some of Flavia's affairs had been, none had been illegal, and as well as sharing the excitement there was the prospect of overturning some of Flavia's assumptions about her. And then there were the practicalities to consider.

Pollen swirled in the declining, coppery light, and when Flavia appeared through the trees she blazed and glowed. Her step was jaunty. She drew closer and waved. 'What's up, Vera Frey?'

Vera waited till they'd kissed. 'I've taken a lover.'

Flavia looked puzzled. 'That's a joke?'

'Would I have asked you here to tell a joke?'

'I don't believe you,' said Flavia, but her face was uncertain.

'Nevertheless.' For years Flavia had teased her about taking a lover, clearly because she thought it could never happen.

'But what about Axel?' she demanded.

'Axel doesn't know.'

'I'm taking that for granted,' snapped Flavia. 'I'm asking have you thought about his feelings.'

'If he doesn't know about it, he needn't have any feelings.'

Astonishing her was one thing, but Flavia looked angry. 'So you've given up on him?'

'I said I've taken a lover, not that I've stopped caring for Axel. To tell you the truth,' she said, hazarding the humour she had pictured Flavia enjoying, 'it's made me fancy him more — I'm worried he might notice a pick-up in tempo.' Once or twice she had wondered if there was such a thing as unfaithfulness to a lover.

'That's revolting. You've violated the sanctity of marriage.'

Vera whooped with tense laughter. She had known that their friendship thrived on mutual recognition — of the bohemian in herself and the *Hausfrau* in Flavia — but hadn't realised that Flavia's alter ego was so priggish.

'But Flavia — pardon me, I have to say it — you regularly sleep with other women's husbands.'

'Not my problem,' she said. 'I've taken no vows — none that count, that is.'

'But I don't feel ashamed, that's the thing. Axel's busy with his usual schemes, and well … I just don't.' Somehow her link with each man seemed separate — Axel was like breathing, Martin an ember in her chest.

'Why are you telling me this, anyway?' asked Flavia.

Vera smiled and attempted a tone of light irony. 'I thought you might be a bit pleased for me.' She knew that Flavia was fond of Axel but had thought she would be titillated and enjoy the skulduggery.

'I'm appalled. I'm disappointed and appalled. Look, I know you're homesick but is this the cure?'

'This has nothing to do with homesickness.'

'It's deceitful and disloyal. This is a very hard time for Axel at the zoo.'

The idea of Flavia making pronouncements about the zoo was laughable. 'To be honest, I think he's happier now than he was before the bombing. The tension is over.'

'All I know is that he doesn't deserve this.'

The fact that Flavia had not asked for a name was unnerving — Vera would never have believed it possible.

'There's something else.' Now that Flavia had made her feelings plain, it was madness to go on, yet Vera knew she would regret not holding to her plan. 'We want to borrow your flat from time to time.'

Flavia violently shook her head. 'No, absolutely not.'

'Just on Sundays, for an hour or two.'

'Over my dead body.'

A quiver of superstition passed through Vera's chest. 'We've nowhere else to go.'

'Doesn't this Romeo have his own apartment?'

'No. He's an *Ostarbeiter*.'

Flavia swayed as if struck. She'd set the tone of this bout, and Vera was unrepentant.

'So you're insane as well,' said Flavia. 'The police will drag you into the street and shave off your hair. Him, they'll just hang from a tree.'

'That's why I'm asking for somewhere safe to go.'

'Screwing *Ostarbeiter* isn't safe anywhere.'

154

Vera breathed deeply. 'You've said yourself that your *Blockleiter* is lax, and the neighbours are used to men coming and going.'

'It's not a brothel.'

'I'm only saying that it won't be as noticeable.' Flavia looked unmoved but Vera was determined. A part of her was observing herself, surprised by how much she needed this. 'Are you going to make me beg?'

'Vera, you've no idea how large a favour you're asking.'

'I realise.'

'No, you don't.'

'So you're not saying no?' she said and smiled, unwilling to believe that Flavia had lost her sense of humour completely.

'Who is he then? One of your zoo men?'

'The Czech, Martin Krypic. We talked about him when you came to dinner.' She explained a little of Martin's background. 'He's twenty-nine,' she concluded.

Flavia looked indignant and began to speak, only to choke back whatever she'd meant to say. Instead she asked, 'So the attraction is simply physical?'

'There's a lot of that,' said Vera, noticing a new airy tone in her voice. Martin's knotted muscularity had surprised her, and his unfamiliarity had lessened her shyness. 'But I also feel alive in his mind. Axel's so preoccupied, whereas Martin wants to know what I'm thinking, how I'm feeling.'

'And you don't mind using a bed that you once shared with Axel?'

'Flavia, it's a bed — your bed, and if that's what's bothering you, we needn't use it.'

'That's not what's bothering me. It's wrong and it's dangerous, and not only to you.'

'But more dangerous than wrong — that's why I'm asking for help.'

'You seem to have done fine without my help.'

'Look, it's not only the risk. We work in a zoo. Martin's a man. In every other way he's treated like livestock.'

'You don't know what you're asking.'

'So you've already made out. Say why.'

Flavia folded her arms.

'Then at least think about it,' continued Vera.

Flavia shut her eyes, shook her head and exhaled. 'You're asking too much.'

The document was a leave pass for a German civilian working somewhere in Russia, but what concerned Krypic was the stamp: a circular design with the word 'Dienststelle' in gothic lettering at the top and 'Feldpostnummer 1017' below. At the centre was a stylised eagle above a swastika.

With tracing paper and a soft pencil he traced the stamp, admiring, despite himself, the eagle's bold lines and the torque of the loathsome symbol. When the image was complete, he used a compass for the border then turned the paper over and traced it a second time, transferring the pencilled outline onto the back of an old photograph. Trial and error had revealed that bromide paper suited his purpose best.

With the design transferred, the job was half done, and he stopped to rest his eyes and stretch his neck. Beyond the toilet door the barracks were quiet. It was Sunday and most of the *Ostarbeiter* were out enjoying the sunshine or doing deals on the blackmarket. Conditions were improving for foreign workers as life harshened for the Germans, a shortage of labour having compelled the authorities to give the workforce enough food to survive, if only just. Security had also eased as former guards were conscripted into the *Wehrmacht*, but even so Krypic took no chances and always worked on documents in the lavatory, using a plank on his knees as a desk. Though the penalty for forgery was death, he had seen people die from many causes, and he was willing to take the chance — the *Ostarbeiter* who did best were those running some scam or other, balancing the risks of breaking the law against the dangers of obedience: hunger and the illnesses that followed in its wake.

He opened a bottle of ink and began filling in the outline on the bromide paper. A mistake here meant starting again. As he worked he hummed Chopin's Waltz in D-flat Major, luxuriating in thoughts of Vera. He could barely believe they were lovers. The happiness she'd brought him was so abrupt that he doubted his own senses, as if he'd stumbled into a world that resembled his own but that in every way was better than the last.

Vera was unlike any woman he'd ever known. As a student, he'd fallen in love with a banker's daughter, and for a year they'd exchanged impassioned letters about poetry and painting, until one glorious summer day they had kissed at the gates of Prague Castle and then walked hand in hand to her house across the river. Yet what seemed like a beginning was in fact the end. For the next two weeks he wrote letters to her that received no reply, and it was only by bribing one of the family's maids that he'd found out that her father had ordered her to break off contact. Krypic's profession, reported the maid, wasn't manly enough.

He'd been inconsolable. He was young and poor and longed for a lover, but not just any woman — he wanted a friend and an equal, a woman with whom he could discuss Raphael or Signorelli without running the risk of sounding patronising. Most of his friends went with prostitutes, and in the following months he consummated two affairs with working-class girls: a laundry woman during his army training, then a maid at a friend's house. On the farm where he worked after the Germans came, there was a girl named Liselotte, a raven-haired beauty whom Vera reminded him of a little. Liselotte had been good company, but he'd still hungered for a love that was entire, and privately he had compared her unfavourably to the banker's daughter. Deciding he was bored, he returned to Prague and the cinema on Kaprova Ulice, remembering too late Liselotte's common sense and generosity.

Captivity had brought an end to his quest for love, or so he had thought, and his most profound cravings had become for bread and warmth and, for a time during his illness, oblivion. Vera's kiss in the tower had restored him to life. She was intelligent, kind and beautiful, and above all she was real — flesh, not figment — an amalgam of the banker's daughter and Liselotte, only much, much more.

When the inner design was done, he used the compass to ink the border, relishing its precise circularity. He lifted the needle and the whole design shivered — the only drawback of bromide paper was its low absorbency. To stop the ink running, he softly blotted it with newspaper.

The stamp was primed. Carefully he placed it face down on the first of several counterfeit passes that the client had produced on a typewriter. He stroked the paper flat with a comb to make the impression, lifted it free then imprinted a second document. With care he'd get four good impressions. The first two were sharp — if anything, better than the original.

With the fourth impression done he dropped the used stamp down the latrine and packed his tools into separate bags. Compass, pen, ink, comb, a pencil and a handful of snapshots — separated, they became innocuous, unrecognisable as tools of crime. It had taken an hour to produce four stamps, leaving plenty of time to rendezvous with the client at Friedrichstrasse and exchange the finished documents for cigarettes — a clear profit, since he never smoked.

Risk came in many forms, and though an *Untermensch* caught defiling an Aryan would be executed, he didn't care. Vera was worth the danger, and in any case the benefits might outweigh the risks: as a German citizen she could be a source not only of extra food and clothing but also of information. He would persist no matter what. Aside from any other consideration, Vera had given him a reason to go on. The best scam of all might be love.

Vera asked how he'd come by his leather boots.

They were in the stables, on a bed of their own clothes and last autumn's leaves. In the stalls the horses scraped and whinnied — among them a kudu, a survivor from the antelope house. He was a buck with corkscrew horns and a noble brow, broad alert ears and white facial patches. Like a creature from myth, Martin had said, in a painting by Titian.

Mention of the boots made him endearingly fraught.

'They must have cost a lot,' she said. 'Do animal rations fetch so much money?' She ran her hand along his neck and into his hair, which had grown soft and wavy.

He looked at her closely, a long assessing gaze. 'If I've taken food, it's been for myself. For that I apologise. As for the boots, I make documents. Ration cards, identity papers.'

Her first reaction was to laugh. He looked so sweetly innocent. 'How? When? I don't believe you.'

He described how he'd decided to work the blackmarket and mastered the art of forgery. 'Drawing is one thing I'm good at.'

'Not the only thing,' she said, and caressed his back. He inhaled and began to stroke her hair.

It would take time to absorb this new information. 'And to think that I was worried about you.'

His fingers traced the chain of her necklace. 'Now I'm the one worried — I've put my life in your hands. What do I get in return?'

His meaning was clear — he was touching her breasts — but she pretended to misconstrue. 'Are you asking for my necklace? You'll take me for all I'm worth!'

'No, no. It's you I want.'

He kissed her and she shivered, already wanting him again, but another idea had come to her. She reached behind her head and unlatched the necklace. 'I want you to put it on.'

He looked uncertain. 'Why?'

'To make you mine.'

He took the necklace, examined the latch and without hesitation secured the chain behind his neck. The penny hung in front of his slender chest. The sight of the chain on his skin was impossibly arousing.

'I want you to have it,' she said.

'You mean keep it?'

She nodded. 'Never to leave that lovely neck.' She leaned forward and pressed her lips on either side of the chain.

'Wouldn't it be missed?'

She guessed he meant by Axel. So far they'd hardly talked about him.

'I've lost everything else. What's one thing more?'

'I couldn't accept it,' he said.

'Please,' she said. 'Giving will be a privilege.'

For a second she wondered if she might regret parting with the coin, but no — losing her last physical connection with home only made the gift more fitting. Imagination was all that connected her to Australia now. Selby would be hurt if he ever learned she had given away his gift, and he wouldn't approve of her affair, and yet he might understand her sympathy for an outsider.

She apologised for the coin's low value. 'But where I come from it's the commonplace that matters.' Martin attempted for a second time to refuse, but Vera was determined and finally he agreed to accept on the condition she wouldn't hesitate to ask for it back. 'And you can view it any time.'

Now that he'd relented he looked pleased, making her even surer that she'd done the right thing. Of the two of them, he was the more sentimental.

'All I ask is that you wear it hidden.' She kissed him again and they began to make love.

She felt reckless and extraordinarily free. The incense of manure rose from the stalls, then she heard movement behind her, looked sharply around and saw the kudu staring at them with long-lashed eyes. 'It's watching us,' she said, quickening.

Martin looked sideways. 'Like a sentinel. A guardian spirit.'

The Uhlandeck's curved façade hugged the corner of the Ku'damm and Uhlandstrasse, but otherwise the restaurant resembled its neighbours: shrapnel-pitted and boarded up. Vera thanked Motz-Wilden for opening the doors and led Flavia and Axel inside. Immediately she was back in pre-war Berlin: mahogany panelling, brass fittings, unbroken mirrors. Dominating the room was a semi-circular counter, and though its glassed-in cabinets were empty of pastries there were spirits and liqueurs on the shelves behind the bar. A ribbed-vault ceiling fanned overhead, and by the bar a pianist in coat-tails played Schubert. The diners were civil-service types, their wives or mistresses, as well as several senior officers. One of them recognised and congratulated Motz-Wilden, who this evening was for the first time wearing the insignia of a *Hauptmann*.

Motz-Wilden signalled an elderly waiter, who seated them at a table beside one of the boarded windows. Goebbels' declaration of Total War had supposedly closed down all restaurants, but to judge by the Uhlandeck there

163

were exceptions for the well-connected, not only Nazis but also scions like Motz-Wilden of the old *Junker* establishment. In her present mood, Vera was happy to accept Motz-Wilden's hospitality, inclined now to overlook any doubts she might have had about him in the past. Axel, too, was in good spirits. Only Flavia seemed out of sorts, no doubt edgy about seeing her and Axel together for the first time since learning about Martin.

The waiter returned with a tray of part-filled brandy balloons. Vera hadn't tasted brandy since shortly after the fall of France. Axel raised his glass to toast Motz-Wilden's promotion, but Motz-Wilden stopped him and announced there was bad news. His pilot friend, Flavia's groom, had been killed over France.

Flavia seized Motz-Wilden's hand, yet he looked calm, the initial shock having passed, perhaps. He unprised Flavia's hand and then proposed a toast. 'Drink up. He wouldn't have wanted us to spoil a good night.'

Vera took a sip of cognac but barely tasted it. She pictured the young airman: blond hair, rosy cheeks and a fatalism that Axel had later claimed he had sometimes seen in the trenches.

The meal was good, in fact exceptional, but despite Motz-Wilden's equanimity the mood was bleak, so that she was almost relieved when the public-address system blared out a fanfare. The waiter stood to attention, the dining clatter fell away and a radio announcer began speaking in a voice that was anonymous yet familiar. Was this the same voice they'd heard for eleven years, or just one of a stable? *Wunderwaffen*, it declared, had been unleashed on London in retaliation against the British and American air-pirates. The weapons — *an invincible armada of rockets* — would pound the enemy into submission. While the voice blustered on, Flavia continued to eat, as if restaking her claim as the reckless one.

The broadcast ended and talking resumed, only louder than before. Flavia put down her spoon. 'Today our weapons rained down on the enemy, annihilating a geranium pot and damaging a lattice. *Heil Hitler!*'

Axel grinned, 'This was always a military town. The Hohenzollerns built a wall to stop the garrison escaping.'

'I'm fed up with it.'

Motz-Wilden said, 'I'd wondered when those missiles would fly. A clever weapon. Rockets will decide the next war but they've come too late to change this one.'

Flavia gaped. 'You knew about them?'

'More or less, yes.'

Vera thought that Flavia had sounded slightly peeved.

For several minutes they talked about the rockets, then Vera excused herself to visit the bathroom. Flavia joined her, closed the door and checked that the cubicles were empty before speaking.

'Yes.'

'Yes, what?'

'Yes, you can use my flat.'

Vera embraced her. 'Oh, Flavia.'

'But I want to meet him first.'

'Martin? Why?'

'I need to see for myself the man for whom you're willing to risk your marriage.'

'I'm not leaving Axel.'

'Then you're that much crazier.'

She tried to make her see how vulnerable such a meeting would make Martin feel. 'And the less you know, the less chance there is of having to lie.'

Flavia's motive was prurience, no matter how she dressed it up, but she was adamant and Vera had to give in. They began to talk through the details, and Flavia's voice betrayed the first tremors of excitement. She was hooked, and there would be no going back.

In an alleyway off Meinekestrasse, behind a pile of rubble, Krypic took off his shirt then replaced it with another, which was badgeless. The frayed strip of lettering on his breast offered protection of sorts, and without it he felt vulnerable, but he planned not to stay on the street for long. Shoving the badged shirt into a drawstring bag, he left the alleyway and crossed to number sixteen.

The building was fully occupied but he saw no one on the stairs. Vera answered her friend's door then bundled him inside. As she'd warned, her friend Flavia was there as well, a tall angular woman who looked him up and down. If this meeting hadn't mattered so much, he might have objected to the inspection, but this was Vera's friend, he reminded himself, and she was putting herself in jeopardy on his behalf.

'All right,' she said, 'I'm finished now.'

Vera looked exasperated. 'Aren't you going to talk with him?'

'I wanted to see the man who'll be using my bed. Beyond that, no. I don't need a new friend.'

Krypic bridled. This was about so much more than a bed, but Vera was saying nothing and he followed her example.

Flavia turned to him and contradicted herself by speaking. 'Why Vera is doing this is beyond me. I just hope you value your own life as much as I do hers.' She strode to the door, tossed a key towards Vera then turned and left the flat.

'Don't worry,' said Vera, 'she'll get used to it. This is a new experience for Flavia — usually I'm the one living vicariously through her.'

Krypic looked around the room in amazement. Since leaving Prague, he hadn't been inside a home, and an armchair, a rug and a coffee table seemed like luxuries. The sight of a few books was exhilarating.

Then Vera was taking him by the hand and leading him through an open doorway, and in front of him lay another wonder: a broad, soft bed.

*

The pebbles on the paths around the zoo seemed more sharply defined than before, and in the trees each leaf looked separate from every other. A glimpse of Vera's black hair made Krypic's heart lurch, and if he hadn't experienced a similar sensation around the banker's daughter he might have worried about his health. Yet even the banker's daughter hadn't had quite this effect. When no one was looking, he'd spring in the air like a boy, and in the barracks at night he would lie on his plank chuckling at something Vera had said until his bunk-mates accused him of becoming unhinged.

With a flat available on Sundays, Vera refused to take as many risks at the zoo, though he would have braved any danger to see her alone. He lived for their Sunday trysts.

In their blessed private moments he would whisper endearments in Czech — cradle talk learned on his mother's knee, which he refused to translate, no matter how much Vera pleaded. What he said to her in German was bad enough, like excerpts from a third-rate romance. He begged her to speak in English and mostly understood when she did, enjoying a thrill of the illicit almost equal to making love.

He hated that they couldn't spend a night together. He had never slept at her side and longed for that privilege, but when he asked her to fall asleep she only laughed and said that she could sleep at home.

But this was a small regret. Most of their time together passed like a dream, making him question what kind of world interrupted suffering with so much joy, though in time he stopped analysing his good luck and gave grudging thanks to God or whatever mechanism had granted him existence. Already he'd led an incomparable life, rich with art and books and pleasures of the senses, so that even if he were to die the next day it would all have been worthwhile.

He tried not to think of her husband, and was jealous of Herr Frey's claim on her history, and in compensation he learned as much as possible about her earlier life. He asked about her childhood in Sydney and she described bright water and sandstone cliffs and lizards that scuttled over baking pavements.

He asked about her family. Vera no longer knew if her mother was alive, a painful predicament they shared. Her mother was a stoical woman, Vera said. 'She had to be. My brother came back changed from the war, and then Father died of the Spanish flu. I'd just turned twelve.'

Her eyes were fixed on memory, and Krypic was torn between wanting to hear more and smothering her with kisses. He held himself still and was rewarded when she began to describe her childhood holidays.

'Father taught me how to surf. At first we'd hold hands. Before each wave he'd yell out whether to dive or jump, and then we'd go under or over together.'

'You make him sound like the perfect parent.'

'He didn't live long enough for me to discover any differently.'

You built love by tearing down obstacles, Krypic decided, the walls of your inner life. With the banker's daughter he'd never had the chance, and with Liselotte the mystery had been over too soon. Vera was a slow and sweet unfolding.

His heart palpitated when he saw her. The fear of death fell away. Her touch felt like consecration.

Illness, madness, a state of grace — love was all three, he decided.

Though the government wouldn't say so, it was clear to Axel that the war was lost, and if the land war came to Berlin the damage to the zoo could be immense — he had seen what an army could do to a city. Surviving would take good luck and clear thinking.

In early June came news of the long-anticipated Allied invasion of northern Europe. The attack had come at Normandy. Axel found himself torn between sympathy for the troops — the sons of his old comrades — and a hope that the western powers and not the Soviets would ultimately take Berlin. Until now, the western Allies' only presence on the mainland had been in Italy and in the skies over Germany, but Normandy had the potential to become a true second front. Axel prayed that the *Wehrmacht* would fold in the west while fending off the Soviets in the east.

The war had been harsh on the Soviets, and if they did arrive first it would be vital that Vera be elsewhere.

At first the *Deutschlandsender* boasted that the British and the Americans would be hurled into the sea, but, as the weeks passed, the place names invoked on the radio — Caen, St Lô, Cherbourg, Honfleur — told their own tale of Allied advances, however slow. Flavia began visiting the zoo and giving breathless summaries of BBC news broadcasts, and Vera, too, was more optimistic. With the summer solstice approaching, there were fewer air raids, as the nights were too short for the British to fly from England and back under cover of darkness, and though the Americans sometimes ventured over Berlin by day, their attacks were less destructive to sleep. Vera's mood improved. She reacted philosophically to the loss of a favourite necklace, and life in the tenements seemed to trouble her less. There had been times when Axel had wondered if they would ever recapture the happiness of the pre-war years, but now he saw that it might only be a matter of waiting. Sometimes in marriage the greatest virtue was endurance.

On the last day of June, Vera arrived home from the zoo and discovered half of the *Stamm* gathered in Erna Eckhardt's flat. Frau Ritter immediately bustled out and announced that a telegram had arrived telling Erna that her son had been killed in Russia. Vera stopped in the doorway. Inside, Erna was sitting stiffly at the table, while her mother was slumped in her bathchair.

Frau Ritter pushed back into the flat. She cleared her throat and suggested that a prayer might be said for the fallen hero, then fell silent when Erna looked up at her and glared. Erna beckoned Vera, pulled her close and asked her to visit that evening. Vera nodded, turned to go and saw a channel of tears on Frau Eckhardt's cheek.

When she visited that night, the Eckhardts were alone. Like she and Axel, they had lost most of what they owned in the November raid, and the flat was pitifully bare: an ancient dresser, hand-hewn chairs and a table with a whorled grain surface.

Erna served tea, sat down and without prompting began to speak. 'I lived for my son.' Her sunken eyes were distant. Vera stole an uneasy glance at Frau Eckhardt, but the old woman was lost in thought or vacancy.

'Before he was born, I hadn't had much to do with boys,' said Erna. 'And his father ...' She waved dismissively. 'I wanted a daughter, a little girl to keep me company, but though at first I was disappointed, it didn't last. He wasn't mollycoddled,' she said firmly, as if defending herself from some old accusation. Vera nodded to show that she understood.

'But from the start he was different,' said Erna. 'Dreamy, but serious. Intense. He took everything to heart: a parrot in a cage, a poisoned rat, and one time a cart-horse that died in the street — he brooded over that for days. And he cried. No matter how hard he tried, he could never stop it happening. His body would tense to hold in the tears but always they came out in the end. And because of this, and because he had no father, the other boys would tease him.'

Now that she'd begun speaking, the words streamed out of her. Vera nodded and murmured.

'When he got older, the Party took him. I don't mean by force,' she said, seeing Vera's expression, 'though it came to the same thing. He got obsessive, *fanatisch*. They all were, I know, but this was something extra. Other boys played the sports, they went to the rallies, but he lived it. He wanted to belong so much that he put himself further apart. He had no friends.'

She paused for a time.

'When he was fifteen — after the victory in France — he told me he was teaching himself Swahili. He wanted to become an administrator in Africa. Africa! What he said to me was … he said, "Mother, I am no Adolf Hitler, but you will be surprised by what your son achieves."'

She smiled bitterly, an expression that Vera had never seen her use.

'He joined the SS — he was a tall boy and strong.' She paused a long time before speaking again.

'I knew that he would die.'

★

Although the fallen were listed in alphabetical order, Vera took a minute to find the name of Erna's son — casualty lists had swollen the newspaper to almost double its pre-war thickness. A small black cross preceded each entry, every page a cemetery of ink. About a quarter of those killed had 'Died for the *Führer*', but Vera was relieved to see that Erna's son had lost his life 'For the Fatherland'. Though that, too, was questionable.

She rolled up the newspaper and pushed it into her string bag, where it sprang open against the containing net. The tram creaked to a halt and a soldier with a walking stick came aboard, his uniform darkened by rain. Vera stood up and offered him her seat, and when he refused she made her way to the front door as if preparing to get off. Glancing back over the heads of the passengers — most of them *Hausfrauen* and factory workers — she saw that the soldier had sat down.

The tram crossed the blade of a canal and lurched into the next stop. Vera grasped a hand strap and the driver turned to her and apologised. He was grey-haired and grizzled, another ancient dragged back into harness.

Ahead, through the rain, she saw that a rainbow had formed, not an arc but a multicoloured prong that ploughed through the wreckage down Kotbusserstrasse. The tram tracks were dull and grey. When she looked up again, the rainbow was fading.

The driver's eyes were on the tracks. In a toneless voice he said, 'How lovely life could be.'

SEVEN

A fistful of mince with shreds of parsley. Some sausage and offal. The butcher's fingers drummed the bench-top, while someone coughed with impatience in the queue. Through curved glass, Vera pointed at a slice of *Rollfleisch*, and at once the butcher plucked it from under her reflection, which was squashed as if by a fairground mirror. He wrapped the meat with three deft folds, stamped her card and handed over the parcel and change.

Outside, the afternoon was hot and still. Around the corner, in Tauenzienstrasse, an army staff car sped past, lifting dust off the road. Trams were the only other traffic. Before the war this had been a fashionable street, busy with cars and pedestrians, but windows were now boarded and the goods on display inside were often tagged NOT FOR SALE. At this time of day the pavements were bare.

In Wittenburgplatz she heard rumbling, and as she reached the top of the *U-Bahn* stairs a tank burst from a side street and slewed into the *Platz*. The tank was grey, decked in camouflage and startlingly fast. It straightened and veered towards her. A man wearing earphones stood erect in the turret, a stalk of flesh in metal. The ground vibrated. The machine filled two lanes. Behind it, a whole column thundered into the *Platz*, cannons level and turrets sealed. The lead tank passed the *U-Bahn* entrance, snorting exhaust from a pipe at the rear. Its wheels screeched. At its prow the teeth of the tracks bit the asphalt, stayed still for a moment then reared at the stern, leaving a trail of indentations on the road. The column headed north into Ansbacherstrasse and the noise of the engines died away.

Unsettled, she hurried down the stairs and caught the *U-Bahn* home, stopping first at the grocery store in Reichenbergerstrasse. She liked to think of the grocer as a friend. He'd nicknamed her the Irishwoman and often allowed her extra morsels of food — Lilliputian deals, he called them, since they were below the counter. Vera had checked with Erna and learned that she received no similar favours.

She'd been home no more than half an hour when Flavia arrived, pounding the door and yelling. Vera let her in and Flavia embraced her, springing up and down.

'He's dead! He's dead!'

'Let go! Who's dead? You're hurting me.'

'Hitler,' she hissed. 'We've killed him. Blasted him to smithereens!' She capered on the spot.

Vera's stomach heaved.

'At Wolf's Lair,' said Flavia. 'A bomb. We blew the bastard to bits.'

'When? When?'

'Earlier today. Freddie told me. It's pandemonium there.'

'Pandemonium where?'

'His office. I surprised him. He was juggling phones and teleprinters. There's a coup d'état! Freddie would only say that Hitler's dead, but I know what's happening. Soon we'll be free!'

'Flavia, this is bound to be dangerous.'

'So?' said Flavia. 'We've done it. Whatever happens now, that can't be changed.'

'You should stay here,' said Vera, then wished she hadn't. Immediately she felt ashamed of her cowardice.

'Freddie has to know where to find me. I'll catch the train home. Give Axel my love and tell him that this war, this fucking war, will be over soon.' She'd started to cry.

'Take care.'

'Never. I'll see you when it's over.'

'When it's over,' repeated Vera. Flavia hugged her and left.

She was basting the *Rollfleisch* in the kitchen when the *Deutschlandsender* announced that the *Führer* had escaped an assassination attempt. The Propaganda Ministry was more than capable of lying, but even so she felt a tremor of dread.

Axel arrived home a short time later and she told him what she knew. He looked troubled and said nothing for a time.

'What if Flavia's mixed up in it?' asked Vera, voicing the thought that had plagued her since Flavia had left.

'I doubt it. What idiot would enlist Flavia in a conspiracy? All the same, I should go and fetch her.'

'No,' said Vera, too forcefully. She felt weak with fear. 'That is, let's first find out what's going on.'

At eight o'clock they stood before the radio, each nursing a schnapps. The bulletin started with news of a failed assassination and finished with a claim that the *Führer* would speak on air 'as soon as practicable'.

'A coup won't succeed if he's alive,' said Axel.

'But it sounds as if they're stalling for time.'

'Perhaps. At least let's hope so.'

She looked at him sidelong. Axel had never supported the regime but this was the first time he'd expressed a wish to see it brought down. If the government collapsed, the country would follow — a terrible prospect for a loyal German.

'An efficient coup would've seized radio transmitters,' he added.

He poured two more schnapps and Vera served dinner. Her stomach was tense, and after eating half the meal she gave the rest to Axel. The *Deutschlandsender* kept repeating the same message: the *Führer* was safe and would address the people soon. Axel convinced her they should try the BBC, but its announcer spoke only of Allied victories, then played Purcell and Tchaikovsky.

By eleven she couldn't stand any more waiting and told Axel she was going to bed. He promised to wake her if anything happened. In the bedroom she undressed and slid beneath the eiderdown, giddy from the hours of nervous tension. The bed seemed to sway. Her belly stewed liquor and pork. In the living room the radio alternated between communiqués and marching tunes — trumpets and drums — until she slept and dreamt of queues that stretched down alleyways and between the desks of her old primary school. Ink on her hands turned to blood that she wiped on her pinafore. She ran into a courtyard strewn with seashells and filled with the roar of an engine, then through a portcullised gate a tank appeared — grey like a rhino, with bristles on its hide. The creature backed her against a wall and the noise of its engine died away. Its cannon dipped and caressed her neck. *Denk an das Fleisch*, the cannon whispered in a sly and nasty tone. *Remember the meat.*

She woke as Axel clambered onto the bed. She asked him the time.

'After one. He's alive.'

'You're sure?'

'He spoke.'

They lay quietly for a time, Vera's mind reeling. 'What will happen now?'

'I don't know. Tomorrow I'll check on Flavia.'

The same fear she'd felt earlier irrigated her stomach — slower, more insidious than terror of bombs. 'Wouldn't it be better to wait?'

'For what?'

She hardly knew, and then it came to her: until Flavia was arrested. She wanted to wait in case Flavia was taken. The realisation appalled her, but recognising the fear made it no less real.

She clutched Axel's hand. 'Let's see how things look tomorrow.'

Axel woke early and again risked tuning in to the BBC, only to turn off in disgust when the announcer gloated about 'Germans killing Germans'. The *Deutschlandsender's* tone was curiously similar: a 'criminal clique of officers' had tried to halt the march of history; some had been shot the day before, the rest would soon be ruthlessly exterminated.

He decided not to ask Vera to come with him to Meinekestrasse. She was a tangle of nerves, her recent poise destroyed, and when he said he was going she even tried to stop him. He'd never seen her so unbalanced, so unlike herself.

He reached Flavia's flat, prepared to knock, but instead announced himself. Flavia answered straight away. She was haggard and red-eyed, and fell sobbing into his arms, then looked up and asked if he'd heard from Friedrich. He shook his head and bustled her inside.

'I've heard nothing,' said Flavia. 'Even if he's safe, I know he won't call, but I can't stand waiting anymore, and it's only been hours. I want to go to him, to call!'

'Don't. He'd want you to be careful.'

Flavia banged the table with her fist. 'I can't bear it.'

'You have to behave as if nothing has happened.' He asked what she was scheduled to do that day.

'A rehearsal at the Rose.'

'Then go,' he said.

'I couldn't.'

'You must.'

He made her eat some toast and she devoured each slice with three or four bites. She dragged a hand across her lips and looked up. 'Why did it fail? How *could* it fail?'

'Because.'

'*Because* what?'

'Just because.'

'That's not good enough!'

'Very well. Because Hitler moved, or didn't. Because the air was too dry or humid. Because there is no God; or if there is, because he's blind, or sees so much further than us.' He gave her a brief and joyless smile. 'You see, I've given the question some thought.'

'I'll never accept it. I won't understand. Not as long as I live!'

'If you're sensible, an eternity. So forget about Hitler. What can we do to find Freddie?'

'Frau Frey, good morning.'

Vera started and spun around. Frau Ritter was standing by the open door, and Vera cursed herself for not having shut it after sweeping.

Frau Ritter crossed the room. 'May I come inside?' Too late Vera saw the radio, and in horror she remembered that Axel had been listening to the BBC. Frau Ritter pretended to look out the window then stole a glance at the radio settings. A flicker of annoyance crossed her face, and Vera mentally blessed Axel for his orderly habits.

Frau Ritter nodded at the flowerbox. 'I came to see how your daffodils are faring. And to check how you're bearing up. That bomb business, I ask you. What a shocking state of affairs.'

'The daffodils are doing nicely.'

'Those traitors will get what's coming to them — those that haven't already, that is.'

'It's terrible,' agreed Vera.

'I heard that some of the plotters were from the Foreign Office.'

Vera steadied herself. 'Is that so?'

'Wasn't your dinner guest seconded to the Foreign Office — that *Luftwaffe* fellow?'

'That's right.'

'How is he?'

'Very well, last I heard.'

'How nice,' said Frau Ritter and returned to the door. 'Remember to pass on my best regards.'

'Why not leap in front of a train instead? If you ask after Friedrich, they'll come for us too.'

Axel had expected concern, anxiety, but not this anger, and certainly not directed at him. 'Vera, we've done nothing wrong.'

'And the Jews did? Which country have you been living in these last ten years?'

A neighbour of Motz-Wilden had seen the police arrest him, though Axel had no idea where he was being held.

'Friedrich's a friend.'

'He's virtually a stranger.'

'But Flavia loves him.'

Vera looked scornful. 'Flavia loves the closest man at hand.'

'Maybe so, though this time I think it's different. And even if it wasn't, Friedrich needs help.'

'He's beyond anyone's help.'

She paused and sighed heavily. 'Axel, please explain to me what you hope to achieve by visiting him. Honestly, what can you hope to do?'

'I don't know yet. That's what we need to find out. Maybe he knows someone who can help his case. I could take books, some food. Perhaps he has a message for Flavia, or Flavia for him.'

Vera looked up sharply. 'Has she asked you to take a message?'

'I offered,' he admitted.

'Because it's not up to you to take risks on her behalf.'

'I offered.'

He paused for a few moments to let her calm down.

'*Liebling*, for all their savagery the Gestapo are methodical. They'll need evidence of a kind, not for justice but good book-keeping.'

'Being acquainted with the accused will be evidence enough.'

'They can't arrest everyone, or where would it stop? The Gestapo are busy enough without chasing the likes of us.'

'People like us are their favourite prey — it's so rare to get a taste.'

Again, stalemate. He could see she was afraid. Fear was natural, but it was distorting her judgment. He owed it to them both to be steady now.

'Vera, when the *Ostarbeiter* arrived, you said our souls were in jeopardy. You might have been right — I admit it — but now we know someone in trouble and our duty is clear. In time you'll see that what I'm doing is right.'

'Oh, I know you're right,' she said bitterly. 'It's your sanity I doubt. What if they question you?'

'I've nothing to hide.'

'Don't you?' Her face screwed into an ugly mask and she launched into a guttural parody of Prussian. 'Herr Frey, you say you're a friend of the prisoner. Who introduced you? Where did you meet? Who else was there?'

It was true that he hadn't considered the possibility of questioning.

'And what if they inject you with some kind of drug?'

'Now you're sounding exactly like Flavia.'

'Maybe Flavia is right about some things. Maybe the truth is worse than we guess.'

'*Liebling*, if it makes you feel any better, I'll speak with Flavia and decide what to say if they question me.'

'The only way you'll make me feel better is by dropping the whole idea.' She crossed her arms. 'You're queuing to be next.'

Krypic was startled when she drew him aside — for a month they hadn't made love at the zoo. This was the same roofless room where he had first undressed her, only today the sun was hot and the bricks lush with weeds. Ordinarily they would have talked, prolonging the moment, but Vera undressed him straight away and, like the first time, she was silent.

The lovemaking was thrilling at first, but by degrees disturbing. She seemed remote, her eyes distant; and half ravished, half provoked, he responded in kind. She held him by the chain around his neck.

Afterwards, they lay still in each other's arms, Krypic unsure whether to be elated or unnerved. Vera was quiet, her eyes shut, then a tear leaked out from under one lid. He asked her what was wrong, but she wouldn't answer. He waited for a while, stroking her forehead, then of her own accord she began to talk. A friend of Flavia Stahl's, an officer, had been arrested, and Axel Frey wanted to intervene. 'He's throwing his life away.'

She railed against her husband's naïvety and innocence, and Krypic listened with alarm. He cared little about the officer, who was doubtlessly brave but whose efforts were at least three years overdue. No, what bothered him was the link to Flavia Stahl, and from Flavia to Vera.

'I can't help admiring his stubborn goodness,' said Vera. 'But it's fatuous — he only understands injustice in person. Politically, he's a simpleton.'

Even the tirade against her husband troubled him. 'You're a heroine too,' he reminded her. 'Every time you kiss me. If there were medals for love, you'd be highly decorated.'

She looked puzzled, as if his German made no sense, much less the joke.

'Axel's not reckless so much as heedless,' she said. 'Insensitive to danger.'

It occurred to Krypic that mentally he had consigned Axel Frey to the category *older*, a thing of the past. Vera's touch had convinced him she no longer cared for her husband, but now the painful thought came to him that vestiges of their love might persist.

Judging by his treatment of workers, Axel Frey was fairminded. He lacked the guardedness you could sense in most men. Krypic had never doubted that Vera once loved him — someone of her sensibility would never have married if she hadn't — but it baffled him why she had chosen to stay in Germany when the regime had first brandished its fist, even as he realised he would never have known her if she'd left.

'He makes the rest of us look cowardly,' she said, 'but he's anaesthetised to fear.'

Her distracted lovemaking had been less troubling than this. He yearned to tell her she'd be safe, that from now on he'd look after her, but the truth was he couldn't promise anything. In Germany he was a zero — worse, a liability. The best thing he could do for her would be to disappear.

'Will you come with me to Prague?' he asked. 'When the war is over?'

She looked irritated and he flinched. To hide the hurt, he tried jauntiness. 'I'd show you the sights. We could sit on the bank of the Vltava eating ice creams. Let's face it, Prague's chances are better than Berlin's.'

'Assuming the Soviets don't wreck it on the way.'

His hackles rose at this. 'Assuming the *Wehrmacht* doesn't fight for it, you mean.'

As if clearing her thoughts, Vera shook her head like a dog. 'I'm sorry. You're right. I hardly know who to blame these days — or who to fear. These round-ups are like the deportation of the Jews, only this time half the victims are *Junker*. Incomprehensible,' she said, then slowly repeated herself. '*Un-vor-stell-bar.*'

This mollified him a little, though she still seemed fixated on the coup, and he cursed himself for the bad timing of his invitation to Prague. At present the offer was laughable, and given his offhand tone her reaction was understandable. His plans were vague — for so long he hadn't expected to live, but now anything was possible. Vera was married, that was true, but there was no saying what might happen over the next few months or years. He tried to forget the flash of scorn on her face.

'I feel like a spectator in a macabre otherworld,' said Vera. 'Alice at the court of the Queen of Hearts. Except the beheadings are real and Alice was braver.'

He took her in his arms and rocked her back and forth, feeling sudden and overwhelming tenderness. Both of them were helpless. He couldn't shield her, was powerless himself, but even so he leaned nearer and whispered he'd look after her. Over and over he chanted the lie, as much to comfort himself as Vera. He cradled her and sang false assurances, then abruptly she rolled on top of him, pinned him down and kissed him hard, forcing a sigh from deep in his chest.

Axel was due to meet Flavia at a local *Kneipe* after a dress rehearsal of Aeschylus's *Herakles* at the Rose. For three days she had heeded his advice and gone to work as usual, but now she claimed she couldn't live with no news of Freddie.

There was time to kill and he decided to walk, since there was little opportunity for recreation these days. Leaving the zoo by the northern gate, he crossed the Tiergarten and entered the Mitte, hardly noticing the latest bomb damage. Vera's fears about trying to find Motz-Wilden preyed on his mind more than he liked to admit. If interrogated, his first instinct would be to tell the truth — by lying, he would only get into a tangle. He felt innocent, that was the thing. *Was* innocent, he reminded himself — already he'd begun to think like a criminal. It was all so absurd.

In Potsdamerplatz the afternoon papers were on sale, and as he passed the newsstand a single word of the *Beobachter*'s headline caught his eye: 'TRAITORS'. Feeling vaguely guilty, he bought a copy of the Party tabloid and stepped out of the stream of people, read the headline 'TRAITORS EXECUTED' and in the list of names saw Friedrich Motz-Wilden's.

The speed of retribution staggered him. He could understand the summary executions of the coup, but in the wake of it he would have expected trials.

The list included a Field Marshal, a General and several other officers. Friedrich had been the most junior. Axel read further and saw that there had been a trial, hastily convened at the People's Court. Friedrich's chances had been nil. The article quoted Heinrich Himmler as vowing to hunt down more conspirators.

Axel would have liked to spare a few thoughts for poor Freddie, but he had to find Flavia and if possible break the news to her in private. He hurried towards Klosterstrasse and arrived a few minutes later at the *Kneipe* where they'd arranged to meet. The bar was rowdy with soldiers and workers, the air dense with the smoke of bad cigarettes. There was no sign of Flavia anywhere.

The Theatre Rose was a small rococo building across the street, and though all its windows were gone it had otherwise survived. Axel entered by the foyer and found the stage crew cleaning up after the dress rehearsal. Most of the crew were women. Three or four actors garbed in togas and gowns were chatting and smoking in the stalls. He'd missed Flavia, they said, by half an hour.

The nearest station was Alexanderplatz. He caught a train to Bahnhof Zoo and within half an hour was climbing the stairs at Meinekestrasse. He called out and seconds later Flavia answered the door, but instead of greeting him as she had a few days before, she walked back into the room and slumped into her armchair. A copy of the *Beobachter* lay on the floor.

'I'm sorry,' he said.

'Everything I touch is destroyed.'

Axel drew nearer, stopped, then picked up the newspaper.

Flavia was very still. 'That animal will pay,' she said.

'Animal?' asked Axel.

'The judge. Freisler. Even if I have to do it myself.'

Axel had hardly registered the judge's name when he'd read the article, but he had heard about Freisler, a man of spittle and bile.

'I've made such a mess of my life,' added Flavia.

Her chain of thoughts was unclear, but Axel chose to let her talk.

'If I'd had any sense, I would have chosen a man like you — decent and dependable.' She gave a mirthless laugh. 'Look at you — you're like a big brown bear.'

He almost smiled but Flavia was serious again. 'Vera's lucky, only she doesn't know it.'

He was at a loss what to do. He offered to get a glass of water, and she nodded. He went to the sink and filled a glass, but when he handed it to her she set it aside. 'Freddie was the only one who knew me.'

Softly she began to cry. Axel hesitated, then stroked her head. 'There, there,' he said. 'There, there, don't cry.'

She began to sob, leaned forward in her chair and wrapped her arms around his legs. She pressed her forehead to his belly. 'It's all right,' he said. She shuddered, drew nearer, then rested her face on his trousers. Her crying stopped.

She was still for a moment then began to stroke his thighs.

'What are you doing?' he asked.

'Don't talk, don't talk.'

She nuzzled his stomach and reached for his belt. He recoiled and backed away.

'Flavia, what are you doing?'

She seemed to register his tone, looked up for a moment, groaned and pulled her arms around her head.

'Flavia?'

'Please, go,' she said, slumping. 'Just go.'

'Are you sure?'

'*Yes.*'

He backed away as far as the door. 'Do you want me to send Vera?'

She said nothing, so he asked her again, and she answered by violently waving him away. He promised to come back in the morning. When he pulled the door shut, she was on the floor, rocking back and forth with her arms about her knees.

They stopped at the African-hunting-dog enclosure. Krypic liked the dogs, their piebald coats and cupped, upright ears, alert like a bat's.

From pails they took seal offal and hurled it over the fence. The dogs gulped whole organs then battled for scraps.

'I can't see you this Sunday,' said Vera.

He looked sharply sideways and searched her face.

She said, 'Flavia's flat is too dangerous now.'

'Dangerous?'

She told him that Flavia's lover had been executed. 'They would have questioned him. We can't take any risks.'

How galling — there was no other way to describe it. A selfish response, certainly, but he couldn't help wishing that Vera had chosen her friends more carefully. How ridiculous that now she found herself in danger not on his account but because of some nincompoop aristocrat. No doubt this was heartless when hundreds were being executed, but hundreds were nothing beside the millions that the war had already claimed.

And what about him? He was only one person, but surely as deserving as any other. He had come to depend on his and Vera's trysts, not for bodily pleasure but the sensation of freedom, for the reminder that he had hopes as well as troubles.

The dogs were eating the last scraps of meat. Their tongues undulated and slapped. What Vera offered, he realised, above all else, was proof that his nature was not only animal but also, for good and ill, legitimately human.

Vera thought carefully about the safest way to meet Flavia. Meinekestrasse was out of the question — she would have spent the whole time with an ear to the staircase, and the prospect of the Rose was almost as bad. Had it been solely up to her she might have postponed the meeting — Flavia would surely understand — but Axel insisted that Flavia needed company.

In the end, at Axel's suggestion, she settled on the *Kneipe* in Klosterstrasse, opposite the Rose. A public place offered comforting anonymity. The most frightening spaces were private.

She called from a public telephone, aiming to catch Flavia at work. A stagehand answered and went to look for her, and minutes passed before Flavia came to the phone. She seemed uninterested in meeting and Vera was riled — if heroics were called for, Flavia could show a little gratitude, but eventually she relented and they arranged to meet the following Saturday before the matinee shift.

Saturday was hot and blustery, the wind blowing grit off the bombsites. Vera pushed open the *Kneipe*'s front door, swapping dust for a pall of cigarette smoke, though the bar was only a quarter full.

Flavia was sitting in a corner booth with a glass of *Weissbier* in front of her. She looked tired but her make-up was perfect. Vera sat down, and to her surprise the barman came out from behind the counter and took her order. He was ancient and doddering. Vera ordered a *Weissbier*.

'A courtesy to the ladies,' explained Flavia as the old man tottered back to the bar.

'He doesn't look strong enough to carry a glass.'

'Gallant to a fault,' said Flavia.

Vera said how sorry she was about Friedrich — and this was true, no matter how reckless he'd been.

'They hanged them slowly,' said Flavia, 'off butcher's hooks. Revived them several times before the end.'

Vera looked at her with incomprehension. She began to speak, but Flavia touched her arm: the barman had brought the beer. She thanked him, waited until he was out of earshot then leaned across the table. 'How do you know?'

'Don't mind about that. I know. All eight of them died that way.'

Vera was speechless. She raised her glass and drank, but the *Weissbier* tasted watery. Flavia might as well have brought news of the underworld. She looked very calm. 'You wanted to see me,' she said.

'I've come to check if you're all right.'

'And am I?'

Outside, a siren cranked into tedious oscillation. Flavia skolled her beer then excused herself and visited the toilet, while Vera watched the other customers leaving the bar. Behind the counter, the old man locked the till. Vera offered to help him get to a shelter, but he refused with an irritable shake of his head.

Flavia emerged from the bathroom and they left at once. The sirens keened. At the end of the street, Vera looked back and saw the barman bolting the front door.

They headed for Alexanderplatz and the station, where streams of people converged and flowed underground down long, central stairs, gloomy after the summer brightness outside. Those who had cardigans or jackets put them on. The walls here were already lined with people, forcing newcomers down to the lower levels. At the bottom of the stairs stood a soldier with a trio of guard dogs on leashes.

On platform three the crush was less. Vera gripped Flavia by an unresisting elbow and sat her down on an empty patch of concrete. Above ground the bombs began to fall, stirring the tunnel's artery of air. Lights overhead dimmed and surged, making minerals glitter in the platform's crust, while dust shivered from the tiles across the tracks. The din of explosions pressed downwards.

Vera surveyed the huddled souls on the platform, as well as latecomers clambering onto the tracks. Most looked bewildered and lost. Flavia had always claimed that the bombing would tell in the end, and now she looked like her own best proof.

The crowd stirred, and on the tracks a man appeared wearing a toga fringed with purple. He held a crown in one hand and his hems in another, revealing hairy shins. Behind him were other actors, all of them costumed, some grave and others laughing. A few of the chorus still carried their masks — papier-mâché likenesses of joy or despair.

Flavia crossed her arms on her knees and shielded her face. Vera peered at her, puzzled. 'Hiding from someone?'

'Everyone,' said Flavia. 'None of them are Freddie.'

An hour later they emerged into daylight and the smoke of burning buildings.

Flavia stopped on the pavement. 'Will you keep seeing your Czech?'

'Maybe,' admitted Vera. 'I'm not sure.'

'He looks a nice boy,' said Flavia, then grasped her hands. 'But Axel's a good man. He needs you more.'

Vera grimaced, yet Axel's supposed neediness pleased her.

Flavia continued, 'Where else would he find a woman crazy enough to spend half her life up to her elbows in manure?'

She turned on her heels, and before Vera could stop her she was striding across the *Platz*.

Later, Vera realised that the arrest must have come only hours after Flavia left Alexanderplatz Station, but it was another two days before Axel dropped by Meinekestrasse and learned that two suited men had taken her away.

Vera's first reaction was terror. Within an hour she had diarrhoea and her heart was racing. The image that racked her was of the guillotine: a prop from nightmares, and the regime's only borrowing from France. She imagined the inexorability of death by execution, and what she saw were fluids. Descriptions were air. Even the word 'death' seemed a euphemism, though the German came closer: *Tod*, a drop of blood on wood.

By evening, the terror had given way to resignation. She felt as though she'd run a marathon. Axel was subdued, but Vera was glad of his composure. She understood without asking that he would do what he could to get Flavia released, and this seemed natural, though she had no doubt what the outcome would be: they would ask Axel about Motz-Wilden, they would question him about Flavia, then ask about his foreign wife. She recalled how as a child she'd heard about the drowning of three men at Manly beach: a rip had dragged the first out to sea and the second had attempted to save the first. The third had died when he tried to rescue the others.

In the night she couldn't sleep for grieving over Flavia. Motz-Wilden had been crazy to draw her into this. She was an innocent, a child. Vera wept — quietly, so as not to wake Axel — trying in vain not to picture what Flavia was enduring. In comparison, dying under a bomb would be easy.

At daybreak she was exhausted. She got out of bed and made a parcel of food and warm clothes in case Axel could hand on something to Flavia. She was calm but knew it wouldn't last.

Axel got up, ate his breakfast and prepared to leave. He put on his only suit. Now that he was ready to leave, she didn't want him to go.

She handed him the parcel. 'Just in case.'

He nodded and kissed her and she returned a brisk

embrace. He said goodbye and promised to see her that evening.

She couldn't face the zoo; Herr Winzens would have to manage alone. Vera doubted she could pretend to the *Ostarbeiter* that all was normal, or even explain herself to Martin. Idly she realised that she hadn't thought of him since Flavia's arrest. Martin believed he needed her, but it wasn't true. If he survived the war, he could make a new life.

For a couple of hours she immersed herself in housework then realised she would have to get groceries. Stocking up seemed strange, a temptation to fate, but the grocer could be relied on for a friendly word. She descended the stairs, and though it had happened a score of times before, she was startled by the sight of Frau Ritter in her doorway.

'Frau Frey, good morning. You look unwell. Is there anything wrong?'

Her voice was sly and knowing.

Gestapo headquarters was a baroque palace on Prinz-Albrechtstrasse, formerly a school for arts and crafts. Secret State Police, *Geheim Staat Polizei* — surely a term of sufficient menace, thought Axel, without the sorcery of fusing those opening syllables. No word had ever swollen so far in excess of the sum of its parts.

He mounted the front steps and entered the building by a door set into a vast iron portal, leaving the morning behind for a cavern in twilight. From the shadows came a policeman who first demanded his identity papers and then started to slap his suit and trousers, a percussive massage that puzzled him until he realised he was undergoing a search. The policeman tore Vera's parcel and looked inside, then handed it back with the contents loose.

All the windows were boarded and as Axel's eyes adjusted to the gloom, he made out a broad marble floor, chequered charcoal and grey. The ceiling was lost in darkness. At the far end of the lobby several people were queuing at a desk staffed by more policemen. Sweat chilled Axel's neck, not all of it from exertion. He wondered if Flavia had passed through here, terrified or glowering.

The policeman waved him forward and he joined the queue. The desk was four-sided and raised so high off the floor that a woman at the counter was tiptoeing to be seen. Beyond the desk a staircase wound around a lift shaft in a cage.

Axel strained to hear the talk at the counter but the voices were hushed. This might have been a bank. When his turn came at the counter, he was served by a bespectacled man in uniform. Axel was tempted to report Flavia as a missing person and see if this functionary was capable of shame, but this was no time for petulance. In an even voice he stated that the Gestapo had arrested one of his friends, and that he'd come to clear up an obvious mistake.

The policeman–clerk looked bemused then asked if he had an appointment. Axel admitted he didn't.

'Then you'll have to come back later.'

'When?'

The man consulted a leather-bound diary. 'September.'

Axel frowned in spite of himself. 'I'm sorry, but I can't wait that long.' The tone came out wrong — peremptory. He would have to be more careful. In a softer voice he tried again. 'Maybe I could wait until someone is free to see me?'

The word 'free' sounded faintly satirical, but the policeman-clerk didn't seem to notice. 'If you were prepared to wait,' he said doubtfully.

Axel assured him that he could.

'Then *Kriminalrat* Gutmann might find time to see you.'

'Ah, *Kriminalrat* Gutmann,' Axel repeated, as if speaking of a friend. Good Man — the name seemed ludicrously allegorical, and for a moment he wondered if it might be a code, a message conveyed by microphone to a tougher type of policeman somewhere else in the building.

'But I can't guarantee anything.'

Axel nodded and said that he understood.

The policeman-clerk took his personal details and asked for Flavia's as well. He pointed upwards: 'Fourth floor, room twenty-nine.'

Axel thanked him and rounded the reception desk. He passed the lift shaft and noticed that the doors were chained. A cold breeze blew from the floors below.

Nursing his mutilated parcel, he climbed the stairs. The upper floors were paved with the same chequered marble as the lobby. Corridors stretched either side and ahead, and there were signs of activity behind the doors — muted conversations, distant teleprinters, a secretary darting from one office to another with a dark-green file tucked under one arm.

He reached the fourth floor and counted off the numbers on the doors — twenty-six ... twenty-seven ... twenty-eight. Room twenty-nine. He opened the door and stepped inside. The room was long and narrow. Three women sat typing at a trestle table with their backs to a series of glassed windows, while three men sat facing them. There were more men on a bench along the nearest wall and a guard at the end of the room. The seated men's posture looked oddly similar, their hands and feet pointing straight ahead, and when Axel looked closer he saw that they were chained.

He hesitated, looked back and saw a second guard by the door — this was an easy room to enter, maybe harder to leave. He wondered if he'd remembered the room number correctly, but the guards seemed to accept his presence and directed him to sit, so he found a place with the others on the bench. On either side he could sense the prisoners glancing at him. Had they too entered the room as free men?

He was feeling light-headed and his hands were shaking, and for a moment he wondered if this was a return of the malaria he'd contracted twenty years ago in Sierra Leone.

Then he remembered — this was the feeling at Passchendaele in 1917 on the morning of the attack in which he'd been wounded: a yawning gap in the pit of the belly.

He shut his eyes, breathed deeply and pictured the sea: the Mediterranean on the day the *Einhorn* left Naples. Open water, warm winds and the prospect of home; Vera in a canvas deckchair at his side, shading her face with a book and smiling into his eyes.

Order thoughts first and the body follows. Courage was a readiness to let go of life — not from apathy but because life was rich enough already. If the worst you faced was death, there was nothing to fear, since death was coming anyway. In the trenches he had seen a good deal of dying. It was commonplace.

The typewriters chattered and chimed, while the men at the table murmured statements or confessions or, for all he knew, the terms of their wills.

The nearest prisoner finished speaking and the woman opposite handed over the transcript, which he read with care. At the bottom of each page, he scribbled a signature — Axel was too far away to decipher the name.

When the man was done, he stood up and looked around, revealing a bruise-marbled face. This too was unexpected, and in confusion Axel avoided the prisoner's eye. His chains made him walk like a penguin. One of the guards escorted him out and another took his place opposite the typewriter.

For the rest of the morning the pattern was the same: prisoners coming and going, dictating their stories. Some were defiant, others cowed, but all spoke carefully, as if their lives depended on it. The women looked uniformly bored.

At lunchtime the typists left with their sheafs of paper, then different women arrived and the process resumed. Axel asked the nearest guard if he knew where *Kriminalrat* Gutmann worked. The man shrugged. 'No one tells me anything.'

Axel wasn't sure how he would explain himself, if it came to that. He'd rehearsed the obvious points but ad-libbing was beyond him, and there was a risk he might contradict Freddie or Flavia.

By mid-afternoon he suspected that the policeman-clerk had either forgotten to mention him to *Kriminalrat* Gutmann or chosen not to — or even that Gutmann was imaginary after all, a laboured joke he was meant to relay to the outside: there is no Good Man at Gestapo headquarters. He was hungry and thirsty and needed to urinate.

It was past five o'clock when they brought in the woman. She was young, about the same age as Flavia, and chained hand and foot like the men, and, when she drew level, Axel saw from the jut of her belly that she was pregnant. The guards and the typists seemed unsurprised, but it was all he could do not to stand up and demand the woman's release. She looked unhealthy and pale. The guard led her to the bench.

Of course he'd known that the regime was arresting women — many of them wives or, like Flavia, lovers of conspirators, but until now he hadn't thought it through, and gradually his anger turned to shock that he was allowed to remain here as a witness — that his opinion mattered so little. Letting him go would prove that they'd lost all decency.

A prisoner signed his statement and the woman got up and took her turn in front of one of the typists. Axel was furious, but also ashamed. For years he'd played down Vera's fears about the direction of the country — she'd come from a happier place, he'd said, and didn't realise that upheaval was normal here. There had been no democracy before the Great War, and during it there'd been hunger. She hadn't experienced the street battles, the hyperinflation.

But Vera had been right. Worse was always possible. Where he had seen only blundering and calamity, she had recognised a journey whose destination was a pregnant woman in chains.

He owed Vera an apology, but not only that — he owed her a measure of security. Already she'd been through too many ordeals, and silently he vowed that after today he would do his utmost to make her safe.

The pregnant woman finished making her statement and signed the transcript, stood up and looked about as if dazed. One of the guards pointed her towards the door.

Axel rose from his seat. '*Gnädige Frau*, excuse me.' She looked at him dully. 'I believe this is yours.'

He held out the food parcel and she stared at it, making no move to accept. 'From a friend,' explained Axel, half to the guard. He placed the parcel in the woman's hands, jangling her chains. 'Take care, it's ripped.' She took it and nodded, but her face was unchanged, so that Axel couldn't tell if she'd understood the nature of the gift, or even that it was one. The guard nudged her arm and she hobbled to the door, clasping the parcel against her belly.

Axel sat down, shaken but no longer afraid. The certainty came to him that he would know how to act if this Gutmann showed himself. Vera had accused him of being an innocent, and so to hell with it — he'd don the armour of innocence. He would say and do whatever it took to get Flavia freed.

He'd been waiting nine hours when a policeman called his name and announced that *Kriminalrat* Gutmann was ready to see him. From the waiting room the policeman led him back down the corridor then knocked on one of the doors Axel had passed that morning. A man answered and the policeman opened the door, ushering him into the glare of arc lights. Axel took one step forward and stopped, seeing no more than the floor and the legs of a desk. A voice in the light called itself *Kriminalrat* Gutmann and ordered him to sit.

'Herr *Kriminalrat*, I'd be glad to, but I must confess that I can't see a thing.' As a first confession it sounded insolent, and the pause across the table was long. Then a chair scraped and Axel heard the click of a switch, leaving a single bulb alight on the ceiling. His pupils dilated.

The first thing he noticed when his sight returned was the *Kriminalrat*'s youth — not so much as a blemish on the pale skin. The face was strikingly triangular and flat, with a lick of brown hair above the forehead. A thin mouth. Half-closed, myopic-looking eyes, though he was wearing no glasses. The broad forehead suggested a formidable brain.

'Herr Frey, in the next hour I'm due for dinner with friends. A dinner, in fact, which is in my honour.'

'I'm grateful for your time.'

'Frankly, I'm curious. It's not often that someone presents himself for questioning.'

'To be honest,' said Axel, 'I've come to ask questions, not to answer them.'

Kriminalrat Gutmann looked amused. 'Concerning Frau Stahl, I take it?'

'That's right.'

'And what would you like to know?'

'Why she is being held. What I can do to clear up any misunderstandings that might have led to her arrest.'

From a drawer the *Kriminalrat* produced several files, one much larger than the rest. 'Herr Frey, you've chosen your friends unwisely. Very unwisely indeed.' He leaned forward. 'Frau Stahl is an idiot. A complete and utter ninny.'

Trottel — an odd, even comical description, and surely encouraging. Would the regime trouble itself with executing ninnies?

'I try to overlook the faults of my friends.'

The *Kriminalrat*'s face darkened. 'Overlook treason? Overlook moronic stupidity, repeated time and time again? Overlook an affair with the foulest kind of traitor, a man bent on murdering the *Führer*, stabbing the nation in the back?'

The squinting eyes brimmed with contempt. There was a stagey quality to the *Kriminalrat*'s rage, but even so Axel could feel his palms begin to dampen.

'Flavia — that is, Frau Stahl,' he said, 'in my opinion loved Friedrich Motz-Wilden very much.'

'You don't deny it, then.'

'No, but she was never political. Flavia is a simple person, and if she has a fault, it's frivolousness. She's the last person to be interested in politics.'

In a way, every word of this was true — for all her rhetoric, Flavia didn't care for ideas. By this measure, Vera was the more political of the two.

'When I heard that Motz-Wilden had plotted against the *Führer*,' he continued, 'I was horrified, and I know that Flavia was too. I would say that her trusting nature blinded her to Motz-Wilden's true character.'

The *Kriminalrat* sneered. 'A pretty speech.' He pointed to the larger of the files: 'The dossier of Friedrich Motz-

Wilden. Every page contains damning evidence of his guilt, and on many I see the name Flavia Stahl.'

He doubted this — the police would have arrested Flavia much earlier. 'As I said, she was very much in love with Motz-Wilden. It's natural she should have spent time with him.' He could only hope that proximity to Freddie was the only evidence against her.

The *Kriminalrat*'s eyes narrowed further. 'Herr Frey, you say you came here out of a concern for Frau Stahl, but may I respectfully suggest that you have problems of your own. You, too, were friendly with Motz-Wilden.'

The *Kriminalrat*'s intentions were out in the open now, the conversation having reached a place where perhaps it had been destined to go all along. Axel wondered if his whole life had been tending to this point.

'That's true,' he admitted. 'And like Flavia I had no inkling of his activities.'

'That remains to be seen.' The *Kriminalrat* opened one of the thinner files, which Axel saw with a shock had his own name on it. 'Herr Frey, I am about to ask you a series of questions, and if you do not answer with absolute truth you'll be playing a very dangerous game.'

Axel nodded. Absolute truth was a standard he could honour.

'How well did you know the traitor Friedrich Motz-Wilden?'

'In hindsight, not well enough. We met for the first time earlier this year.' With a start he realised that this was not only vague but untrue, since he'd first met Freddie on New Year's Eve.

'When exactly did you meet?'

Axel recalled the party. How many guests had there been? Twenty? Twenty-five? He remembered the elation of the night, the spirit of goodwill.

'It would have been in January, the seventh or the eighth. He helped my wife and I move to our flat in Kreuzberg.'

The *Kriminalrat*'s face did not change, and Axel allowed himself guarded relief. Perhaps the Gestapo lacked the clairvoyance everyone attributed to it. The *Kriminalrat* asked who else had been there, and Axel answered without hesitation — after all, Freddie and his pilot friend were both dead, and that left only himself and Vera and Flavia.

The *Kriminalrat* consulted the file. 'On March the seventeenth of this year you hosted a dinner party for Frau Stahl and Motz-Wilden.'

This was more unnerving. Had Freddie or Flavia revealed this, or someone else? 'I don't remember the exact date, but yes, there was a dinner party.'

'And what did you discuss?'

Sedition, mostly, if he remembered rightly — from the *Führer*'s carpet-eating to the supposed mass-killing of Jews.

'The conversation was light.'

'Light?'

'Playful. Trivial.'

'Come now, there must have been moments of seriousness. The nation is at war.'

'Herr *Kriminalrat*, you're right. At one stage I did express dismay that the Soviets had crossed the Polish border.'

'You discussed politics?'

'Not that I recall. As I said, Flavia is not a political animal. She would have been bored by talk of politics.'

Kriminalrat Gutmann looked sceptical but didn't press the point. Instead he opened another of the files. 'I see here that your wife is British.'

This was expected, but still his spirits flagged. So far Vera had been correct about what to expect in here.

'British dominion,' he corrected.

Kriminalrat Gutmann looked puzzled by this distinction.

'She's Australian,' said Axel.

'But Australia is a part of the British Empire.'

'Was.' In truth, he was hazy about the constitutional nuances.

Kriminalrat Gutmann looked impatient. 'Australia is at war with Germany, is that so?'

He sounded a little uncertain, and Axel was tempted to deny it, but facts were easily checked. Australia was indeed at war with Germany, he admitted. 'But only technically. I don't think they've fought against Germans. Their main enemy is Japan.'

The *Kriminalrat* looked no more enlightened than before. He peered at the file then began to ask a series of questions about Vera: how she and Axel had met, who her parents were, her relatives, what her profession had been. His manner was calmer and almost seemed friendly, as if they'd just met at a party and were swapping small talk. Axel was mystified. When he revealed that Vera had taught German to schoolgirls, the *Kriminalrat* looked interested and wanted to know what sort of school it had been. Had Vera known any of the parents? Were some of the fathers influential?

A suspicion was dawning, an idea so startling that at first he dismissed it, only to return with repressed excitement. At the very least he could put the theory to the test.

'There was a high-up civil servant whom Vera knew. She'd met his wife through the school and Vera became a regular guest of theirs. Now, what was his name?' He pursed his eyebrows, the strain of thought terrifyingly real — the only English names that came to mind were Churchill and Roosevelt, and the latter was Dutch. 'Smith,' he said at last. 'That was it. Smith.'

Kriminalrat Gutmann's expression was derisive.

'Selby Smith,' continued Axel. 'He was influential in the government of New South Wales, but later he moved into national government — First-Secretary for the army, or similar. In the late '30s he led a delegation to Britain and made connections with the military there. Vera corresponded with his wife till the start of the war. He was knighted and became Sir Selby Smith.' He wondered if this was overdoing it a bit, but the *Kriminalrat* seemed interested, even eager.

'This Selby Smith, did you meet him yourself?'

'Oh, certainly. Vera was by that stage a firm family friend. I can still picture Sir Selby: he was a vigorous man with a walrus moustache and an egg-bald head. He had a booming laugh,' added Axel, laughing himself and picturing other features of Reinhardt Schiefer that he could add to the portrait. This was almost enjoyable. 'He was a great admirer of Germany.'

'Really? Why was that?'

'He believed that the Allies had dealt harshly with Germany at Versailles. I remember him saying that Britain had made a big mistake and would have to rectify it one day.'

'He said that to you?'

'That's right. Of course, this was before he became well known, though I doubt his views have changed since then. He was very interested to hear about my experiences on the western front. In fact, we discovered that he'd commanded a regiment opposite my own at the time I was wounded in 1917.'

'What a coincidence,' said the *Kriminalrat*, his voice guarded again.

'Not really,' said Axel. 'Australian troops held big sectors of the Allied line.'

'I thought you said that they hadn't fought against Germany.'

'In this war. In the last we were great adversaries. Some even say that the Australians tipped the scales in the final battles of 1918.'

The *Kriminalrat* suddenly looked furious again. 'That's a lie. The war would never have been lost if Jews and communists hadn't stabbed us in the back.'

'I wouldn't know,' said Axel. 'I was a frontline soldier.'

He was tired now and fed up with games, dangerous or otherwise. One of them would have to take a chance. It was possible the room was microphoned, so he would have to watch his words.

'Selby Smith is a significant man,' he said, freighting his voice with promise, 'and when this unfortunate war is over, my wife will no doubt renew the acquaintance.'

The *Kriminalrat* regarded him closely, stood up then put away the files. 'Herr Frey, the dinner I am attending tonight is a farewell of sorts. I have volunteered to join the *Wehrmacht* and will soon be leaving my position here, however I can promise you that before I go I will deal with Frau Stahl's case.'

He held out his hand and Axel shook it. Whatever his political beliefs, *Kriminalrat* Gutmann knew which way the wind was blowing — field-grey would be much easier to explain to the Allies than the uniform he was wearing now. He would have to survive the battlefield first, but no doubt he'd attached himself to some general's HQ. Axel expressed his gratitude and the *Kriminalrat* showed him out of the office.

The stairs were dimly lit and Axel descended in a daze. He had no idea of the time, and no energy to lift his watch and check. The front desk was empty. He crossed the lobby and a guard showed him out. It was twilight and Venus was sinking to a skyline that for all he could tell had been cut with scissors from blackout paper. He walked down the steps and set out for home.

EIGHT

Krypic was worried. He hadn't seen Vera in days.

On the first day neither Vera nor her husband had showed, and he had convinced himself that both had been arrested. In the first few hours he had learned that Vera's life meant more to him than his own, and that he would have died to save her. But this was a fantasy. All he could do was wait.

Axel Frey appeared the next day, looking uncharacteristically worried. Vera was unwell, he announced to the work team, touching his mouth and glancing sideways as he spoke. When the Poles left to go about their duties, Krypic hesitated, seized by an impulse to collar him and demand the truth. What use was caution now? Only an infuriating sense of powerlessness stopped him — knowing the facts wouldn't make it easier to help.

For the next two days he lived in torment. While Herr Frey arrived as usual each morning at the zoo, he said nothing more about Vera. The uncertainty was agonising.

Sunday came. The moment the doors of the barracks were unlocked, Krypic left for Bahnhof Zoo, arriving soon after eight o'clock. On Sundays the Director usually arrived late, and sure enough he emerged from the station at nine, crossed Hardenbergplatz and entered the zoo. Losing no time, Krypic set out for Kreuzberg.

His only option was to walk. It was a fine late-summer day, and trudging between screes of tiles and bricks reminded him of hiking in the Carpathians. In the Mitte, some of the buildings were no more than rock formations.

In Kreuzberg the damage was marginally less. He had never been to this part of Berlin and had only seen Vera's address on letters at the zoo. He walked at random without finding Reichenbergerstrasse, saw an old man and decided to risk asking for directions. The man answered laboriously then began to tell the story of his life, which as far as Krypic could tell had been mostly spent in the surrounding streets. He seemed too shortsighted to notice the badge, and the pleasure of being spoken to as a normal human being was so unexpected that Krypic let him ramble.

After a few false starts he was able to say goodbye then headed the way the old man had pointed. Reichenbergerstrasse was close — he'd crossed it already, but rubble or blasts had swallowed the street signs.

Beyond finding Vera's block, he had no firm plan. He'd pictured seeing her convalescing at an open window, or maybe strolling the street — a glimpse would be enough. In fact, if she was at home, she might not be pleased to see him. For a number of reasons, it was best to be careful.

He walked only a few doors before noticing that for every block that faced the street there were up to five others in rear courtyards, which were linked by archways as though in infinite regress. Number 412 was one of those set back from the street. Krypic paused on the pavement. It was one thing to saunter past a building on a public street, another to venture into the tenements. He needed time to think, and so as not to loiter he turned down a cross street, arriving two minutes later at a broad canal.

In the shadows beneath a bridge he swapped shirts and emerged on the other side as an unmarked citizen. Thanks to forgery, he wasn't too badly dressed. The walk back to Reichenbergerstrasse was longer than any he had taken in Berlin without the ambiguous protection of a badge, but the streets were sparsely peopled and he tried to look purposeful.

He turned off Reichenberger and walked under the archways until he came to 412. The block was dismal, and he found it hard to believe that this was Vera's home. Some of the upper windows were open but revealed only ceiling, and he didn't wish to draw attention to himself by backing into the middle of the courtyard. There was nothing for it but to go inside.

Neither of the ground-floor flats was Vera's, so he climbed the stairs until he reached the third floor and came to number six. The door was shut. He'd hoped to find it ajar and hear movement inside.

He went nearer and pressed his ear to the door. The flat was silent. If Vera was unwell, she might be asleep — though this would not explain why Axel Frey was on edge.

How keenly he had hoped to find her here! At the end of his pilgrimage it seemed a small thing to ask. A sign would have done, the merest trace — no need for the gaudy proof of a flesh-and-blood woman.

He turned away and then paused, looked again at the door and almost as an afterthought he raised his hand and knocked.

The flat was the first place the police would come looking, but nowhere would be safe if they did choose to come, and having started out by hating the flat, Vera now drew comfort from its smallness.

Axel came and went, radiating hope. This helped, but there was still no word of Flavia.

For three days she wrote letters or cleaned the flat, and when there was nothing left to scrub she turned to sewing. From time to time she stopped and stared into space, immobilised by a sense of futility.

She was stitching the hem of a skirt when the knock came, punching the soft of her chest. She sat still. The visitor could be anyone — Erna Eckhardt or even Flavia. She stood up and crossed the room, unlocked and threw open the door.

Martin looked surprised, which later she would think was odd. For now she was only dumbfounded. Her instinct was to snarl at him to go, but the thought of him returning down the stairs was as terrifying as letting him in. She wrenched him across the threshold, glanced back at the landing and saw Frau Ritter. Vera paused, her hand still on Martin's arm, nodded brusquely at the smirking woman and slammed the door.

Martin was blabbering apologies. 'I didn't think you'd be here.'

'Who did you expect?' she hissed. 'Hermann Göring?'

'So you're feeling better?'

She glared at him, baffled, and pressed a finger to his lips. She had no idea how he'd found her. At least he wasn't wearing the badge, though this only emphasised the risk he was running.

She put her ear to the door and heard nothing outside, though she was sure Frau Ritter was still there, probably centimetres away.

She led Martin into the bedroom and whispered in his ear: he had to leave immediately, she would see him tomorrow. He was not to speak with the woman outside, even if she tried to make him. She asked if he understood.

Martin nodded, looking miserable, and she marched

him to the door. Outside there was scuffling. To emphasise her point, Vera jabbed a finger towards the stairs, then she opened the door and showed Martin out. Frau Ritter was waiting on the stairs, openly spying. Vera watched until Martin was safely past, stared at Frau Ritter and shut the door.

'What on earth did you think you were doing?'

The question had raged in her for twenty-four hours, and she was ready for an answer. The boiler room was hot, the generator loud, and a smell of petrol filled the air. A rack of spare gas cylinders lined one wall, like bombs as she imagined them in the belly of an aircraft.

Martin squirmed — there was no other word. With his curly hair and compressed red lips he might have been a schoolboy stung with remorse. The light globe pulsed. Martin was angst-tossed. 'Vera, I'm so sorry. I was worried.'

'So you handed an extra worry to me.'

The term 'worry' fell far short of what she'd experienced overnight. The generator throbbed on the soundboard of her skull.

Martin composed himself. His face was solemn. 'Vera, I would never hurt you. I love you. I'd do anything to protect our love.'

Their love. He made it sound so concrete, so *thinglike*. She wondered if her emotions had ever coagulated this way. Martin had compelled and intrigued her, that was true, and in return she had lusted and empathised, at times even adored.

He said, 'We don't speak the way we did at first.'

If she'd loved him at all, it had been as an action. Her feelings were quicksilver, not the monument he described as love.

'Your soul — it's elsewhere.' He was sounding more and more plaintive. 'We've never once spent the night together.'

She was about to point out that this was his fault, but stopped herself in time, perplexed that she'd come so close to blaming him.

He clasped both her hands. 'If you let them, they'll kill us.'

He meant their love, their ponderous love, laid out like a seal for men with clubs. She let him wrap his arms about her.

In many ways she understood him better than she did Axel. There was a vulnerability about Martin that she recognised all too well, a sensibility that she would have called feminine had she not met other men with the same quality, and many women without.

Perhaps what she had sought in Martin was herself. If so, she doubted that the affair could be justified — if infidelity was ever defensible. Self-discovery was surely a peacetime luxury.

'Things will improve,' said Martin. 'The war will end. Until then, let's hold on to one another.'

She pulled him nearer, hoping this would do as a reply, but from his tautness she could sense that he wanted her to speak. Gently she trailed her fingers through his hair, cradled his head then drew it to her neck.

'Martin, how could I do without you?'

Thanks to the summer reprieve from overnight air raids, Axel had been seeing very little of the *Stamm*, and so he was surprised when Frau Ritter stopped him in the vestibule. She began with ritual complaints about shortages of food, discussed how many socks her daughter had knitted for the troops and boasted of her son-in-law becoming District Party boss. He was already halfway out the door when she added a sentence that struck him as odd, as if it were meant for someone else. He paused on the steps, unsure if he'd even heard correctly — something about Vera and a good-looking young man. 'They seem like such good friends,' said Frau Ritter. 'Isn't it comforting having people to rely on in tough times.'

He mumbled agreement and hastily said goodbye, feeling as if he'd just pried into someone else's business. Mainly he was confused — Vera didn't know any young men, at least not anymore. Even the younger actors they'd met through Flavia had long ago all been sent to the front. He ran through possible explanations, but whether Frau Ritter had meant to imply it or not, there was only one.

Even before the thought had settled, he'd rejected it. Except for the tension over trying to help Friedrich, he and Vera had been getting on well enough. Despite a heavy workload and rationing, the physical side of their relationship was flourishing. And Vera was too deliberate, too serious-minded, to stray.

But the question remained of why Frau Ritter would lie. Vera had always said that the woman bore a grudge against her, and maybe she'd been right.

Another thought came to him. At Prinz-Albrechtstrasse he had wondered how Gutmann had known about the dinner party with Friedrich and Flavia, and in Frau Ritter he could well have an answer. He recalled she'd been stationed at her door late that night, and that the following day she'd quizzed Vera. Anxiety about her captured son might have driven the poor woman to the brink, and possibly Vera's accent had done the rest. Whatever the cause, there seemed a strong chance that Vera had been right about her.

Steering a wheelbarrow piled high with cattle shanks, Krypic approached the African hunting dogs. The bones were stripped of meat and included a pair of antlers. Already the dogs were bobbing and barking. He put down the barrow and threw the bones one by one across the fence. There were tussles for the first few of them, then each dog settled down and chewed a shank of its own.

He rested against the mesh. The sun was soft. From the shade of a kennel a lone dog, a bitch, tottered into the sunlight. She was darting her head from side to side and breathing fast, growling each exhalation. Her jaws were ajar and hooped with slobber. The other dogs' ears swivelled towards her and several looked up.

Krypic backed away from the mesh, and leaving the wheelbarrow at the fence he set off at a run to find Vera. He found her outside the primate house and described what he'd seen, keeping his diagnosis to himself, and together they hurried back. Air laved his lungs, which felt stronger than at any other time since his capture. Sunlight bathed his arms and neck.

They reached the pen, where the bitch was guarding a circle of abandoned bones. Fur ridged her back and she panted and foamed at the mouth. Three of the males were baring their fangs at her, among them the top dog. Vera swore in English, warned him to let no one near, and walked swiftly away. She looked compact and purposeful.

In the pen the bitch snarled and fell on the top dog, which yelped and backed away, his neck in a noose of saliva. The rest of the pack kept its distance, one or two scampering forward for a bone. The bitch growled but left the shanks untouched.

Vera reappeared around the viewing tower with a rifle on her arm.

Krypic straightened. 'Can't your husband do this?'

'He's at the Ministry.'

'Then wait till he gets back.'

'Can't risk it.'

'Then let me,' he said.

She smiled cheerlessly. 'Hand a weapon to a foreign worker? I could land myself in serious trouble.'

He wanted to save her from this. 'It's no job for a woman.'

She frowned. 'If that were once true, Martin, it's rubbish now.' She approached the fence, drew the bolt of the weapon and raised it to her shoulder. From his army days he recognised the rifle as a Mauser, about forty years old but in good condition. Vera thrust the barrel through the mesh and aimed at the bitch, who sprang at the fence. The Mauser discharged and the bitch sat down, whined, then dragged her haunches like a sack. Vera recocked the rifle. Krypic felt a tenderness for her, an obligation not to look away.

The second bullet struck the bitch's neck, driving her body sideways to the ground. Krypic reached for Vera's arm and felt it trembling. She warned him to step back, then re-levelled the rifle through the fence. The other dogs had scattered. Using the mesh to steady her aim, she shot each of them in turn, stopping twice to reload. The recoil jerked her backwards. She looked too small to take such a battering.

He made himself witness it all. At the end there were fourteen carcasses. He was breathing hard.

'They'll have to be burned,' said Vera, gesturing at the bodies. 'Would you organise it?'

He nodded.

'Use firewood,' she said, 'as little as possible. Kerosene, if you need it.' She turned to go.

'I'll come with you,' he said. 'To the storeroom.'

She agreed and they walked in silence to the kitchens. Dead leaves dodged their feet. He imagined her distress and wondered what consolation he could offer. After upsetting her so badly by going to Kreuzberg, it was vital now to prove his worth.

The kitchens were empty. Vera locked away the gun, and as she turned to leave he took her by the hand. As if scorched, she wrenched it free. 'What's wrong with you? Are you mad? I'm not in the mood.'

He stared at her, aghast. 'It wasn't that.'

'Then what?'

It would have been easier to list what he wasn't seeking from her. He wanted a lover with whom he could laugh or converse, and who returned his devotion. He yearned for a commingling of souls.

'I wanted to comfort you, to show how much I care. And yes, you're right, I'd hoped for affection in return.'

Her face was disfigured by a scowl, and he saw with a shock that she was no longer quite young.

'Then today you want to be loved against impossible odds.'

★

The concert hall was one part of the zoo that Axel planned to restore in the original style. If ever life got back to normal, people would need music to help forget what they'd been through. Where the money would come from was another question.

He picked his way through the charred timber, then saw Herr Winzens in the foyer.

'There's someone here to see you.' As usual, the old man's tone was dour.

Axel asked who the visitor was, then in the sunlit entrance he saw Flavia's silhouette.

'What's up, Axel Frey?'

He must have hurdled the intervening beams, then scooped her up at full tilt and spun her in circles. He was jabbering like an idiot. 'Are you all right? Are you hurt?' Then even more inanely, 'Is it really you?

'Of course it's me. Put me down! You're crushing me to death.' Then quietly, so Herr Winzens wouldn't hear, 'This is worse than the Gestapo.'

He set her down quickly, stricken with concern.

She rolled her eyes. 'For goodness sake, I'm joking.'

He nodded at her chin, which was grazed, and raised a quizzical eyebrow.

'Partly joking, then,' said Flavia.

He'd ruffled her hair, making her look so

uncharacteristically scruffy that he burst out laughing, wondering if this was hysteria. Herr Winzens was eyeing him in alarm.

'What are you laughing at?' asked Flavia. She was spiky and undaunted.

For good measure he hugged her a second time. 'Come, let's look for Vera.'

They found her near the roundabout, Herr Krypic in tow. She saw Flavia from a distance and was already crying by the time they embraced.

Flavia grinned. 'You'd have thought I'd snuffed it.' She was rubbing Vera's back. 'I'd always wondered what my own funeral would be like, and now I needn't die to find out.'

Flavia was peering oddly at Herr Krypic, and, guessing that she wanted to speak in private, Axel asked the Czech to allow the women a few minutes alone. Krypic hesitated, nodded, and left.

'Those cells are busier than a *U-Bahn* station,' said Flavia over Vera's still-trembling frame. 'My guess is that the police have choked on their victims and been forced to spit a few of us out.'

Axel beamed and nodded. Anything was possible. The logistics of state security were easier to guess at than the reckonings of one man's mind.

★　★　★

With Flavia back, decided Vera, life was simpler, but a week later a letter came from the Reich Labour Front that destroyed this illusion. Two-thirds of the zoo's *Ostarbeiter* faced redeployment.

Axel lodged a formal protest in person, but in vain. An official revealed in confidence that with France lost and the Soviets massing in Poland, the *Ostarbeiter* were needed for building fortifications around Berlin.

'The way I see it,' Axel told her when he returned from the Ministry, 'we either keep a single team or select our four best men.'

There was a week to decide.

Without meaning to, she had grown used to having slave labour, and the prospect of making do with less was daunting. Four *Ostarbeiter* plus Axel, herself and Herr Winzens made seven — too few, even for a zoo fast losing its stock, yet four too many for a clean, or less soiled, conscience.

And then there was Martin. Just the thought of him was troubling. Her zeal for him had passed, which perhaps was normal, but whereas a marriage might go on from here and deepen, an affair appeared to have nowhere else to go. It was atrocious to think of hurting him, but Axel's news had freed a nasty genie in her mind, and by turns she was fascinated and horrified by the ease with which she could expel Martin from her life. The idea was unconscionable, and she could never act on it. The problem was how to keep Martin at the zoo without betraying herself to Axel.

Beside Neptune's Pool, she told Martin about the redeployment, making it clear he would stay at the zoo. He was silent, as thoughtful as the god on the water, who looked intent on some revenge or *amour*.

Martin looked up. 'Do you want me to stay?'

The question surprised her. 'Of course.'

'Because if you don't, I'll go.'

'Martin, I don't want you to go.'

He looked unconvinced and she tried to stay calm. If only he'd just accept his luck.

'What if they'd conscripted all of us?' asked Martin. 'How would you have felt?'

'Exhausted,' she said and tried to smile. Martin looked annoyed, and this irritated her. 'What do you expect from hypothetical questions?'

'I don't think you love me. Not as I love you.'

So they were back to love. Vera grew cautious. 'It seems to me we're not as happy as we were.'

'You're the one who's unhappy.'

She doubted this was true. If Martin weren't so demanding, there would be no crisis.

'You think less of me now,' he said. 'Admit it.'

'That's not it.'

'I want the truth.'

'As you wish, Martin: I think less of you.' She'd spoken with weary irony, but the whiplash of hurt on his face was real enough. Each time he courted cruelty, some law of nature seemed to force her to provide it.

He stared down at the ground and Vera thought he might cry, but instead he looked up with new determination. 'Vera, come with me to Prague. Now, not later.' She began to shake her head, but he kept talking in a rush. 'We'd be safer in Prague — it hasn't been bombed and won't be fought over like Berlin. I'll make travel passes and all the other documents we'll need, and once we're there we can live on forged ration cards.'

'Martin, that's crazy. I can't leave Berlin.'

He seemed to lose height, to deflate. 'Can't? Or won't? And is it Berlin you won't leave, or Axel?'

It was the first time she'd heard him use Axel's name, and she could see that the effort had cost him. 'Both,' she said. 'I'm sorry. Both.'

He looked sideways at the pool, and now he did begin to cry.

'How can you bear to be among them?' he asked.

How many times had she asked herself the same question? Martin was still looking out over the water, and she followed his gaze. Wind corrugated the pool.

'Because I have no choice.'

'But before the war. When you were free to choose. The propaganda, the *Lager*, the anti-Semitism — how could you go on with these people?'

He deserved an answer, but what kind? She could try to

tell him that the crimes committed here weren't German in nature but human, yet this would be unforgivably glib. She had witnessed how the regime had persecuted others and been appalled, but as a German woman she had been able to remain a spectator.

'Martin, there is no excuse. My decision was personal. I would have stayed with Axel no matter what. I loved him. Nothing else mattered but being together.'

He nodded once and shut his eyes. She wanted to comfort him but couldn't. They were out in the open, but it wasn't only that. Touching him might only do further harm.

Despite living opposite the stenographer and the engineer for nine months, Axel knew little about them, though he did recall that their old home had been hit early in the war. Of all the refugees in the block, they'd known Frau Ritter the longest.

Vera was visiting Flavia, and taking advantage of her absence, Axel crossed the landing and knocked on the door of flat number five. After a lengthy pause it opened slightly, revealing a door chain and the stenographer's face in the gap. Despite knowing him from the cellar, she looked guarded and the chain stayed in place, and with a start Axel realised that she saw him as a threat. He stepped backwards and smiled. Her husband was out, she said. In his friendliest tone he explained that he wanted to discuss matters concerning the block. Her husband was due home soon, she replied.

Her nervousness was making him uneasy. Nothing would induce him to harm this woman, not if he were to live his life ten times over, yet there was another part of his mind, detached and speculative, that saw how easy it would be to reach through the gap, rip the chain off the socket and force his way inside.

He wondered if the stenographer had somehow sensed what he was thinking, perhaps including the fact she was perfectly safe, yet even if she were to unchain the door and invite him in for coffee, the other possibility would stay lodged between them.

Axel suggested that he could come back after dinner, and the stenographer nodded. He thanked her, went back to the flat and busied himself until eight o'clock. When he returned, it was the engineer who opened the door, though the chain was still latched to the jamb. The engineer unhooked it and invited him inside, peering onto the landing before shutting the door.

The flat was a mirror image of their own, though the furnishings were better than he and Vera had managed, perhaps because the couple had moved in earlier. They looked ill at ease but were welcoming enough. The stenographer even greeted him with a smile. Refusing her offer of a drink, he got straight to the point, or one part of it at least — he wouldn't mention a young man. A friend had been in trouble with the police, he said, and he suspected that Frau Ritter might have played a part. For his and Vera's safety, he wanted to ask their opinion.

The couple didn't look surprised — if anything they seemed to have expected it. They glanced at each other, and Axel had the impression that an agreement of some kind passed between them. It was the engineer who spoke. 'You're right to be concerned.'

Flat number six was never condemned, said the engineer, like Schiefer's and the Eckhardts', but had been occupied until a week before he and Vera had moved in. A midwife whose husband had gone missing in Russia had lived there with her three young children. A talkative woman, the midwife had made everyone's business her own and helped in whatever ways she could.

'She was the only one in the building who wasn't scared of Frau Ritter,' said the engineer. 'She knew Frau Ritter hated her, and liked to annoy her with friendliness: cheerful greetings, even offers of milk — sometimes she had extra, thanks to the children's rations.'

In December of the previous year, the midwife had been arrested for listening to Soviet radio. She'd tuned in to a broadcast of the names of German prisoners, hoping to hear her husband's.

'She didn't,' said the engineer. 'But there was another familiar name: Norbert Ritter's. Naturally she went straight to Frau Ritter and told her that her son was still alive, and later that day Frau Ritter reported her to the police. She was executed two days before you arrived. The children were handed on to relatives.'

Axel sat quietly, trying to absorb what he'd just heard, knowing that the effort was pointless.

The stenographer asked if he wanted to stay for a while, but politely he refused. He thanked them both, said goodbye and crossed the landing, re-entered flat number six and lit a solitary candle. A draught touched the flame and the living room shivered. It felt less like home.

He found the gift in an old-style pharmacy in the Mitte, an ark for glass that was situated a few crucial steps below the pavement. The pharmacist placed the bottle in a tiny box and wrapped it in faded green paper.

At home that night after dinner he presented the box to Vera. She looked up from the armchair in surprise.

'An apology,' he explained. 'Go on, open it.'

She unwrapped the green paper then opened the box and pulled out the small blue bottle.

'Sniff,' he said.

She unscrewed the lid, raised the bottle to her nose, closed her eyes and went still. With alarm he saw that her eyelashes were watering and wondered whether eucalyptus was too poignant. He should have realised that the aroma of home might upset her. Abruptly she stood up and embraced him, murmuring endearments on his neck.

'As I said,' he repeated, 'an apology.'

She pulled back her head, looking quizzical, and he told her what he knew about Frau Ritter and the midwife. She heard him out in silence and sighed deeply at the end.

'You warned me,' he said, 'and I should have listened. I'm sorry. For everything.'

This seemed to trouble her, yet when she looked at him he knew he was forgiven. For several seconds they held each other's gaze — after ten years of marriage still a potent act — then she inhaled the oil one last time and tightened the lid.

It was late, and there were other pressing matters to discuss. He mentioned the *Ostarbeiter* and Vera screwed up her face, and gently he reminded her that the Reich Labour Front needed an answer soon.

'I'd like to keep Martin Krypic,' she said. 'He's the smartest in my team and speaks fluent German.'

It was a pity to break up the work teams, but there seemed little choice. 'Then Herr Krypic stays. We'll distil a single work team from the existing three.'

He felt relieved to get this particular decision behind him. Compared to ruling on the fate of others, surviving a war was straightforward — you planned, stockpiled, ducked at the right time and trusted your luck. In the east the Soviets were poised outside Warsaw, while the western Allies had re-conquered Paris and Brussels. At home, Himmler had created the *Volkssturm*, a reserve army from which a Z-card would offer no exemption.

He took Vera by the hands. '*Liebling*, the war's drawing closer. It's time we decided what to do if it gets here.'

She looked at him oddly and he asked what was wrong. She collected herself. 'Nothing. I wasn't expecting this now.'

'Any later might be too late.'

He outlined the plan he'd been dwelling on for months. If the Soviets neared Berlin, Vera would go to Freiburg and take refuge with his sister. 'You'll be safer in the west.'

She paused. 'What about *your* safety?'

'It's different for a man.'

'Different how?'

Axel guessed she knew very well what he was talking about. 'The risks are different.'

Vera looked sceptical. 'Even if you're right and the western Allies are gentler invaders, I wouldn't leave you here. What if you're mobilised?'

'I doubt it'll come to that.'

'But the likelihood of it coming to that is the reason you want to send me away.'

He tried to gather his thoughts. There were times when he could understand why some men prized dim-witted wives.

'Vera, I have to stay. Someone has to look after the animals.'

She said nothing at first, only looked at him impassively, a sign she was displeased but willing to overlook it. She replied in a steady tone: 'Axel, it's too late to pose as a defender of the animals.'

Care was needed not to squander her recent affection. '*Liebling*, do I have to spell out the risks here?'

'No. Because I agree with you. It would be prudent to go.'

At last, progress.

'But what's true for me is true for us both, and I'll never go without you.' She fixed him with unblinking eyes.

Leave the zoo — the idea was unimaginable. There were choices that would tear up your life by the roots, making your own story meaningless.

But could he afford to ignore Vera's wishes again? Her willingness to abandon the animals was sobering, and he recalled his vow at Gestapo headquarters to shield her from harm. When the time came, it was essential she leave Berlin. Ten years ago, to be with him, she'd made the city her home, and to return the favour he would have to go with her to the west, however illogical it might be for him personally. 'Very well,' he said. 'We'll go together.'

Whatever happened, Krypic knew he would always remember this day. The light and the air were perfect — this was autumn as Renoir would have painted it. The leaves of the trees had become beautiful by dying: claret ash beside goldening elms, like demijohns of red wine and riesling; liquidambars in flames. Poplars yellowed down their western flanks. Only the plane trees yielded gracelessly, their leaves shading to a sullen brown before falling and snagging in the skirts of conifers.

At the primate house he seized the chance to speak with Vera alone. Her face, her dear dark eyes, told him nothing at all, but in the background the lemurs screeched derision. He was a fool, they cried, an idiot, a clown.

Vera smiled and said that she had good news: he could stay at the zoo.

But he'd known this already. It wasn't enough. Safety was meaningless without the assurance of her love.

He had to be certain. Staring into her eyes, he extended his hands, palms upward — apart from himself, he had nothing to give.

Vera studied his hands then slowly shook her head, and, even as the primate house fractured with shrieks, he saw the irony: she'd understood him with ease.

He thanked her, and in a fit of gallows humour even smiled a little. 'I've decided to leave.'

'What are you talking about?'

'The zoo. And us. Staying would be pointless.'

She looked alarmed, and this pleased him.

'You can't leave.'

'No? And why not?'

'The risk,' said Vera. 'I won't let you.'

As if what mattered most wasn't lost already. He tried to smile but suspected he'd smirked. 'Labour's too scarce for the authorities to kill us off at random. We've never had it so good.'

One by one she listed objections — he'd starve without extra food from the zoo, freeze without the uniform, get randomly thrashed. Point by point he tried to set her mind at rest, or nearly — a little angst would serve as retaliation for his misery.

Vera cajoled, reasoned, begged, but he managed to hold firm. Renunciation was the only worthy way of losing love.

What he hadn't expected was a tiny frisson of freedom, and even as Vera tried to persuade him to stay he was amazed to find his mind turning to the future. Though he now had the means to get away, he would stay in Berlin. He had contacts here. In the past few weeks he'd neglected forgery, and it was time to get back to it — demand was high, and the destruction of printeries and government offices meant that the format of documents was changing constantly.

'What will I say to Axel?' asked Vera. 'I've already told him I want you to stay.'

'Tell him I prefer to go with the Poles. God knows, I've become fond of them.'

Again she begged him to change his mind, and though tempted he reminded himself of her curt refusal to go to Prague.

To forestall the risk of wavering, he picked up his pail and carried it to the white-cheeked gibbons' cage. Vera joined him and together they fed the gibbons, a respite from speaking. The female was cream-coloured, the male and the juvenile black. Vera had described how the young of the species were born creamy like their mothers and later turned black, then how the females reverted to cream in adolescence.

When the feed was gone, the gibbons took to the ropes, whooping and swinging parabolas on arms twice the length of their bodies, their holds as easy as dancers' steps. They paused and dangled, the male by one hand.

'A few days ago you asked me why I stayed in Berlin,' said Vera. She pointed at the gibbons. 'Another kind of answer.'

The black juvenile waltzed along the ropes then wound herself to the bar at Krypic's nose. She tilted her head and peered at him, the rounded eyes intensely human.

Vera's mood had shifted from pensive to downright nostalgic. 'Who'd have thought I'd be left by a Slav subhuman?'

Krypic bristled at her levity. It was as if she were remembering a love affair that had ended not minutes ago but years.

She said, 'To be truthful, I'm glad it was your decision. Did I ever tell you what I missed most about my father when he died?'

He shook his head. He wouldn't give her this. 'Vera, I don't want to know about your father.'

She looked taken aback, another cause for morose satisfaction, then she lowered her eyes, as if acknowledging his rebuke and its justice. This was poor consolation. In the silence that followed he felt amputated from everything hopeful, tender and good.

NINE

At nightfall, a slit moon rose over the ruins of the aquarium. Axel left the zoo with Vera, chaining the gate on a place he barely recognised. The new year had ushered in further air raids, eroding the zoo so quickly that disorientation dogged his every visit.

He took Vera's gloved hand and they crossed the street. On the pavements around Kaiser Wilhelm church, refugees from Pomerania and Silesia were huddled against the cold. He felt a tightening of Vera's hold and pressed her fingers in reply. Two women were swinging a child to sleep in a blanket.

Number sixteen Meinekestrasse had partly collapsed. The outer wall of the stairwell had gone, revealing nearby houses and the rear of the old synagogue. No lights shone anywhere. Stairs climbed into a void from the fourth-floor landing and came to rest on the Milky Way.

Flavia answered his knock and hugged him, then hurled her arms around Vera. 'Freisler's dead! Killed!'

'So there is a God,' said Axel. 'That's excellent news.'

Flavia showed them into the flat and told the story in a rush. In the big raid of the day before, Judge Freisler had been the sole casualty at the People's Court. Flavia was exultant. 'Justice! And in that place. He would've been one of the first against the wall, but the Americans have saved the workers the bullet.'

Lately she had become a communist, and boasted mysteriously of 'acts of sabotage'. She had a new lexicon of abuse against the bourgeoisie, adapting Motz-Wilden's aristocratic disdain into a new and more viable idiom. Axel was thankful that she appeared to exempt him and Vera.

She began to brew chicory on an upturned electric iron and Axel examined her repairs to the flat, which now resembled a burrow, making him think of the English term 'digs'. Flavia had rebuilt an entire wall without mortar and reconnected the electricity with a neighbour's help, but most of the plaster was gone and the balcony doorway was bricked in for warmth. Thanks to a makeshift fireplace, the flat was heated — for the last two months the destruction of the furniture in raids had gone some way to meeting Berlin's need for wood.

Flavia poured the chicory and toasted Freisler's death. Axel raised his mug then nodded to Vera — they'd agreed that she should do the talking.

'When the time is right,' said Vera, 'Axel and I plan to go westwards. We want you to come with us.'

Flavia looked incredulous. 'And miss the fascists getting their comeuppance? The wife of your *Blockleiter*, for instance — don't you want to see her pay?'

'I'd prefer not to see her at all,' said Vera. 'More importantly, we'll be safer in the west.'

Flavia was sceptical. 'As refugees?'

'Safer with the western Allies than the Soviets,' said Axel. To purge the comment of ideological bias, he added, 'The comrades have more to forgive.'

Flavia crossed her arms. 'I disagree that the Red Army will behave worse than any other.'

'Be serious,' said Vera. 'What about the atrocities in Silesia?'

Flavia answered calmly. 'Propaganda exaggerations.'

Axel could see that Vera was already annoyed. Quickly he reminded Flavia that he'd fought against the British. 'They're resolute but fair.'

'Men are men,' said Flavia. 'Nationality makes no difference.'

This was a simplification, thought Axel.

'Men are schooled by circumstance,' he said, sounding more pompous than he'd planned.

An argument set in. Once or twice he thought he'd cornered Flavia with logic, only to see her wriggle free with jokes or sloganeering. She could only ever manage one emotion at a time, and for now it was flippancy. Vera laboured on for a while, but it was clear they would have to catch Flavia in another mood.

The war would get serious, ran the latest joke, when the frontline could be visited by *U-Bahn*. Sooner or later, Flavia would have to see sense.

★ ★ ★

For six weeks the Red Army stalled on the river Oder, sixty kilometres to the east, giving Berlin an unexpected reprieve. The *Wehrmacht* was fighting hard against the Soviets, while troops in the west were surrendering en masse, reviving Axel's hopes that the western Allies would take Berlin first, though as yet they hadn't penetrated far beyond the German border. For now he was willing to wait and hope, and any escape to the west would have to be last-minute in any case, since exit permits were hard to come by.

On Sunday 18 March, mid-morning, a fleet of Flying Fortresses struck the city for two hours. Axel took refuge with Vera in the tower-bunker, and when they emerged spent the rest of the day fighting fires and putting down injured animals, reminding him of November 1943.

That evening they arrived at 412 Reichenberger to find the rear of the tenement pulverised. No one was hurt, but over half the *Stamm* — the bus driver and his family, the factory girls, the family from the Ukraine, as well as the engineer and the stenographer — were now left homeless. Most took refuge with friends or family, while the mother and her five children were at last evacuated to the west. During a follow-up raid that night, the cellar was eerily spacious: apart from themselves, the only people who remained were Erna Eckhardt and her mother, Schiefer and the Ritters. To boost morale, the *Blockleiter* produced gifts of window boxes planted with bulbs for the spring.

The next morning Axel stopped at a *litfass* column plastered with roughly printed posters:

Berliners!
Every building
Every floor
Every hedge
Every crater
Every sewer
Will be defended to the utmost!

Under the message was a map of Berlin superimposed with concentric rings, meant to suggest a fortress but more closely resembling a target. The bullseye was labelled 'Zone Z', *die Zitadelle*, and Axel saw that it included the zoo. He looked from side to side, tore the poster loose and shoved it into a pocket.

He found Flavia at the Rose. The little theatre had survived, though the only male actors left were all elderly, allowing Flavia to step in at short notice and play the Moor in Johann Schiller's *The Robbers*. Her spirits were high.

Axel made her take off a false beard and step out the back of the theatre. He unfolded the poster. 'Seems that Adolf has included your neighbourhood and my zoo in preparations for a final stand.'

She peered at the map and whistled. 'We're sure in for a pounding.'

'Flavia, staying is madness. Please change your mind.'

She looked distractedly at her watch. 'The play runs for two more weeks. I couldn't go before then.'

It was the first sign of a concession, and hastily he agreed. 'Two weeks then.'

She grinned. 'After all, someone has to look after you two.' It was as if she'd just agreed to a picnic at Wannsee.

For the next few days Axel threw himself into planning their escape. Vera was already stockpiling food and packing essentials, but exit permits would be the key to travelling, and so he went to the military command post in Wilmersdorf and joined a queue two blocks long for permits. After lodging an application he was told to come back the following Monday.

For the next week the bombing was relentless: Americans by day, the British by night, though so far the city had been spared the kind of firestorm that had swallowed Dresden. In the cellar, Schiefer no longer invoked the *Wunderwaffen*. His factory was a ruin. Even Frau Ritter admitted that if necessary she'd flee westwards with her daughter and son-in-law. The *Deutschlandsender* sounded more and more hysterical and often talked of the dictator's 'unbendable will'.

Axel returned to Wilmersdorf on the appointed day and was told that as 'established householders' he and Vera and Flavia were ineligible to leave. He went to the zoo and told Vera the bad news.

She seemed undaunted. 'Then we'll find another way.'

That evening they pored over a map of Berlin, seeking a safe route out of the city on foot. What the map didn't show were the barriers that old men, boys and foreign workers like their own former *Ostarbeiter* were preparing on the outskirts of Berlin. Police patrolled train stations and roads to the west.

'This is pointless,' Vera said at last. 'We'd be turned back, or worse. We have to leave with permission, if possible in style — confidence makes the wearer invisible.'

'But how?' For the first time he faced the possibility they might be trapped. 'Apply again for permits?'

'No,' she said. 'Forge them.'

Vera passed the message through one of the remaining *Ostarbeiter*, buying his discretion with cigarettes. Several times in the last four months she'd asked after the departed workers, learning little except that all were alive. She had no idea if Martin would be able to reply, or want to, but the next day the *Ostarbeiter* returned with the message that Martin Krypic would be waiting near the tower-bunker at eleven on Sunday. Vera nodded, suppressing a smile.

On Sunday she reached the bunker at the appointed time and saw a man she didn't recognise under the trees. He raised a hand and she went a little nearer. His head was shaven.

She had loved those locks. She pointed at his scalp and Martin explained that he'd cut the hair himself. 'To look less healthy.'

It was a weak disguise — he radiated vigour. His cheeks shone where he'd shaved, and he was wearing a greatcoat with the ease of a man in a light cotton shirt, making her picture the plaited muscles on his ribs. Along with the coat he wore a scarf, a pair of serge trousers and his hobnail boots. She hoped he wouldn't look at her disintegrating shoes.

They walked deeper into the park between craters and blackened trees with shaggy new growth.

She asked how he was faring. The work was hard, he said, and the food terrible.

'On the good side, a lot of the guards have left for the *Wehrmacht* or the *Volkssturm*, and others take bribes. The cracks are widening. Plenty aren't making it, but if you're smart you have a chance. A few even flourish.'

He asked after her health, and even Axel's. He enquired about the zoo and looked pained by her answer.

It was time to explain herself. 'I'm looking for papers,' she said. 'Exit permits. For myself and Axel and Flavia.'

Martin appraised her. 'The going rate is fifteen thousand Reichsmark. Gold or jewellery is better again.'

This was an unexpected blow.

'We could raise maybe half. I have earrings. My wedding ring.' She raised her left hand.

Martin shook his head. 'A few cigarettes should cover costs.' His smile was openly cheeky. 'Leaving Berlin is the right decision. It's good you've come to me.'

He took a notebook from his pocket and took down the details: names, dates of birth, and identity-card numbers.

'If you want sympathy from the Allies, I can get authentic Jewish stars.'

'Just the permits will do.'

He snapped shut the notebook. 'We'll meet here this time next week.'

'A whole week?' She tried to hide her disappointment.

'I can only make Sundays. Officially I work every day — twelve-hour shifts — but one of the guards is pious and on Sundays takes bribes.'

She said that Sunday would be fine.

It was time to go and she had to stifle a kiss. As Martin turned to leave, he tripped on a rock and gave a self-mocking salute. Vera waved and walked away between the craters.

★

The following day a sound like thunder rolled in from the east, and within hours news spread that the Soviets had launched an assault from the Oder. Vera thought of ways of meeting Martin sooner but decided she could do nothing but wait.

In Sydney she'd met communists — not at university, but later at pubs in Pyrmont and Leichhardt — and had even considered joining the Party, only to be repelled by the comrades' iron convictions. Even so, she'd continued to regard the Soviet Union as a noble experiment, and if the results didn't resemble her own idea of utopia, it was still comforting that someone was trying.

Her approval had lasted until Hitler and Stalin's carve-up of Poland; and later, when the *Wehrmacht* suffered its first reversals in Russia, she'd been relieved there was one country resisting the Reich on land; but militarism had never been part of what she had admired about the Soviet Union, and the advance of the Red Army frightened her.

On the second day of the offensive, the Ritters' daughter and son-in-law decamped to the west in a private car, leaving Frau Ritter stricken with rage and disbelief. Vera felt almost sorry for her. In the cellar she glowered at everyone, making Vera glad of the extra space but more anxious than ever to get away. Workmen from Schiefer's saucepan factory arrived to reinforce his door with steel.

In the streets and shops, people were querulous, like children on the verge of tears. The only military in evidence were rickety *Volkssturm*, as well as SS flying courts-martial empowered to execute deserters. From the distance, the rumble of artillery grew louder. Propaganda posters multiplied. In Lützowplatz, under 'We All Pull on the Same Rope', someone had scrawled 'Up the *Führer*!', and on Friday morning Vera found the slogan '*Nein*' painted on walls and pavements around the zoo. She visited Flavia and found her paint-spattered and exultant.

'The answer is *nein*!' she declared.

'What's the question?'

'Take your pick.'

'Just don't take any more risks,' said Vera. 'We're so close to the end.'

For the third or fourth time she went over the plan. On Saturday, she and Axel would bring their luggage to Meinekestrasse, where all three of them would spend the night after Flavia's last performance at the Rose; the following morning, Vera would rendezvous with Martin and then return with the permits to Flavia's flat, and from there they'd go straight to the Anhalter Station and catch the afternoon train. The timing was tight but couldn't be helped. They'd done everything possible. Only the wait remained.

With Herr Winzens at his side, Axel farewelled the zoo, enclosure by enclosure. They'd given the last food to the surviving animals and put herbivores in pens where grass might grow. Herr Winzens had offered to keep the zoo running, but only a miracle would save the stock. Artillery rumbled from afar, a sound that Axel remembered all too clearly — someone at the front was getting it in the neck.

At the wallaby enclosure he apologised to Herr Winzens for abandoning the zoo. The old man cut him short. 'If I had a wife, Herr Director, I'd get out as well.'

'What about your niece?'

'Her! She's a brute and can look after herself. She'd turn me out if she had the chance. Labels the food that I'm not allowed to eat, and last week she turned my best shirt blue in the wash.'

'Where do you stand with the *Volkssturm*?'

Herr Winzens looked sideways.

'Go on, you can speak plainly with me.'

'I was too old for the last war, and now they say I'm needed in the second levy. If there were guns to go around, I'd consider it. Or uniforms — what'll the Ruskies do to a man out of uniform? String him up as a partisan, that's what. That's not for me. It's an idiot's game.'

Axel asked what he'd do.

'Go back to Kreuzberg and batten down. The world will turn.'

They shook hands and then Axel embraced him, remembering that no one had known him longer than this old man. His frame was unyielding. Axel let go and Herr

Winzens stepped backwards, cleared his throat, then ran a hand through his iron-grey hair.

The place under the trees was empty when Vera arrived. She stopped. There was no fall-back plan.

She took a calming breath. A couple of minutes still remained till the meeting time. She loitered then began to feel conspicuous and sat down on a park bench. This corner of the Tiergarten was empty, yet if anyone did pass this way she would have no explanation for why she was sitting in the cold with artillery thumping in the distance.

After twenty minutes and still no sign of Martin, she grew afraid. Though the train didn't leave until the afternoon the station would be crowded. At forty-five minutes, a feeling of calm enveloped her. He wasn't coming. The idea was manageable if it didn't include what came after.

She was wording excuses to Axel and Flavia when Martin materialised, crossing the park from Charlottenburger Chausee. She could have run into his arms.

He reached her side and apologised — he'd had to bribe a different guard. From his greatcoat he gave her a thick brown envelope. She handed him half a carton of cigarettes and Martin shook his head.

'To cover the bribe,' she insisted.

He shrugged and tucked the package into his coat. 'I hope you make it.'

Torn now between leaving and lingering, she asked how he planned to survive the coming battle.

'Except for our rations,' he said, 'we're the privileged ones now — the only men in Berlin not expected to fight, since they know we'd turn the guns on them. With luck, I ought to make it.'

'Visit me after the war.'

'I doubt I'll ever come back to Berlin.'

'Then I'll come to Prague.'

He looked sceptical. 'And talk about old times? Me, you and Herr Frey?'

'Maybe. Who knows?'

'Who knows,' he said. He pointed at the envelope. 'Vera, that's for you. Remember that: only for you.'

Not for Flavia, and definitely not for Axel. A parting gift for her alone. She thanked him, leaned forward and kissed his cheek. 'Goodbye, Martin Krypic.'

Martin mumbled a farewell. She squeezed his hand and turned away, took several steps then heard him call her name. She looked back. He hadn't moved.

'What did you miss about your father? I didn't let you tell me.'

She hesitated, trying to find the right word. 'Counsel. Whether to go under or over the waves.'

He nodded. 'Under, I'd say. This time at least.'

He raised his hand then walked away, and it struck her she might never see him again. She turned and began walking in the opposite direction.

She felt the presence of the permits inside her bag and would have liked to check them straight away, yet she was too afraid to open the envelope in public. With so many refugees about, the police were stopping civilians at random.

And time was short. She ran half the way to Meinekestrasse and arrived out of breath. Flavia looked excitable, Axel tense. He was tightening the straps of Vera's rucksack and their solitary suitcase. Vera plucked the envelope from her handbag and dropped it on the table.

Later she would wonder if it was negligence or a habit of helpfulness that made her cross to Axel's side when he began to struggle with the buckle of a strap. Too late she saw Flavia tear the seal of the envelope, yet even now she wasn't anxious.

Flavia spread the exit permits on the table. 'Superb! Your man's an artist. These are utterly convincing.' She reached further into the envelope and pulled out a square of folded paper, unwrapped it and held up a coin on a chain.

Her arm stiffened. The coin seemed to mesmerise her. Axel was silent.

Vera reached the table just as Flavia returned the coin to the envelope. Her face was clownishly mortified. Vera retrieved the coin and latched the chain around her neck. 'I was wondering where that had got to.'

Even to her, this sounded weak. She picked up the permits and made a pretence of admiring them, then Axel was at her side. Flavia excused herself and left the flat.

Axel waited, saying nothing. Frantically Vera tried to think of explanations — tales of loss and recovery.

Axel said, 'Are you having an affair with him?'

She gripped the edge of the table, aggrieved that he'd come so near the truth with so little evidence. Was this how he thought of her? 'No, I'm not,' she said.

'Then why?' asked Axel. He pointed at the penny.

'I gave it to him.'

He looked perplexed, and suddenly she lost the will to lie. 'There was an affair, but it ended months ago.'

She watched the words eating into his face.

'I'm so sorry,' she said.

He looked at the floor and she apologised again. 'It's never happened before and it won't again.' She pictured herself saying sorry forever. Less than a minute had passed and already she was weary.

Axel looked up and the questions began. How had it started? Where? When? His face was composed, and somehow his self-possession made her feel worse. She felt the pull of the train at Anhalter Station.

Axel's questions narrowed. Was the affair going on when she tried to keep Martin Krypic at the zoo? Had he been to Reichenbergerstrasse? She hesitated at this and Axel stared hard. Once, she admitted, but he'd arrived uninvited and she'd sent him away. Axel frowned but seemed to accept this answer.

Then he asked her why.

She shut her eyes for a moment. 'Axel, I don't know. I can't explain. You might find this hard to believe, but I love you.'

He made a choked, mocking noise and turned away. 'We're late,' he said. 'I'll go and get Flavia.' He crossed the room and went outside, leaving the door unlatched.

Vera sat down, the penny hot against her chest. For you, alone, Martin had said. The paper in which he'd wrapped the coin was still lying on the table, and she saw that it was a note, a single line of English. *Darling Vera, for your safe passage home.*

They walked directly to the station, Axel limping with the heavy suitcase at his side. Vera couldn't bear to meet his eye, and even Flavia was silent. Her hair was bound in a scarlet scarf and she wore sunglasses, though the sky was heavily overcast. The sound of artillery had stopped, leaving the city strangely calm.

Beneath the mangled façade of the Anhalter Station, they joined a horde of refugees pushing up the front steps. The concourse seethed with people talking and shouting. The glass vault ceiling had long since shattered, leaving fronds of steel hanging off the frame. There were craters in the marble floor and a smell of coal and engine oil. A girl sat weeping on a cairn of luggage, while an old man clung to a pillar in the crush.

At the platform gate, several police were checking papers. Beyond the barrier, a series of rail lines terminated between the prongs of platforms. A single train was getting up steam.

Axel led them deeper into the throng and for the next half-hour they edged towards the gate. Vera's heart punched at the permit in her pocket. The police were examining every document and sending most people away. Flavia gazed above the crowd, apparently relaxed behind her sunglasses.

Axel reached the barrier first and handed over the three permits and their identity papers. The policeman read each document in detail, as if examining every letter of the gothic script. Vera felt herself trembling, then abruptly he returned the papers and waved them through.

She could have cried out in relief, and as she took her first steps along the platform she had a sense of drawing a line between her old life and the new — having come so close to losing Axel, she would never again put her marriage in jeopardy.

The rear carriages were full and Flavia galloped ahead along the platform. Vera and Axel followed her to a carriage that was peppered with shrapnel holes, climbed aboard and barged down the corridor until they reached an empty compartment. One window pane was missing. Flavia pounced on a seat and Axel stowed their luggage on the rack as a large family group crowded in behind. Others peered enviously into the full compartment, until pressure in the corridor forced an elderly couple through the door, followed by three young women with suitcases.

Fifteen people now crammed the compartment. Reaching the toilet would be next to impossible. Vera stood up and offered the old woman her seat and Axel did the same for the man — plainly they couldn't stand all the way to Frankfurt.

Vera tried to take hold of Axel's hand, and though he pulled away, it was gently — in their private language of touch, a hesitant refusal. She leaned out through the empty pane and watched as still more passengers climbed aboard.

An hour passed. 'Why don't we *leave*?' whined Flavia. It occurred to Vera that the Soviets had been silent for hours.

A few minutes later she noticed mechanics tinkering with the locomotive. Flavia began abusing the railways, making Vera afraid that she would start on the regime. Axel's face was abstracted and pained.

From the concourse, she heard steel crash against concrete and turned to see the crowd surging over the barrier. There were whistles then gunshots, but the crowd kept coming. Flavia asked what was happening, but Vera could only watch in amazement as the wave of refugees broke against the side of the train, laying siege to windows and doors. A man swung on one hand from the side of the carriage and with the other plucked luggage from someone below. Boxes and then a wailing boy were pushed through open windows. A woman with a baby met Vera's gaze, held it, then darted forward and pitched the baby into her arms. Vera lunged, caught the bundle and reeled backwards, striking her head. She called out but the woman was already battling with the others trying to get on board. The baby screamed.

Vera craned forward as the woman clawed to a doorway, where a man threw a punch that jerked her head sideways, but as if nothing had happened she clambered up the steps, gave Vera a beseeching look then disappeared inside.

Three more people squeezed into the compartment and Vera braced herself to protect the howling child, who was no more than six months old. A man in the corridor relayed a message from the mother, and Vera gratefully passed the baby onto a river of hands.

A few minutes later a voice on the loudspeaker ordered everyone off the train, and the police began clearing the rear carriages. No one in the compartment moved, then the loudspeaker announced that anyone left on board would be shot. Passengers streamed back onto the platform. Flavia was swearing. Axel looked sombre.

They were among the last to disembark and were herded towards the gate and back to the concourse. At the barrier, three bodies lay in puddles of blood.

The police set up two new checkpoints and began refiltering the crowd. Vera held on to Axel's arm and this time he didn't pull away. Her belly chewed. They were near the front, and within ten minutes they reached the head of the queue and handed over their documents. The policeman gave the papers a cursory glance.

'No.'

'What do you mean no?' asked Flavia.

'These documents are faked. Get out of here.'

Axel shouldered Flavia aside. 'Officer, we were let on board earlier. Your colleague over there had no problem with these documents.'

'I don't care what happened before.'

People behind demanded they get out of the way.

'These documents are authentic,' said Axel.

'Tell your forger he is too conscientious. It's been over a week since Wilmersdorf used paper of this quality.' Abruptly he tore the permits in half.

'You oaf!' cried Flavia. 'Who's your commanding officer?'

The policeman unbuttoned his holster. Vera leaned forward: 'Look, what does this matter to you? Let us through, for God's sake.' She unclasped her purse but the policeman raised his pistol.

'Listen, Frau, I don't want your worthless marks. Move or I'll put a bullet through you.'

Vera looked at his empty face.

'You arsehole!' hissed Flavia. 'You cretin!'

Axel dragged her back.

'Next!' cried the policeman. Someone shouldered them aside.

They struggled back through the crowd, Flavia cursing furiously. 'The bastard. Moron! His time will come, and soon.' A woman ran into her and Flavia shoved her backwards.

At the entrance, Axel put down the suitcase, sat on the steps and massaged his bad leg, saying nothing. Vera heard bellowing like the start of a siren, looked up and saw two soldiers driving cattle up Stresemannstrasse — an attempt, she supposed, to keep livestock out of Soviet hands. Her head felt light, as if the confusion of the street might fade in an instant, leaving her standing on a beach looking out to sea.

The sun was sinking. 'What now?' asked Axel.

Vera collected herself. 'Home.' She turned to Flavia. 'You'd better come with us. The Ku'damm and the Mitte will be far too dangerous.'

Flavia shrugged. 'Any port in a firestorm.'

They'd gone a few hundred metres when Axel threw himself on the pavement and gestured them down, then Vera heard whistling, higher than a bomb's, hurled herself down and felt the earth heave. The blast was deafening. Fragments whizzed overhead. 'Artillery!' cried Axel. 'The gutter! The gutter!' He bellied off the pavement and Vera wriggled after him. The concrete was wet and smelt of urine and manure. She felt Flavia's hands on her ankles and took hold of Axel's, and for minutes they lay in a chain until the barrage crossed the railway tracks, belching smoke and dust.

Axel clambered to his feet and urged them forward at a run, still hefting the suitcase. Vera's rucksack juddered on her back.

They hadn't gone far when another barrage rolled in from the east, a roar that advanced across entire suburbs. They dived into a bomb-site just as shells struck again.

'Back to the station?' called Flavia.

'No point,' Axel yelled. 'The whole Mitte's in range.'

They waited until the bombardment eased, then Axel took off again, limping. Vera followed with Flavia as far as Mehringplatz, where they tumbled into a bus shelter and cowered under the seats as the road vented geysers of dirt.

To the north the Reich Chancellery stood on a plinth of dust between a column of smoke and a column of fire. Again the shelling paused and Vera sprang to her feet, turned towards home and ran.

TEN

The blast-door slammed shut. Axel met the gaze of what was left of the *Stamm*: Erna and her mother; Reinhardt Schiefer; Frau Ritter and the *Blockleiter* — the last three as usual playing skat.

Frau Ritter laid her cards face down on the table and pointed at Flavia. 'Why is she here?'

'For relaxation,' said Flavia. 'I might stay a while, so you can ask me any more questions in person.' She tossed her bag onto a spare stretcher bed.

Frau Ritter chortled, shook her head and turned to Vera. 'A pleasant outing?'

'Lovely,' said Vera, taking Flavia's cue in sarcasm.

'Let's just thank the good Lord you got back safely, *nicht*?'

Axel limped to the beds, too tired to follow this piece of theatre. His whole body ached, particularly the leg. He dropped the suitcase on the cobbles. From now on, Vera could fight her own battles. For more than a year he'd done his best to protect her, only to learn he'd been standing on sand.

'Come now,' said Schiefer, 'that's no way to talk to one another. We're a family now.'

Above ground, the shelling had stopped.

Axel sat down on his stretcher bed, while beside him Vera began rummaging in her rucksack. She took out a face washer, dampened it and wiped her face, then presented him with the other side. Mechanically he took the rough wet towelling and kneaded his face and neck, the dank cellar air chilling sweat on his back.

For months Vera had warned him to be on guard against Frau Ritter, yet he knew now it was Vera he'd had least cause to trust.

At six o'clock the bombardment resumed — blasts and shrieking shells. The floor shuddered and plaster puffed off the ceiling onto blankets and pillows and clothes. Vera longed to run her hands through Axel's hair but couldn't bear a rebuff in front of the *Stamm*.

Because the British had always come at night, the cellar had been a place for sleeping and sometimes talking, but now the *Stamm* faced its first mealtime together. Frau Ritter brought out food and Erna did the same: rye bread, cabbage and cheese. Vera's reserves fitted into a single rucksack. Alongside the other food she put a can of herrings and some radishes then sat down with Axel and Flavia. At the other end of the table, Schiefer joined Frau Ritter and the *Blockleiter*, while in the middle Erna sat opposite her mother, making awkward offers to share food with all. Vera took her first bite just as Erna lowered her head and said grace, making everyone pause. A shell fell close and rocked the lamp, swaying the shadows of the four brick columns.

The meal began with limited talk — the shelling was thunderous, and in any case there were few safe topics. Schiefer looked morose. Vera guessed that his enthusiasm for National Socialism had stemmed more from pragmatism than ideology, and like a supporter of a failing football team he'd lost interest in the fate of his nation. Frau Ritter nipped at bratwurst, while her husband seemed lost. Axel, too, looked miserable. Using the table for cover, Vera put a hand on his knee and felt encouraged when he didn't object.

Halfway through the meal the bombardment stopped, leaving quietness that cut the last link with elsewhere. Beyond the blast-door, Vera imagined the vacuum of space and wheeling galaxies.

Schiefer fetched a bottle of schnapps, filled the *Stamm*'s glasses and passed them around. He proposed no toasts. For Schiefer there was nothing apart from survival still worth drinking to. He brought the glass to his mouth and threw back his head as if shot.

'I've been considering our position,' said Schiefer, 'our location.' His voice was clipped and rasping. 'Because the building is back from the street, we have a low tactical value. I'll make this clear to any troops who show up.'

Frau Ritter nodded vigorously, and Schiefer leaned back in his chair. Frau Eckhardt pulled a face and spat out some gristle, then Erna mopped her mother's mouth with a handkerchief. A head-cold had mottled Erna's nose, so that it seemed unrelated to her pale face. She shook her head. 'Our poor soldiers.' Her voice barely carried across the table.

'Not our *poor* soldiers,' snapped Frau Ritter. 'Brave!'

'Stupid, is how I'd put it,' said Flavia. 'Fighting to the death, and for what? The war is lost.'

Vera caught her breath, and the whole table fell silent. Frau Ritter glared. At this late stage it would be hard for her to make a denunciation, but if she succeeded the consequences would be dire. Her husband glanced from side to side, unnerved by such a frank expression of defeatism. Schiefer stooped and re-tied his laces.

Frau Ritter squared her narrow shoulders. 'I resent that. Who are we to doubt the *Führer*?'

'Who are we?' Flavia replied, mock sweetly. 'We are the ones with high explosives dropping on our heads.'

There was another pause, then braying at the end of the table, and in astonishment the *Stamm* turned and saw the *Blockleiter* unwinding in spasms of laughter that left him panting over his dinner plate. His plump face was cerise.

Frau Ritter lunged and jabbed her husband in the chest. 'I'll give you funny, you clown! You won't be laughing, let me tell you, when the Russians are stringing you up from a lamppost.'

The scar on the *Blockleiter's* forehead compressed, and he straightened in his chair. A shell exploded nearby, shaking the floor.

Old Frau Eckhardt looked up from chasing peas on her plate with a fork. 'It's a joke.'

'That's just what I say,' cried Flavia. She turned to Frau Ritter. 'Listen to what the old lady is telling you.'

Frau Ritter responded with a look of loathing. Vera had never expected the two women would be thrown together, and she regretted telling Frau Ritter's history to Flavia, who was growing more reckless as the war neared its end.

She felt like crawling into a corner and weeping. None of this was what she'd intended — not for Flavia, not for Axel, and not for herself. Fear wasn't meant to mar the joy of liberation.

With Flavia she made plans to scrounge for food above ground. It would be wiser for the men to stay hidden. Now that a direct attack had started, Axel was liable for service in the *Volkssturm*, and even Schiefer and the *Blockleiter*, both holders of full exemptions, were cautiously staying inside.

Frau Ritter claimed to be supplied well enough already, but a plucky Erna agreed to come along for water. At eight o'clock, Vera led Erna and Flavia up the stairs to the vestibule. Erna carried four pails, Flavia a shopping bag. Outside it was windy and raining. A shell had gouged the courtyard, scouring the stone steps with shrapnel, and from a muddy pool at the bottom of the crater two pipes strained skywards. Against scudding clouds the tenements seemed to topple.

In the next courtyard an entire wall had fallen, exposing a termite maze of rooms. On the top floor an oven jutted into space. Anyone alive had joined the dead underground.

They stepped onto Reichenbergerstrasse, where whole buildings had slumped onto the cobblestones. Beside an oak tree growing from a strip of grass, about thirty women were queuing at the pump. Erna begged Vera to come back as soon as possible, then shuffling as if her pails were already full she joined the queue.

Vera set out with Flavia to the grocery story, tacking between embankments of wreckage. Timber, bricks, tiles, drainpipes, power lines and wrought-iron balcony rails; splintered glass and strewn belongings: a teapot, a lamp, saucepans and books, shards of terracotta flowerpots. Chalk and mortar mixed with rainwater, streaking the middens with filth. The odour of leaking gas fluttered on the wind. Cloud swept low, spitting darts of rain.

They passed other women with shopping bags, and halfway along the street two soldiers appeared. The first was pushing a pram piled with boxes and rags. He was short and plump and his balding head was lowered like a charging bull's. The other was younger and towered above his comrade. A grey forage cap clung to the back of his head. He wore wire-thin glasses and a saffron scarf and carried a ginger cat. The tubby soldier pushed the pram through a puddle while the tall one tiptoed around the edge. Flavia watched them go with frank delight. Neither was carrying a weapon.

The bakery was boarded up but the grocery store was open, and a queue was sheltering in the lee of a neighbouring building. The shoppers were all women, and the talk was of food and the shelling. No one mentioned the Soviets.

Flavia turned and made a face of remorse, and Vera guessed what was coming next.

'Sorry for my stupidity of yesterday.'

'Not your fault. Or even Martin's. This time I only have myself to blame.'

Somewhere to the north a shell exploded and a flock of pigeons burst from a building across the street. The rumble of a bombardment rolled through the rain, but the sound was distant and the queue stood its ground. In close formation the pigeons wheeled then fluttered back onto their perch.

'What worries me now,' she went on, 'is what to do about Axel. That cool correctness of his is worse than rage. I'd feel better if he was able to bellow at me. God knows, I suppose I deserve it.'

'Yes you do, but ranting isn't Axel's style. Maybe I should speak with him on your behalf. I do feel responsible, whatever you say.'

The thought of Flavia trying to save her marriage filled Vera with alarm, and she chose her next words carefully. 'Maybe later. Let me try first.'

And there were other pressing problems. 'Flavia, about Ritter. You'll have to stop baiting her, at least until she can't do us any harm.'

'Ha! Let her try and see what happens.'

'Please, for my sake. The war's nearly over.'

Flavia fumed and made more threats, but Vera made her promise to restrain herself in the cellar.

Ten minutes later they entered the store. With the windows boarded, Vera could barely see the scattering of goods behind the counter. 'I hope they have soap.'

'Don't worry,' said Flavia. 'When the Ruskies arrive, we'll wash our hands in innocence.'

'It's not my hands that are dirty,' said Vera, 'it's my clothes.'

In front of them, a woman demanded five *Pfennig*'s change. The grocer spread his hands. 'Sorry, *gnädige Frau*, but I'm out of coins.'

'I'm not leaving without my five *Pfennig*!'

The grocer tucked a pencil above his ear, opened the till and handed over a one-Reichsmark note. He peered at Flavia. 'What can I get you?'

The woman jabbed the note into her purse and stalked away. Flavia slid a sheaf of ration cards across the counter. 'Whatever you've got.'

'As little as that, eh?' He smiled grimly, took Flavia's bag and filled it with half-rotting potatoes and onions. He tipped ersatz coffee into a paper bag.

'No milk?'

'Not since the shelling started.'

He smiled wearily at Vera and gathered her rations. She asked if there was soap and he shook his head, but when he handed her the change she felt a gritty cube among the coins. He leaned across the counter. 'The way I see it, you're the last one to blame.'

She thanked him, feeling an urge to weep.

Outside the shelling was louder. She joined Flavia and hurried back to Erna, who was standing against a wall near the pump, her hands pressing and parting like componentry. Vera and Flavia picked up their share of the pails, and all three women returned to the cellar.

The *Stamm* waited, Axel thankful for the moratorium on talk imposed by the shelling. At the table, the skat players reordered cards in what was surely a finite set of combinations. Erna was dusting, a futile task, while her mother studied the juddering of the overhead lamp. On a stretcher bed, Flavia was reading *The Armoured Bear*, the city's week-old emergency news-sheet, from time to time yelping with impatience or disgust.

And Vera. Vera, whose name meant truth. From his stretcher bed, Axel observed her washing their clothes in a pail beside the bathtub. She was using soap that disintegrated, leaving scum around the rim. Just to look at her caused him physical pain, a clenching of stomach and chest.

He interrogated his faults, searching for the shortcoming that might have driven her to adultery. His unwillingness, perhaps, as Vera saw it, to save the last of the animals. Or his slowness to recognise the true odiousness of the regime. In the past she had always forgiven his mistakes.

As he'd forgiven hers.

Vera wrung out the washing and then rigged a clothesline over the bathtub. She pegged up their clothes, glancing at him once or twice as if checking he'd noticed her labours. The shelling faltered, and by coincidence or otherwise his bowels began clamouring for release. He rose reluctantly and left the cellar, taking brief satisfaction in not letting Vera know why.

The lavatory was a plank and a can in a cupboard at the end of the corridor. His own stench smelt alien to him, a version of the can's communal reek. He wiped himself with *The Armoured Bear* then tipped water on his hands from a bottle clamped between his knees.

Outside the cellar, Vera was waiting for him.

'I had to speak with you,' she said.

To shelter his face he looked sideways.

She said, 'What can I say that will make a difference?'

'There's nothing you can say.'

She reached for his face and her hand brushed his forehead as he tried to step around her, and feeling the skin reverberate he strode to the blast-door, pulled it open and re-entered the cellar. The *Stamm* glanced up, Flavia more intently than the rest. He lay down on the stretcher bed.

So inconsequential a touch, yet it had almost unmanned him. Beneath the exhilaration of walking away was a sickening sense of having inflicted pain. The thought of Vera standing alone in the corridor was wrenching.

He disgusted himself. Histrionics had never been his show, and now in particular he needed to think clearly. Vera had tried to say sorry and even claimed she still loved him, and the obvious response was to try to put the past behind them. Some signal, a touch, would be enough to start again.

The blast-door opened and then closed, but as if set in cement he kept staring at the ceiling. It was his body baulking, and enraged by his own irrationality he scoured his mind for an explanation, testing each conjecture on a gauge of pain. He considered Vera's scheming. Her duplicity. If a particular thought hurt more than another he homed in on it, burrowing into the distress. He saw his wife in the arms of the Czech: her lips on his, the meeting of their tongues. He pictured — had this really happened? — their nakedness, and the anguish escalated in his chest.

He pushed on, the point of perseverance now forgotten. If naked, then joined — she had put her body at another man's disposal.

But even this was too cowardly. What Vera had done, rather, was to take another man into herself. His penis. His cock. At last, in a crucible of pain, the answer. Her labia and vagina, and the liquid there. Intolerable fire.

For this he would never be able to forgive her.

Flavia came back from the lavatory with news shouted by neighbours: cigarettes and food and drink for the taking. The *Stamm* snatched bags and scrambled for the door.

Vera pounded up the stairs and into the courtyard, looked back at Axel and saw him waving her on. With Flavia she ran onto the street and headed west, passing fully laden looters coming the other way, until they reached a mass of floury footmarks at the front of the grocery store. A man came out and grinned at them, brandished two satchels then loped away.

She followed Flavia inside and stopped to adjust her eyes to the gloom. The shelves, never full, were empty now, and on the floorboards a trail of mud and flour rounded the counter and entered a curtained door at the back of the shop. From behind the curtain a *Hausfrau* appeared and staggered into the shop with a heavy bag. Flavia made way for her then plunged past the curtain.

Vera started forward then saw a motionless figure at the cash register. The grocer was resting his fingers on the till as if halfway through a transaction. He nodded at her, unsurprised. She held his gaze for a moment, owing at least this, then turned and tugged the curtain aside.

A short landing jutted into darkness, and beyond it was a stairway into a pitch-dark cellar. There were collisions of glass and steel and wood and the cries of marauding ghosts. Vera gripped Flavia by the hand and they descended together, stopping once to press against the wall as someone barged upwards.

The cellar was utterly black. Vera smelt cabbage and dust and schnapps. She gagged on a powder that tasted like flour, and slipped on a rink of what she guessed were peas. Reaching for a wall, she collided with another's bare arm and brushed it aside like kelp. She gripped a shelf and tried to steady herself, then from nowhere came a blow to her ribs and she buckled, collapsing the shelf and cascading apples down her body. Close by, a woman cursed. Vera's ribs were throbbing. Flavia arrived and called her name and then helped her up.

While she caught her breath, Flavia made her hold open a shopping bag and half filled it with apples. Gingerly, she started probing the shelves, found nothing and then tried the floor. There she found several sacks the size of sandbags and collected two.

Overhead there were footfalls and curses on the stairs, then Schiefer yelled out and Flavia called back. Vera could hear Axel's voice and called his name, and a few moments later he was by her side. Impulsively she clasped his fingers and drew them to her ribs. Just bruised, she said, but his touch felt good. Axel said nothing and she let him go.

Schiefer was barking orders, and the *Stamm* seized a corner and swept the shelves. Vera found bottles and a truncheon of sausage and dropped them in her bag.

When all the others were finished, Vera ascended with the *Stamm* into the comparative radiance of the store. The grocer had left the register. Vera hoped he had joined the looting, salvaging a fraction of the stockpile for himself.

On the pavement, an impromptu exchange market had formed. Vera opened her rucksack and was disappointed to find that the bottles contained vinegar, then an elderly woman clutched at her elbow and begged for them in exchange for three bottles of riesling. Before the woman could change her mind, Vera closed the deal.

Schiefer was predicting disaster if they didn't keep moving, but the rest of the *Stamm* was triumphant. Flavia was sorting through packets of dried food, and Erna was smiling, her arms akimbo, a rucksack hanging from her narrow shoulders. Frau Ritter was scrutinising a pair of string bags stuffed with black bread and onions. Her face was pinched and white. Vera hadn't seen her above ground for days.

The *Blockleiter* became visible at the moment of his death, abandoning a stance of unnatural rigidity and toppling face down across the gutter. His skull rang on the cobbles like a hammer on an anvil, and the suitcase he had carried released a torrent of cans. Bystanders flinched, but no shot had been fired.

Erna reached him first, then Schiefer. Axel arrived and they rolled the *Blockleiter* onto his back, accidentally crossing his legs and making him look like a man restraining his bladder, then a stain spread around the crotch of his trousers and the body released a guttural fart. Schiefer recoiled just as the stink reached Vera. The face was pulpy and red down one side. No one could doubt he was dead.

Passers-by rippled around the *Stamm*. The stillest of all was Frau Ritter. Flavia prised the string bags from her hands and led her towards the body, but after only two paces Frau Ritter halted, wailed. Her cries were jagged and thin.

Cans lay scattered about the corpse like provisions for a voyage to a field-grey afterlife.

At twilight they gathered to bury the *Blockleiter* in the courtyard. Artillery rumbled distantly. Beside the crater skewered by twin metal pipes lay a broom cupboard, and in it the body.

Vera would have preferred not to come back above ground, yet pity for the dead man had brought her here with the rest. They were a sorry sight. Efforts to dress respectably had only emphasised the group's dishevelment. Schiefer, in a crumpled suit and navy tie, read a speech off an envelope about the *Blockleiter's* good nature. Though normally a keen talker, Schiefer's delivery was halting. Axel stood beside the cupboard, a crest of hair protruding from the back of his head. Only Frau Ritter had managed to dress wholly in black — with a veil draped over a broad-brimmed hat and a silk dress under her sable coat. Precious kohl rimmed her eyes.

Schiefer's oration came to an end. He crushed the envelope in his pocket and signalled Axel to pick up the other end of the cupboard. A struggle followed to manoeuvre it between the uprooted pipes, but when Vera stepped forwards, Schiefer shook his head vehemently. He lowered one end into the crater and circled around to help Axel, who was leaning over the grave with only the cupboard for support, then together they laid it level below ground. Underneath was a gap and a pool of filthy water. On either side rose the pipes.

Filling the crater would be the work of a couple of hours. Vera disliked the thought of Axel remaining outside so long. The *Blockleiter's* death, though of natural causes, had destroyed her last expectations of order. There were no longer any inquests, obsequies or certificates to paper the void beneath everyone's feet.

Clutching a handful of lilacs, Erna approached the crater, stopped at the edge and tossed the posy like a quoit. The flowers landed on the cupboard but skittered off, splashing into the pool amid cinders and ash.

The *Stamm* peered expectedly at Frau Ritter, who stepped forward a few paces. Her pointed chin was high. Leaning down, she sank her fingernails into the mud, straightened up and spattered it onto the cupboard.

Overhead, Vera heard the breathy flight of rockets, sending her scampering with the rest of the *Stamm* into the vestibule. From a nearby street came the sound of explosions. Frau Ritter adjusted her veil and stepped inside.

The task of backfilling would have to wait. From the open grave the pipes seemed to wave like a drowning man in a trough beyond breakers.

The booty from the grocery store, some of it the *Blockleiter*'s, dominated the menu at his wake. When Axel surveyed the *Stamm*, he couldn't help thinking that no one, not even the dead man's wife, looked particularly undone by grief. Chastened, perhaps, but not sorrowful. Vera and Flavia were labouring over plates of potato and cabbage, each crowned by a miraculous fried egg. Schiefer poured wine and schnapps. Frau Eckhardt dribbled soup and her daughter scraped it back into her mouth with a spoon. Frau Ritter was neater. Her forkfuls seemed bigger than the opening of her mouth, yet without smudging her lipstick she kept pace with the rest.

Schiefer poured another round of drinks, and Axel excused himself from the table. Private contemplation seemed a better tribute to a man with whom he'd shared the brotherhood of battle, however little they had known one another personally.

At the table, he noted, the mood was turning convivial. Frau Ritter said that all they needed were cigarettes, and Schiefer replied with a joke about an irate general, his batman and a butt discarded on the floor — 'It's yours, Herr General, you saw it first.' Axel turned away from the merriment, and so he was surprised when Flavia sat down beside him on a stretcher bed. At the table, Vera was pulling a face that was clearly meant to warn Flavia off, but Flavia wasn't looking, and instead Vera smiled at him ruefully, as if sharing her exasperation with all things Stahl.

Flavia seized his arm and gave it a shake. 'I've come to tell you to stop being such a blockhead and start speaking with Vera again.'

Ever the diplomat. 'Am I right in saying you're here without authority?'

'Vera asked me not to interfere, but I feel responsible.'

'Don't. One way or another it would have come to light.'

It — the faithlessness of Vera's body. At the table, she was talking loudly, no doubt wishing to distract the others from a conversation she couldn't stop.

'Possibly,' conceded Flavia.

A new suspicion occurred to him. 'Did you know what was going on?'

Flavia hesitated. 'Not at first.' She went on briskly, 'Later, yes of course. And it's no use looking like that. What choice did I have? Vera's my closest friend.'

'Then maybe you should have taken her advice and left me alone.'

'Why don't *you* listen to her? She wants you back, and in my opinion you'd be mad not to take her. Your wife's as rare as oranges. And loyal too.'

It was one thing to exaggerate, quite another to call an elephant a giraffe. 'Flavia, how can you possibly say that?'

'She's still here, isn't she?'

'I don't see that she has much choice.'

'What would you know about her choices? Look Axel, as it happens, I didn't agree with what she was doing, and I told her so, but one reason I didn't come bleating to you was that I knew it wouldn't last. Believe me, I'm an expert. There are two kinds of infidelities: one that's a bridge to someone new, and another that takes you back to yourself. Vera's was the second. She's had a fling, that's all, and in the end she's chosen you. If anything, you should be flattered.'

As a defender of the indefensible, she was second to none. 'Flavia, you should have gone into propaganda.'

'Thanks, but I haven't finished with you yet.' She waved at the ceiling. 'In case you haven't noticed, we're in the

285

middle of a war. This is a wake, remember — never mind he died naturally; we could be killed any time. Make it up with Vera. When I think of Freddie, I tell myself that at least he was loved.' Her voice faltered. 'And died knowing it.' She paused. 'But if that's not enough, and you're too proud to help yourself, for pity's sake, spare a thought for me: I don't want a ham-fisted act of mine to bring about the end of your marriage.' She gave a sad little smile. 'After all, I wasn't even trying this time.'

He was puzzled for a moment then recalled Flavia on her knees, fumbling with his flies and weeping for Motz-Wilden. At the time he had known she was disoriented, and he certainly hadn't been tempted to take advantage of her, but now he asked himself if this had been a genuine test of virtue. What if she'd come to him in another mood, in different circumstances? From time to time over the years he had registered her charms, and however mechanical his reactions might have been to the glimpse of a garter or the outline of a breast, it was undeniable that occasionally he had desired his wife's best friend, a woman, moreover, who was young enough to be his daughter.

At the table, he realised, conversation had stopped. Flavia, too, had noticed and turned around, yet it was clear that the hush was not for them but for Frau Ritter, who was staring into the depths of her mug.

'Such a good man,' she declared.

Even Schiefer looked contrite.

'So good,' repeated Frau Ritter, and began sobbing into a handkerchief. Schiefer reached to touch her shoulders then hovered like a mountaineer seeking a better hold. He looked pleadingly at Erna, who got up and put her arms around the weeping woman. Schiefer plucked his serviette from his collar and folded it in front of him on the table.

'Where would I be now if it weren't for him?' sobbed Frau Ritter. 'Just tell me that.'

No one answered. Abruptly she broke Erna's embrace and took another draught of schnapps. She slapped down the mug and answered her own question. 'Nowhere. Taking in laundry. Or worse.'

Erna, who Axel knew had done her share of others' laundry, looked mystified. Frau Ritter mopped her eyes, smearing kohl on her face. Holding herself tight, she began to rock.

'Up there now,' she wailed. 'Above us. Above us and unburied.' Even Erna seemed unsure how to offer consolation.

The next morning Flavia announced it was Wednesday — to Vera, a giddyingly humdrum statement. The deployment of days into ranks of seven had surely lapsed. Day and night were indistinguishable in their clammy kiln.

Hours later the shelling stopped, and she agreed with Erna and Flavia to go up for more water. It was raining outside. In the courtyard a new crater was leaking smoke, and Vera imagined the water in the drains and gutters tasting of nitroglycerine. From the distance came the typewriter chatter of small arms, a new and chilling sound.

Reichenbergerstrasse at first seemed deserted, but at the water pump the usual queue was waiting, and Vera caught sight of two SS men near the pump, one standing and the other bent over double. Both carried submachine guns, the first weapons Vera had seen since the start of the shelling, but instead of field uniforms they were dressed in ceremonial black. The guns were the same shade of grey as the clouds — a colour repeated in the cobblestones, on the pails of the *Hausfrauen* queued at the pump, and in their scarves and stockings and coats. Only the men's black uniforms were unequivocal.

The man who was standing was middle-aged and looked more like a stevedore than a member of a military elite. The second man was hunching over a pool of vomit, while his comrade consoled him and stroked his nape. Slowly he stood up. He was young and in other circumstances might have been good-looking, but his blue eyes were bloodshot and his face was flushed.

The women in the queue weren't looking at the soldiers but at the pavement or the strip of park out of Vera's line of sight. As she drew nearer, the oak tree came into view, revealing a man hanging by the neck from a branch.

She joined the end of the queue, put down the pails and linked arms with her friends, comforting one and restraining the other. The younger soldier was pale and laid his forearms on his weapon, which was hanging on a strap from his shoulders. The older man dabbed a cigarette paper onto his lower lip. He opened a leather pouch, unplucked the paper from his lips and packed it with tobacco, then with thumbs and fingers rolled a cylinder that he sealed with his tongue and tapped on his palm. He passed the cigarette to his comrade, who accepted and lit up without looking at his hands.

They seemed in no hurry to leave, and this was perhaps intentional. Vera tried not to look at the hanging man, and instead examined the unmown grass, then a shark's yawn of glass in a background window. The crown of the oak was primed with buds.

The man was dangling by a frayed electric cord and facing the other way. A power plug sprouted from the knot of the noose, and above a cord-notch in the neck the skin was blue. Vera was glad she could not see a face.

The body was slight and clad in brown trousers, a sleeveless jumper and a once-white shirt that had been laundered blue. The hair was iron-grey. On the man's back hung a square of masonite with 'I refused to fight' inscribed on it in charcoal. The motto, its precise formation of tense, had been scrawled with trembling fingers.

Though the air was still, the hanged man swayed.

★

Axel guessed he was the only one left in the *Stamm* who could meaningfully picture the fighting. Machine-gun and rifle fire was constant now. Unlike air raids, there was an intimacy to combat on the ground, where a man might kill with his teeth, or like a chicken keep running without a head.

The *Stamm* was listless, all except Erna, who was busy stirring flurries of plaster with a broom. After sweeping, she arranged shovels in order of size, then prowled behind the skat players seated at the table. A stray salt-shaker seemed to catch her eye, but when she reached for it Frau Ritter slapped her hand.

'Be still, for God's sake!'

Erna rubbed her hand. 'I was only helping.'

'Just mind your own business.'

At the other end of the table, Flavia stirred, and from the eager thrust of her shoulders Axel guessed what was coming.

'Why not mind your own business?' she said. 'Get in training for life after National Socialism.'

Frau Ritter looked incredulous and then outraged, and even to Axel it seemed unkind to needle her so soon after the *Blockleiter's* death.

She swivelled at Flavia. 'Looking forward to it, are we?' She pointed at Vera. 'Knowing that one helps, I bet. Enemy alien. Probably a spy. Should've been sent to a *Lager* years ago.'

Axel had never heard anyone attack Vera so openly, but though troubled he felt strangely detached. This was how a ghost might feel: mute, yet tremulous with emotion. Vera looked fierce and self-possessed.

'Only a *Lager*?' asked Flavia. 'Where's the fun in that? I've heard you prefer something stiffer — say, the guillotine.'

Frau Ritter hesitated, then answered firmly: 'Whatever I've done in the past, I've done for the Fatherland. The pity is there's not more like me.'

Flavia scoffed, and Frau Ritter's voice turned shrill. 'It's you acrobats of the intellect who've brought us down! Spies and traitors, the lot of you. Undermining the Reich from inside, and when your filthy work is done you try hightailing it to the west. Well, I can only thank the good Lord you failed in that.'

'Not like your daughter,' said Flavia.

Frau Ritter went rigid but recovered quickly. 'That was different. She left Berlin in support of her husband. He was heading to the Alpine Redoubt to pursue the war.'

'*Gluwein*,' said Frau Eckhardt, who was parked in her bathchair by the stretcher beds. The whole *Stamm* turned to her and the old woman beamed.

Axel looked back towards the table and saw Frau Ritter's eyes fix on him.

'And what are *you* doing here, skulking underground? Should've been up there days ago, fighting for the

291

Fatherland! Defending us all.' Her voice turned sarcastically hearty. 'Make no mistake, my friend, we all know the law. We can see what you are. The lowest, the *merde de la merde*. The shit that'll fill up your pants when our troops arrive.'

He looked at the floor. The woman was right: he was probably fitter than most of the poor devils in the *Volkssturm*.

He cleared his throat, then Vera was on her feet. 'You witch! How *dare* you speak to my husband that way!'

Lines from a melodrama, he thought. Why so much anger about the truth?

'A veteran! And wounded! He won't be dying, let me tell you, for your lost cause!'

Astonishingly, she was crying. Flavia put an arm about her.

'It's no business of yours,' said Frau Ritter. 'You're a foreigner here. Reinhardt, what do you think?'

Schiefer looked startled, but composed himself and furrowed his brow. As Axel waited, his sense of detachment returned, as if Schiefer's deliberations concerned someone else altogether. Stranger still was the sudden conviction that Schiefer was about to speak the truth — not as himself but as the voice of German manhood. His bulk, his baldness, the winged moustache — the sheer ridiculousness of the man seemed to make him a likely oracle.

'Well,' said Schiefer, 'no doubt there are others more crippled who are up there fighting.'

'Exactly!' said Frau Ritter.

'And he's not an old man, is he? Not like me,' he added.

Self-justification, bogus gravitas — the style was all Schiefer, yet even so Axel couldn't shake the sense that here was uncontaminated judgment.

'So, why not?' continued Schiefer. 'Why not answer the call?'

'There!' crowed Frau Ritter.

A verdict, then. Or so it seemed. As if surprised to be taken at his word, Schiefer now seemed anxious to clarify. 'At any rate, that's one view. You could also argue that Herr Frey should choose. After all, the decision is a serious one.'

'Very serious,' said Frau Ritter. Axel noticed her piercing eyes, and recalled how months ago he'd teased Vera for making the same observation.

'This is absurd,' said Flavia. 'Axel, pay no attention.'

Frau Ritter's gaze was fixed. 'So tell me, Herr Frey, when will you do your duty?'

In the background he glimpsed Vera, whose own expression was a blend of entreaty and warning. It seemed he would have to choose after all. The *Stamm* was waiting, but an illusion gripped him that an answer would leave his mouth not as sound but as vapour.

'You heard the woman,' said Vera. 'If she can, she'll denounce you.'

'Perhaps she's right. I've fought before — why not again?'

Axel's fatalism was unnerving, though if apathy made him more compliant then perhaps it was a blessing.

They reached the third-floor landing and Axel pulled out his keys.

'Too obvious,' said Vera. She led him up the stairs.

Between the third and fourth floors one wall had gone, revealing a view of rooftops and steeples linked to clouds by cords of smoke. She kept clear of the edge, cautious now in every action. Like the *Blockleiter*, there would be many people dying at the end.

The bus-driver's flat had made peace with the sky. A gap in the ceiling invited weather inside, and starlings had nested in broken crockery in the kitchen. The sound of gunfire spattered the walls. Apart from some shattered furniture, few signs of the bus-driver's family remained. A strong smell of mildew filled the air. Fleur-de-lis wallpaper unravelled in strips, as if driven by some failure of will to join the rubbish on the floor.

In the half of the flat that still had a ceiling, wreckage blocked the door to the bedroom. Axel was ready to return downstairs but Vera found a way in through a hole on the landing.

In the bedroom they found a bed frame with sagging wire mesh. Vera pushed it beneath a storage loft. She pointed at the bedhead and motioned him up.

'This is ridiculous,' he said.

'Better embarrassed than dead.'

He gave a sceptical grunt. 'Just don't leave me here longer than necessary.'

Using the bedhead as a ladder, he climbed up to the hatch, opened it and slithered into the loft. Vera handed him a pair of blankets, one of which he shoved under his hip as a cushion. She passed up a satchel of food and water.

It was exposed to shells and not much of a hiding place, but it would have to do.

'Is this so bad?' she asked.

'I've slept in worse.'

'Defending you, I mean.'

'Your choice,' he said.

She paused to gauge his tone, then gave up and turned away. Behind her the hatch closed, and the sound of wood on wood was a relief. She made her way across the rubble and onto the landing.

Their own flat was a ruin, though not as bad as upstairs. The window frame splayed. Ribbons of blackout paper wafted in the breeze. Plaster had fallen in sheets from the ceiling, and tufts in the floorboards marked the resting points of shrapnel. The battle was still some distance away, and on an impulse she sat down in the solitary armchair.

She felt a need to make plans but couldn't concentrate. The window box was flying daffodils like flags, and the flapping of the petals echoed in her chest. Now that Axel was as safe as possible, she was aware of feeling frightened for herself, and her greatest fear was not of death but of rape.

Naming the danger only made her feel worse, but the task now was to live, and survival might mean facing even the vilest possibilities. She cried a little, then got up and surveyed the space that for over a year had passed as her home. It was almost dear to her now. She locked up and descended the stairs.

Outside the cellar she knocked and announced herself. Schiefer opened the door, peered over her shoulder and asked after Axel. He was safe, she replied. Frau Ritter gazed at her over a stockade of playing cards.

Hammering on the blast-door stopped and in German a man demanded entry. Before Vera could stop her, Frau Ritter had darted to the door and pulled it open, revealing several soldiers in grey uniforms, though the perspective of the scene seemed weirdly awry, as if the troops were standing further away than the size of the corridor allowed. The nearest of them stepped into the light of the lamp.

He was perhaps fourteen years old, square-jawed but downy-cheeked. Lips so thin they were barely visible. The brim of a forage cap shadowed his eyes, and on his throat the lamplight showed his adam's apple. He carried a light machine gun with a bipod, and across his chest a belt of ammunition. By his thigh he held a *Luger*. A stick-grenade on each hip, and on his uniform the insignia of a Hitler Youth *Leutnant*. As he peered around the cellar, his armoury clanked.

Three of the youth's comrades followed him into the cellar, while a fourth, whose face was pitted with acne, stood in the doorway nursing a submachine gun. One of the other boys was taller, gawky and stooped. He was older than the others by at least two years but watched the *Leutnant* with an expression between fear and devotion. He was clasping a rifle.

The last two boys were barely pubescent. The first had a head of tousled hair that spilt over a bandage stiff with gore. Granules of blood smeared his face and neck and uniform, which was rucked like the costume of a clown. He had the muzzle of a rocket launcher balanced on one boot, while the other end reached as high as his neck.

His companion was also toting a *Panzerfaust*. He had bright-blue eyes, ruddy cheeks and delicately flared pink lips. An oversized helmet framed his face. A greatcoat draped his body to the ankles.

Frau Ritter took a step towards the *Leutnant*. 'I wish to inform you there's a deserter in this building.'

'You bitch,' said Flavia. Vera said nothing, coolly aware that if anything happened to Axel she would kill Frau Ritter.

The *Leutnant* asked for details in a wayward, imperfectly broken voice. The accent was cultured, Prussian and privileged.

'Axel Frey,' said Frau Ritter, 'a deserter from the *Volkssturm*. Fifty years old, or thereabouts, hiding somewhere in this building.'

A knife would be simplest. She would go to the baggage and take out Erna's carving knife, catch Frau Ritter unawares and sink the blade into her chest.

The *Leutnant* looked scornful. 'Fifty? We're not here to play hide-and-seek with oldies.'

Vera gripped Flavia by the arm, as if by clutching her she could also hold the boy to his decision. Frau Ritter looked incredulous.

'My platoon needs rations,' said the boy. His tone brooked no refusal. A platoon should have been more numerous than this.

'We don't have much,' said Schiefer.

'I'm not asking how much you have.'

There was the briefest pause while Schiefer took this in. The youth's eyes were still in shadow. Schiefer looked at the rest of the *Stamm* and nodded at their belongings. Erna opened a hessian sack and took out two loaves of bread, while Flavia fetched potatoes and a cabbage, which she loaded into a bag. Vera gave apples, spilling several on the floor, anxious for the boys to leave as fast as possible. Frau Ritter sat rigid and alone at the table.

The *Leutnant* asked for water, and Vera saw that the group meant to stay, at least for as long as it took to eat a meal. The *Leutnant* and the guard in the doorway ate upright, while the others squatted on the cobbles, savaging apples and cabbage and chunks of bread. Their gazes were glassy. The *Leutnant* chewed steadily, his eyes raking the room. Vera had never seen a group so heavily armed. Armed — as if weapons were limbs.

The lanky youth held out a crust to Frau Eckhardt then snatched it away when she reached for it. Frau Eckhardt stared the youth in the eyes. 'Growing bones,' she said. The lanky youth sniggered.

One by one the boys finished eating and the *Leutnant* nodded and they rose to leave. They were already moving when Flavia stopped them. 'Where are you going? It's crazy!' She appealed to the *Stamm*. 'We can't let them leave. They're children.'

'They can decide for themselves,' said Schiefer.

'Can they?' She pointed at the bandaged boy. 'You! Do you want to go?'

The boy glanced at the others. 'It's my duty,' he piped. His accent was middle-class, and Vera wondered for the first time where the children were from. They'd materialised so suddenly. With an effort, she could imagine parents crouched somewhere in a hole like this one.

Flavia turned to the helmeted child. 'What do you want to do?'

'The same as the others.' Like the other boy, his voice was unbroken, and as if resting her case Flavia turned to the *Stamm*.

The *Leutnant* waved his *Luger* like a wand. 'That's enough. We're going.'

'Isn't it time to call off the war?' said Flavia. 'Why not get older? Visit some day and we'll drink *Weissbier* at a *Kneipe.*'

Vera saw the youth hesitate, and the acne-faced henchman looked at him in amazement. The other boys were also watching. The *Leutnant* appraised Flavia. Light fell on his eyes. One iris was green, the other brown.

'You're forgetting we have no clothes for them,' said Schiefer. 'They can't stay here in uniform.'

'Then lend them your clothes,' said Flavia.

Schiefer was dubious. 'For the taller lad, perhaps. The others, no.'

Everyone peered at the lanky youth, who looked about in alarm, but the *Leutnant* had lost interest and stepped into the corridor. Flavia swore, but Vera felt relieved. The youth with acne waved his gun and the other boys filed into the corridor. They seemed resigned rather than disappointed, and their fatalism revived Vera's pity. Surely there was an instinct against risking the lives of boys too young to father children of their own. Even now she could argue, beg them not to leave.

But time was too pressing. There'd been no chance to prepare, to clear the clutter of fear. Flavia had at least tried to act.

For a moment, all five boys were visible through the doorway. They were a rabble, disjointed. Elongating bones and burgeoning flesh. The patches of hair on the older boys' napes were like the tufts of a lion-cub's mane. Their weaponry gleamed in the lamplight and rattled as they moved. Seconds later they were gone.

The sound of gunfire and explosions intensified. Vera visualised the Soviet advance as a wave, like one of the breakers at Manly beach after cyclones to the north. On days like those, in rapier sunshine, with the water glassy between each swell, she had loved as a child to defy the ocean, at first with her father and later on her own. She would swim alone beyond the broken water and skim down the face of an accumulating wave, riding out the collapse and surfing to the shore, though always there were bigger waves that broke further out, or the kind that trapped you on a sand bar, devouring all the water between your shoulders and your thighs until the mottled mouth gulped and rolled you under. The secret was not to resist. Struggling only emptied your lungs. Easier to swirl in the belly of the water until the churning slowed and you could swim upwards, plunging into air.

The *Stamm* was tense, even skat suspended. Erna was washing clothes in the tub, while Vera waited nearby for her turn to use the water. Abruptly Frau Ritter left her place at the table, crossed the cellar and sat down beside them. Vera was amazed. Erna continued to pummel her laundry, while from her stretcher bed Flavia cast a cold eye on Frau Ritter, who beamed as if surrounded by friends.

'Time to be frank,' murmured Frau Ritter. 'There's no use pretending. None of us is a virgin, *nicht*? No innocent maidens here.'

Vera shivered. Frau Ritter's face reminded her of the fear grimace of a chimpanzee.

'Better a Ruski on the belly than a shell on the head, that's what I say!' She threw back her head and shrieked with laughter, blinking like a doll with swivel eyes. At the table, Schiefer was pretending not to notice a conversation from which he was excluded.

'The way I see it,' said Frau Ritter, 'there's no use worrying. If it happens, it happens.'

No one else spoke.

ELEVEN

Vera's eyes jerked open to the glare of the lamp and she sat up in bed. Schiefer yelled. Bricks clattered onto the cobbles, a hand thrust out of the escape tunnel and the wall disgorged a Red Army soldier.

The Russian, an officer, scrambled to his feet and shone a torch across the *Stamm*, exposing the shadows behind the columns. The light blinked in Vera's eyes, leaving a swooping after-image. The Russian lowered the torch and bid them good evening in accented German. Fair-skinned, lean, neither tall nor short, and perhaps thirty years of age. He wore a peaked cap the width of a dinner plate, and his uniform was mustard-brown. As well as the torch, he held a submachine gun with a circular magazine like a gangster's.

The *Stamm* gaped at the conqueror, who spoke back into the tunnel. The stream of Russian hit Vera like water. Other than snatches of Russian on the radio, she had heard little of the language since the years before the war, when it had been common in the streets and cafés.

Another man emerged, followed rapidly by others, all of them armed with the same archaic-looking Tommy guns. Wanting to meet them standing, Vera edged out of bed, intensely thankful to be wearing street clothes. The soldiers squirmed out of the wall and fanned across the cellar until the *Stamm* was heavily outnumbered.

A young, freckled man pushed Schiefer in the chest, forcing him back between the stretcher beds, then the soldiers started rifling through the *Stamm*'s possessions, chatting and laughing as they went. They wore baggy breeches and mustard-brown tunics that tapered at the waist and flared about the hips, and except for the officer they all wore forage caps. Thickset, scrawny, youthful or weather-beaten, dark, Asiatic or blond. If the unit once came from a single district, it had long since recruited from elsewhere.

Flavia was motionless as a lizard. Erna's eyes were shut, while her mother was still asleep and snoring, her mouth a ridge of gums. Frau Ritter was saucer-eyed. Her sting was drawn, and it occurred to Vera that their differences were now less than what they had in common.

In front of her, a soldier stripped back the blankets and tossed them aside. From the rucksacks he took most of their remaining food, then in mangled German he demanded Vera's watch. She handed it over and he buckled it below a dozen or so others strapped to his forearm. He was young, not much older than the boys of the Hitler Youth. A cowlick of hair escaped his cap, which he wore at a tilt, and though he was trying to look fierce, a smile kept tugging his lips.

The officer ordered his men to search the wall behind Schiefer, who cleared his throat and in a respectful tone explained that there was no second tunnel. He pointed at the wall and shook his head. He said no in German and repeated the word in Russian. The officer thanked him but the soldiers inspected each wall in turn, stepping over the sleeping old woman.

The officer pointed at the ceiling and raised his eyebrows. '*Wehrmacht*?'

Schiefer explained that no German troops had taken up positions in the building, but then fluttered one hand to show he couldn't be sure. Vera had never seen him more obliging. The officer thanked him and went to the blast-door, where a soldier had readied himself by the handle. He opened it and the officer peered around the doorjamb, probed the darkness with his torch then slipped into the corridor. A second man left, followed one at a time by the others.

The soldier who had stolen her watch was among the last to leave. He flicked open a satchel and took out a hammer with the same oblong head as the one on the Soviet flag, so that for a moment Vera expected him to produce a sickle and perform some kind of ideological pantomime. Instead he struck the door-lock a single blow that sent the cylinder clattering into the corridor. He turned to the *Stamm*, doffed his forage cap and bowed, eddying the cap through the air until it paused by his toes. His comrades laughed and bundled him through the door.

For a time the *Stamm* was motionless, then Schiefer shut the door. This was no more than a gesture. The air seemed warmer and Vera's heart raced. Frau Eckhardt was still snoring, and from the tunnel to the next cellar came urgent talk. The liberation had come and seemingly gone, leaving the *Stamm* like fish dumped onto a deck.

After a fitful sleep through what was left of the night, Vera rose early with the others. She yearned for tea but there was only water. The Hitler Youth boys had taken much of their food.

Schiefer picked up his cards from the table and tapped them into their box, crossed to his bed and started packing his suitcase. 'That's it, then,' he said when he was done.

'You're *going*?' said Frau Ritter.

'If it's safe,' he said. 'I don't hear any shooting.'

'But so soon?'

For once, Vera felt that Frau Ritter was speaking on her behalf, and she felt ashamed of her cowardice. As Flavia had long ago predicted, living like worms had come to feel normal, and the idea of a sky free of steel seemed far-fetched.

Schiefer gestured at the mutilated lock. 'There's no point staying.'

'What about the rest of us?' asked Frau Ritter. Her voice was quavering. 'What'll we do?'

Vera pictured Schiefer's reinforced door. It was natural that a man with a key to such a door should be the first to abandon the *Stamm*.

Frau Ritter started whimpering, then cried aloud when Schiefer made a move to the door. He stopped and scrutinised the weeping woman, narrowed his eyes and suggested she could join him. Frau Ritter clapped her hands together, then collected herself and smoothed her skirt and thanked him for his hospitality. The rest of the *Stamm* was silent. Frau Ritter packed up her belongings, Schiefer opened the door, and with a show of nonchalance Frau Ritter followed him into the corridor.

Vera turned to Flavia. 'It's time I got Axel.'

'I'd better go with you.'

'Will you stay in your flat?' asked Erna. She looked forlorn.

'I don't know,' admitted Vera. 'I'll see what Axel thinks. Would you and your mother like to come upstairs for a few days?'

Erna considered this offer then shook her head. 'Better off in our own place, don't you think? And your flat is too small for five.'

Vera let her know she could change her mind, aware she had hurried to take no for an answer, though Erna was right about the size of the flat. Another thought nagged at her, more calculating and callous: she wanted to be as unobtrusive as possible.

Vera promised to send Axel to help Frau Eckhardt up the stairs, then with Flavia she left the cellar. The sound of battle was diffuse and distant, no longer the roar of the day before. They peered into the courtyard and saw no sign of movement. The sky was clogged with cloud. Though she tried to tread softly, her shoes clopped like hoofs.

On the second-floor landing, Schiefer appeared with a bundle of sheets in his arms.

'Dirty already?' asked Flavia.

'To hang from windows,' said Schiefer, pretending not to hear. He handed some of the sheets to Vera. 'We don't want anyone shooting at us.'

Vera agreed to drape the sheets from the upper-level windows, then she and Flavia climbed the stairs to the bus-driver's flat. Axel had escaped the loft and was sitting at the demolished brink of the living room.

'Our lot has gone?' he asked.

'Yes. And the others have arrived.'

'You're both ... safe?'

'We're all right, yes.'

She explained that the *Stamm* was abandoning the cellar, and Axel agreed that Flavia should join them in the flat.

He pointed at the sheets and asked what they were for.

'To remind the Soviets we've surrendered. Schiefer's idea.'

With Flavia's help she unfurled a sheet above the courtyard and secured it with broken masonry. The fabric barely rippled on the bricks. From this high up it was possible to trace the noise of the fighting in the north and west — the Mitte, the zoo.

'I feel like a medieval bride after my wedding night,' said Flavia.

'Let's hope the Soviets see it,' said Axel.

Vera turned and saw his face colouring. He opened his mouth as if to explain, seemed to think better of it and said nothing.

The sheet hung limply in the stagnant air.

When the water ran out, Vera announced she'd get more.

'I'll go,' said Axel.

She was ready for this. 'You should stay till we know what's going on. You might be rounded up.'

'That's just speculation,' said Axel.

'Maybe. But I haven't fended off the *Wehrmacht* to see you taken for forced labour in the Soviet Union.'

'I can't allow it.'

'Axel, please.'

He looked at Flavia. 'Do you want to go?'

Flavia shrugged. 'I'm game for anything.'

Axel kept arguing. Vera sympathised. One way or another he'd been powerless from the time he'd learned of her affair, yet having held on to him then she was determined not to lose him through an act of carelessness now. At last he relented, though vowing to ignore her the next time. Schiefer and Frau Ritter refused to venture out, but Erna agreed, and fetched two pails.

In the courtyard, sunshine crowned the top half of the northern wall, though in the shadows the cobbles remained slippery and cold. Sheets were hanging from several windows, and overhead the sky was a pale-blue square.

Apart from their own footfalls, she realised, there were few sounds of any kind — the noise of gunfire had ceased, and when a moment later the meaning of this silence became clear, she could barely stop herself crying out in jubilation and waltzing Flavia across the cobbles. The high band of sunlight on the northern wall made do as a symbol of radiant peace.

In the next courtyard she saw that Reichenbergerstrasse was alive with troops and horses, and her stomach rolled. Erna trod on her heel, blurted an apology then stepped on the other, so that Vera reached the street still stomping back into her shoes. She felt unshucked, exposed. Two soldiers looked up from a team of horses hitched to an artillery piece, stared for several seconds then returned to their work. The tableau of horse and cannon was Napoleonic, yet this was the army that had crushed the panzers.

The conquerors had turned the street into a bivouac. Scores of soldiers lay asleep on the cobbles or lolled in their singlets in the sunshine, and several eyed the women with open curiosity. Brown overcoats and tunics hung from timber in the wreckage. After days of gunfire, the noiseless sky seemed unreal.

Near the pump, about twenty troops were sitting on ammunition boxes around a bonfire. Bottles of schnapps bobbed from hand to hand, and there was shouting and laughter. A giant ox of a man in a padded jacket bellowed to a friend as the two of them launched furniture onto the flames, adding scorched varnish to odours of horse dung and petrol. Behind the veil of fire, the giant's flesh seemed to ripple.

Locals huddled in a queue at the pump. The body of the hanged man was gone from the oak tree, though the electric cord, now severed, still dangled from its branch. The queue was shorter than usual and included men of Axel's age whose presence, Vera noted, seemed of no interest to the Soviets. Some of the locals wore white ragged armbands of surrender.

Vera stole glances at the Soviet soldiers and saw that two of them were women. Both wore thick brown skirts and stockings, as well as tunics and caps the same as those of their comrades. Hair tied in buns. Plump cheeks flushed red. They swigged the schnapps as often as the men and their shouts were equally loud, and Vera envied these joking, laughing women. In their mustard-brown uniforms they should have seemed anonymous, but instead it was she who felt bland, just one more head in the civilian herd. Her cotton dress felt flimsy compared to the women's tunics. Their shoes were battered but polished. Vera was filled with admiration for their travel-worn shoes.

The pump was damaged and would have fallen apart already if someone hadn't bound it up with wire. Half of the water spilled onto the pavement. A *Hausfrau* at the head of the queue asked an old man behind her to steady the pump while she worked the handle. He bent down, clutched the column of the pump and sank to his knees. Water soused the man's hands and sleeves. His knees ground the pavement, wetting the fabric of his trousers.

The revelry around the bonfire grew louder. A soldier backed away from the fire, paused and then sprinted towards the flames, leaping at the last moment between the two women then skimming the fire and slapping feet-first onto the cobbles. He pulled up at a jog, his comrades cheering. Immediately several others backed away at different angles, waving their arms to clear an approach, only to howl in protest when the giant soldier lumbered forward and hurled a bookcase on the fire, spilling books and spraying cinders on the superheated air.

To Vera the leap looked impossible now, but one by one the soldiers ran at the flames, until men were hurtling, moments apart, over the apex of the fire. Several capered as far as the pump and, to the cheers of their comrades, raised their arms above their heads before turning and scraping the cobbles with their toes.

At the fire, a soldier with a cavalryman's moustache challenged the giant to jump, and though clearly drunk he thumped his chest and drew backwards to charge. His comrades doubled over with laughter, and the other leapers paused. Some way up the street he stopped and rocked on one heel, brayed and then set off across the cobbles, gaining pace only to tire and mince through the last few steps. He took to the air with his legs askew, demolished the bonfire then crashed belly-down and skidded to a halt. Friends rushed over and brushed embers off his breeches before hoisting him upright. He looked stunned but unhurt and ventured a smile.

The moustached soldier slapped the giant on the back, gripped him by the wrist and raised his arm. The pair swivelled towards the pump and beamed at the locals, then with exaggerated thoroughness Moustache dusted off the giant's uniform, tidied his fringe and started spruiking him in Russian to the women in the queue, pointing out the girth of his biceps and thighs. The giant looked sheepish and ludicrously flattered.

The *Hausfrau* at the pump snatched her pails and hurried away, bringing up the turn of the elderly man. Vera steadied the pump, but when the old man failed to raise more than a dribble Flavia elbowed him aside and filled his pail. The pump handle whimpered.

Flavia handed the man his pail and set to work on the first of the *Stamm*'s. Leaking cold water numbed Vera's fingers. From the corner of one eye she saw the moustached soldier draw nearer, then he jabbered in Flavia's face and started mimicking her movements, raising howls of laughter from around the bonfire. Moustache levered his arm in front of the giant's groin, causing further guffaws.

Two or three *Hausfrauen* dropped off the back of the queue. Vera searched Flavia's face for a sign that she wanted to leave, but though scowling she continued to pump.

A hand touched Vera's arm and she jolted. She turned and looked up. Their tormentor was older than she'd thought — about the age of the century — though the moustache harked back to an earlier era. His eyes were bloodshot. He was swaying heavily, then he snatched the giant's hand and lunged it at her face. She smelt soot and sweat and drinker's reek, reared away then realised that her throat was bared and forced herself to look back. Moustache turned the great paw upwards, a courtly burlesque, then thrust it onto her breasts. She locked her arms together. Immediately Moustache started scooping at her ribcage, then he saw that the hand had fallen limp and let it go. The giant rubbed his wrist, looking uneasy. His comrades laughed.

Vera scoured all emotion from her face. She picked up a pail and passed it to Erna, who looked terrified. Vera nodded to reassure her, then took a turn at the handle, though what she wanted most of all was to leave.

When the pails were filled the women moved off in tight formation. Wolf whistles split the air. Vera looked around as Moustache made a show of pursuit, egged on by his comrades. The loudest of them were the two soldier women, and Vera felt strangely betrayed. If not for Flavia and Erna, she would have started to run — as a group they were clumsy and unkiltered. The handles of the pails crushed her finger pads.

Moustache and the giant were following at a walk, then a third soldier caught up and handed over two Tommy guns before returning to the bonfire.

Vera wheeled beneath the tenement archway and hurried with the others through the outermost courtyard. 'What'll we do?' said Erna in a high breathy voice, 'What'll we do?'

'Walk fast,' said Flavia, 'keep together.'

'Leave the water?' suggested Vera. 'Come back for it later?'

Flavia scoffed. 'And lose the pails?'

Vera looked backwards as the two soldiers jogged into the courtyard. Erna started sobbing and Flavia told her to shut up. The water smacked in Vera's pails and splashed her skirt, gluing the fabric to her calves.

At the front of the block she looked behind her and saw the Soviets a dozen paces away. The giant was scanning the tenements and clearly wanted to be elsewhere, while Moustache looked ungainly, his joints unyoked.

She crossed the threshold, stumbling under the dead weight of water, then while the others rushed inside she lowered both pails and stopped. Flavia beckoned her furiously, but Vera shook her head. 'I'm going that way,' she said, pointing outside, then with less conviction, 'I'll be all right.'

The soldiers arrived and Vera smiled, then Flavia was at her side. 'What the hell happens now?'

Vera wasn't sure but knew she couldn't bear to be degraded in front of Axel.

'Simper,' she said, hoping the soldiers spoke no German. 'Follow me and get ready to run.'

Taking Flavia by the hand, she brushed past the two men and re-entered the courtyard, sauntering between the craters. The soldiers followed. From the vestibule of the opposite block she led them into another courtyard, a place she had never visited but that in desolation looked much like the rest. Moustache protested. He wanted to know where they were going. She smiled at him, pointed at the nearest block, and then hand-in-hand with Flavia she entered the gloom. The building's layout was the same as their own, and the wrecked rooftops were a maze.

'What do you say?' she asked Flavia, still smiling at the men. 'On the stairs we go?'

'Suits me,' said Flavia. 'Lead the way.'

There was no time to argue with this act of courage, and with a sultry gaze towards the men she led Flavia onto the stairs. Moustache leered and nudged the giant, who shook his head. His comrade chuckled and said something sharp, and looking stung the giant followed him up the stairs, scanning about with his Tommy gun raised.

Vera's breaths were wing beats. She reached the second flight, tapped Flavia's arm and started running, bounding two steps at a time and hauling on the balustrade, with Flavia close behind her. Moustache yelled and came after them, hollering abuse. Vera kept her head low, terrified of bullets, then saw that the giant was unsighted and that Moustache's gun was still slung on his back. She lunged onto the next flight and heard clattering metal, looked past Flavia and saw Moustache sprawled on the steps. The giant was a flight further back. On the fifth-floor landing, Flavia skittered past, and between the banisters Vera glimpsed Moustache waving goodbye, his parting smile a dart of admiration.

Down corridors and stairs they made for the block, pausing often to survey the way ahead, and giving a wide berth to some soldiers they glimpsed in a courtyard. All the doors of the flats they passed were shut.

They reached the block, entered the vestibule and saw Axel standing at Erna's door. His face was grim. The jamb was splintered, the door ajar. He thrust a finger to his lips and motioned to the stairs, shaking his head fiercely when

Flavia tried to get the pails. Beyond Erna's door, Vera heard the laughing of men.

Obeying Axel's urgent gestures, she crossed the vestibule and let herself be herded with Flavia up the stairs. On the third floor they paused, but Axel urged them higher and led them into the bus-driver's flat. 'There are two of them,' he whispered. 'I did what I could.'

'You're saying what?' asked Vera.

'I asked them to stop.'

'Asked them?' she whispered, appalled he'd run such a risk.

'They had guns,' he said, misunderstanding her. 'There wasn't anything else I could do.'

'And Erna?'

'She told me to leave.'

Vera tried to imagine this and failed.

'Was she hurt?'

'I don't think so. I'll go back when they're gone.'

'Frau Eckhardt?'

'... Was there too.'

Axel looked pained and Vera guessed how excruciating he would have found it to stand by and do nothing.

'What did they look like?' she asked.

He was puzzled by this but went on to describe two soldiers who were clearly not the same men she and Flavia had escaped.

'We have to hide both of you,' said Axel.

Flavia held up her palms. 'Not me.'

'What are you talking about?' asked Vera.

'I'll be off home.'

Vera seized her by the arm. 'It's not safe.'

'I'll take my chances. Vera, please — don't look so wretched. I'll be back soon enough. One of us has to get food, you know.'

Vera turned to Axel. 'Tell her she can't go.'

'You can't go,' he said. 'And Vera's right — why risk it?'

'You know how I fidget — hiding would be torture.'

Her flippancy was ominous. 'Look, you can't mean this,' said Vera. She pointed to the stairs. 'You've seen what's happening.'

Flavia embraced her. 'Vera, darling, there's more than one way to get by. This is Berlin — you'll find we're the world's best accommodators. I'll be back in a few days, I promise.'

'You'll go in daylight?'

'There's bound to be a curfew after dark.'

Flavia turned and hugged Axel. 'You'll look after Vera?'

'She'll be as safe as possible.'

The loft was coffin-sized and dusty, and despite the cushioning of a blanket, her body ached within hours of Axel closing the hatch.

Light by day frilled the edge of the hatch but at night the blackness was absolute, taunting the eye to detect more

319

than its own projections, the floating amoebae of lesser darknesses. Into the pitch-black capsule came noises from outside: creaking beams, the scurrying of rats, breeze in the rooftops, an occasional gunshot, breakneck tunes from a far-away harmonica.

Axel brought water and morsels of food: boiled barley, potato broth, an onion garnished with dandelion leaves. He emptied the pail she relieved herself in, the only function he would let her perform outside the loft. So far the Soviets had shown no sign of distributing rations to the populace, and she fretted that the city would be left to starve, though Axel professed an inexplicable faith that rations would arrive. He couldn't explain why the conquerors should be generous after the *Wehrmacht*'s devastation of the Soviet Union. More talkative than in the cellar, he was at times even cheerful, though frustrated that checkpoints had blocked his attempts to reach the zoo.

She asked after Erna and he said she was coping. Two days later he mentioned in passing that the Soviets were everywhere, then seeing her alarm he hurriedly explained that their own flat lay outside, or above, the soldiers' range. 'Not so at ease above ground level, is my guess.'

'So it's safe for me to come down.'

He looked alarmed. 'No, no. Not yet.'

Soon she began to feel seriously hungry, her stomach astew with expectant acids. Her navel was a notch in a shallow dip. Asleep or awake, her legs were restless, and headaches sloshed in treacle-slow waves from her eyes to the stern of her skull. She daydreamed of dying here, four storeys high, her skin left to cure into leather.

On the third evening, Axel appeared with a wad of meat on a plate he held balanced on his fingertips. 'Roof rabbit,' he said, and raised the plate to the open hatch. She wrested her gaze from the meat. '*Berlinisch* for cat,' he explained.

'My God, you're not serious?'

'Eat up. The others have. This is all that's left.'

She inhaled the fragrance and her stomach dilated. Saliva drenched her tongue.

'Go ahead. Use fingers.'

She nibbled at first and then chewed. The flesh was tough and stringy and did taste a little like rabbit, though its sharpness was more suggestive of carnivore's flesh. As she ate, she devoured the image of the meat, as though taste and touch and smell weren't means enough to experience it — until she forgot to blink and her eyes blurred with tears.

Axel grinned, delighted by her savagery. She asked if he'd eaten enough himself, and was glad when he said yes. She chewed a while longer then stopped again.

'Where did it come from? The cat.'

'The rubble. Alive, that is. Alive. Sunbathing on rubble in the middle courtyard.'

She wished he hadn't told her this, or that she hadn't asked. An image entered her mind of him befriending the cat, of his hand stroking from the small of its back to its neck. It was too late not to know — she asked how he'd killed it.

'Not me,' said Axel. 'I couldn't get close.'

'Then how?'

'I asked a Russian to shoot it for me.'

She paused to take this in. 'A pal of yours?'

She hadn't meant to sound so accusatory.

'Not a pal, but with some of them it's possible to talk.'

'This is safe?'

'I think so. They don't give me any trouble.'

She went back to gnawing what was left of the meat — as Erna had once said, too little to live on, too much to die.

What shocked her was how easily Axel was able to fraternise with men she was doing her utmost to avoid. Not that she blamed him — no, she admired his boldness — but keenly she felt her difference, the tyranny of physique.

'One of the Russians told me that Hitler's dead,' said Axel. 'Suicided, if I understood the sign language.'

She blinked, preparing space in her mind for the immensity of this death, only to be left feeling empty. Just one more among multitudes. The news seemed familiar, historical — thanks maybe to months of jokes and speculation about how the dictator would meet his end. No, she was more surprised that Axel had convinced a Russian to kill a cat.

TWELVE

When news came that Germany had surrendered, Axel agreed she could leave the loft. There was less risk of rape, he said — releasing the word that till now they'd contained — as the timing of the soldiers' visits had become more predictable: midday and early evening — the feeding hours. Locks were useless, so at mealtimes she would have to return to the loft.

Though her encloisterment had lasted less than a week, she felt as if she'd been gone for years. Axel had said little about the *Stamm*.

Vera stopped outside Erna's flat. She knocked, called hello, and the door drifted inwards.

Erna stood in the middle of the room. She was a terrible sight. Her left eye was bruised and her face drawn. Her hair was lank. With a weary smile she invited Vera in and announced to her mother that a guest had arrived. The old woman looked up from a crocheted rug that was draped across her legs. 'Lost again?'

'It seems so,' said Vera, unsure if Frau Eckhardt was talking about her or the war. The old woman smiled.

Erna invited Vera to sit and poured three glasses of water, splashing her dress.

'Well?' she asked.

'Well what?'

'Did you take it?'

At first the question made no sense, and then Vera was speechless. To play for time, she pretended not to understand.

'From the Ivans,' explained Erna. 'Did you take it from the Ivans?'

Vera glanced sideways — Frau Eckhardt was staring at the ceiling.

'I hid in a loft,' said Vera, 'in the flat above ours. Axel looked after me. I'm well.'

Erna seemed almost to grimace. 'Like Frau Ritter, then, behind her steel door. I suppose your husband told you that I wasn't so lucky.' She sounded defiant, in arms against sympathy. 'And it wasn't only the once.' Vera felt a pang of shame.

'It's been worse for others,' said Erna. 'They're no joke, the Ivans, the nastiest ones. No joke at all.'

Vera nodded helplessly. It was as if her friend were on first-name terms with her attackers.

'When they want you, do you know what they say?'

Vera could only shake her head.

'*Kommen.* They tell you to come. *Frau, kommen.*'

'It must have been awful.'

In a falling tone, Erna said, 'I'm lucky — it could have been worse. The good Lord is merciful.'

Vera preferred not to imagine a worse. She said, 'I know that words aren't much help, but Erna — I'm sorry.'

Erna turned away. 'Don't be. It's just what happens. You think it's the worst, the end of everything, then you realise that it isn't.'

'All the same …' said Vera.

But Erna wasn't listening. 'Why they have to do it is a mystery to me, but do you want to know something? I doubt our men behaved much better over there.'

An engine in the courtyard broke the late-morning calm. Vera hurried to the window, looked below, and saw a rangy motorcyclist in goggles and a brown leather helmet circling the craters. As the motorbike cornered, it sputtered like gunfire, then accelerated to a roar made thunderous between the walls.

Axel joined her at the sill, and in the windows around the courtyard other people appeared. It was hard to believe there were so many survivors.

The motorcycle skidded to a halt at the *Blockleiter*'s grave. The rider dismounted, removed the goggles and gloves, and liberated a head of neck-length hair from the helmet.

'My God,' said Axel. 'It's Flavia.'

Vera couldn't speak. Flavia tossed her head, resharpening the blades of hair beside her cheeks. She looked up and Vera waved.

'Come down!' cried Flavia, ignoring the spectators.

Vera signalled her to wait and left the window. 'What gear!' said Axel, clearly impressed. 'And where did she come by a motorbike?'

They rushed downstairs and into the courtyard, where Flavia was waiting by the bike, dressed in what looked like a pair of Red Army breeches.

'Can't stay long,' she said, jabbing a thumb at the bike. 'At present there are people who'll cut your throat for less. Your best defence is speed.'

Vera stepped forwards and embraced her, but Flavia wriggled free. 'No time for that!' She pointed at two bulky panniers on the back of the bike. 'Supplies. They're wrapped, but better get them inside.'

Beneath the jacket she wore a red satin blouse. The rest of the outfit was Soviet issue. She opened the panniers and handed over two brown hessian bags. 'Flour, apples, potatoes, bread, cured pork, cigarettes and vodka.'

Vera was overwhelmed. 'Can you afford this? Have you enough for yourself?'

'And more. Courtesy of a nice Russian major.'

'And the motorbike?' asked Axel.

'A liberated BMW, on loan from the major. He'd kill me if I lost it. Figuratively, that is — he's really rather sweet.'

Two adolescent boys emerged from the opposite block and crossed the courtyard to look at the motorcycle. Axel went and stood guard, feigning interest in the engine.

'This major ...' said Vera. 'How can I put this? Are you with him voluntarily? Are you all right?'

Flavia pursed her lips. 'Every girl needs a protector. And you? Has Axel guarded your honour?'

'Ceaselessly.'

'There! We each have our knight.'

'I'm married to mine.'

A hint of annoyance crossed her face. 'Vera, I'm fine. Really, you don't have to worry.'

'All right, but what about earlier? When they first arrived?'

'Was I raped? No. Though my neighbours were, even the young girls. Unspeakable — you were right about that after all. Me, I was lucky: I found the major first.'

'And these?' asked Vera, pointing at Flavia's clothes.

'The latest fashion.'

The boys near the motorbike were joined by two men — enthusiasts, probably, but Flavia was nervous. 'I have to go.' She kissed Vera's forehead and returned to the bike, and the boys and the men stepped aside. With the tips of her fingers she relayed a kiss to Axel's cheek, sat astride the bike, donned helmet and goggles, and pulled on the gloves, tugging each finger for a perfect fit. Not for the first time it occurred to Vera that Flavia was never meant for the stage — her over-acting was more in keeping with reality.

She kick-started the engine and tucked in the stand, and the motor roared off the tenement walls. She let go of the handlebars and cupped her mouth. 'See you soon!'

Vera waved and Flavia flexed the throttle, spraying loose gravel in a backwards arc until the tyre bit the cobbles and she leapt away in a cloud of exhaust. She headed for the archway, skirting the rubble, then swerved and doubled back for another lap, gunning the engine as she braked on the corners, then with a final wave she straightened up, opened the throttle and accelerated, hunched over the fuel tank like a Valkyrie in flight. The bike speared the archway and vanished from sight.

After lunch, as usual, Axel fetched her from the loft.

'There were Russians,' he said. 'Three of them on Schiefer's landing.'

'Is everyone safe?'

He helped her across the wreckage. 'Schiefer's door was open and the soldiers pushed inside.'

'My God.'

'They were armed.'

'How is Frau Ritter?'

They reached the third-floor landing and Vera heard voices, including Frau Ritter's, coming from the floor below. Axel beamed. 'Schiefer sent them packing.'

'The *soldiers*?'

'Ejected them.'

'Ejected? How?'

'Went berserk and sent them running.'

Axel beckoned her downstairs, where Erna, Schiefer and Frau Ritter were gathered on the second-floor landing. Frau Ritter was veering from talk to laughter. She stretched forward and stroked the dome of Schiefer's head, then glimpsed Vera and held him out at arm's length. 'You should have *seen* this man! Like a tiger, he was. Like a lion.'

'So I heard.'

'When the Ivans barged in I thought, this is it. They had guns. Then he exploded — my God — just like that. Spread both arms. Charged. Not a young man, either. Howling like a demon!' She looked at Erna. 'Did you hear the noise he made? Like nothing I've ever heard. Too much for the Ivans, at any rate. Vamoosed, the lot of 'em.'

Schiefer looked rattled. He was wet with sweat. Between nervous smiles he glanced over the banister.

'I wouldn't worry,' Vera told him. 'By the sound of it they'll keep running till they reach the Russian border.'

Frau Ritter glared at her. 'You can sneer all you like, but if we had more men like this, the Reich wouldn't be in such a state.' She turned to Schiefer. 'Ignore her, Reinhardt. If I had my way, you'd be given a medal.'

She stalked into the flat and waited by the door. Schiefer hesitated, as if about to speak, then turned and followed, trailing body odour. As soon as he was over the threshhold, Frau Ritter closed the door, jarring the steel-plated frame.

'She was wrapped around him like a scarf,' said Erna. 'And her husband barely two weeks in the ground!'

Vera took another mouthful of soup. Since yesterday, she had wondered more than once whether Axel would have defended her as ferociously as Schiefer had Frau Ritter.

For several minutes, Erna marvelled at the scandal of their neighbours, but when Vera refused to join in she changed the subject to Hitler. The poor man must have been desperate, she said, to have taken his own life.

Vera was astonished. 'You feel sorry for him?'

'Why not?' asked Erna.

'But *that* man? You feel pity for *him*?'

'Oh, I suppose he was bad. They all are, those politicians. Have to be. But does that mean he deserved it? The man never did anything to me.'

Vera considered pointing out to Erna that the dictator had caused the death of her son, but she had no wish to be brutal and instead returned to her soup, recalling again that it was made from horse. She asked Erna how she'd found the meat.

'Some men were butchering on the street. I hung about till one of them took pity and gave me the head. Almost died getting it home.' She chortled. 'Mutti, she's a funny one. Wouldn't let me take a knife to it till I'd brushed its teeth, God bless her. Dental paste and all. My own brush, mind. The pony on a platter, its mouth all foamy, and me brushing away for all I'm worth.'

She took several spoonfuls and her smile disappeared.

'Vera, the other day when I told you what had happened, you said, "It must have been awful."' She frowned. Her black eye had turned plum coloured. Frau Eckhardt's snoring rumbled from the bedroom.

'I remember,' prompted Vera.

'Do you know why I'm telling you this?'

Vera shook her head. Had Erna become a little crazed? She seemed suddenly determined.

'It wasn't only me the soldiers did it to. They did it to my mother too. Did your husband say?'

Vera shook her head, fighting to control her face. Erna would need calmness now, a show of normality. Why else would she choose to confide this thing? Vera clasped her friend's hands. Though outwardly calm, her own steadiness was the poise of a spinning top.

'How did she take it?' Too late she heard herself, but Erna seemed not to notice.

'As far as I could tell, she didn't realise, but was — what's the word? — oblivious. She hasn't spoken of it once.'

'She may not have known what was happening to her,' said Vera. 'Can't remember it, maybe.' She paused to let the idea grow. If Erna's mother had been spared the memory, her suffering perhaps had been only fleeting.

Erna was nodding furiously. 'That's what I thought. I knew you'd see it that way. She mightn't have known.'

Vera relaxed in her chair. 'Yes, very likely.'

'Was oblivious, *nicht*?'

'Oblivious.'

'It's the mercy of the Lord.'

Vera merely nodded.

'His loving kindness.'

'A good thing, too, that you've told me this, I think. For your own peace of mind.'

A gust of irritation crossed Erna's face.

'When the soldiers — there were four of them — when the soldiers were here the first time, I looked sideways across the room. Like so.' Here she twisted her neck to one side. 'The one on my mother, this soldier, he smiled at me. He smiled, then he spat, but slowly. Not at me. A dribble, *nicht*?' She leaned forward, bunched her lips, though withholding her saliva. 'Not at me but down, into my mother's mouth. He lowered it down. Into her mouth he hung it like rope.'

★　★　★

Flavia's major was square-built, about thirty years old, with dark hair, a broad face and blue-shaven cheeks. His eyebrows turned down on either side, giving him an anxious but open expression. It was a likeable face, which along with his good manners and generosity had caught Vera off-guard: it would have been easier to dislike a man who belonged to the army that now occupied Berlin.

A peaked cap hung on the back of the door, where the comrade-major had left it soon after he'd arrived. He hadn't likewise offered to part with his pistol, but neither Axel nor Flavia had seemed to mind, and the major had not only brought food and the candles that burned on the table but spent much of the time asking questions about animals. He spoke impressive German, having studied it as a boy and later trained in the language, he admitted, to monitor enemy radio traffic. His tone was sincere, almost gauche at times, and he showed far more interest in zookeeping than politics, dispelling her suspicion that he might be an intelligence officer on the lookout for recruits.

When she wasn't observing the major, Vera watched Flavia for signs of distress about an arrangement that rescued her from rape but which resembled prostitution, with one man supplying both protection and pay. Yet apart from some tiredness around the eyes, Flavia seemed cheerful. The unending war was over, and while the Red Army's conduct had been disillusioning, she would no doubt be poised to seize the slightest freedom — already she'd sent the major's eyebrows rearing by asking for his help to stage Brecht at the Rose. Like much of the Mitte, the theatre had been destroyed, but Flavia argued that ruins were eloquent.

After dinner, the major conjured coffee from his bag, reminding Vera of a similar meal a year ago when Friedrich Motz-Wilden had played providore. The comrade-major, as an enemy of Friedrich's enemy, was by definition a friend. He had clearly charmed Axel, and while Vera brewed coffee and Flavia smoked, the two men rehearsed basic Russian phrases, Axel a model of concentration. His brown hair was longer than usual, endearingly scruffy. Though trimmer than before, his sturdy core seemed untouched.

How he might be in spirit was another matter. Vera supposed a time might come when they would talk again about Martin Krypic, but not now. Silence had worked like a tourniquet, and she was worried what might happen if they spoke again — however exasperating Martin had been by the end, she couldn't say that she wholly regretted the affair, and weirdly she had an impulse to explain this to Axel, not from cruelty but a yearning to share everything.

The men embarked on the verb *to be*, their recitations sounding like Gregorian chant, and again Vera was struck by the strangeness of having a Soviet officer seated at her table.

When the pot boiled, the conjugating stopped, and Vera served the coffee. She swapped thanks with the major, sat

down and drank. The taste was raw and bitter —
unpleasant for Axel, who would be longing for sugar. For
herself, she could do without. With each sip she listened to
the rippling of her throat.

Axel asked the major about his life before the war, and
he told them he was from Leningrad, the old St Petersburg,
where he had taught mathematics to schoolchildren. He
had two older sisters, he said, both widowed by the war, as
well as several nieces and nephews, all of whom had
survived. At the age of five he had lost his own father in the
civil war that had followed the Revolution — fighting for
which side, he didn't say — forcing his mother to earn a
living washing bottles in a factory. He paused and smiled at
his own solemnity. There had also been good times, he said.

He leaned back and roamed a hand on Flavia's thigh,
and all at once Vera's heart began to thud — in the ease of
the gesture she was sure she had glimpsed the arrogance of
a conqueror. Flavia's face was unchanged, but this was small
reassurance. The man across the table might be innocent of
the worst abuses taking place in Berlin, but as an officer he
was adding to a mood of impunity, and who else might be
made to answer for crimes which, for all Vera knew, were
being carried out by men under his direct command?

The veins in her temples palpitated. The major began to
describe how he had spent the summers of his childhood
swimming in lakes edged with pines, and how in
wintertime he had skated on Leningrad's canals. Thanks to

335

his father, he'd mastered chess before he could read, and had passed thousands of hours in adolescence poised forehead to forehead over chessboards with friends. Axel asked how he'd come to teach mathematics, and the major grinned: inability had prevented him becoming a physicist.

Vera calmed herself. This was no spokesman for an army but a fellow human being, a man who dreamed in a language she did not know. On the skeleton of his story she could drape imagined detail — scent of lake water and the ooze of mud between toes; chunk-ice bumping down the Neva in spring; the sacrifices of felt-footed pawns — yet this was far from complete understanding. And he was only one man. She could not hope to comprehend the tens of thousands of his comrades spread out across the city.

Axel asked about the major's unit, and he replied that he commanded a battalion. 'My men are camped south and west of the zoo.'

At the mention of his troops, Vera felt her composure vanish. 'Your men,' she said, 'what measures control them?'

'Control?' asked the major.

'What do you do to stop them harassing civilians? Women, I mean.'

Flavia's eyes flashed a warning.

'I don't mean to be unpleasant,' added Vera, unnerved. She forced herself to look the major in the face. 'You've been very kind, and of course we're thankful ... '

'Let's change the subject,' said Flavia.

The major made a calming gesture, then like a policeman directing traffic invited Vera to go on. His manner was polite but she hesitated. Was it naïve to think that a tolerant man could reach an army's middle ranks?

'It seems shortsighted,' she continued. 'Politically inept.'

This last phrase appeared to test the major's German.

'She means clumsy,' said Axel.

She tried again, aiming for a tone of exasperation and regret: 'It's just that you're squandering any goodwill you might have found here.'

The major deliberated, then answered slowly. 'On our way here we found very little goodwill.'

'That was war,' she countered, 'soldier to soldier. Now there is peace, and as victors you have a duty to civilians.'

She hadn't planned to sound so adamant, but the major merely nodded, while Flavia looked not so much worried as annoyed. In the past she'd made plenty of scenes herself, and surely somebody had to speak for Erna.

'I agree with you,' said the major at last. 'But Frau Frey, with respect, you hope for too much. The war is our teacher,' he added, then promptly looked abashed, and when he spoke again his voice was brisker. 'For the last four years my people have been bent on only one task: killing Germans — or, more exactly, the German fighting-man. What you see now is the ugly upshot of that passion. The killing may be over, but for some of my comrades the time has come to humiliate the enemy. Regrettably, they choose to do this through his women.'

'War by other means,' said Axel quietly.

'That's nonsense,' said Vera. 'This is males on females. War is the excuse. These are boys in a wonderland of revenge against some girl in their past who stopped them grappling her breasts.'

The major looked uncertain. 'I'm no psychologist ...'

'What's more, I'll bet there are German men who are out there taking advantage too.'

'I can't speak for civilians,' said the major, 'but I can say this: order will be restored.'

Vera wasn't sure she liked the implications of *restored*. Flavia intervened: 'Can you tell us when?'

The major turned to her. 'The truth?'

'Always,' said Flavia.

'When Moscow chooses.'

Flavia frowned. The first to speak was Axel. 'There are orders to rape?'

The major shook his head. 'No, just no orders *not* to. But they will come. They must. I'm sure of that.'

He didn't sound in the least bit sure, but Vera sensed that his sympathy was real.

'You're an officer,' she said, surprised by her own persistence. 'Issue orders of your own.'

He gave a rueful smile. 'The best orders are those that men will obey.'

The only scorn she could manage at short notice was a stare, but when the major saw it he responded again, scanning the ceiling for suitable words. 'I am only, understand, a particle. A speck.'

He seemed pleased by the idea of his own insignificance, and this provoked Vera further. 'That's very convenient.'

Axel rested a hand on her arm. 'We've harassed the poor lad enough, don't you think.'

But the major seemed uninterested in rescue. 'Maybe you're right, Frau Frey, and I'm just looking for excuses. It would be better simply to tell you what I've seen.'

'Let's forget it,' said Flavia, all her energy for the topic apparently sapped.

'No,' said the major, 'Frau Frey's accusation deserves an answer.' His voice was strained and his eyebrows hunched, yet there was also a look of abstraction in his eyes, as if any anger she'd caused had sunk inwards.

'I have no wish to minimise,' he began. 'Four months ago, near Breslau, I saw a German girl — she must have been about fifteen — with human bites on her breasts and thighs. This was after our troops had been through. One of my medics claimed that the bites were from more than one man.'

He paused. 'You will think us savages, so I will also say that in Hellersdorf two weeks ago I saw one of my men swim a canal under fire to rescue a crying baby beside the body of his mother. Perhaps we'd killed the mother — I'm not sure — there was a good deal of crossfire.

'But I should go further back. A year ago I saw a village near Minsk from which the Germans had just retreated. Ashes, a few chimneys. My men were thirsty and the village had a well, but sticking from the wellhead were arms and legs.'

His voice was incantatory, as if the dead were muttering from the shadows at his back, and Vera sensed that if she tried to interrupt, to protest that these reports, this testimony, was unnecessary, he would be compelled to ignore her and go on talking.

'I saw a freed prisoner-of-war whose knees were wider than his legs, and another who tried to fight off a comrade who took away the rat he'd been gnawing on. I saw both these men given guns and told to fight. That was in Poland, and later at the German frontier I saw a signboard scrawled in diesel oil with the message, *You are now in Goddamn Germany*.

'I could go on,' he said, then stopped, seeming almost embarrassed. 'You know I could.'

She didn't doubt it, and somehow the intimacy of his comment seemed natural and proper.

'I could also talk to you of Stalingrad,' he continued, 'where I had the good luck not to fight, or of Leningrad, besieged for nine hundred days. Even if the stories my sisters pass on are wrong, the fact that they believe them is all I need to know.'

He gazed into his mug and was quiet for a time, then as if struck by an afterthought he looked up again. 'And of course there are the death camps.'

'The death camps?' asked Flavia.

The major looked at her strangely. 'You haven't heard?'

Flavia admitted she hadn't and then Axel said the same, and by the time the major turned to Vera, her gut was tight with foreboding. Her denial sounded strangled.

'None of you?' asked the major. Like schoolchildren cowed by a difficult question, they shook their heads.

And so he told them.

The sun was high and warm, a foretaste of summer. Axel followed Vera and Flavia into the courtyard, where the major and a driver were waiting beside an off-road military vehicle: small, open-topped, with camouflage markings and tyres with a hoof-like tread. It occurred to Axel how useful a vehicle like this would be in Africa — an effect of the savannah-brown paintwork, perhaps, or the heat of the sun.

The major introduced the driver, a small, pudgy man of middle years, then he stepped through a gap that served as a door. Axel clambered into the seat behind him, pressing against the wheel-well in order to leave space for Vera and Flavia. The driver took his place and they got underway, pulling out beneath the archways and turning on to the street.

Along Reichenbergerstrasse the going was slow, but the road was clearer beside the overhead railway and the driver picked up speed. To the right, the railway buckled and sagged where its pylons had snapped, and when Axel followed the tracks with his eyes he could imagine himself on a rollercoaster. At this rate they would reach the zoo in twenty minutes, though a part of him would have preferred to leave the ruined city for the countryside and never turn back.

He glanced sideways at the women. Both were wearing summer dresses, but colour and sunshine had not been enough to dispel the horror of the night before. Nothing ever would, he realised, not completely. For the rest of his days a brooding black crow would cling to his shoulder.

The view alone was enough to stifle conversation. Most of the remaining buildings were shells, and the streets had an air of somnolence that reminded him of Pompeii. Here and there survivors scratched at mounds of bricks, and in the shade of some spiral stairs he glimpsed a woman squatting with her skirts raised and legs apart.

The bridge over the Canal at Lindenstrasse had fallen into the water, and at the approaches, in the shade of the railway, they passed several rows of graves in torn-up pavement, each marked with a small white star on a stake — Soviet, no doubt, though the major said nothing, probably feeling, quite rightly, there was no need to comment.

Near Potsdamer Bridge the streets were busier, and, though the bridge was down, there were lorries and civilians crossing a pontoon bridge with guards at either end. The driver edged into the stream of traffic and then nosed onto the pontoon's plate-steel surface, which heaved. Pedestrians jostled along an edge without railings. Through a roar of engines and grinding gears they climbed to street level, before continuing west beside the Canal. At Lützowplatz they passed another crop of stars, the graves as regimented as plough lines, then Axel glimpsed the top of the burnt-out concert hall at the eastern end of the zoo.

Five minutes later they reached the eagle gate and clambered out. The gate was locked, but there were several breaches in the wall. The major gave instructions to the driver then invited Axel to lead the way.

Littering the ground beyond the wall were several coils of human waste, some still glossy and writhing with flies. There was a stench of decomposing flesh, and from a pile of bricks jutted a corkscrew horn, unmistakably a kudu's. The animal had died half a kilometre from the stables. Axel hurried onwards, keen to get away, then looked back and saw that Vera had stopped. Behind her, Flavia clambered through the gap, made a face of revulsion, then elbowed past, bringing a spike of annoyance to Vera's face.

The four of them passed Neptune and his escort of dolphins, then the burned-out rotunda and the aquarium. Fighting and shelling had finished the work of the air raids, leaving the zoo a ruin. The hooped frame of the aviary was a stack of bangles. The bird house had been levelled. Axel had primed himself to expect the worst, yet around every corner was a sight to shock.

At the monkey rocks they saw the first living animals: the hamadryas baboons. The tribe was lolling and grooming in the sunshine. A lookout spotted them and the tribe rushed to the ledge, but Axel could only stretch out empty hands, intensifying the screams. Otto eyed him grimly. Vera asked the major if feed could be arranged, and he answered that he'd see, though when Axel thanked him, the major added that he could guarantee nothing. In his eyes there was a hint of reproach or accusation, and Axel remembered the night's black news. No one as perceptive as the major could fail to compare the wrecked enclosures with those *Lager* he'd described in such abominable detail.

They passed the rodent house, destroyed before the shelling began, then arrived at the Four Forests Lake. Beyond the sun-streaked water lay a panorama of ruins. Axel sensed that Vera was watching him, assessing his reaction. He noticed hints of grey in her hair and was somehow comforted, as if the youthful woman he'd married had been somehow incomplete.

With a show of purposefulness he led the group onwards, tracing the shore of the lake to the bovine enclosures, where three domestic yaks were still alive. By the water trough he found several pails and, taking a pair each, he and Vera went down to the lake. On the embankment, Flavia lay down in the sun and invited the major to join her. Axel waved his assent. He would have liked to do the same.

Leaving Flavia and the major to their sunbathing, he and Vera carried water to the primate house: an act of dogged optimism, as he had no idea what they would find inside. In the shattered atrium they put down the pails and entered the southern wing. There was no sign of life. An artillery shell had brought down the roof, letting sunlight in on a naval snarl of beams and climbing ropes. For several seconds they stood and stared, then Vera cried out and pointed. At first Axel saw nothing, then Vera pointed again, and suddenly he glimpsed movement and saw the gibbons, the youngest dangling by a finger. Her fur had shaded to cream. The eyes were neither friendly nor hostile.

Vera left to get a pail, and Axel gazed into the wreckage. They would have to clear the lot. At last there would be space, no more bricks and bars, just enclosures as near to nature as possible. It would not *be* nature — he had no illusions about that — but nor did it have to be a *Lager* for animals. Such distinctions were surely possible. Intentions mattered, and so did heart. He had to believe they could create something good here, something that on balance would be worthwhile.

Vera returned and waded into the debris, looking for somewhere to leave the pail. She tried to shift an iron bar but it wouldn't budge, and Axel joined her and took hold from the other side. He counted to three and they hauled together until the trapped end wrenched free and rang on the floor, and at once the gibbons were on the move through thickets of rope and sunlight, a warp and weft of arms and legs that might have been reconciled with laws of motion but whose loveliness could only be felt.

THIRTEEN

It happened in the tranquil reaches of mid-morning, a holy time of day that reminded her of convalescing on a sofa as a child and listening to her mother at work in the kitchen. Axel was sitting in the armchair, which he'd turned into a makeshift desk, arguing a case for the zoo in a letter to the Soviet military governor. Vera sat at the empty window darning a pair of stockings. She tied a thread, rested the sewing on her knees, closed her eyes and heard the hush of the building, the scratch of Axel's pen and the creaking of his chair, and from outside on the rooftops the singing of birds. Spring air and sunshine entered the window and mingled in her hair, each sensation sharpening the other. She was not due to hide in the loft for an hour.

A man laughed in the courtyard and Vera thrust her head outside in time to see a soldier entering the building. Axel caught her eye and must have seen her alarm, because immediately he opened the door and windmilled her onto the landing. She heard the tread of boots and wavered, and Axel urged her upwards. There was no choice but to run, yet instantly their scramble triggered whoops of glee and the drumming of boots on the stairs. They were heavy, arrhythmic, from more than one man. Rage reddened her terror, and on the landing she would have stopped to make a stand if Axel hadn't shoved her into the abandoned flat and pointed to the loft. Making a springboard of his interlocked hands, she jumped through the open hatch, hitting her shoulder on the upper edge. Ignoring the pain, she bellied all the way in, closed the hatch and tried to make herself still, battling the heaving of her chest.

On the landing she heard bricks clattering underfoot, then a lengthy pause in which she held her breath, deepening the debt already owed to her lungs. She pictured the soldiers taking stock of the room — debris, rubbish, a middle-aged man, an iron bed and a cupboard high on the wall. She'd been stupid, *stupid* to give in to hope, and asked herself whether deep down she had always known it would end like this.

'*Tovarishchi*! Comrades!' Axel's voice was warm. Vera breathed in and listened in amazement as Axel rattled off several phrases of Russian — small talk, by the sound of it, picked up from the major or soldiers on the street. There was another silence, then a one-word reply: *Frauen* — part question and part demand. The voice was hostile, slurred with drink, and she raised her shoes to stop them tapping on the wood. How many men were there? Two? Three? Not the end of life, maybe, but if Axel tried to stay she would threaten to kill herself.

'Women?' repeated Axel — his tone was rueful, almost ribald: *Oh to get my hands on a woman*. He said no and laughed, a chuckle of male connivance, and though Vera knew it was acting, her armpits crawled. He sighed, and this too was eloquent: *No, more's the pity, there are no women here*; then suddenly he brightened and suggested vodka — sly, this time, disclosing a secret. He was running the risk of being taken for a thief.

A rapid exchange of Russian followed, confirming the presence of another man. This voice was higher than the first, and like the other man he sounded young. Both voices were bleary with booze.

The chatter finished and the men started moving again, turning her muscles into wood. At first the bustle made no sense, and then she could not believe what she was hearing: footsteps, including Axel's, returning to the landing, the noise of laughter ebbing on the stairs. The room had fallen silent, she was certain of it. She tried to breathe smoothly, not daring to hope. Not yet. She would not believe that she'd been spared.

Consciously Axel slowed his heart. A close-run thing, a mighty close thing — had his visitors been sober, they would have easily twigged. It was even possible that in

349

some addled way they knew they'd been conned but chose the sidetrack to drink.

He opened the flat and invited both soldiers inside, crossed the room and bent down to open the drinks cabinet, causing one of them to yell out and aim his rifle. No sudden moves, then. Gently he smoothed the air before stooping and placing the vodka on the table. '*Kommunist*,' he explained, pointing from the bottle to himself, causing the smaller of his guests to giggle. They were no more than boys. Axel mentioned the name of the major but they seemed uninterested, more intent on the bottle than where it had come from. So much the better. He put two tumblers on the table, hesitated, then added a third and poured. The vodka danced three rapid jigs. He handed a glass each to the Soviets and raised the third in the air.

'*Na zdorovye!*'

His guests returned the toast then sniffed their drinks before draining them at a gulp, then rapidly a second serving went the way of the first. Once or twice the boys glanced furtively sideways, gauging or tuning their effect on one another, and when by chance they met each other's eyes, they broke into grins. Such heroic drinking was strictly for the young, and the demonstration had a touching air of innocence, making the threat they had posed to Vera seem alarmist. What worried him now was the careless way they were handling their rifles — ignominious to die in an accident after getting through a second war.

Without weapons, these boys would have been harmless enough. One of them was pudgy in a sickly-looking way, as if overfed on potatoes. A rind of whiskers on his cheeks. A black wavy head of hair. The second boy was not only thinner but shorter, and in all probability weighed less than Vera. A high-pitched voice. Red hair and acne. Axel smiled, aiming for a kindly, fraternal effect — a friendly barman at a local *Kneipe*.

The black-haired lad shoved his tumbler in a trouser pocket then began to poke around the room. He picked up the receiver of the unconnected telephone, said hello and began talking to an imaginary caller, paralysing his friend with laughter. Apart from a few prepositions and conjunctions, the only word that Axel could make out was 'Mama'. Abruptly the prankster roared in mock rage, rapped the receiver on the wall and hurled the telephone aside. With a sidelong glance he sauntered into the kitchen, where he clattered the plates and cutlery then reappeared with a mixing bowl — a bourgeois remnant from the villa — that he held aloft. The redhead squealed, and as if on cue his friend smashed the bowl on the floor, skittering pieces about the room. He looked up and smiled, perhaps with a hint of uncertainty. Like any delinquent, he was aiming to goad, and Axel was tempted to react. A stern word might be enough to bring the lad to his senses, but with only rudimentary Russian it was impossible to know which word to select, leaving mime or a full-blooded assault like Schiefer's as the only ways to protest.

He shrugged, persevering with good humour. The black-haired soldier grinned then stalked past the window. There was something familiar about all this that Axel couldn't place, some mood or echo, a remembrance of tedium. As the black-haired soldier searched for something else to break, the redhead's face tracked him, joyfully agog. At the bedroom door the black-haired soldier leaned against the jamb, and in his self-regarding, callow slouch Axel had the answer: the schoolyard and its petty abuses. The waving of guns had rolled back time, and despite the passage of years, he remembered the rules: keep calm, show no fear and stay on your feet. As a child he had mostly succeeded at this, ducking persecution without joining the tormentors, and in adolescence he had sometimes managed to jolly the strong into sparing the weak.

The black-haired soldier strolled into the bedroom, whose only decoration was a print of a dinghy upside-down on a beach. Beside his mustard-brown uniform the eiderdown looked starkly white. He noticed the chest in which Vera kept her few remaining clothes, pulled back the lid and began delving through the contents, lingering over the undergarments. From the redhead, a drawn-out, smutty yodel. Having thoroughly fingered each one in turn, the intruder folded them away with dainty care. He came to the doorway, pointed and beckoned.

'*Frau, kommen!*'

Redhead howled with laughter, and to prove he liked a joke, Axel chuckled along, but then the black-haired boy levelled his gun, and Axel felt his smile yield to cold inner fury. The urge to call the boy's bluff was powerful this time, yet still he hesitated — guns and drink were a volatile mixture. Safer, on balance, to show neither anger nor fear, but instead stay patient and watchful.

With his rifle, the black-haired boy made a herding motion through the bedroom door, and to humour him, as well as to ward off the gun, Axel did as directed, half expecting that by the logic of drink he would have to march right out again. But no, he was now required to stand. Redhead joined his comrade at the door, idiotically grinning, then the black-haired boy made more gestures with his rifle, as if trying to write two-handed with a hoe. Baffled now and angry, Axel stared at the barrel, convinced its calligraphy was meaningless, then with a sudden commotion of nerves and blood he understood he was meant to strip.

He stared at each boy in turn. Their faces were unchanged: one inane, the other sardonically amused. Did they mean to kill him? Somehow he doubted it, however strange the request. There was nothing murderous in their eyes, just juvenile swagger, and if they had anything in mind at all — in Redhead's case this was doubtful — it was likely to resemble a student jape: stealing his clothes, or tying him in his underwear to a lamppost. The late regime had done worse to the Jews — and this had been years before the deportations had begun. Inexcusable, in retrospect, to have missed the signs, though it was beyond him how anyone could have predicted what had followed. At any rate, embarrassment was trivial penance. His persecutors were in no state for complex tasks, and at worst he would be forced to borrow a pair of trousers from Schiefer.

The black-haired soldier made more tossing motions with his rifle, and his mate began to cackle. Pointedly Axel rolled his eyes, then with a dismissive smile and a shake of the head he began to undo the buttons of his shirt. Instantly the redhead yelped, a noise that stabbed at Axel's inner ear. He wrenched off his shirt and undershirt, and when the rifle kept flicking he removed his shoes and trousers. He hoped that this would be humiliation enough and made a face of tired forbearance, but finding the black-haired boy unmoved he shrugged and took off his underwear. Redhead screeched at this and covered his eyes, as if genuinely embarrassed, while the other boy lowered his rifle and kept staring with the same air of amused detachment. Often at school and in the army Axel had been naked around other males, though generally they had been naked too, and it was only by an effort of will that he now resisted cupping his genitals, standing instead with his hands on his hips, less defiant than frankly impatient. Despite the sunlight outside, the flat was cool, and

354

goosebumps roughened his skin. Too late it occurred to him that by not removing his socks he had made himself absurd. Redhead was pointing and wildly laughing at his penis, which was shrivelled from anger and cold.

Again the black-haired boy raised the rifle, telling him this time to turn around. A moment of freefall and roaring in the ears, erasing any memory of which language had been spoken. Carefully he searched the puffy face for signs that he'd miscalculated. This was how people went meekly to their deaths, he realised, snatching at dwindling chances of mercy till the moment came when, naked and shivering, they found themselves staring at the muzzle of a gun. Forcefully he repeated the major's name, and when neither boy reacted he opened one hand, pointed the other at himself and claimed again to be a communist. This time both boys laughed. Then Redhead stepped close and shoved him on the shoulder, forcing him to throw a hand onto the bed for support. Even now it seemed foolish to retaliate, yet he was damned if he would ever turn around. A premonition came to him of Vera finding his body, and keeping his eyes trained on the gun he unpeeled the first of his socks. As he was reaching for the other, the smaller boy pushed him, then Axel glimpsed a rifle butt swooping at his skull.

An age of blackness followed, a time of sluggish convection, then he woke with the weight of a knee on his back. His head was hurting and he needed to vomit, but recalling the eiderdown, he consciously tensed, tightening a drawstring of muscle in his gut. He tried to rise, felt pain in one shoulder and realised that his arm was pinned behind his back. Opening his eyes he saw white — the eiderdown — and beyond it the dirty white sky of the wall. The print of a boat kept sliding out of view, and when he tried to fix his gaze on a single point, his body seemed to roll as if turning on a spit.

There was movement behind him and a warbled acclamation. The noise sounded familiar, though he wasn't sure why. The voice, his pounding head, the twisting of his shoulder — these were separate and incongruous pieces of what seemed to be a larger puzzle. He tried to peer up at whoever was holding him in place, but this was impossible, so instead he craned over his jack-knifed shoulder and saw a pair of breeches rucked below two knees. This was perplexing, yet before he could make sense of it someone yanked him by the hair and thrust a pillow under his throat and chin, actions in which he suddenly sensed a presiding intellect and practised skill, and for the first time since waking he became afraid.

The metal edge of the bed frame pressed into his thighs, robbing him of leverage when he tried to struggle. Another weight disfigured the bed. There was a hawking noise, the shock of fingers smearing phlegm, then a clarifying panic. He reared but the knee on his spine pressed down, pulling his upper-arm on its socket. The block of the pillow held his neck in place, and now it was the room that began to move, rotating on the axis of his body. Again the fingers, and his skin contracted. The underlying muscles tensed. He could not believe in this — around each instant, each sensation, hung shiver and blur. The idea came to him of voiding his bowels, but the shame of explaining to Vera was inconceivable, and in any case there was nothing to give. Instead he demanded, '*Bitte*! Please!' — indignantly, refusing to plead, only to hear the word flung back with mocking emphasis, making him determined to say nothing more.

The fingers withdrew, only to be replaced by blunter probing, and, though hideous, it convinced him that the act was impossible. His eyes and the muscles of his face were clenched, and his teeth were interlocked. There were curses, grunts of concentration, then a punch to his head, which seemed a hopeful sign. His attacker floundered, muttered and withdrew, letting in cleansing air, but then the pain returned, sharper and stronger than before, aided by a buttressing hand. The breach, when it came, was abrasive and fierce. He gagged. The mattress heaved. He could smell the other's sweat, along with horse stink, vodka, cigarettes, and he clamped his teeth against nausea. Red circles swelled on his shuttered eyes, and the bedsprings squawked like crows. Erratic, jagged agony burst from lesser pain, and consciously he tried to inhabit the troughs, waiting for an aftertime — for everything to end. Above the cries of the bedsprings he heard words and yapping laughter — a joke of some kind — and against his will the words took on meaning. Papa. They were calling him Papa.

He fled inwards, seeking refuge in stillness. A creature being eaten was said to enter a trance. Somewhere there was sanctuary, and he strove to reach it, to be nothing but spirit. The outer world fell away, but something other than pain was nagging at him, and suddenly he realised there was stirring in his groin. In anguished incredulity he hunted his senses for evidence of pleasure, but there was none, he was certain — just hydraulic obedience, cruel and blind.

Like a corpse on waves he rolled on shame, till with cries and grunts it reached an end, or seemed to. There was a feeling of cold evacuation, then a vile, loose sensation of warmth. The pressure eased on his shoulder, his arm was freed and the touch of flesh disappeared, but though separate at last he was unwilling to move, afraid of exposing his self's betrayal. They could kill him, it wouldn't matter — what happened now was irrelevant. For years he'd recognised the possibility of violent death, but never this abomination. This had been the furthest, the furthest thing from his mind.

The room fell quiet: boots shuffling, someone straining for breath, a click of metal that might have been the buckling of a belt. He turned his head and rested it sideways on the pillow, as if readying himself for sleep. There was a muffled phrase of Russian, and from the tone or a burr of suggestive syllables he understood that his body was on offer. Instantly he was startled by a new impulse to resist, though his eyes were shut and any force would be unleashed without a target. He heard a squeal of distaste and further laughter. There was a slap on his buttocks and he prepared to lash out, then a gust of foul breath made him open his eyes, revealing an oval face, pale and faintly flushed. Iron filings of stubble swirled on the skin. The eyes were moist and brown. From the mouth flowed words Axel couldn't decipher, though the tone was tender, and in the syrup of his thoughts self-pity blended with revulsion. He turned from the doe-like eyes to the door, then an object, a packet, landed on the pillow. Nougat, Swiss. A hand rubbed his bicep, making him flinch, then the face floated back into view and spoke. '*Stalin gut, ja? Ruskies gut!*' The smile was good-natured, empty of irony. A hand cuffed his shoulder blade, the face disappeared, and briefly two figures blocked the light from the doorway. In the living room the intruders turned and the smaller of them waved, then both ambled out of the flat. The noise of their boots on the stairs fell away.

Axel rose on one elbow, setting the room in orbit. Blood pumping from his heart hurt the side of his head. He was utterly shrunken. He felt slither on his thighs, smelt the alkaline reek of semen and struggled off the bed. The floor bucked and he staggered into the living room, locked the front door and forced a chair under the doorknob. He was desperate to wash. In the kitchen he filled the basin, seized a sponge and tried to flush away the filth, wincing with every touch. He guessed there was damage but only wanted to be clean, and when he'd done what he could between his legs he started on his torso, using untainted water from the bucket. Gingerly he scrubbed his arms and face, then he hoisted the bucket upwards and rinsed, slapping water on the floor. He still wore a sock, but it was drenched and he removed it. The dizziness was bad. He tottered into the bedroom, gathering grit on his soles, dried off with a towel and put on his clothes. They smelt stale, but a remedy was beyond him. He couldn't find another pair of socks and put his shoes onto his bare feet. What to do next was unclear. He felt a vague sense of duty but did not know why, or how to respond.

On the pillow he saw the nougat, which had come from them, but which was blameless, inanimate. Logic was vital — now more than ever. He picked up the packet, unpeeled the wrapping, bit into the nougat and savoured the sweetness, a taste he'd all but forgotten. His tongue massaged the sticky paste, extruding sugar, but the bolus was unwieldy and meshed his teeth, and the nausea returned. He seized a glass of water from beside the bed and drank, loosening gobbets of nut, then his gorge rose up and he covered his mouth, stumbled to the kitchen and slipped and fell. Once, twice, his gut convulsed, ejecting bitter liquid and pulp on the floor. Stunned and winded, he gazed at the mess. At the other end of the room the doorknob turned.

Gripping the bench for support, he lurched to his feet and stared as the door pressed against the lock. There was a pause, then the rattling of a key and new confusion. The chair that was lodged under the doorknob jolted. He heard Vera calling his name, took a step forward, then stopped. He had forgotten she was here. She asked if he was on his own; he said yes, approached the door and pulled away the chair.

In Rudow, on the southern outskirts of Berlin, Krypic encountered a Soviet checkpoint, and inwardly cursing he joined a queue of refugees being herded by soldiers onto the grassed and muddy verge of the road, ensuring space for a procession of lorries. Though impatient, he was not particularly alarmed — already that morning he had passed through two similar posts, his way smoothed by the badge sewn onto his shirt and the card that branded him as a foreign worker.

The people in front of him had lowered their bundles and bags, and he followed their example and shrugged off his rucksack and undid the straps, taking care not to muddy his greatcoat, which he'd lashed to the top like a bedroll. He opened the flap and pulled out a canteen, took a swig of water and looked about. The checkpoint was manned by ten or so soldiers, half on the righthand side of the road and half on the left, where an equally long line of people were awaiting permission to enter Berlin. 'Displaced' was the term he'd heard applied to the thousands like himself who wanted to leave the city, and now he pictured the whole continent on the move, as if Europe were a pool convulsed by hippos, sending small-fry roiling in all directions. He could not grasp what force would drive people towards Berlin, and considered warning those coming the other way, the women especially, to turn around and go back. But pity flagged in the face of such widespread distress.

He returned the canteen to the rucksack, in which he also carried a spare shirt, a pair of socks and a pair of underwear, some potatoes and a loaf of bread. He'd brought three packets of cigarettes to barter for more food — not enough for what he'd need to walk as far as Prague, but all the same he felt confident. The road would provide. He'd never felt so strong, so free and, despite the rucksack, so unencumbered. The Soviets had positioned their checkpoint on a rise, and beyond the warehouses and bombed-out factories, the railway signals and sagging power lines, he could see the road stretching into open fields and fancied that amidst the fumes of the lorries he could smell the fragrance of fresh grass, and once on that road he felt as though it would be possible to march clear through to Prague, sustained if necessary by nothing more than the warmth of the sun on his face. He would find his mother and search for his friends, get useful work and devote himself, by day and by night, to rebuilding the culture of his homeland.

The Soviets, he noticed, were turning some people back — according to what criteria he wasn't sure. Before leaving the barracks he had thought of forging his own identity, of augmenting his Nazi-issued identity card with false evidence of his life in Czechoslovakia. What had stopped him, aside from the risk of carrying fake papers, was an intuition that if he forged a document now he might never quite recover the habit of honesty. He was tired of deception, and to banish temptation he had dropped the tools of his old trade down the throat of a latrine. From now on he would be himself without complication. There was no reason to feel any shame. He would not attempt, if turned back now, to slip by in the night like a criminal, but would return the next day or try a different checkpoint until his right to leave was recognised.

As he drew closer to the soldiers at the head of the queue, he saw that alongside the presiding officer was a female interpreter, herself in uniform. She was lithe and young and strikingly blonde, all the more so against the drab of her tunic. Her hair was tied in a bun, though wisps had escaped at the nape of her Raphaelite neck, while a tilt gave her forage cap an air of haute couture. His knowledge of Russian was limited, and was mostly based on its kinship with Czech, so he guessed that within the next few minutes he was likely to be talking with this remarkable creature. He thought she looked humane. When the refugees were speaking, her expression was attentive, though he also noticed that she related their answers in a cooler manner, as if some strain existed between her and the interrogator, a florid-faced lieutenant about ten years her senior. As far as Krypic could make out, he was refusing passage to every male of military age. Beyond the checkpoint the road narrowed to a distant rise through which an endless file of lorries lurched, fringed by two columns of refugees.

Krypic reached the soldiers and presented his identity card, curbing an urge to gaze at the interpreter. Clearly it was the officer he needed to impress. The lieutenant took the card between stubby fingers, frowned at the German script and passed it to his lovely comrade, who recited the contents in melodious Russian. The lieutenant was staring at him with blunt antagonism, and when the interpreter stopped speaking he asked a question whose function, Krypic gathered, was to confirm his nationality. He answered quickly, interrupting the young woman, then involuntarily smiled in apology, shrugging to show that he made no great claims for his Russian but that equally he was not linguistically helpless.

The lieutenant's next question baffled him, though he heard the word 'German' and turned to the interpreter, who now smiled herself, but teasingly, as if enjoying his embarrassment. Her eyes were a celestial blue. In German she said, 'He's asking why you think you can pass as Czech.'

'I *am* Czech.'

In a deadpan tone she translated this answer word for word, drawing a chuckle from a nearby comrade. The lieutenant glared at her, and in response she batted her lengthy lashes. The face was Aryan but the accent unambiguously Russian.

The lieutenant spoke again, and abandoning any pretence of comprehending Russian, Krypic looked again to the interpreter.

'He wants to see your Czechoslovakian papers,' she said. 'Anyone could get a worker's card, he says. Anyone could steal a shirt with a badge.'

'The Germans took my papers. He should know that. I've stolen nothing.'

'He thinks you might be German. A dangerous German war criminal.'

She raised one blonde eyebrow and looked askance, leaving Krypic in no doubt she was inviting him to join her in mocking the lieutenant. At the same time she'd unnerved him — he had no idea if there were any limits to the authority that Soviet officers had over civilians.

'Just tell him I'm Czech,' he said, feigning weary amusement. 'It's the Germans who've stolen from me.'

She translated and the lieutenant asked another question. The interpreter explained, 'He wants to know where you're from in Czechoslovakia.'

'Prague,' he said, addressing the lieutenant directly. 'I'm from Prague.'

The lieutenant scoffed then replied to the effect that anyone could say that they came from Prague.

'We've just been there ourselves,' said the interpreter. 'A wonderful city. Such lovely bridges.'

'Is there damage?' Krypic asked.

'Just a little at the edges. The old town is intact.'

She raised a palm to placate the lieutenant, who was puffing with impatience.

'I especially loved all the statues,' she said. 'The angel on the clock. Those huge horses at the castle gates.'

Krypic looked at her carefully. 'There are no horses. Not that I recall.'

She grinned. 'I'm sorry. Just thought I'd check.' She gestured at the lieutenant. 'His imagination isn't the only place where war criminals are on the loose.'

She spoke to the lieutenant and a dispute began, and Krypic realised that she was arguing his case, countering the lieutenant's peevishness with calm assertion. Her chances of succeeding were unclear, but he was moved that she had roused herself from scenes of mass destitution to intercede on his behalf, and he recalled the kindness of Vera Frey in wrenching him back from death. His bond with Vera had grown gradually, but from the moment he'd met the interpreter's eye he'd sensed an understanding with her, a quiver of complicity, and now he was wholly in her hands.

And what hands they were: smooth and elegant, the faintly pink nails trimmed short and kept meticulously clean. Distractedly she stroked the side of her hair in a failed attempt to tidy loose strands. He knew nothing about her, not her name or where she came from or how she'd learned German — what she planned to do now the war was over. He imagined her as a translator at some international conference, a new League of Nations charged with making a better world.

The lieutenant left off arguing and ordered him to step away from his rucksack while a soldier rummaged through it. The interpreter was searching his face as if doubting him after all, or maybe — a more hopeful thought — as if speculating about him as he had about her. While he was still trying to decide, the soldier straightened up and signalled there was nothing compromising in the rucksack — though not, Krypic noticed, before spiriting all three packets of cigarettes into his trouser pockets.

The lieutenant had already turned to the next person in line, and in confusion Krypic waited for several seconds before realising he was free to go. The interpreter, too, was busy with the next refugee, but as Krypic picked up the rucksack she looked back once more and bestowed on him a rich and soulful smile. He thought of asking for her name, an address he could write to, some thread to find a way back to her. But no, the lieutenant was demanding her attention, and in any case that luminous smile was enough — wanting more would only spoil its perfection. There would be other chances to find love. He raised a hand in farewell and then strode away in the sunshine, lifting his gaze above the lorries and the trudging people to the point where the road and the horizon met.

Vera hesitated. 'Are they gone?'

Axel nodded. His hair was wet. She asked him what had happened.

'I'm all right,' he said.

She smelt vomit, looked into the kitchen and saw a sludge of it on the floor. 'You've been sick?'

Sounding mournful he said, 'I'm not wearing any socks.'

Along with the vomit there was water on the kitchen floor. One soggy sock lay crumpled on the boards.

'Are you ill?'

'They hit me. A rifle. I think I'm concussed.'

Instinctively she clasped both his shoulders to steady him.

'You should sit down.'

'I don't want to sit.'

'But you must.' She began to manouevre him to the armchair but he shook her off, then as if to apologise he offered the side of his head for inspection. He pointed: 'Somewhere here.'

She delved into his hair and he flinched, then as gently as possible she tried again, picturing the hamadryas females at work on Otto's mane.

The scalp was swollen and there was a nasty graze. 'It's not bleeding, at least. But you should lie down straight away.'

He glanced into the bedroom. 'I'm all right now.'

'Axel, you have to lie down.'

She took him by the wrist and tried to tow him to the bedroom door, but with a sudden cry he tore away his arm. The noise frightened her, but also it proved that Axel was confused and she realised she would have to take charge.

Axel seemed abashed. 'I'm better, you see. It's the water.'

He turned around, strode into the kitchen and was picking up an empty pail when Vera saw a wet splash of blood on his trousers. Her swallowed cry made Axel spin round. 'Can't you see I'm cleaning up?'

'Are you hurt?'

'I'm better. I told you that.'

She pointed at his trousers. 'There's blood. Are you hurt?'

He looked behind him. 'I'm all right, I've told you.'

'But the blood, is it yours?'

He swatted the seat of his pants. 'I'm not sure. I don't think so.'

'Perhaps I ought to check.'

'It's nothing.'

'Should we try to find a doctor?'

'No doctor!'

She took a steadying breath. 'Axel, please tell me what happened. We went upstairs. I hid in the loft. The soldiers arrived but you led them away. You were extraordinary.'

He seemed not to have heard.

'Axel?'

A great weariness settled on his face and limbs. 'Don't you see?'

She waited for more, growing frightened.

He said, 'Do I have to make it clear? What they planned to do to you — what they wanted you for — one of them did to me instead.'

She stared for a moment. Comprehension felt like falling.

'Are you all right?' she asked and instantly felt the question's gross inadequacy.

He grimaced. 'What do you want me to say?'

She could barely think, much less answer. At each mental turning a wall was waiting.

'Please leave,' said Axel.

She blinked as if slapped.

'Go,' he said. 'Go downstairs.'

She stretched out a hand and he parried her at the wrist.

He said, 'You can only make it worse.'

'I won't go,' she said, fending hurt off her face.

'Leave. I want to be alone.'

She stepped backwards, hesitated, then went into the kitchen. Axel had emptied one of the pails but there was another one full. She found a mug and thrust it below the surface, felt it gulp to the brim and then lifted it free, showering droplets on the water. To stop and imagine what he was feeling would be the end of her — whatever world she had fallen into, the only way forward was to act. She returned to the living room and handed Axel the mug, which he took before lowering himself into the armchair. Again she suggested he lie down, if not on the bed then on the floor, and when he did not reply she fetched the eiderdown and draped it round his shoulders. He hadn't drunk any of the water and so she nudged his arm, prompting the mug to his lips.

For now this would have to be enough. He was no longer asking her to leave. She took a chair and sat at an angle to the armchair, ready to wait till he could tolerate more care. As yet she couldn't contemplate that splash of blood.

Whatever Axel had been through, it had been on her behalf. He had taken her place, and the injustice of it staggered her.

Several minutes passed. Axel finished drinking the water then reached beside him and retrieved the panel of wood he used as a desk, along with his pen and writing paper. He glanced in her direction then smoothed the pages, and as if only seconds had passed since abandoning the letter he returned to his plea in support of the zoo. The pen stuttered then began to loop across the page. Vera felt a fraction of the strain leave her limbs.

From where she was sitting she could see out the window. Sunlight buttered the flowerbox, and despite the nodding of the *Blockleiter*'s daffodils, there was barely any breeze. In the armchair, Axel coughed. The urge to go to him was strong, yet Vera sensed that it was wiser to wait. Noon had passed, but only just — if needs be, she would wait hours for Axel to relent. In the air above the courtyard, sparrows bickered and swooped, and in the distance she could hear the droning of lorries whose freight was the future. She felt oddly secure, immune from more harm, but knew this was an illusion. They called this time peace. She gazed across the roofs and pictured Berlin, the plain to the north and beyond it a sea in which fish and birds and mammals preyed, and over the waters she imagined a ceiling of pale-blue, empty sky.

ACKNOWLEDGMENTS

The Zookeeper's War draws on a number of books about animals and zoos: *Beasts and Men* (1909) by Carl Hagenbeck, *Animals are My Life* (1956) by Lorenz Hagenbeck, *Animals and Architecture* (1971) by David Hancocks, *Zoo Culture* (1987) by Bob Mullen and Garry Marvin, *Zoos and Animal Rights: the Ethics of Keeping Animals* (1993) by Stephen St. C. Bostock, *The Zoo Story* (1995) by Catherine de Courcey, and H-G. Klos' history of the Berlin Zoo, *Von der Menagerie zum Tierparadies* (1969).

A variety of books relating to the Third Reich also contributed to the novel. They include *A Social History of the Third Reich* (1971) by Richard Grunberger, *The Fall of Berlin* (1992) by Anthony Read and David Fisher, *While Berlin Burns* (1964) by Hans-Georg von Studnitz, *Diary of a Nightmare* (1965) by Ursula von Kardorff, *The Berlin Diaries 1940–45* (1987) by Marie Vassiltchikov, *Outwitting Hitler* (2002) by Marian Pretzel, the anonymously written

A *Woman of Berlin* (1955), and Alison Owings' *Frauen* (1993). Especially useful were the memoirs of three Anglophone women who married Germans and spent the war in Germany: Christabel Bielenberg's *The Past is Myself* (1984), *The Alien Years* (1963) by Sarah Mabel Collins, and *Thy People, My People* (1950) by Elizabeth Hoemberg. An episode described by Sarah Mabel Collins inspired the scene that begins on page 174, and words spoken by the tram driver on the same page are borrowed verbatim. Axel's visit to Gestapo headquarters is based on an experience described by Christabel Bielenberg.

In the early stages of writing the novel I received financial support from Arts Victoria in the form of an arts development grant. I also wish to acknowledge the Victorian Writers' Centre, whose mentorship program brought the discerning eye of Andrea Goldsmith to the manuscript.

I am indebted to several others who read and commented on the novel's various drafts: Emma Farley, Anita Harris, Kate Manton and Sari Smith. Susan Gray, in particular, was an attentive reader at the outset and the end. At the University of Melbourne I was the lucky recipient of the advice and friendship of Kevin Brophy, as well as patronage in the form of a postgraduate scholarship.